Meet the Weavils

by Bill Ryan

For Rachel

"Pursue your passions"

Listen to the "Meet the Weavils!" Spotify playlist at:

https://open.spotify.com/playlist/1055y84t9iakrPbRzM7YEM?si=KpJyXczGTDqLbN8Y4UHlYw

If you enjoyed the music in this novel please consider going to Music Cares at https://www.grammy.com/musicares/donations and making a donation. Many of the musicians and songwriters of the time were not appropriately paid for their contributions to the art and Music Cares works to help those in need.

Check out the "Meet the Weavils!" website: https://meettheweavilsnovel.wordpress.com

***Table of Contents*:**

The Hook

It was a Sunday night. Donna was the babysitter. Donna wasn't a good babysitter, but sure, she could use the money; at fifteen in 1956, Donna wasn't about to find a real job. So, it was either babysitting or asking her cheap pop for a raise in allowance, but that's not why she took this job to babysit Franny Walsh. She took this job because Miss Walsh had a television set and her family didn't. It didn't take all of Franny's nine years of life to understand that Donna wanted to watch the tv.

For Franny, the black and white Zenith television was something that her mom would let her watch when she was busy. Whether it was because Joanie Walsh, Franny's mom, was washing her hair, or making dinner, or talking to her friend "Ginny" on the telephone, the tv came on only when it was needed to remove Franny from her mom's adult business. Now she was watching it with a teenage girl, who was also busy talking to her friend on the phone. Most likely, it was not Joanie's friend, Ginny.

"I will die if he sings *Love Me Tender*. I will, Louise, I swear I will." Suddenly, the show came back from commercial, but this time, it was an old man standing there on the screen. Charles Laughton was his name. It was Ed Sullivan's show, but he wasn't on the show that night. It was the English actor that Franny remembered who gave her nightmares when he played "The

Hunchback of Notre Dame." Tonight, he was just a fat English guy in a suit introducing Elvis in Los Angeles while he was in New York.

Donna jumped suddenly and yelled into the phone receiver, "He's on. Gotta go!" and slammed the phone down. "Please welcome," requested Charles, the Hunchback, "Elvis Presley!" The girls at the television show started yelling at the top of their lungs, and Donna jumped up onto her feet. The television screen was filled with an awkward-looking boy, his bushy hair in a pompadour and sideburns for days. He was wearing an awkwardly fitted plaid suit, holding an emblazoned acoustic guitar. He politely thanked Charles Laughton for "the opportunity" and then started singing, *"Don't Be Cruel."* Donna screamed, "Elvis, I love you" and started dancing in front of the television, mimicking the moves that Elvis was doing in front of his backup singers, but you couldn't actually see them on television.

Franny stared at Donna, then at Elvis on the television, and she felt it… or maybe heard it… or even saw it. Franny didn't know what it was, but it felt good. It was the same feeling when Buffalo Bob would ask, "Hey kids, what time is it?" and everyone would start singing, "It's Howdy Dowdy Time," but this was different. It wasn't just a bunch of kids brought in to laugh at a puppet and a guy dressed like a cowboy or a clown. It was exciting, but it also felt dirty– like something her mother wouldn't like her doing.

Donna was still dancing when she suddenly turned and reached down for Franny, who was sitting mesmerized by Elvis on the black and white screen, snow-flecked from bad reception. Franny gave Donna her hands and stood up. With Donna leading, she and Franny danced around the small apartment, happily singing along.

♫♫♫

Jim didn't really like Terry. Terry talked too much, and it was never anything interesting. Usually, it was some nervous talk about the weather or who was the toughest boy in the fourth grade. Jim wasn't there to play with Terry; he was at Terry's house to watch Terry's television. Terry was saying something to Jim when that guy came on the screen. One thing Jim knew was that the guy wasn't Ed Sullivan, but he didn't care. He wanted to see Elvis Presley, Jim's older sisters had some of Elvis's records, and he really liked them. He usually had to listen to them when his sisters weren't around. They didn't like him using their record player since Kathleen and Peggy had used their own money to buy the turntable and the few records they owned. Jim had wanted to see Elvis for himself, and since his family didn't have a television, he had to be friends with Terry for this one night... at least.

Terry kept on talking, but finally, the show returned from commercial. Jim didn't really get the commercials. "Who would want to interrupt the program so someone could tell how great it is to smoke after dinner," he thought. The adults in the commercials didn't look anything like the adults he knew. They had very clean kitchens and wore aprons over their church clothes. "I don't like this show," Terry whispered, but Jim wasn't really listening. "Let's go into the kitchen. My mom will make us a frappe." Then Elvis was suddenly on the screen. Jim jumped up and ran to the television. "I want to see this," he announced.

Jim turned up the volume (using the same knob that Terry's mom used to turn it down after she switched the television on) and watched the show as Elvis started singing *Don't Be Cruel*. Terry slumped down on the couch and crossed his arms. This wasn't his idea of having a friend over. Jim stood in front of the television, listening and watching Elvis Presley sing, strum his guitar, and shake. Jim didn't recognize the song, but he did recognize Elvis' voice. It was young and breathy; his words almost chomped at the end of every last syllable.

"Let's get something to eat?" whined Terry, from the couch. Jim stood mesmerized as he watched the images on the screen. Elvis was now even more animated, playing, or not playing his guitar– Jim couldn't tell. He couldn't take his eyes off of this country boy. Who was this guy? How could he do that in front of so many people? Elvis looked so sure and relaxed as he sang and strummed that beautifully ornamented guitar he was holding. The guitar looked like it had a hundred different stories in it alone, never mind the songs it could play. Jim didn't want to be cruel. He just wanted to sing that song, play the guitar like Elvis (or pretend to play it). Jim could tell that Elvis was dancing along to the song, but he wasn't sure because the camera only displayed his face and shoulders. However, it appeared as if something was happening down there, Jim knew it… and it was making all the young girls scream like they were crazy. Jim began to snap his fingers along with the song. "Let's do something," whimpered Terry.

♫♫♫

Lenny was bored. The house was quiet; he was hoping that Grammy Ham would wake up from her nap and make him dinner, but he knew Grammy Ham wasn't going to wake up soon, if at all that night. Grammy Ham had her friend Evelyn over that afternoon, and after four gin and tonics (the last two Lenny had made himself), Grammy Ham passed out in her bedroom. Lenny thought maybe he would go into the kitchen and see if he could find something to eat. He hated when Grammy Ham looked after him. His mother and Harry, her new husband, had taken the Boston train to New York City for the weekend. Grammy Ham said that they would be home in the morning. Until then, Lenny was pretty much on his own.

Lenny got up from the musty smelling couch that Harry must have owned for like twenty years and started to flip through the three television channels. Lenny watched "Shane" on The Million Dollar Movie, but it was boring, and Shane looked like he was queer. He switched to another station where he came across some guy singing about "Being Cruel" while holding a guitar. It didn't take Lenny long to realize that this guy was kind of 'cool' as the older boys would say while listening to Frank Sinatra, smoking cigarettes outside of Benny's Barbershop.

Lenny got up from the musty smelling couch that Harry must have owned for like twenty years and started to flip through the three television channels. Lenny watched "Shane" on The Million Dollar Movie, but it was boring, and Shane looked like he was queer. He switched to another station where he came across some guy singing about "Being Cruel" while holding a guitar. It didn't take Lenny long to realize that this guy was kind of 'cool' as the older boys would say while listening to Frank Sinatra, smoking cigarettes outside of Benny's Barbershop.

Lenny stared, listening to what the boy was singing and the way he sang it. It sounded almost like a growl, yet with so much confidence, it made the song difficult to understand, but you still had to believe him. The boy actually meant what he was saying. The singing was all well and good, but the way that boy looked caught Lenny's interest. He looked like he couldn't care what people thought of him. He wore a large plaid jacket, and his hair was long; it looked as if he had not been to the barber in weeks, yet he didn't care. He just wanted to sing his song for you. There was something in this guy that made you want to follow him around, to be his friend, and listen to him while he tells you about some girl who was cruel to him. Elvis was so cool that even the thought of some girls not liking this guy was almost outrageous. Lenny watched him with a totally dumbstruck expression on his face. This is what he wanted to do. He wanted to wear sideburns, sing and dance in front of people and have girls yell his name every time that he did, why hadn't he thought of this yet.

He watched Elvis sing his second song, *Love Me Tender*. It was more of a slow, syrupy ballad but even singing that song, Elvis looked cool. The girls were going wild for him. Lenny decided right there that this is what he was going to do– he was going to make those girls go wild and scream for him.

♫♫♫

Franny lay in bed. The two songs that Elvis had sung chimed in her head. *Don't Be Cruel* and yes, to Donna's great excitement, *Love Me Tender* (Donna screamed so loud Franny thought she had been stung by a spider). Donna and Franny watched Elvis as if he was the burning bush. It was almost like Elvis had whispered to her a secret, a secret about what was to come, about a new world, about what her life could become. When her mom came home, Joanie paid Donna, and Donna gave Franny a hug good-bye. They had shared something. Franny didn't know what it was at the time, but she was sure it was something special.

♫♫♫

Saint Anthony's is a towering church on Haverhill Street. Catholic by denomination, it was mostly made up of French, Irish, Italian, and Polish working-class families. The wooden pews and large, rectangle altar, surrounded by four stained-glass windows, set in the front of the church depicted the stations of the cross, Jesus' march to his crucifixion, on each side. A much larger stain-colored depiction of Christ in the arms of his mother, the Virgin Mary, looking down at the altar and congregation spread out before them. Franny sat in a pew beside her mom, Joanie, an attractive woman in her early thirties, wearing a dark dress, with a large bow attached to the shoulder. "Oh, what's he doing here?" asked Joanie, in a whisper to her daughter. "You would think a lightning bolt would zap him as he walked through the door." Franny followed her gaze to Richard, or Uncle Rich, as she was introduced to him last year … or maybe it was the year before that? Franny could feel her mother squirm beside her. Suddenly, Uncle Rich turned and caught Joanie looking at him.

Franny could feel her mother trying to scrunch down in the pew, but it was too late; Uncle Rich waved at them. Joanie gave him a stiff nod. "Oh, now you want to be friends," she groused. "Is that your sad little wife there with you?" A hand whacked Franny in the back of her head; she turned quickly to confront her attacker. She recognized Mary Catherine Dewey, a girl who was in Franny's class. Mary Catherine stuck out her tongue at Franny and followed her family to an empty pew. Franny wasn't friends with Mary Catherine, but she knew her and was even familiar with Mary Catherine's family. Mary Catherine's father was a notorious drunk. Everyone had heard the stories of his binges and drunken antics. Franny could feel her mother shaking her head sadly as Da Dewey pushed Mary Catherine into a pew, a few rows in front of them.

♫♫♫

Jim Dewey didn't mind going to church. It was just the whole deal of getting ready for church that he didn't like. Usually, Jim's family went to church because his da had done something in the previous week that had gotten his ma mad. Early Sunday morning, Jim's da would drag himself and everyone else out of bed and force them to doll up in their Sunday clothes intimidating the family with outright physical threats to get them moving. Ma always made a big thing about going to church as "a family." No one else seemed to really care. It was better to go than it was to get kicked by Da.

Jim's da wasn't a big man, but almost everyone agreed on Paddy Hill that he kicked like a mule. So as not to get kicked, everyone went to church. Jim liked it when they played the large pipe organ at the back of the church. The melodic groans of the organ would send chills through his body, just like the night when he had seen Elvis on Terry's tv. The organ hadn't started playing yet, but Jim knew it would, to alert everyone that the mass would soon be starting.

Jim peered at the pews behind him and noticed the girl that Mary Catherine had hit on the way in. Mary Catherine hit a lot of people. Ma said it was because she was a "busy" baby before she was born. Jim thought that it was because she was just mean. Jim recognized the girl as Franny Walsh, a year younger than him, and in Mary Catherine's grade at school. "Ya got a thing for Frumpy Walsh?" whispered Mary Catherine, "She doesn't have a father, ya know. Her mother can't be sure who it was that made her…" She added. "Shush," hissed Jim's ma. "You're in church, don't talk of such things." "I was only telling Jimmy we should feel sorry for them since they don't have a real family," whispered Mary Catherine. "No talkin' -- shush," scolded Ma.

♫♫♫

Franny noticed Jim Dewey staring at her. She didn't like Mary Catherine, but she didn't really have an opinion of Jim. He was just another stupid boy in her school. Suddenly, the church rang with the loud groan of the organ warming up. Jim looked up to the balcony at the back of the church, where old Mrs. Warren would be playing the enormous keyboard, pumping the pedals for generating the air to fill the sanctuary with melodious sounds. Franny also turned to her. Mrs. Warren was a bit deaf, but she sure knew how to work those keys and pedals. Old Mrs. Warren opened with *When the Saints Go Marching In*. The sound gave her goose flesh, just like the night she saw Elvis with Donna.

♫♫♫

Lenny stood in the sacristy of Saint Anthony's. He liked wearing the vestments of an altar boy, the long black cassock with the white surplice draped over it. He waited beside Ralph Murphy, holding an empty chalice to assist Father Nelson. Ralph, or Ratsie, as everyone else called him, was the senior altar boy. He was a heavy kid, with coke-bottle glasses and the always fashionable piece of Scotch Tape on the hinge, wearing his vestments, he looked like a comfortable club chair. Lenny was excited, even if it was just his third mass. Father Nelson waited as Mrs. Warren played *When the Saints Go Marching in*. Lenny liked the sound of the organ, but all he could think of was old Mrs. Warren.

Years earlier, Lenny's mother had asked Mrs. Warren if he could sit with her during a mass. Mrs. Warren said that she would look forward to having young Leonard's company in the organ loft. On the designated Sunday, Lenny went up and sat behind Mrs. Warren as she played. That Sunday was particularly cold, and Mrs. Warren was in the early stages of the sniffles. Lenny was impressed by Mrs. Warren's musicianship until she sneezed during a rendition of *Closer to Thee*. When Mrs. Warren sneezed, she couldn't stop playing, so she continued on with the song, even while sneezing another three times. Finally, almost sick to his stomach, Lenny offered Mrs. Warren his pocket handkerchief to wipe the snot, which was dripping off her trembling hairy upper lip.

Mrs. Warren, now fully dedicated to finishing the song, signaled Lenny to wipe her nose, which Lenny did, going against all decency that he could think of. "Beautiful," Father Nelson declared. "Obviously," thought Lenny, still holding the holy water like it was… holy water, "He had never seen old Mrs. Warren play the organ in the loft." Lenny was not sure which was worse; Mrs. Warren's hairy lip or the snot running off it. That was the reason Leonard declined any of Mrs. Warren's further invitations to visit the loft. "Let's go, boys," Father Nelson ordered. Father Nelson entered the church, followed by Lenny and Ratsie, walking slowly and holy-ily to the altar.

♫♫♫

Franny turned and watched as Father Nelson entered the sanctuary, followed by two altar boys. Franny recognized one, but the other seemed new. He was younger and had a certain look to him. Maybe his hair was a little longer, or maybe it just wasn't recently cut, but there was something different– something interesting in him. When Lenny turned to face the congregation, Franny was suddenly taken by his soft brown eyes. They seemed more open than any others in all of Lawrence -- more inviting. Franny and Joanie were in a pew a good two hundred yards down the nave from the altar, but still, there was something in this new altar boy's face that took Franny's breath away. Realizing that she was staring, Franny looked away… at the strange boy who was Mary Catherine's brother.

♫♫♫

Jim was staring up at the organ loft still, or at least where he thought the organ loft was. To him, the music from the large pipe vessel was the most wondrous sound in the world. Jim could stand there and listen to the music all day long. The booming chords echoed throughout the building.

Suddenly, Jim felt a shooting pain in his groin. "Sit down, dummy," Mary Catherine hissed, after whacking him in the balls. Jim crumpled to the pew, his face all red and pained. "What's goin' on down there?" Da's harsh whisper sounded. "M.C. just smacked Jimmy in the nuts," reported Kevin, the next oldest boy to Jim, who was sitting beside him. "Shhhh," hissed Ma Dewey, "That's no way to talk in church." Jim squeezed his eyes closed, trying to make the pain go away. "Why not?" asked Kathy, the girl who was a year older than Jim, "God made his nuts; why can't we talk about 'em?"

Ma turned away, trying to ignore the stupid question. "Because Jim's nuts even make God want to puke," injected Mary Catherine. "If you don't shut up down there, I'm comin' to kick someone, split-tail or not," cautioned Da, ending the conversation right there.

♫♫♫

Lenny stood behind Father Nelson, displaying the holy water, and waited. He liked being an altar boy. He liked being in front of the congregation. It was fun ringing the bells during the Eucharist and singing the hymns. A few weeks before, Father Nelson had complimented Lenny on his singing voice. He said that it was strong and could 'wake angels.' Lenny liked being up in the front.

♫♫♫

Franny watched Mary Catherine's brother struggle in the pew. It was obvious he was crying, his face all red and scrunched. He was trying not to cry, but Franny could see his body quiver as he sat beside his sister and brother. Ma Dewey leaned over and said something to the boy, and the other kids tried not to laugh.

Franny was an only child; she always wondered what it was like to have a brother or a sister. Or even, in that case, many brothers and sisters. It must be fun to have other children to share your life with. Da glared down the pew at Mary Catherine and her troubled brother.

This morning, Da Dewey looked like he was paying for something bad. Let alone the fact that he was in church today was just one thing. He also had the look of Franny's Uncle Mike, who never seemed well until he could eventually drink a beer, "for that hair of the dog that bit him." Da Dewey looked as if he had shaved too closely, and his shirt collar was too tight, and he also needed a hair of that dog. Da stared down at his children, all seven of them, ready to throw up if needed.

♫♫♫

"Stop cryin'. You big baby," scolded Mary Catherine. "Why'd you do that?" croaked Jim. Ma Dewey angrily turned to her other children, who were trying not to laugh at their brother. "And all of you stop it…, or we're going home right now." "But it hurts, Ma," moaned Jim through his tears. "There's no crying in church," answered Ma. "Everyone cries in church?" questioned Kathy, "Remember Booby Doyle's funeral? Everybody was cryin' then." "Shut up and listen to Father Nelson, miss smarty-pants." "Yeah, listen to Father Nelson," goaded Mary Catherine, "He's talking about Jesus blessin' the Lepers. Maybe he'll bless Jimmy's balls?" "Shuddup, down there," warned Da, swinging his leg to warm it up in case he had to use it after mass.

♫♫♫

Donna was again babysitting Franny, but this time Franny was excited to see her turning on the television set. "You don't mind watching what I wanna watch, do-ya?" Franny nodded that it was okay. She was hoping that Elvis would be on tv, but this time, it was some other show with Steve Allen, a very good piano player, Franny remembered. Donna talked to Franny about school and boys (Donna mostly talked about boys) and even asked Franny what she liked to do. When Franny was about to tell her, suddenly, Donna said, "Shhhh, there he is." This boy was playing the piano or more like he was beating the piano keys up. He sat and sang wildly into the microphone on the piano top. His hair was flying all over the place as he pawed the keys, this boy was wearing a baggy suit that waving all over the place.

Donna watched the television like she was judging his performance for a talent show. Suddenly, this boy, Jerry Lee Lewis, as it said on the bottom of the black and white television screen, stood and kicked his piano stool away, dancing awkwardly while still beating the piano keys hard with his hands. He sang about a W*hole Lot of Shaking Going On*. As much as Franny liked his piano playing, she thought he was doing a lot more than shaking; he seemed to be trying to break everything. Franny couldn't help but to stand up and play an imaginary piano, just like the boy on television. Donna got up and started dancing the "Twist" to Franny and Jerry Lee's wild piano playing. Donna started singing the song, and Franny kept playing as if she was accompanying Donna. When they finished, Donna told Franny that she should learn how to play the piano because she looked like a natural.

Donna let Franny stay up past the bedtime that Joanie had told her before leaving. They ate ice cream and giggled at Jerry Lee Lewis singing and all the *Whole Lot of Shaking Going On*. Later that night, while she lay in bed, Franny thought about learning to play the piano. Maybe someday, she and Donna could really sing together as she played a fun song on the piano, but Franny had a feeling that her mom wouldn't let her take lessons. The lessons would cost money, and Joanie didn't get that raise at the mill she hoped for. Besides, ever since she tried to take up the clarinet in the third grade, her mom was not too keen on learning an instrument. Franny asked, no, begged to learn to play it, but after finding out how difficult it was to put the reed in correctly and get it wet enough to make noise and then getting the right noise to come out, she had lost interest. When Franny suggested that maybe she should try the flute, Joanie suggested that she wait for a while, at least till she got a little older and more responsible.

♫♫♫

Old Mrs. Dunphy sat in her favorite chair, a blanket wrapped around her shoulders. "I finished bringin' the wood in," announced Jim. He was wrapped in his warmest coat and had a pair of old socks on his hands to keep them from freezing. "Thank ya, boy," said Mrs. Dunphy, watching some news show on television. Jim looked around anxiously, "Mind if we put on my show now?" Mrs. Dunphy didn't move. She thought about the idea of changing the station. "You said you would…if I got you some wood," reminded Jim, now looking more anxious. "I was hopin' you would start the fire for me," said the old woman. Jim looked over at the television and then to the clock on the mantel over the fireplace; the show had already started. Jim moved quickly to the hearth and tossed in the small logs he had taken from the pile in the backyard and carried into the house. "You get a good fire goin', and we'll see if ya program is on," answered Mrs. Dunphy.

Jim stacked the wood the best he could in the fireplace. He stuffed old newspaper in between the logs and lit them on fire. It was just looking like the logs were beginning to catch when Mrs. Dunphy relented, "You can try to find ya program now." Jim shot over to the television and started turning the knob through the three available stations. Finally, finding Ed Sullivan on the last turn of the knob, Ed stood in front of three young men, interviewing the closest boy. The boy wore dark frame glasses and held an impressive looking electric guitar slung over his left shoulder. The boy's hair was curly, and he wore an old-fashioned suit and a skinny tie. "Ladies and Gentleman, Buddy Holly and the Crickets," introduced Ed.

The boy, Buddy Holly, started playing the guitar and tapping his foot. "They don't look like no crickets to me," snorted Mrs. Dunphy. Jim didn't hear her. All he could hear was Buddy Holly's music as he watched him shimmying with his guitar. "It was a nice guitar," thought Jim. Jim's sister, Peggy, the oldest one, had gotten a Buddy Holly .45 as a gift from some boy. The song was called *Peggy Sue,* and this was the song that Buddy was singing on Ed Sullivan. Jim would sit in his sister's room and listen to the record over and over again. When he heard at school from Terry that Buddy Holly was going to be on Ed Sullivan, Jim knew he had to see him. The Deweys did not have a television set of their own (Da thought it was only good to watch the fights on and that everything else was just to sell some guy's crap – Da was way ahead of his time on that matter). Jim knew he had to sweet talk Terry into having him over.

Unfortunately, Terry got the measles leaving Jim to change plans, which left Mrs. Dunphy, who Jim would occasionally do chores for. Even more occasionally, Mrs. Dunphy would actually pay him for it. Jim watched Buddy Holly and the Crickets perform the song standing since Mrs. Dunphy never offered him a seat. Jim was able to coax Mrs. Dunphy into letting him stay and watch Buddy sing *Oh, Boy*. She didn't really care. Mrs. Dunphy wasn't as desperate for the company as Terry, but she did like having someone over every once in a while. It was nice to have the company even if she suspected the Dewey boy of having brain damage but then that Mick Dewey was of terrible moral character. He used to run with Mrs. Dunphy's son, who was serving time in the Billerica House of Correction for sticking up an armored car.

Mrs. Dunphy didn't really understand the music that kids listen to today, but on the other hand, the older she got, the less she seemed to understand anyway. She was able to get the boy to make her a cup of tea before he left. She hated getting up from in front of the television once she was comfortable in her chair.

The Dewey boy looked like his father, the Black Irish type; he had dark wiry hair, jug-handle ears but with hazel-brown, green eyes. Not the green eyes like his sister, that one was bad. She had those serpent eyes-- Mrs. Dunphy had seen her hanging out downtown with some rough-looking girls. The girl's cat eyes sent chills down her spine. The boy had more of a puny look, like his old man. Mick Dewey should be in jail with her son, thought Mrs. Dunphy, as she watched the television. The Dewey kid made an awful cup of tea.

♫♫♫

Lenny sat in his room, spinning records on the portable turntable he had bought down at W.T. Grant on Essex Street. He kept playing the same record over and over. Lenny thought the songs were silly, but there was something in the way the guy on the record sang them. The singer was a colored guy, or a Negro, as his mom had told him to call them. The guy played the piano and sang about *Slippin' and a Slidin'*, *Ready Teddy*, and *Lucille*. It wasn't really the songs that Lenny liked; it was what the guy did with his voice, raising it in different sounds and intonations. At times Lenny would pretend to play the piano and sing with his voice raising into almost a falsetto sound. He didn't do it as good as Little Richard, but it did make him feel good listening to the sound coming from his record player. Lenny decided that he liked playing the piano and would like to play in front of people. It would be like church but without having to watch Mrs. Warren's runny nose.

♫♫♫

Joanie sat at the kitchen table reading the Lawrence Eagle-Tribune. She grimaced at the newspaper; it was becoming more and more a world she didn't understand. Franny watched her mom from across the table. Franny wanted to ask her, but she wasn't sure that it would be the best time. Mr. Arlequeew, the landlord, had dropped by to remind Joanie that the rent was two weeks late, but Franny knew she had to ask her, or her world would crash in… or something like that.

"Can I get piano lessons?" she blurted out. Her mom kept slowly reading her newspaper. Franny wasn't sure her mom had heard her. Franny waited, debating whether she should ask again, "We don't have the money" was the answer. Franny sighed, was this really about the money, or was it about the clarinet? "I'll go– I promise," she begged.

"We don't have the money, Frances," said her mom, finally looking up at her. Franny hated it when her mom used her real name. It made her feel eighty years old --- she was a child with an old person name. "I'll go– I want to learn how to play." "It's not about you wanting to play; we don't have the money. Did you hear me?" Franny heard her, but she was hoping her mom would change her mind. "There's a lot of things I would like also, but I can't buy them because we don't have enough money." "Can I take lessons if I don't have to pay for them?" Franny asked in desperation and in an attempt to show her mom how serious she was. Joanie snorted and laughed, "If you can find someone who will teach you for nothin', then go ahead." It wasn't much, but Franny felt that she had won a little bit of a victory. "How she was going to take lessons without paying for them?" was the question she didn't have the answer to.

♫♫♫

Franny prepared herself. She was just going to walk up to Mary Catherine and ask her straightaway. Mary Catherine came around the corner and walked towards her, down the school's empty hallway. Mary Catherine was surrounded by the girls who usually swirled around her, all done up and prepared to do as Mary Catherine told. The girls made their way down the hall of Saint Mary of the Assumption Elementary School. It was now or never; Mary Catherine would never be alone, not even in the lavatory. "Mary Catherine, can I talk to you for a minute?" she heard her voice weakly ask.

Mary Catherine stopped in front of her. Franny noticed how Mary Catherine's shirttails were hanging out of her pleated skirt and draped over, making her uniform look as if it had two sets of skirts, a complete violation of the school's dress code. "What is it, Frumpy? Ya wanna tell me ya love me?" she asked, looking to her followers for approval. "I would like to talk to you alone." Mary Catherine looked back at her friends. "Sure, Frumpy. Let's find a quiet place." Mary Catherine grabbed the sleeve of Franny's sweater and pushed her to the meeting spot under the south stairs.

This was where Mary Catherine sold other students cigarettes or bubble gum. It was where you would meet Mary Catherine if she wanted to talk to you. It was remote so that if she had to hit you or knock you down, she could do it without the nuns seeing. That was why Franny wanted to see her there. This way, Mary Catherine would feel safe and not feel that she had to make a statement. "I want to know if you could ask your mom if I could take piano lessons from her."

The other girls who had followed Mary Catherine and Franny to the meeting place started laughing. Mary Catherine looked back at them to signal it was all right.

"Jesus, Walsh. I thought you were knocked up or somethin'," gwarfed Mary Catherine. "Sure, my ma will teach ya, but you're gonna have to have money to pay for 'em," answered Mary Catherine. "I don't have any money, but I was thinking maybe I could take it out in trade," questioned Franny. "Trade?" snickered Mary Catherine, suddenly making Franny realize what a stupid idea it was. "What kind of trade do you have?" asked Mary Catherine, "We don't need any goats or chickens." "Maybe I could do some errands?" stated Franny. "Errands? There's seven kids in my family. My da works our asses off. What errands are ya gonna do, draw pictures for the refrigerator?" "Isn't that your dink brother's job," laughed Janet, one of the girls.

Mary Catherine started to walk away, leading her band of bad girls behind her. "Ya can ask my ma," Mary Catherine tossed over her shoulder, on her way down the hall. "But you better have money. My da ain't lettin' it go for free." Franny didn't know what was worse, getting beat up or feeling like the dope that she felt like now. It was probably better than being beaten up.

♫♫♫

The Dewey's lived on a high hill on Haverhill Street. Their house over-looked most of Lawrence and the mills that ran along the banks of the Merrimack River, in an area of town known as Paddy Hill– Little Dublin, or Irish Town. Franny stood in front of the large wooden door, waiting. She had pressed the doorbell but wasn't sure that it actually worked. She had been waiting in the cold for what felt like five minutes before she knocked on the door. Again, there was no answer. She thought about maybe kicking the door to rouse someone inside (she could hear people walking and yelling in the house), but she was afraid she would lose her balance and fall down the steep, railing-less front steps of the house, landing in the middle of the busy street.

She knocked again, and suddenly the door opened. Behind it was the face of one of the younger girls, Teresa. Teresa looked at her and asked, "Ya here about the piano?"' "Yeah," answered Franny, but before she could say anything else, Teresa yelled into the house, "It's another 'tudent, Ma!" Then the little girl ran away, leaving the massive door open.

Ma Dewey came trudging to the door, wiping her hands on an old apron. Ma Dewey didn't look like Mary Catherine or even Jimmy. She was a big-boned woman with dark skin and a full bosom, her short dark hair tied up in a kerchief on the top of her head, not fair-skinned and freckled like Jim and Mary Catherine. "You're not one of my students," she answered, drying her hands on the apron from in front of her print house dress. "No, ma'am. I wanted to ask about piano lessons," retorted Franny, the fear welling up inside her. "I've got enough students now. I don't have time for anymore." Franny stood frozen. She didn't know what to do. "I…I… go to school with Mary Catherine…" was all she could choke out.

Ma Dewey finished drying her hands and smoothed out her apron. She gave Franny a good looking over. "You're that Walsh kid, aren't ya?" Franny nodded that she was. "Ya ever play the piano?" asked Ma. "No, I tried to play the clarinet once," answered Franny. Ma Dewey shook her head, "The clarinet's not like the piano. Do ya have one at home?" Franny shook her head, "I don't." "How're ya gonna practice?" "I don't know," answered Franny, honestly.

Ma looked her over some more. "Can ya pay? It's fifty cents a lesson." Franny shook her head again, remembering what Mary Catherine had said. Inside the house, down a hall, a girl's voice yelled, "Ma, somethin's boilin' over." Ma turned from Franny and yelled back down the hall, "Dorrie, take it off the burner. It's done." Ma turned back to Franny and said, "I can't be givin' away lessons. I want my students to wanna learn how to play." "Ma, it's still boilin'," Dorrie yelled again. "Just let it sit awhile." Ma thought about it some more; finally, she asked, "You'll do chores?" "Yes," answered Franny, realizing that there may be a chance. "Come by tomorrow after school. I'll fit you in somewhere." "Ma, it's still boilin'… and now smoke's coming from the top," yelled the same voice from the back of the house. "Oh goodness cakes!" stated Ma Dewey as she turned to make her way to the kitchen. "I need as much help as I can get."

♫♫♫

Franny walked through the cold crisp night. Scenes of her playing a large white piano, with a candelabra set on top ran through her head. Except that the music she was playing wasn't Leonard Bernstein -- who had grown up in Lawrence -- as anyone in town would tell you, but Jerry Lee Lewis. At one point in her imagination, she stood up from the piano and kicked away the piano bench, still playing and singing. She made her way through the muddy streets of Lawrence with a smile on her face. It was a good feeling, like a promise that was about to be fulfilled– she would learn to play the piano, she would be a musician.

♫♫♫

The next day Franny stood at the large door again, and finally, after knocking a few times, it was opened by another girl. Franny could tell by the sound of her voice that it was Dorrie, or Doreen, as she would later learn. Dorrie was a darker-skinned Mary Catherine, her ma's olive color covering the fair Dewey skin. "I'm here for my lesson," she informed Dorrie. Dorrie turned without saying anything and bolted up the stairs, leaving Franny to let herself in and close the front door.

Franny stood patiently in the front hallway, waiting. She could hear people upstairs running. Behind the door to her right, she could hear someone awkwardly hitting piano keys. Franny couldn't help wondering while she stood there what it must be like to live in such a busy household. An older boy came out of a room upstairs, slapping a baseball mitt; he looked down the stairs at Franny but kept on his way into another doorway. Mary Catherine entered from the back hallway, with three of her sisters from the room that Franny assumed was the kitchen. "What are ya, doin,' Walsh?" asked Mary Catherine, "Waitin' for a bus?" "I'm here to take piano lessons from your ma," answered Franny. "Good luck with that," replied Mary Catherine, in the manner that meant she had seen new students come and go. Mary

Catherine led her followers away up the steep stairway (it always seemed that Mary Catherine had some kind of group following her.)

Franny grew more anxious; maybe Ma Dewey forgot that she had told her to come today. Maybe it was a joke that Mary Catherine had put her mom up to. Franny heard a creak in the railing above her. She looked up in time to spot Jim staring down at her. When Jim realized she was looking up at him, he tried to rear back and disappear from her sight. Jim didn't see his older brother Kevin speed out of a bedroom and down the hall at him. Kevin kicked Jim as he ran by, "Get out of the way, dopey," he yelled, sliding his way into another room. Jim rubbed his calf, where he was kicked. He peered down at Franny, still waiting in the front hall. She was dressed in her winter coat and Saint Mary of Ass uniform. Franny looked up at him again. Jim slid back away from the railing; he didn't want Franny to see him again.

Finally, the plucking of the piano keys stopped, and the large door to the front room slid open. Ma Dewey stood there with the previous student, a spindly boy with a tall cowlick. Ma told him to "mind his wrists." The boy nodded, his cowlick waving at the top of his head. Ma turned to Franny, "Are you ready to start?" Franny nodded anxiously; she wanted to play but hoped she could get enough nerve together to try. Ma led her into the front room, where the piano was about the only thing that looked as if it had any value in the house. The rest of the furniture looked to have been rescued from the dump or the side of the road, a quilted blanket strewn across the cushions to hide the worn couch and its previous life. The piano was an old upright with its top open.

Franny took the place beside Ma Dewey on the bench. Ma ran her hands expertly across the keys, describing notes and chords. Franny felt overwhelmed. There was so much to learn; she wasn't sure she could move her hands like Ma's, and she realized that she couldn't reach the three pedals on the floor without sliding halfway off the seat. Franny watched as Ma Dewey ran her hands up and down the keyboard, making different chords and keeping rhythm with her left hand. Franny realized that she couldn't learn anything because she had never been so close to music before. She tried to pay attention, but the sound and vibrations of the music left her disoriented.

Ma Dewey played a bit for Franny. Franny watched her hands at first, delicately bouncing up and down on the keys. The light touch of her fingers as they found the piano key they were looking for adding another wonderful sound to whatever Ma was playing. Franny glanced up at Ma's face, her delicate features starting to gather creases and losing its elasticity. Ma's eyes were closed. She played as if she was reading the music from somewhere deep in her mind. Her face was relaxed; only the small flap of skin under her chin moved so slightly. Ma opened her eyes and realized that Franny was watching her. "Hands on the keys, please," she ordered, wanting to get to work. Franny set her hands on some keys. Ma moved them to a scale. "Okay, that's a C, that's a D, that's your E…" Ma began to show her the foundation of a scale.

Franny tried to follow along with Ma's instruction, but it was hard to understand. Though the chords were in A, B, C, D, E, F, and G, it was confusing what notes made which chords. Franny practiced the scale that Ma had shown her. Just before she was supposed to leave, Ma took out some cardboard and placed it on the piano bench. "My boy, Jimmy, made this. You take it home and practice with it." When folded out at length, it was a keyboard on the back of cardboard cereal boxes, taped together. The keys had been drawn in with black crayon, and the black keys were colored in to look like a piano's keyboard. "I want you to practice the scale on this keyboard at home." Ma added, "Then I'll see you next week at the same time." Franny stood and looked at her. "What about my chores?" she asked. "I'll think of some next week. This week you only have to practice," Ma said and led Franny out.

♫♫♫

Franny sat at the kitchen table; her new cardboard keyboard laid out in front of her. She tried to place her fingers on the keys, as Ma had told her. It was hard holding her wrists up like Ma said and still hit the right keys with her fingers. She practiced her silent scales. At one point, Joanie entered, dressed for a date, clipping an earring on to one of her earlobes. Franny concentrated on her scales, but she could still feel Joanie's smirk that said she didn't expect to see Franny practicing on the cardboard too long. Franny focused harder on her cardboard piano keys.

♫♫♫

Franny was getting used to being in the Dewey house. From where she sat in the front hall, she could feel the busy movement in the house outside of the front room. Boys and girls were walking and running up and down the stairs, while some were banging things around in the kitchen; maybe a young Dewey would walk by her and climb the steep stairs to the second floor, pretending not to notice, or even not noticing her waiting for her lesson. Behind the large sliding door, Franny could hear someone playing the piano but not like the way Ma Dewey wanted the piano to be played. They were pounding and in rhythm, not melodic like the last lesson. Occasionally, she would glance up above her to see if Jimmy was staring down at her, but there was no one there.

Franny stood up and decided she would try to have a peek in the room and see if it was, in fact, Ma Dewey playing the rolling melody that was coming out of the old piano. Franny tried to slide the door slightly to have a look, but the door was heavy and seemed stubborn; she pulled again, but this time, the door slid more than she had planned, and it suddenly opened. Inside the front room, the music stopped. Franny looked in, and Jimmy looked up at her from the piano bench. He stood and backed away from the door. They looked at each other. Franny was surprised that the music came from a child, and Jim was surprised that someone was obviously listening to him play. "Is my ma waiting?" Jim asked anxiously. "No," Franny answered, "You're pretty good." "Not as good as Ma," replied Jim.

"Have you been playing long?" asked Franny. Jim suddenly looked past her and into the hall. He didn't reply; he just sprinted past her and out of the room. Franny turned to follow him when suddenly, Jim ran into his father, just getting home. Da blocked him and turned Jim away. "I'm doin' my chores, Da," answered Jim, even though he wasn't asked. Franny stared at Da, who was dressed in work pants and a heavy watch coat, his large ears red from the cold and, at 3:30 in the afternoon, already smelled like many of Joanie's men, like beer. Da scowled at Jim. "Who's this?" he grumbled. "She's Ma's three-thirty," said Jim, turning and running up the stairs. Ma Dewey entered from the kitchen. "She's payin', right?" asked Da. Ma wiped her hands on her apron and answered, "Of course– get to the piano, Tommy." Franny followed Ma Dewey into the front room. "My name's Franny," she reminded her. "I'm sorry. I knew it was a boy's name."

♫♫♫

Franny and Ma Dewey sat at the piano. Franny plucked out the notes of her first scale. When the lesson was finished, Ma told Franny that she needed to keep practicing on her cardboard keyboard and instructed her to keep her wrists up. Franny promised Ma that she would and put on her coat to leave. Ma Dewey led Franny to the front door. Franny couldn't help but glance up the stairs and spotted Jim staring down at her from behind the rickety spindles of the staircase railing. Suddenly Jim screamed in pain and recoiled from Franny's sight. "Get off the floor, boy," scolded Da Dewey, kicking at his son. Jim jumped up quickly and disappeared into one of the bedrooms.

Ma Dewey looked a bit embarrassed as she opened the front door for Franny, "See you next week– and Franky, practice." Just as Ma Dewey opened the door, a boy barreled in, "Am I late? Reynolds got lost. He doesn't know Paddy Town." Lenny stood by the door to the front room, ready to take his piano lesson. "Franky was just leavin'," reported Ma. Suddenly Franny realized that it was the altar boy from Saint Tony's. Franny suddenly felt very self-conscious and could only nod to the boy – she indeed was leaving. "Good," answered Lenny, surveying the house. "Do you know, Franky?" Ma asked Lenny. Lenny quickly glanced back at Franny, "I think I've seen her around." "Do you know, Leonard?" Ma asked Franny. Franny could only shake her head and quickly bolted out the door-- without even correcting her name to the boy.

As soon as the door closed behind her, Franny started cursing herself. "Why didn't she say something? Shake his hand? Smile at him? Tell him her name is Franny?" She knew that she didn't usually act this way. This was exactly how her mother acted around men she liked. They would run into someone at the grocery store or the laundromat, and Joanie would then scold herself all the way home about what she should have said or done after the fact. Now Franny found herself doing the same thing as she walked home down Haverhill Street. He was just a boy– like any other boy, but he did have that hair… and those sad, soft brown, lost-puppy-dog eyes and that smile. Franny felt worried; what was she turning into? Her mother?

♫♫♫

Jim's side hurt where his father had kicked him. He had seen his da wind up to kick him but couldn't get out of the way in time. Jim rubbed his leg and whimpered softly, hiding in his brothers' closet. It was the only place he felt safe in the house. He knew that the hall was a terrible place to lie down, but he wanted to see the girl come out of her lesson. He had spent most of the last hour trying to find a reason to be near the hall doorway to the front room. He tried to understand why he wanted to hear her. She certainly wasn't a good piano player, and he really didn't think she was so pretty. She seemed kind of plain, with buck teeth, wearing the same school uniform that his sisters wore but despite that, there was something interesting about her. Maybe it was her curly blond hair and the way she wore it, tied with a bow in the back. Jim had learned from listening to Mary Catherine and Doreen, talking that Franny had no father, and her mother was a whore. Maybe her mother being a whore was what interested him. Jim knew many people in the neighborhood, but none seemed to be obviously going to hell like Franny's mom would. Franny wasn't going to hell because it wasn't her fault; she was a bastard; she was going to Purgatory, or someplace like that. Jim couldn't help wondering what a relief it must be not to have a da.

Jim figured he would stay in the safety of the closet until that boy was finished. He knew of Lenny through his brother Kevin, who once beat up Lenny at the park. Lenny must have thought he had a good reason to kick their football into the woods, "Because only queers played with balls." Of course, Kevin and his friends had to beat his bum, but it was such a stupid reason to get your bum beaten. Lenny still gave Kev a good shiner, but of course, Kev still beat his bum.

Jim didn't like fighting his brothers, they were all bigger than him, and he never won. He didn't like fighting with his sisters either, most of whom could also beat his bum, except for the little ones, maybe Teresa and Annie; he wasn't really sure about Dorrie. He had been doing better in his fights with Mary Catherine, but she would grab his dingle-berries, and that wasn't fair since she was a girl and didn't have any to grab back, but Mary Catherine had no problem in grabbing your dingle-berries, even if you told Ma. Jim knew that you didn't tell Da that you fought a girl, then he would fight you, and if he's been to Barnaby's, then there's a good chance you're going to get more than your bum beaten.

Jim dug into the back of the closet and pulled out an old guitar hidden behind a pile of clothes. It was an Harmony Supertone from Sears. Jim fingered the guitar strings and gently strummed them with his thumb, playing quietly. He knew the strings were out of tune, but he didn't know how to tune them or knew anyone who would do that for him. Jim gently caressed the guitar. The rosewood body was scarred and nicked by years of abuse and neglect. It was a smaller body instrument, sometimes called a "parlor guitar," which actually felt more compatible to him. It wasn't much of a guitar, but to an eleven-year-old Jim Dewey, it was beautiful.

♫♫♫

Franny was disappointed that she hadn't seen Lenny at Ma Dewey's since that first time. Her scales had gotten a bit better, they didn't sound like just clumsy notes anymore, but the piano lessons had opened her ears to all kinds of music around her. It seemed like there was music everywhere. She started going through her mother's records, listening to the Andrews Sisters, Frank Sinatra, Bing Crosby, Doo Wop groups, Broadway Musicals, or whatever Joanie had.

Franny's Aunt Lucy one day showed up with her records -- Elvis, Jerry Lee, Richie Valens, the Big Bopper, Fats Domino, Little Richard. Aunt Lucy was more than ten years younger than Joanie. When she had heard that Franny was listening to Elvis and learning to play the piano, she had to show her niece her collection. Franny and Lucy poured over the albums. Franny would read everything on the album cover and the record.

Whenever she had the chance, Franny would read the music magazines at the Rexall. Lucy would talk about how much she loved Elvis and how Elvis was in the army and how she missed him like she really knew him. Franny felt sad knowing that she would never know these men. That most likely, she was going to be like her aunt, a woman in love with a man she had never met, a woman in love with the sound of a man's voice on a record. It seemed so sad and disappointing. So much like her mother, constantly looking for a husband, one who was better than Franny's father, whom Franny didn't know and whom her mother wouldn't tell her about. Looking so hard, it appeared that she was desperate to find one, and it also seemed that she was the only person who didn't recognize her own desperation.

Franny could usually tell when Joanie was going out with someone new. First, the house was clean. Second, Joanie was usually singing and humming, trying to get into a good mood or staying in one. Everything had to be just right, including Franny. clean dress, clean underwear, shined shoes, and her hair combed perfectly. Then Donna would arrive to babysit, or Franny would be taken to her grandfather's house to be looked after. Sometimes, Franny was actually allowed to meet the guy. Most times, the man would back away as if she had cooties or something. One guy just smiled and stared at her, making her feel all uncomfortable and having that feeling that the hair on her neck was standing up (she looked in the bathroom mirror, and it wasn't really).

One time, Joanie went out with a man that Franny liked. His name was "Slim," or at least that's what Joanie called him. The first couple of times that Franny met Slim, he was quiet and really didn't make an impression on her. He and Joanie would sit on the couch and drink their drinks and talk the way adults do, but one night, Slim showed up with a guitar case and a guitar in it. Fascinated, Franny asked to see the instrument. Slim suddenly looked very pleased to show it to her.

It was a big instrument shiny with pearl set in the neck. Franny stared at it, mesmerized. Slim asked her if she would like him to play a song. Franny said that she would. Slim played two songs, both by a guy named Hank Williams. Both songs were different, but they had a real honest sound to them. Though she couldn't remember all the words, it sounded like Slim really meant what he was singing. Like some of the Broadway albums Joanie owned. Slim and Joanie left to go Barnaby's, a bar where Slim was scheduled to play that night. Even after they left, Franny could still hear Slim singing and the rich, beautiful sound of that big guitar ringing in her ears.

♫♫♫

Jim was home doing homework for Mrs. Angeleri's English class when his brothers, Kevin and Patrick, entered the room and started teasing him about not wanting to play baseball. To Kevin and Patrick, and Michael even, baseball was a boy's game, but all Jim wanted to do was stay home and listen to records in the girl's room. Peggy and Kathleen complained about his listening to their records. Ma Dewey came in and cut their fun short by instructing her older sons to go to Barnaby's to get their da out of there before the police came to take him away. Someone from the bar had sent word to Ma to come and get Da. Jim volunteered immediately to go with them. Ma thought about it for a minute and figured it would be best to let Jim go so that he could familiarize himself with the family curse firsthand.

Jim followed Kevin, Patrick, and Michael to Barnaby's. It was a cold night, and they all wore their heavy coats and boots. The older boys joked about how many times they had to pull Da from local bars and how they were getting well-known in most of the Lawrence rum-joints. Jim felt very grown up with his big older brothers, even though they acted like he wasn't even there.

When they entered the bar, it was like the world had exploded. Inside Barnaby's, it was the world of men, but with one interesting difference, there was a skiffle band playing there that night. Patrick, Michael, and Kevin searched the crowd of mill men for their da while Jim stood at the doorway, watching the band onstage. Patrick, Michael, and Kevin found their father, where else, at the bar. Pat and Mike spoke to Da, while the bartender took Da's mug of beer away from him. It seemed like Da was having another argument with a couple of tough-looking mill men next to him.

Suddenly, Da's arm shot out and swung a punch at one of the tough-looking guys. The mill man grabbed Da's arm and swung him around. Da tried to take another swing but the second man pushed him into the first man, who pushed Da into another man drinking at the bar. That man pushed Da back to the first man, and they continued to push Da around like a pinball. Da was turning red in the face. Jim recognized his father getting angry, but unlike when Da got angry at home, these men were laughing at him.

Jim was angry that the men were laughing at his da, but at the same time, Jim couldn't help listening to the band on stage and the wonderful music they were making. "Jimmy, c'mon– we're leavin'," yelled Kevin, fighting his da out the door. "Get yer mitts offa me," screamed Da

Dewey, "No boy of mine tells me when to go or not to go!" "Ma says you have to come home," added Patrick. Just as the boys got Da out the door, Kevin reached back in and pulled Jim out by his collar, "You're a big help– get Da's foot." "No," replied Jim, suddenly aware of what was happening, "He'll kick me." "He's gonna kick ya anyways. At least try to hold him." The boys dragged their drunk and struggling father down the street. The magic skiffle music echoing down Methuen Street, "Watch out. He's got a hand free," warned Patrick.

♫♫♫

It was a different band at Barnaby's from the previous night. They were close to finishing their set; a crowd of drinkers and mill men stood around the bar trying to talk over the noise the band was making. In the audience were a half dozen men and women trying to listen to music. Outside, Jim peered into the dirty window, watching the performance. Jim couldn't help but stare at the big guitar player, holding a large-body guitar with the jewels embedded in the neck. Jim waited outside until the show ended and the band slowly filed off the stage. He watched the band walk towards the back door of Barnaby's. Jim ran around to meet the band at the back door of the bar.

Slim and his bandmates stood outside the back door, sipping bottles of beer. Some of the players were grabbing a smoke of a cigarette before the next set, while others drank from a bottle in a brown paper bag that was being passed around. Jim cautiously turned the corner, watching his footing in the slushy snow. Slowly he walked up to Slim– holding the guitar from the closet. "I was..." started Jim, "I want to know… I wanted to ask you… Could ya?" Slim smiled and took a drag from the cigarette that he had just lit, "Look at that gee-tar, you got there." Jim held the guitar up to show Slim, "It's a beauty." Jim didn't think it was a beauty, but he liked hearing Slim say it. Slim strummed and then plucked a string. From the tone, Slim realized that the instrument was out of tune. Jim indicated that he wanted him to tune it. Slim smiled; he started to pluck strings and turn the tuning pegs at the top of the guitar neck. Jim watched Slim as he tuned the guitar.

Jim listened to each string as Slim plucked it, then turned the pegs till it sounded right.

Eventually, Slim finished tuning all six strings. "Here you are, little fella," said Slim, handing the guitar back to Jim. "Can ya show me how to play it?" asked Jim. Slim showed him how to place his index finger on the third string from the bottom in the middle of the first fret, his middle finger on the second string from the top, on the second fret, and Jim's ring-finger on the third string from the top, also in the second fret. "That's an E chord," instructed Slim. Jim strummed the recently tuned instrument and recognized the sound from his piano. Slim was able to show Jim an A chord, D chord, and G chord before he was needed back on stage. Jim realized he was probably going to have to find the C chord and F chord on his own. "Learn those chords, boy. They'll free ya," said Slim, before entering the bar for his next set. Jim was determined to do as Slim said.

♫♫♫

Franny finished her piano class with Ma Dewey. Ma commented about how she was coming on with her scales and that they would do more song work the next time she came. Happily, Franny slid the heavy door to the front hall open and discovered Lenny, sitting on the stairs, waiting. Lenny smiled at her, "That was very pretty, little lady." Franny was frozen; it was the first time Lenny had even noticed her. She stared at him, registering how perfect his nose was. His hair, though disheveled, seemed to have a personality of its own. Lenny's hair had a way of saying, "follow us, we know where all the fun is." Franny stared into Lenny's warm brown eyes, looking as liquid as Elvis'. "Elvis," that's where she had seen those eyes, in Aunt Lucy's pictures of Elvis. They were so mysterious….

"Are you ready, Leonard?" asked Ma. Lenny stood up and smiled a crooked smile at Franny and then followed Ma into the front room. "I wanna play like her," Lenny stated, as he slid the heavy door closed. "Thank you," said Franny, to no one. No matter how scared she was at this surprise meeting, it had been a success. Franny knew his name now --- Leonard.

♫♫♫

Franny lay in her bed, or more like the couch in the living room of her and Joanie's apartment. It was dark, and she could hear the sounds of the traffic racing by far-away on Route 495. The apartment faced Marston Street, and every once in a while, a headlight would speed across the ceiling, one way and then the other. She couldn't get Lenny's smile out of her head. She looked deeply into his Elvis eyes and his' floppy hair; Franny imagined that she was singing a song to him. It sounded like a Billie Holiday song while Leonard was elegantly playing the piano behind her; they were a musical act, like Ruby Keillor and Louis Prima. Franny was in an evening dress with many sparkles, and Leonard was in a tuxedo, tickling the ivories. They made a beautiful couple (as they say in the movies). Leonard got up and took her in his arms, like the way Fred Astaire did with Ginger Rogers, and they spun around the dance floor of the club where they were playing. Suddenly, Franny realized this wasn't what she wanted; it was something she had seen in a movie. What Franny wanted was something real, not some stupid Hollywood picture. She wanted a real-life romance.

Franny was startled by a noise down the hall. She knew that Slim and Joanie were in the apartment. She had pretended to be asleep when she heard them come home, and Joanie had paid Donna and let her go home. Franny knew that she wasn't supposed to bother the adults when they were in Joanie's bedroom. Franny knew that she shouldn't get up, but she did need to use the bathroom. Finally, she decided she had to go and slipped out of bed, then tiptoed away from the couch to the bathroom. When she got into the bathroom, she sat quietly on the toilet, with the sound of her pee hitting the water in the bowl being the only noise. She could hear movement in Joanie's bedroom. Franny finished and wiped herself. She rinsed her hands and quietly slipped out of the bathroom without turning on the bare light bulb in the ceiling. Franny started to her bed when she realized that Joanie's bedroom door wasn't closed, or as closed as it could be because the lock never really worked as long as Franny could remember.

There had never been much privacy between her and her mother. Now that Franny had turned eleven and was developing breasts, she wished that she could get dressed without being in the middle of the living room. Sometimes, even when it was just her and Joanie at home, she would dress in the bathroom. The door to Joanie's room was slightly open. Franny watched the door; she could hear the movements of the blankets in the room. Not understanding why, she moved closer to the opening in the door and peered into the darkened room.

She could make out two figures in the bed. Franny could hear Slim and Joanie breathing in the room. They undulated on the bed; their bodies clasped together. She could make out the bare backside of Slim and realized both people were naked. Franny recognized Joanie, making some low moaning sounds, not the sound of pain but the sound her mom sometimes made when she was eating ice cream. The bodies moved faster, and the breathing got louder. Franny could see her mother's face, her eyes were closed, and her mouth was opened. At one point, without opening her eyes, Joanie gently kissed Slim on the side of the neck. As Franny's eyes adjusted to the dark, she could see Joanie's naked breast bounce back and forth in rhythm to Slim's movement. Scared and confused, Franny realized that she should get back to bed. Laying there, she started to understand what Mary Catherine was telling the other girls that she had seen once when she had walked up to a couple in a car on River Road and what they were doing when she was looking for her da during one of his benders.

Mary Catherine had gone to the car and noticed that it was rocking back and forth; she peered into the window that was all fogged up and saw Mr. Shaunnessy, the science teacher at their school, with a high school girl who was friends with Mary Catherine's oldest brother, Patrick. Franny deduced that it was the same as what Mary Catherine reported on. It was that thing that adults did but didn't want kids to know about. It was the thing that the men talked about and got all quiet when you walked by them. Franny watched the door to Joanie's room from where she laid on the couch.

She couldn't help peeking at it to see if a light went on, or maybe she should get up and watch some more, but she knew that Joanie would be livid if she caught her looking, like the time that Joanie caught her reading those letters from that man at Joanie's office. Franny couldn't understand why her mom would do such a thing, rub up against a man like that – was it for Slim's guitar? She wouldn't want to lay with any boy over a guitar. It had to be an adult thing, like drinking beer. For some reason, Franny suddenly wished she hadn't seen it. She now wished she could go to sleep.

Suddenly, the door to Joanie's room opened. Franny closed her eyes to make it look like she was sleeping. Joanie stepped out of the room and stared over at her daughter. When she was sure Franny was asleep, she signaled behind her into the room. Franny knew this because, though she pretended to have her eyes closed, she was actually watching as Slim hurried out of the room, naked, his long flute, still wet, shining in the car headlights going by; Slim and his instrument hurried into the bathroom. Franny shut her eyes now. She had seen one once before but really wasn't sure what it was for. Some girls had told her it was the difference between boys and girls. But Slim's was big… and stiff… and shiny.

Franny tried to go to sleep. Quickly, she heard the toilet flush, and Slim hurried back into the bedroom. Then again, someone went into the bathroom and flushed the toilet. Franny guessed that was her mom; Joanie usually had to go at least once a night, sometimes twice if she was drinking beer with Aunt Lucy or Ginny. For a short time, she heard hushed voices in the bedroom but eventually, they were quiet. Franny found herself wondering what it would be like to rub against Leonard's body.

♫♫♫

Jim kept going back to Barnaby's to ask questions of that tall guitar player. "Can you show me what a "G" is? "How 'bout a "B"? What's a bar chord? Can you tune this again? It doesn't sound, right." The tall guitar player would sip his bottle of beer and help Jim, occasionally showing him a strumming pattern or chord progression.

One night, Jim went back to Barnaby's looking for the tall guitar player. He thought maybe he would show up at the bar early and catch the band before the show started. Jim left Saint Tony's right after school ended and ran to Barnaby's. He realized that he had to beat the first shift of mill men there. The place was empty. Jim slipped inside the door because he could hear someone banging on the drums, hoping that it was the drummer of the tall guy's band. Jim was disappointed to find that it was an older boy. He was a friend or at least someone his brother Kevin knew from school; he was a Webster. Barnaby Webster once owned the bar, but now the bar belonged to the Webster family. Jim knew that the older boy was a Webster. Jim also knew right away that the boy couldn't play the drums. He banged hard, and he banged often, but it wasn't in rhythm or on any kind of beat. The older boy was just flailing around with the drums and cymbals.

"Are they here?" yelled Jim over the boy's banging. The older boy stopped and glared, embarrassed at first, and then angrily, at Jim. Holding his suspected out of tune guitar, "Are they here?" Jim repeated. The older boy slammed down the drum sticks he was using. He stood and looked straight at Jim. "You're not supposed to be in here," he ordered. "I'm looking for the guitar player who was here last week," answered Jim. "They're not here anymore," growled the boy, getting more and more bothered by Jim, "They left last night." Jim looked over the drums that the older boy was trying to play. "Are those your drums?" he asked.

The Webster boy stepped away from the drums and walked towards Jim. "You didn't see anything here," he instructed, "I know who you are, and I know where you live." Jim started to back out of the bar's front door. "I was just looking for the band," he answered. "They're not here; I said," hollered the boy. Jim didn't need to be told twice; he turned with his guitar and ran out the front door into

Methuen Street. He would have to learn how to tune his guitar by himself.

♫♫♫

Jim would watch that boy, "Leonard," go into the parlor with his ma and try to play the piano. Jim could tell, even standing outside in the hall, that the boy wasn't any good. He played too fast and, at times, too hard, pounding the keys like his da would when he caught Jim playing the piano. Pounding on it to scare him as he tried to chase Jim outside to play with the other kids and get away from this "sissy" piano.

Da Dewey felt that instruments were fine for women but not for men or his boys. He liked the way Ma played when they first met, and he really liked the money that Ma's teaching brought in, but he didn't side with any of his boys taking part. Sure, a tenor singing "Danny Boy" could make him cry, but it made all Irish men cry– especially if they had a pint on, but men did not play the piano. Jim Dewey liked to play, and he was pretty sure that his ma liked the way he played. Sometimes, when his da was at work or had a job to go to, Ma would let Jim play, reminding him to keep his "wrists up."

She would sit beside him and listen, all the time watching his hands. If he made a mistake, she would correct him– at times; she would turn the well-worn pages on the "Today's Hits" music book for him. Jim was by far the best at playing the piano among her children. Kathy and Ann played well enough, but neither of them spent the time practicing that Jim did. Whenever he could jump on and be sure that his father couldn't hear, he would.

At times, Jim would sit by his mother's feet and watch her press the three pedals with her feet as she played to herself, usually waiting for Leonard to arrive for his lesson. Jim liked to watch his mother play, she would close her eyes, and Jim was sure that she had gone somewhere else. He would imagine where she went, was it Barnaby's down the street, where Da would tie a pint on? Was it some stage in Lowell, or Boston, or maybe even New York City? Was she playing in Carnegie Hall like she would jokingly tell her students where they will one day end up if they practiced? Or was it the rich man's house that she grew up in- Master Woods? It wasn't here on Haverhill Street in Lawrence, Massachusetts. Jim was sure of that.

Suddenly the door opened, and Leonard entered, snapping both Jim and his ma from their individual trances of thought. Ma Dewey smiled at him and offered Lenny a piece of the piano bench she was sitting on, at the same time nudging Jim to the door. "There ya are," she exclaimed, back to reality, "I hope you've been practicin'." Jim slipped from under his mother's feet and to the door. Lenny smiled at him, as one would do with a bothersome dog. Jim slipped out of the room and closed the door. Remembering his da wasn't home (if he was, he surely would have checked to see if Jim was at the piano), Jim thought this might be a great time to sneak up the stairs to his sister's bedroom. He scurried up the steep staircase to his sisters' room and the only phonograph in the house.

Jim dropped the needle on the round black grooved disk. The familiar hiss began, and then with a flourish, the music flowed out of the small speaker on the side of the phonograph case. Bing Crosby's crooning voice swirled out, singing about a woodchuck with high hopes. Jim surveyed the dozen or so records that his family owned. Most of them were crooners of the previous era, Crosby, Dean Martin, Frank Sinatra, his mother's music. There were a few Irish tenors, the Irish Rovers, and the occasional Broadway musical album like "*Oklahoma*" and "*The Sound of Music*." But Jim also knew where his sisters hid the other records. The albums full of smoky music, of jazz, made by Negroes, "race" albums as his father called them, or "Jigaboo" or "nigger" music. Records full of songs sung by the Isley Brothers, Nat King Cole, Johnny Mathis, and the Ink Spots.

Jim took out one of his favorite albums, Ray Charles. He set it on the turntable and let it play. The sound of Ray's husky voice and the driving vocals filled the room. Jim sat listening and staring at the back of the album. The voice startled him at first, thinking it was his da about to beat him, "Is that Brother Ray?" the voice asked. Jim recoiled and stared in panic at Lenny, standing in the doorway of his sister's room. "Yeah," mumbled Jim, as he usually did when he was scared. "Which one is it?" Jim displayed the album cover for the strange boy to see. Lenny slid down onto the floor and started digging through the small collection of albums. "Do you have any more of his?" Jim told him that they didn't have any other Ray Charles albums, but it didn't seem to matter to Lenny, who was just as pleased with the other records he found.

One by one, Lenny laid them on the turntable and played them. Enthusiastically telling Jim everything he knew about the song, the music, the album, and the musicians who made them. Lenny knew a lot about records. Jim spent the whole afternoon listening to him and the records. The whole time Jim expected his da to walk in and beat both of them. Just as they got to the last Nat King Cole record (because he wasn't too much of a favorite of Lenny's), Mary Catherine walked in and kicked them out of her room, making sure that they both knew that she suspected them of kissing each other.

♫♫♫

Franny continued to take lessons with Ma Dewey, though it was hard to learn to play the piano by practicing on a cardboard mock-up of a keyboard. Whenever she went over to the Dewey house, she would always feel like she had been caught in a violent wind. There would be Dewey kids running up and down the stairs and out the front door, or someone yelling in a backroom, or the sound of kids arguing upstairs. She used to wonder how anyone could live in this hurricane of movement and sound. Sometimes, she would see Mary Catherine with one of her sisters. Mary Catherine would raise her hands, limply and say, "Lift your wrists, darlin'," and giggle, mocking her mother's reminder. The rest of the Dewey family seemed unaware of her, even Da Dewey.

Once when leaving, Franny almost tripped over Mister Dewey outside of the front door. Da was drunk and passed out. Ma Dewey came out and yelled for the boys. Two of Mary Catherine's older brothers came out and dragged their drunken father back into the house. Franny knew of Da Dewey's drinking as most other local neighbors did. He would sometimes stay away from home for days and weeks on end, but always, eventually, made his way back home. Da Dewey rarely held a job for long, or at least till he got paid and then went to Barnaby's, The River Boat, or any of the other gin joints on Methuen Street.

For Franny, though, Da Dewey was the man she saw while walking home from a friend's house (Joanie had to work late and therefore couldn't accompany her home) who was swaying in front of the old fence by Mulligan's Motors.

When he heard her coming up from behind him, Da turned around to face her, still holding his spraying flute in his hand. It shocked Franny, being of a two-woman household and never having met her father; it was the first time she saw a man's penis. Da stood in the streetlight smiling, waving his dripping member at her. Franny would never forget the strangeness of it. It looked like a root, or hot dog, with pee coming out of the end (on the other hand, Franny wasn't really sure what it looked like where the pee came out of her. She knew when to go and how to go but had never really checked to see where it came from, later she would use a hand mirror from Joanie's purse to see. She still wasn't all that sure where it came out). Finally, Da shook the strip of flesh and pushed it back into his pants, "Hoo-boy, you're a wee blondie lass," he said. "Better not be showin' you my tally-whacker." He stumbled off singing some Irish song, but the sight had always bothered Franny, even if she didn't know why. Now, Da Dewey would mumble something in his Irish lilt, ignore her, and probably already had forgotten the incident outside of Mulligan's.

Franny sat at the piano with Ma, watching her play. Ma Dewey had her eyes closed and sang softly to herself, in accompaniment with the music she was making. Franny started to feel uncomfortable watching. It was like watching someone pray silently, something deeply personal. Ma stopped and paused. She removed her hands from the piano keys, "See, can you try to listen to the music inside you?" Franny was confused. The music inside her sounded like other musician's music, not hers. Her own music on the piano sounded stilted and off-key, like listening to a child read to you when they were first starting out. "I'll try," Franny answered, pulling her winter coat on. Franny said "Goodnight" to Ma Dewey and pushed the heavy door to the front hall open. "Keep your wrists up, darling," coached Ma, as the next student, a younger boy in a ski suit, passed her going into the room. "Hello, Andrew," greeted Ma, leading Andrew to the piano for his lesson.

Franny bundled herself up for the cold night, buttoning each button on her coat, and started to leave when music had wafted down from upstairs. Franny looked around; she couldn't see any of the Deweys. Franny started up the steep old stairs of the Dewey house, listening to the music drifting down to her. Curious, as if almost drawn to the music, Franny tip-toed up the stairs, not knowing what she was going to do when she found the origin of the music. All she hoped was that Da Dewey wasn't nearby. She followed the music down the hall at the top of the stairs, past two empty bedrooms. Franny cautiously glanced into the dark rooms, one had a single, double bed, and the other room held two large mattresses on the floor.

Franny realized that the music was coming from the room at the end of the hall. Slowly she crept to the door and looked in on the only room with a light on. The two boys laid on their backs, listening to a record playing on a small second-hand phonograph. Lenny was the first to catch her looking in, "Hey, did ya come up to hear the Crickets?" Jim was startled and jumped away from the door that he was lying in front of. He couldn't help but to assume that it was Da who had caught him and the strange boy listening to the girl's records, or maybe it was his sisters, angry that he was using their records and would scratch them. He stared at Franny with the expression of a dog caught in headlights. Franny couldn't help herself now--- she had come this far. At her most lady-like, she took a seat on the floor to listen to Buddy Holly. "I really like him," Franny added, with no other way to introduce herself to the boys. "He's hep," was Lenny's answer. Jim nodded in agreement.

♫♫♫

An hour later, Ma Dewey approached the door to the girl's room. She could hear the music, so she wanted to warn her daughters to turn off that phonograph before their da got home. When she looked in, she was surprised to find two of her recent piano students listening with Jimmy. Franny gave a small wave to Ma when she happened to look up and noticed her in the doorway; Lenny wasn't paying attention; his eyes were closed, bobbing his head along with the beat of the Cricket's drummer, Jerry Allison.

Jim looked up at her, at first embarrassed but quickly shifted his attention back to what Buddy Holly was singing. Ma just smiled at them and left. She knew the problems that Jimmy had making friends. Jim was just like her as a girl; her father used to say she spent too much time in her head. That the world was going by as she listened to the music between her ears. She realized that this was his first chance to have friends over. Ma went down the stairs, smiling to herself.

♫♫♫

"You ever hear this one?" Lenny asked Franny, handing her a worn-out album. "Jerry Lee Lewis, I've heard "*Great Balls of Fire.*" "Boy, can he sing," answered Lenny. "Not like Buddy Holly," argued Jim, in his first real disagreement with his new friends. "Buddy writes songs anyone can sing and sing good. But Little Richard writes songs that only he can sing and make real," Jim added, "Like Jerry Lee, you can't sing a Jerry Lee song." Franny and Lenny turned to Jim because of the sudden conviction in his voice. "I can sing Jerry Lee, pallee." confirmed Lenny, "I can sing Buddy Holly." Lenny placed a record on the turntable, "I'll show you I can sing Jerry Lee." Lenny got to his feet and waited for the song to come on.

Lenny sang along with Jerry Lee to *Great Balls of Fire*. Lenny had all Jerry Lee's moves down, even pretending to shoot the piano stool out from under him and play the piano standing up. Jim and Franny watched him shake and shiver.

It was interesting for Jim how Lenny could dance in front of them without any sense of fear of other people judging him. Lenny could shimmy and never even break a smile as he sang along with The Killer (Jerry Lee's nick-name). Franny was stunned– not by the performance as much as her body's reaction to the performance. Suddenly her heart started beating faster; she could feel the perspiration gather around the neck of her cotton shirt under her school sweater. Her face felt flushed, and for a moment, she felt like she had stopped breathing. Lenny continued to dance like Jerry Lee while singing with the record. Franny was sure that if he didn't stop soon, she was going to pass out.

"What's goin' on 'ere?" a voice echoed from the hallway. Lenny missed his beat and accidentally kicked the phonograph, sending the needle scratching across the record, in a blood-freezing sound. "Da," announced Jim, panicked.

Da Dewey swung into the doorway, glassy-eyed and staggering. "What do ya have here, boyo?" he asked his son. Jim stood frozen. Franny stood, also suddenly afraid of Mr. Dewey, her hands clenched tightly in front of her Catholic school uniform. "We're listening to records," Lenny warmly reported to Da, reaching out to shake his hand, "Sir." Confounded by this boy being in his house or at least muddled by the beer he had drunk at Barnaby's Da Dewey extended his hand back. "Leonard Hamilton, the third." Lenny introduced himself. "Dares three of ya, ya say?" retorted Da. "Yes, my stepfather, my grandfather, and me, number three," answered Lenny, still pumping the drunken man's hand. "Are you the Hamilton that own the hardware store downtown on Hampshire Street?" "And soon to open one on Route 114, too," added Lenny.

"Your people sell crap. I wouldn't use nuthin' from there to fix anything in this house," chided Da. "I suggest you use Vernon's in Groveland. They have a better selection," instructed Lenny. Da spat on the floor and rubbed it into the wood with his shoe, "They're all a bunch of crooks." "I couldn't agree with you more," shot Lenny, "My folks are the biggest crooks."

Da stared at Lenny, drunkenly confused. He grumbled and warned them to keep that "Gar-darned music down." Lenny put the Buddy Holly record back on, but Franny and Jim remained standing. "Maybe ya should go," motioned Jim, hoping his da wouldn't come back. Franny started to gather her things, "Maybe we should." Lenny ran his hands through his hair, almost making Franny swoon right there. "Aw, we didn't finish Buddy Holly," he groused. Franny reached over and awkwardly shook Jim's hand, "Thank you for letting me listen to your records." Jim shook her hand and added, "They're really my sister's records." "Yeah, thanks, kid," Lenny replied, patting Jim on the back like a good pony. Franny led them downstairs and out of the house into the cold Massachusetts night.

Franny and Lenny stepped outside the front door, they looked back in at Jim, who had no expression and seemed unable to send them off. Franny gave a meek wave, and Jim closed the door. Franny looked down at Lenny at the bottom of the stairs trying to maneuver through the slush of Haverhill Street. Lenny glanced up at her and smiled but made no attempt to wait for her. Franny realized that she would have to walk home alone. Even as Lenny slogged a half a block ahead of her to Chelmsford Road, she could wonder what it would be like to walk with him…to maybe have him hold her hand.

♫♫♫

School was difficult for Jim. It was a big game of hide and stay hidden. Nothing good came of the teachers recognizing you in the back of the room, not paying attention. Nothing good came of having your fellow students recognize you as Mick Dewey's son. "Your

Dad's a drunk," they would hiss. "Not all the time," he would answer. "He's not drunk when he's sleeping it off," they would taunt him. Nothing good came from going to school, but he knew he had to go-- it was the law.

Jim had already witnessed Patrick's, Michael's, Kevin's, and even Mary Catherine's battles with Ma to stay home. Ma would not give in– if you were healthy enough to get out of bed, you were healthy enough to go to school, and if she discovered you were faking it, Ma would drag the truant child, and the rest of the younger children who were not of school-age yet down to the school and turn you over to the ladies in the office. Trapped, as in most decisions in his young life, Jim tried to blend into the walls of John Quincy Adams Junior High and not be bothered, at least until high school graduation.

It was one of those days that Jim was hiding in plain sight when he became aware that something had happened. As other students passed, they whispered between themselves. Many looked concerned- others laughed. Suddenly, Franny ran up behind him and tapped Jim on the shoulder. Jim was surprised; he thought they had an agreement. They wouldn't be friends at school, only listening to records in his sister's bedroom. Neither Lenny nor Franny ever made any advances to Jim in the halls of John Q. Adams before. Jim looked at Franny; he could tell she was trying to say something but nothing was coming out. Her robin-egg blue eyes were brimming with emotion, welling up so that she could only croak, "Buddy Holly's dead."

Jim didn't understand at first, "Buddy Holly's dead?" "Yes," replied Franny, choking back her tears. "It's awful; it was a plane crash." "Were the Crickets with him?" asked Jim, trying to understand what she was so upset about. "No, he was with the Big Bopper and Richie Valens. They crashed in a field in Iowa." Franny leaned forward into Jim's arms and started crying on his shoulder. Jim couldn't understand how Buddy Holly could die. He didn't know Buddy Holly, but he was sure that Buddy Holly was supposed to play that cool guitar with the Crickets. Forever! He would write a bunch of songs about girls and love, and they would play them on the radio, and he, Franny, and Lenny would listen to them in his sister's bedroom after their piano lessons. Jim couldn't believe it; he so looked forward to listening to records with Lenny and Franny. Now, with Buddy Holly gone…well, he just couldn't think about it. He wanted to cry like Franny, but he was a boy and couldn't-- if his da ever found out.

He realized that he didn't know what to do with Franny crying on his shoulder. He tried patting her gently on the shoulder, the way Ma would comfort him when he was crying. Franny squeezed him tighter as she sobbed. Jim could feel her body tense as she sobbed harder. He could feel her breathing… her small, budding breasts pressing against his chest, through their sweaters. Even in his sudden grief of hearing that Buddy Holly had died, Jim realized that he was also having a reaction that he couldn't control. His erection pressed against his underpants. The bible talked about wanton behavior, but of course, it never mentioned what to do when you had a boner in the school's hallway.

The grief Franny had felt about the passing of Buddy Holly strained through her body. Though she had never met him or even seen him in concert, she had always had a connection with him. Maybe it was his ugly-duckling looks that Franny understood. She was no fool and knew that she was never going to have the feminine sexiness that Joanie held over men. In fact, the last thing she wanted was to be considered because of her looks. She wanted to be considered because she was smart and talented (even if she felt she wasn't smart nor talented), not because she looked good on someone's arm. Or maybe she connected with Buddy Holly in the way he looked at love like there was one someone out there for everyone. All you had to do was find him. Or maybe like Buddy, Franny had to wear glasses most of the time. She hated being called "four eyes," but Joanie said that she had to wear them, so she did.

Franny held Jim, not even really caring who it was. She just needed someone to hold and was sure Jim would share her grief. She could feel his body recoil as she wrapped her arms around his shoulders. She cried into the nape of his neck, the wool from his sweater itching her face. Slowly, Jim gave in to her hug and wrapped his arms around her waist; she could feel his hands shaking. What bothered her was the realization that she would never hear another song by Buddy Holly. That would be all his music, everything that had been released, and there would be no chance to see him in person. That every time she would hear a Buddy Holly song, she would know that he would never sing it again. Franny sadly thought about Buddy's young wife and child. She remembered seeing a picture of them in Life magazine; they seemed so happy. Then suddenly, she felt something poke her thigh. It was hard, like a stick or a branch…

Franny pulled back from Jim and stared at his face. Jim seemed as surprised as she was about the little poker. She had heard about erections but assumed that it happened just before intercourse, not during a grief-stricken hug. Jim smiled awkwardly and tried to back away. Franny couldn't help but to look down at the bulge in Jim's pants. Jim quickly moved his hand in front to block the view of his crotch. He didn't know what to do. He remembered the embarrassment of his brother, Patrick, when Mary Catherine accused him of getting "excited" one time when she was sitting on his lap. Pat said that Mary Catherine had been rubbing his "hog" and she made it like that. Except that Franny hadn't rubbed his "hog." It had something do with a feeling Jim had while holding Franny. Maybe it was the fresh smell of her hair or the feeling of her small bumps touching his chest through his sweater, shirt, and undershirt. The truth was that he didn't really know why he had a boner. He just knew that he did and had better hide it before anyone else noticed it.

Franny looked at him, stunned because she didn't think that would be Jim's reaction to the grim news of Buddy Holly's death. She thought that he would be the one person who would want to grieve with her. But he was obviously thinking about something else. She thought about running home and crying in the comfort of her own house, but Joanie would be all over her for leaving school, and how could she explain her absence when she would eventually come back. She hoped that maybe she could find Lenny, and he would understand and share sympathy with her. Lenny was usually dawdling to his math class (that was how well she knew his class schedule). She realized all she could do was to turn and run away from Jim, that he could never understand her pain.

Nor could she understand his. Jim reached out to stop her-- to explain to her that he had no control over his hog. It just did these things on its own, and he couldn't stop it, whether it was getting large in an innocent hug or retreating into his body when the bath was cold. He had no idea what it would do next. Jim watched Franny run away down the hallway while trying to stop her own sobbing. Jim then noticed that everyone around was staring at him. "There's Da Dewey's kid again– scarin' girls."

♫♫♫

Jim kept his distance from Franny, it seemed like she wasn't interested in talking to him, and he didn't want to explain what it was that poked her during their hug if she asked. Sometimes, he would enter the front door, and Ma would be leading Franny into the front room to start her lesson. Occasionally, he would see her around the house, helping with chores to pay off her piano lessons. Jim couldn't really understand why Ma had asked her to do chores. He had six brothers and sisters, all of whom, except for baby Ann, had their own chores to do. Jim also noticed that some of Franny's tasks were the same chores that belonged to one of his siblings, but it was done twice... and sometimes it didn't need to be done at all.

One time while hiding in a closet, Jim had heard his da scolding his ma for not making Franny pay for her lessons (Da called her "That tramp's bastard"). Ma had said that she felt that Franny was talented and one of her best students. She had also said that she felt sorry for

Franny because she didn't have no father and no man in the house. Da had just snarled and said, "If they don't have no man in the house, it's because that whore drives 'em away." Ma got really angry and stormed downstairs, the way she did when Da got under her skin. But Franny wasn't talking to him.

Sometimes, Jim would stand outside the door to the living room and listen to Franny play. Ma was right; Franny was getting good (not as good as Jim, in his opinion, but good for a girl). Jim could imagine her hands moving slowly, cautiously, sometimes picking out keys on the old piano keyboard. He could imagine her soft blue eyes, behind her horn-rimmed glasses, following the music on the page. He knew that his ma was following along with her, occasionally telling her to pick up her tempo. Jim could hear the parts where Franny struggled and where she was more familiar. Sometimes when he was standing listening outside in the front hall, Mary Catherine would come by and bounce his forehead into the door, calling him a "busy-body." Jim would notice that Ma and Franny had heard the sound of his head hitting against the door and had stopped for a few seconds. In moments like that, he would quickly tear up the stairs to escape from getting caught.

♫♫♫

Ma would glance over at the heavy door to the front room. Then, she would give a little start and turn back to Franny, her heavy woolen sweater keeping her warm, but the sleeves sometimes got in her way. "Let's try that again," Ma would then continue. For Franny, those piano lessons had become a time to look forward to during the week. Joanie had been working more and wasn't at home. And when she was, it seemed as if they couldn't stop fighting. It was like Joanie wanted to live her life and make her decisions. She always had some criticism for Franny. This one hour a week, going through her lessons was her time to herself. Franny could hear the improvement in her playing. She could recognize a note or chord that was played correctly and one that she had missed. The sound was getting there, but the songs didn't sound quite right. She could hear the song in what she was playing, but it would drift in and out, like the moon on a cloudy night.

What she looked forward to was when Ma Dewey played. There was something in Ma's music and the way she played that captivated her. The songs were older--many of them were pop songs from around World-War II while some of them were more recent Broadway tunes, but all of them had this thing, that sound in them. She was so much more than a woman who had raised seven children, had a drunk for a husband, and taught piano lessons to neighborhood children. Franny didn't know what it was, but she wished she knew what it was and how to get it.

Once again, there was pounding on the hallway door, followed by the sound of footsteps running up the stairs. "Continue, darlin'," Ma scolded. Franny played her piece of practice music with a feeling of relief. Even though she wasn't exactly mad at Jim, she didn't want to see him and assumed that it was his footsteps that ran up the stairs. It wasn't his reaction to the hug that bothered her but her own recognition that she wanted to share that sad news with the person she cared for, Lenny, and when she couldn't find him, she sought out Jim, who was her second choice. Maybe she deserved to be jabbed by an angry piece of anatomy. "Pay attention, Frances," scolded Ma, "Feel the music in your hands."

♫♫♫

Franny put on her heavy wool coat. "Make sure you're warm," said Ma Dewey, as she helped Franny tie her scarf around her neck. Franny smiled at Ma's kindness. "It's a long walk home from here. I hope your mom is there to make dinner for you." "Probably," answered Franny, realizing that she couldn't help but glance up the stairs to see if Jim was peering down at them. "I hope so," reaffirmed Ma. If Jim was up there, Franny couldn't see him. Suddenly, Mary Catherine appeared at the top of the stairs in a short skirt. "Frances, I hope you're not looking up my skirt. I don't have any knickers on." Mary Catherine only called her "Frances" when she was taking the piss out of her, but it was better than being called Frumpy. "It's getting pretty bushy down there," announced Mary Catherine. "You're so fresh. Go away, you little brat," yelled Ma, not finding anything funny in what her daughter had said.

Ma opened the great front door and let Franny out. "Keep working, Franny," Ma shouted after her. Franny pulled her scarf tight around her throat and tucked it into her winter coat. The air was crisp, and she could see her breath, but somewhere in the distance, someone was playing a guitar. Franny stopped at the bottom of the Dewey's front steps and listened intently. It sounded like Buddy Holly's *Peggy Sue.* A cold numbing sensation tightened in her chest. She wondered how long it would be like this. Would every song remind her of what once was and what will never be? Would she ever feel that way about another musician again? She started down the icy hill on her way home. The strains of what was maybe *Peggy Sue* blowing down Haverhill Street.

♫♫♫

As Jim played, he thought about Franny in his front room. He wondered what she thought about him. Was he just some icky boy, or did he even register in her mind? Did she clutch him when she found out about Buddy's death because she knew he would care or because he was the only one who she knew was a fan of his? He couldn't help but remember how her body felt as he held her- the bones in her back under her shirt, her shoulder blades, her breasts touching his chest. Suddenly, the shame set back in. He knew he was supposed to go to confession and tell of his sins, but he was afraid Father Nelson would ask who it was that he had these thoughts about, and he didn't want to give Father Nelson any wrong impressions of Franny; they were his thoughts after all.

Jim continued playing and singing *Peggy Sue* on his guitar. Occasionally, he would tap his foot from habit, but he would quickly stop, remembering that he was using his foot to brace on the shingles of the precariously tilted roof over the kitchen. The cold night nipped at his cheeks as he continued to play and sing to himself. He knew he was in danger of falling off the roof that looked over the lowlands of Lawrence, eventually spilling into the

Merrimack River, a deep blackness far away from his crazy family, his house, and his world. He was in danger of falling off the roof and in having his da discover him playing the guitar. Jim had been able to keep it hidden in the house and practiced whenever he could find the time when there was no one in hearing distance. But it was difficult to find those moments in a house that was always filled with eight other people and students that came and went throughout the week. Sometimes, he would play up in the attic, but he was always afraid of pulling up the drop-down stairs and not being able to open them again (he could be stuck up there forever)... or even worse, dropping them on someone as they were passing by.

Jim had tried to play in the basement, but the echo was too loud, and he was constantly afraid that he would get caught, and his parents would ask him where he had gotten the beat-up instrument from. Sometimes he would find a quiet closet to play in, but for the time being, the best place was outside his room's window high above the cement backyard where the other children played. He couldn't help thinking about Franny. What it would be like to be an only child, what her world was like, where did she go after school or when she wasn't taking lessons or working around his house. He wondered if she ever thought of him, if she ever thought she loved someone? Jim played in the still night and wondered.

♫♫♫

Da Dewey stood at the top of the stairs, holding the old guitar. "What is this?" he bellowed. Jim stood in the middle of the staircase, frozen. "What is this, boyo?" Da asked. Jim strained to find some kind of reason why he had a guitar in the house and, more importantly, how he got the guitar in the first place. Jim wanted to lie, but he couldn't come up with a good excuse; he wasn't even sure if he was more afraid of Da hitting him or of Da smashing his instrument. "Your sister found this in your closet. What is it?" "I don't know," Jim lied to him. Jim had taken the guitar from under the eaves because he had heard it was supposed to rain, and he didn't want the neck to warp.

"It looks like a guitar," Jim answered, innocently. "Goddamn it, boy– I know it's a feckin' guitar. What do I look like? Where did ye get it?" Da's brogue was becoming heavier and heavier as he got angrier. "I got it from a kid," Jim winced. "He traded me for it." Da threateningly swung the Sears Harmony Supertone over the stairs. "What do ya have that ya could trade for this?" yelled Da. "It was mine," answered Jim, in fear for his instrument. Da winded up and prepared to throw the guitar down to the first floor, where it would smash for sure. "Don't!!!" yelled a voice from behind Jim.

Jim turned to his mother, who pushed the heavy door open and stepped into the front hall. "Don't you drop that," warned Ma. "He got this from thievery," complained Da. By then, most of the other Dewey children were gawking at their father from their rooms or up from the hall leading to the kitchen. "This is ill-gotten gain; he nicked it," reassured Da. "No, it's not," answered Jim. He turned to his ma and pleaded, "I traded my baseball mitt for it." "For what???" demanded Da. Jim knew how proud Da was to be able to afford new baseball mitts for all four of his boys a few Christmases back (The Dewey boys would later learn that the mitts had fallen off a truck in the loading dock of G.T. Grant). Jim could only imagine how angry his father was going to be when he found out that he traded Munchie Breen the mitt for Munchie's old guitar that he got from his older brother when he went into the army.

"Ya did what, boyo?" "I traded my baseball mitt for that guitar." There was a silence that hung over the whole family. All the Dewey children knew what the silence was; it was that stillness which usually led to some violence on Da's part toward whichever child that had initiated it. Da's face turned red; his dark black eyes started to bulge out; Da pulled back his arm, holding the guitar and prepared to wing it in Jim's direction. "Don't you dare, Michael!" shouted Ma. Da stopped in mid-motion. "Who are ya talkin' to, woman?" shouted Da at Ma. "Don't smash that instrument," warned Ma, now standing over Jim, like a protective mother dog. "He shouldn't have traded his mitt, but you're not gonna smash that guitar. What kinda example is that?"

Da lowered the guitar to his side; Jim could smell the old beer wafting down from his father's breath. "I don't want no boy of mine lyin' to me. That's the kind of example it is," fumed Da. Ma turned to Jim and said, "Go up and get that instrument." Jim ran up the stairs and reached for the guitar. Da held it by the neck, and for a moment, he thought about tossing it down the stairs just to teach Jim a lesson. But finally, he relented and let Jim take the guitar. Jim ran down the stairs, clutching his guitar with tears running down his face. "He'll keep the guitar," instructed Ma, "But he's not gonna do anymore lyin'. Right, James?" Jim clutched the guitar to his chest, "Yes, Ma'am." "Feckin' sissy," Da tossed down at Jim, in disgust, and turned to go into his bedroom.

Jim followed Ma into the front room, past the young student whose lesson was interrupted by the fight over the guitar. "Come on back to the piano, Christopher," coached Ma, "Let's keep those wrists up." The rest of the family watched their father enter his and Ma's bedroom. "Ya should've smashed it, Da," shouted Mary Catherine, "It would've been wicked pissah!"

♫♫♫

Lenny sat at the piano. He lightly tapped a few keys. He wished he had continued his piano lessons. He wished he could just start playing. He thought about all the songs he would play if he knew how to. He was alone in the house; it seemed like he was alone all the time now; every once in a while, his ma and Harry would turn up, but usually, it was only him and Grammy Ham, living in the big old house, alone. Lenny felt good that his ma seemed happy in her life with Harry; God knows she was miserable when his father was alive. Lenny's dad, Milton Suggs, or Milty by all those who knew him, was a tough man to live with. A mill man, he believed when he came home from work that his home was his castle and everyone else, including Lenny and his mother, were peasants who could be pushed around and be ordered to do things.

When his dad was crushed by the pile of skids on a loading dock of the Malden Mills, Lenny was saddened that he wouldn't have a dad anymore but to be honest, he never really had a dad. Milty liked to spend his time in the beer joints of Lawrence. He was a mill man's mill man. He worked long hours, moving large quantities of fabric and material from the looms to the different rooms to be treated and rolled out to the loading dock to be loaded on the trucks to be taken to Boston, New York, Halifax, and New Bedford. He shipped materials that were made into clothes, furniture, fabric, and bedding. After work, Milty would follow the other men down to the bars on Merrimack and Methuen Streets and drink their cheap beer until they closed or the fear of facing his mother was too much. Then Milty would stagger home and try to slip into bed, unnoticed. But Lenny's ma would be waiting for him. No matter how late it was, she would wait to hear him turn that knob on the old apartment on Pelham Street. Lenny's ma would yell at him, and occasionally, there would be a real fight, but Milty would finally slip into the bedroom and pass out, drunk.

Lenny sometimes sat with his ma when she would cry and lament her bad luck in ever meeting Milty Suggs all those years ago. At other times she talked about her plans of doing something else except waiting for her drunken husband to come home. She wanted to travel or maybe finish high school and go on to college or business school.

After Milty was crushed by the wooden skids, she never went back to school. Instead, she went to work in the same mill that her deceased husband had died in. She worked in the billing office; the billing manager often dealt with Hamilton Hardware on Hampshire Street. Within a short time, Lenny's ma came home and told him she was going to dinner with a man–"a nice man." Then a short time after that, she didn't come home one night. This was followed by another night of a no-show.

One Sunday, Harry Hamilton showed up for Sunday dinner, in an expensive suit, with his mother, Grammy Ham, to have a meal with Lenny and his ma. The next thing he knew, his ma and Harry were getting married at the Copley Plaza in Boston after which, they would be off to Paris for a honeymoon. Later that year, Harry adopted Lenny and changed his last name to Hamilton. Lenny didn't really mind; he liked that everyone thought he owned the three hardware stores around town. Also, Lenny wasn't that crazy with the old "Suggs" name either; it was too close to sounding like a slug. Those worms you find under a rock. Lenny didn't mind the name Leonard Hamilton, and he even added 'the Third' at the end so that people wouldn't suspect that he was a fill-in. No one ever checked to see if there was ever a Leonard the Second or a Leonard Junior, just Leonard the Third. Louise, Lenny's mom, and Harry traveled a lot. They seemed to be traveling more than they were at home.

Lenny dreamed of the good things that his ma and Harry enjoyed on their trips. The restaurants and hotels that they stayed in, the cars they rode around in, and the fancy parties they went to. Lenny was never invited on these trips; Harry said that they were for business where he met buyers and sellers of materials and tools for his family's stores. His ma and Harry had once taken him to dinner at the Ritz in Boston, and another time, they all went to New York City for New Year's Eve, but Lenny and Grammy Ham had stayed in the hotel while Harry and his ma went to a fancy party. Grammy Ham got plied on some gin and puked in the hotel bed. Little Richard was on the tv that night. Boy, he could sing.

Lenny had been told that those black boys could reach the high notes because they didn't have any testicles. Lenny thought that Richard was a bit of a pansy, but he really liked his singing. He wished he could hit those notes that Richard sang. Lenny got up and went down to the kitchen to see if he could find something to eat. He looked forward to mass on Sunday morning, he was going to be the first altar boy. Father Nelson would work directly with him during the mass's Eucharist.

♫♫♫

Jim hurried down Essex Street, clutching his guitar. He scanned the corners, looking for the familiar figure that entertained the shoppers. It was Christmas time, and the stores on the street were all dressed in red, green, and white, with Santa mannequins in the windows. The gray slush and snow on the sidewalks added a sad look to the decked-out avenue as if even in the joyous season, it couldn't hide the decrepit-ness of Jim's hometown. It was getting dark, and Jim was looking for Smilin' Leo, who made his business on the street by playing songs and singing for dimes and nickels, competing with the Salvation Army's Santa, ringing his bell. Busking, Leo called it. Jim always thought that it was a strange name, Smilin' Leo.

The first thing most people noticed about Leo was that he was black, as black as licorice, and also that he was blind. Leo wore dark, wrap-around sunglasses, even at night. He had them on all the time. Like his beat-up fedora, or the moth-eaten woolen coat, or even the layers of sweaters that he wore, Leo was, for most Lawrencesonians, their only familiarity with a Negro. They smiled back at Leo and left money in his open guitar case; sometimes they would doff their hats or nod in Smilin' Leo's direction (which was kind of silly, since everyone knew Leo was blind and couldn't see them). Jim needed to find Smilin' Leo quick; he needed someone to tune his guitar.

Jim had been playing the guitar for almost a year. Although he was starting to sound a bit fluid on the instrument, he still couldn't tune the strings by ear. They always seemed to be out of tune. Lately, Jim had been using his mother's piano to tune the guitar, but no matter how much he tried, he couldn't get it in tune enough for it to sound right. At least not like the way Smilin' Leo could. Jim knew that at some point, his da would come home again (he always did), and he wouldn't be allowed to play in the house. Jim's Da had disappeared and hadn't come home in weeks. It wasn't unusual for him; he would disappear a couple of times a year. Sometimes he would meet some guys in a bar, and they would head somewhere in hopes of searching for work. Of course, they would never really find work and end up drinking whatever they made. Other times, Ma would discover that he was in jail somewhere, in Boston or Worcester, maybe. Whenever Jim's da was gone, there was almost a festive atmosphere in the house, like Christmas but without having to go to Midnight Mass.

Ma ran the house most days, and when Da was missing, it ran better and without any violence. Even Ma seemed happier when Da was gone. When he came back, she had to pretend that she missed him and was worried. She would bug him about letting her know where he'd gone, but you could tell she never really had her heart in it. For the kids, it was always easier to have to deal with the family and not always be judging Da's mood. Maybe if he was sober (and that wasn't often), he could joke and kid around, but if he had a snoot-full, they knew better not to try anything, buddy. You could get your bum beat.

Jim looked across the street and spotted Smilin' Leo on the opposite corner. Leo stood with his beautiful 1953 acoustic guitar, slung over his right shoulder, and a big smile as he rocked back and forth on the only bare spot of sidewalk across from the Strand Theatre that wasn't covered with snow. Jim waited for the cars to go by and then crossed Essex Street. Leo was in his old hat and ragged jacket, playing his guitar and singing about *Nobody Loves You When You're Down and Out*. In front of Leo, on the sidewalk, was his guitar case, open, a few coins resting on the blue velvet, inviting other denominations to join them as pedestrians passed by.

Jim had seen Ray Charles on Ed Sullivan, who was a blind piano player. Ray had worn the same black sunglasses that Leo wore, and he also smiled like Leo. Maybe they should've called him Smilin' Ray. When Jim got a few feet away from Leo, he suddenly turned his head to the boy and smiled wide, his bright white teeth flashing big across his black face.

"Hey, Strings," Leo called. Strings was the name that Leo had given to Jim because he would usually ask him to tune his strings or fix a broken one. Jim was always surprised that Leo could recognize him before he even spoke to the old man. "Hi, Leo," Jim started, he hated interrupting Leo in the middle of a song, but nobody was really listening anyway. Leo would talk to Jim without having to stop playing. Leo would strum or pick the same riff and hold a discussion with anyone on the street. Jim would watch him and hope that one day he would be able to play without even paying any attention to it.

Jim's uncle Christopher was a stripper in the Boot Mill; he could shear cloth without even looking at it. Using the large shears, Christy could carry on a conversation without even looking at the work he was doing (Christy had lost a few fingers on his left hand, but that was to a mortar when he was in the Philippines during the war, "not freezing his arse off," as Da would have to point out). Leo could play while he was talking or "attending to the ladies," as he used to call it.

"Can ya take a look at it?" Jim asked, never really noticing he was asking for the impossible. "I'll see what I can do," answered Leo smilin'. He swung his worn guitar around his shoulder and held Jim's beat-up Harmony guitar in his large, cracked hands. Leo plucked each string, listening to it over the din of the traffic on Essex Street. After he plucked the string, Leo would then turn the tuning peg until the string stretched into tune. Leo tuned the guitar for Jim. Jim liked to stay and listen to Smilin' Leo play. He also liked to look at Leo's guitar; it was a 1953 Guild F-20 Hoboken Troubadour, acoustic guitar, made of Maple, with an Ebony fingerboard and Mother-of-Pearl fingerboard inlays on the neck. It was time-worn, a working instrument, but in the evening, it kind of shimmered in the light of the evening dusk.

Leo got sounds out of that guitar that Jim couldn't imagine a regular guitar could make. Smilin' Leo played the blues, though most of the people on Essex Street that heard it just thought it was nigger music; Leo called it all the blues. He had told Jim about his growing up in Alabama and Mississippi, where it was always warm. Leo told him about learning the guitar from some boys he knew in Mobile and coming north with them to Chicago. Smilin' Leo told him of playing the blues clubs on the 'Southside of Chi-town,' as he called it. He talked about playing with Howlin' Wolf, Muddy Waters, and Slim Harpo and even recorded a record with Buddy Guy at Blue Bird Sound. Most of the names Jim didn't know, but he found the music interesting and tried to learn how to play *I'm a King Bee* from Smilin' Leo. But Jim didn't have the strength in his fingers yet to make the slides and not have them come out screechy.

Leo handed the guitar back to Jim. He took it and listened to the newly tuned strings. Leo swung his guitar back and started to strum on it. "Good as new," Leo added. Jim thanked him. He wished he could stay around and listen to Leo, but he knew he had to get home. It was getting dark, and he had to go through Spickville to get back to Paddy Hill. Jim reached into his pocket and dropped ten cents into Smilin' Leo's case. Leo stopped playing and turned angrily to Jim. "Take that out, boy." "I thought I'd give ya that for tuning my guitar," answered Jim innocently. "Take it out, Strings," ordered Leo, "We're musicians; we take care of our own." Jim removed the two nickels and said good-bye to Smilin' Leo. Leo turned and played S*poonful* as the people made their way home after work and Christmas shopping. It made Jim feel good to have Smilin' Leo call him a musician, even though he guessed that Leo wasn't really saying that Jim was as good as him, but it made Jim feel good anyway.

♫♫♫

Jim rushed up the hill to Haverhill Street and his house. He was aware that he was in Spickville, but he was on the main street, so it was pretty safe, as safe as you were going to be in Spickville. Paddy Hill was above Spickville, sitting in the Lawrence Highlands. Jim made his way up the hill; in spots, the sidewalk was icy. The moisture on the cement was starting to freeze over as the day faded, and it became colder. Jim was concentrating on his footing when he was shoved from behind. All of a sudden, he found himself tumbling to the ground. Jim clutched his guitar, holding it up so that it wouldn't scrape on the sidewalk. That's when he was shoved again, "Pinche pendejo. Get in there!" Three sets of hands grabbed his coat and dragged him into a small alley between two double-decker houses. "I've got no money," yelled Jim, hoping that it was all they wanted. One of the boys pushed him to the ground, but again Jim was able to avoid scraping the guitar. "I don't have any!" he shouted again. Another boy grabbed for the guitar in Jim's raised hands.

"We'll take this then," was the answer. Jim tried to recognize the boys; many of the Puerto Ricans in this neighborhood went to John Quincy Adams Junior High School with him. Maybe they will realize that they went to school with him and let him keep his guitar. But Jim couldn't recognize any of the three boys. They sounded older than him; maybe they were in high school. But with the darkness in the alley and with the hoods of their coats over their heads, Jim couldn't make out who they were. The boy pulled the guitar free.

The Hispanic teen-ager stood over Jim, holding the guitar over his head. "Don't!" screamed Jim, fearing he was going to smash the guitar on the cement. One of the boys kicked Jim in the back, but Jim could only reach for his Sears Harmony Supertone and beg the boy holding his instrument. "Please don't. It's old, and it keeps goin' out of tune. Don't take it!" The third boy ran up and kicked Jim in the ribs, making him crumple up into a ball on the icy alleyway. "Hey there, pendejo-- how 'bout I smash this against the building? What you say to that?" Jim couldn't answer, the kick had taken the air out of his lungs, and he couldn't breathe. The second boy swung down at Jim with his fist, bouncing a jab off the back of Jim's head. "How 'bout it? Should I smash it?" threatened the first Puerto Rican boy.

"If you do, your friends there will be picking you up in pieces," came a voice from behind the attacking boys. The Puerto Ricans turned and faced the owner of the voice, blocking the exit of the alley. "Give him his guitar back," ordered the voice. Jim looked up from the ground.

At first, he couldn't make out the voice's face in the shadows of the alley. "We were jus' messin' with our friend here," answered the first of Jim's attackers. "Give him his guitar back," replied the voice. This time the shadowed figure threw down a baseball mitt and raised the baseball bat that he was holding. "Do it fast," the figure ordered.

The Puerto Ricans looked at each other. It was obvious that they didn't plan this out, and since the exit was blocked by some guy with a bat, it had suddenly taken a more serious turn. The first boy lowered the guitar down to Jim on the ground, "We were jus' messin' with 'im." Jim grabbed the guitar as it got close to him and pulled it to his body. "You don't want me messin' you," said the figure as Jim stood and started to walk towards the exit of the alley.

The Puerto Rican boys watched Jim shuffle by, checking over his guitar for any collateral damage. When Jim got close enough to the figure, he looked up and stared into his savior's face. He recognized the boy, who may have been a few years older, but he still couldn't place the face with where he knew him from. Jim nodded to the boy who saved him and his guitar and mumbled a quick "thanks" but kept walking out to Haverhill Street. When Jim got to the street, he turned left quickly and continued to make his way up the hill.

The boy didn't react; he just watched the three Puerto Rican boys. Feeling he was safe from another attack, Jim stopped and turned around to look down the hill from where he came. He saw the boy with the bat resting on his shoulder, walking the other way. The baseball mitt hanging off the end of the bat, it was at that moment that Jim remembered where he had seen the boy; he was the guy at Barnaby's who was playing the drums. He was the Webster boy, who told him that he didn't see him playing the drums on stage. Jim watched the Webster boy walk away down towards Main Street.

♫♫♫

Midnight mass didn't go well. It was a big thing for Lenny since it was his first Christmas assisting in the biggest celebration of the year. Saint Tonys was decked out in all its yuletide beauty, and as it was every year, the mass was packed. Standing room only, the parish turned out to enjoy this most special mass. Unfortunately, Father Nelson had started celebrating a whole lot earlier than he should have. By the time Lenny had arrived in the sacristy to prepare, Father Nelson already was flushed and had a goofy smile on his face. Both Lenny and Ratsie could tell that the priest had already started in on the sacramental wine. The priest also had a sway in his walk that Lenny had never seen before. Father Nelson had been known amongst the altar-boys to like to indulge in a bit of the wine stored in the locked cabinet in the sacristy. But tonight, it was obvious that Father Nelson wasn't the most sober shepherd to administer mass to his flock.

As they were getting into their cassocks, Lenny whispered to Ratsie, "You think we should say something?" Ratsie shook his head, the flesh under his chin waving back and forth, "I'm not saying anything. The last thing my pop wants to hear when he's soused is that he looks like he's soused." "What will we do?" asked Lenny. "Pray," was Ratsie's suggestion, "If he falls down, we'll help him up." It was a good idea if Father Nelson fell down, but he didn't... he did everything but that.

Father Nelson started out by slurring his words during the first reading. His reading of the birth of baby Jesus was rambling, and he had to stop a number of times to find his place. Then during the Gospel, he became so quiet that even Ratsie and Lenny couldn't hear him, and they were kneeling only few feet away. In the Homily, he openly slurred his words and, at times, wasn't even understandable; the Mystery of Faith was left a mystery since he was almost incoherent. During communion, he kept dropping the host. Poor Ratsie looked like a Red Sox outfielder shagging flies. The Epistle sounded slurred; even though it was spoken in Latin (Most people assumed the clergy was just talking gibberish, anyways).

Father Nelson would occasionally reach down into a cubby hole in the altar and take a drink from a paper cup that Lenny was sure wasn't water. The fortunate thing about a Midnight Mass was that most of the Parish couldn't wait to get home and open their presents or to sleep it off. It didn't seem to bother the parishioners leaving that it was obvious that Father Nelson had over-done the blood of Christ on his birthday.

Now in the sacristy, Ratsie and Lenny undressed quickly, hoping to get away before Father Nelson came back. "Merry Christmas, Leonard," said Ratsie, making his exit out a back door. Lenny had just swung his arm through his winter coat's sleeve when suddenly Father Nelson appeared. He stood in the doorway, staring at Lenny, who recognized the stare from Grammy Ham after Lenny had made her more than three gin and tonics. He buttoned up his coat to make it obvious that he was on his way out. "You know, Leonard. We're a lot alike," started Father Nelson. Lenny nodded in agreement, feeling a real urgency to leave as fast as he could. "I have always liked you, my boy," added Father Nelson, as he swayed into the room. Lenny backed up as the Holy Father approached him.

"What would you like to do when you grow up?' he asked. Lenny started to stutter, it was unusual for him to stutter, but suddenly, he couldn't stop. "I-I-I-I was thinking about be-be-becoming a priest. Like you, Father." "You would make a fine seminarian," slurred the priest, making seminarian sound like "sud-marion."

Father Nelson kept stalking towards Lenny, who was slowly trying to back away. "You have a voice like an angel," the priest purred. Lenny backed up against the counter where the wine and communion hosts were stored. Father Nelson reached his hand out from his cassock and placed it familiarly against Lenny's bare cheek. "I hope you understand how much I appreciate you, Leonard. If you took your orders, we could spend a lot of time together."

Lenny smiled uneasily. It pleased him that Father Nelson had this kind of affection for him, but the feeling of the man's hand on his face made him feel creepy. He could smell the wine on the priest's breath, heavy and sweet. Father Nelson leaned forward, closer to him. Lenny could hear him whisper, "We're so alike." Before Lenny could understand, Father Nelson kissed him on the lips.

Lenny froze. Father Nelson's lips pressed against his– Lenny stood motionless, confused about what to do next. He kissed back, the smell of the wine pushing up his nostrils. Suddenly, Father Nelson held his arm, and something brushed against his prick, which Lenny suddenly realized was erect and pushing against his pants. Father Nelson rubbed his prick again.

Lenny pushed the priest's hand away. Father Nelson stopped kissing him and embraced him around the waist. The priest buried his face in Lenny's shoulder. They stood that way for what seemed to Lenny like an hour. "I'm sorry, son," whimpered Father Nelson. Lenny could feel Father gently rocking. At first, Lenny thought the priest was crying, but then he realized that whatever was moving was below the clergy man's waist. Suddenly a hand hit Lenny in the thigh; that was when he realized what was moving. At one point, Father Nelson rubbed his prick on Lenny's thigh, trying to move closer to Lenny's fly, but Lenny pulled his leg away.

Lenny wanted to look down but was afraid to. He had never seen another prick, only his own. Lenny was excited, but he was confused as to why. He knew nothing about what Father Nelson was doing to him… on this most holy day. Lenny wanted to run, but he didn't want to make Father Nelson angry. That's when the priest wretched and almost collapsed on him. Lenny was practically holding the father up; the holy man had orgasmed.

Lenny looked down at his pants leg and saw what he felt, the oozing ejaculation that Father Nelson had shot on him. Lenny had no idea of what had just happened or where did the gooey stuff on his corduroy trousers came from. Father Nelson stood up and apologized. He had a hand cloth and wiped Lenny's church pants.

The priest turned away from him and pulled his pants up. Lenny noticed the white boxer shorts that the clergyman was wearing. He thought it was strange that with all the special vestments they wore, Father Nelson wore regular underwear, like every other guy wear; white boxer shorts. Father Nelson buttoned his cassock down and stared at the wall, where a single depiction of the crucifixion of Christ hung. It looked like Father Nelson was crying from behind, but Lenny couldn't be sure. "I'm sorry, Leonard," apologized the priest, without turning around, "Merry Christmas…"

Lenny didn't know what to do or to say. He could only just mumble "Merry Christmas, Father," and left. Walking down the hallway to the door to Saint Anthony's parking lot, Lenny started to become more aware of what had happened. When he exited from the church, a blast of cold December air hit him in the face. He walked a few steps into the parking lot and suddenly became sick. Bracing himself on a rear panel of a car, he threw up. When he finished, he wiped his mouth on the sleeve of his winter coat. As he walked home, he realized that he and Father Nelson were not alike… and he didn't want to become a priest.

♫♫♫

Franny sat at the long table surrounded by the Deweys. Ma brought the large pot of spaghetti and butter sauce from the kitchen while Kathleen started dishing it out in bowls. Franny wasn't used to the loud dinners that the Deweys had, but she did enjoy them more than eating at home alone. Joanie had met Uncle Mutt at The Commodore Ballroom, a night club in Lowell, and Joanie was spending a lot of time with Uncle Mutt. He was a manager at the club, so Joanie and her friend, Ginny, could drink for free and even have dinner with Mutt, leaving Franny on her own. When Ma Dewey found out that Franny was eating alone, she was invited to dinner. Franny had been taking lessons from Ma for three years and was doing well with her piano playing. In fact, Ma told Franny that she was her best student.

Though Jim was her son and easily the most talented musically among her children, it was Franny who Ma felt was most gifted by her musical ability. Ma had been teaching piano most of her adult life, almost thirty years, but Franny was the one that would leave Ma smiling and hoping that she would continue to play. Ma could hear how well Franny could keep rhythm even while other students and her children bustled in and out of the room. Ma also realized that Franny had perfect pitch. Even Jim realized he could go to Franny, and she could tune his guitar with only the piano. Ma would tell Franny that she had to keep playing and keep practicing, that she could be very good one day– maybe even get a scholarship to a good music school, like the Berklee School of Music or Julliard even. The problem was that, unfortunately, Franny assumed Ma said that to every student.

Franny realized that she was getting good on the piano. At times, she and Jim would sit at the keyboard and play together. She noticed that she wasn't struggling as much, trying to keep up with Jimmy, who felt he had to prove he was faster and more proficient at his playing. No matter how fast they played *Chopsticks,* she could keep up. It was usually Jim who got lost or fell behind. Jim would get up and announce that a piano was a "girl's instrument," and he would go off somewhere in the house and play his guitar. The thing was that Franny wanted to try to learn how to play the guitar next.

Franny took her bowl of spaghetti and sat next to Mary Catherine. Mary Catherine glared at Franny and filled her mouth with spaghetti, with long strands of the pasta dangling out, she asked, "Are you still here?" Ma Dewey interrupted her. "She's a guest, Mary Catherine. Let her eat her dinner." Jim entered the kitchen carrying his guitar. He carefully placed the instrument in a corner and sat at the table. Franny thought it was strange seeing Jim without a guitar hanging on his neck. Jim took a bowl away from Kevin, who had taken two and was trying to finish his dinner fast so he could to start on the other. "Give it to me, Kev," whined Jim, pulling the bowl from his older brother. "Take another," growled Kevin, as the bowl slipped from his grip. Jim sat down across from

Franny. She watched Jim eat his spaghetti while trying to push Kevin's hands away from his dinner. Franny couldn't help but remember the night at church during Mass when Jim had started crying (of course, she didn't know that Mary Catherine had punched him in the nuts). Franny thought about Lenny; she had last seen him the past Christmas at Midnight Mass.

Franny still dreamed of Lenny. He was usually wearing a floppy sweater and was lying on the floor of the girl's room, in this house, listening to records with her. She and Jim still listened to records together. The Deweys had a lot more records since the last time Lenny had been over. Mary Catherine had found that she had a real talent for kleptomania. She could go into W.T. Grant and come out with at least three layers of new clothing and a dozen records. Unfortunately, Mary Catherine had no taste or interest in music, and with her poor reading skills, the instructions of purloining the most recent Everly Brothers album could produce a Beverly Sills opera record.

Mary Catherine did take her "nicking" (as Da referred to shoplifting) seriously, having fashioned a large pouch from one of Ma's aprons to wear under her overcoat. Mary Catherine could go down an aisle filling it up. Once in a while, some unfortunate store employee or manager would try to stop her, but Mary Catherine would just refute everything they accused her of until they tried to reach into her coat. Then Mary Catherine would scream bloody murder or more like bloody "He's grabbing my tit!" Most store employees and store managers would retreat back to the office after being accused of molesting a young girl.

It was always hard to keep up with the conversations at the Dewey dinner table. Most of the talk was usually about something that Mary Catherine had done. Franny did enjoy the dinners with the Deweys, even when Da Dewey came home to eat. This wasn't often, but occasionally Da would stagger in and stare at everyone at the table. His own children didn't give much thought to him; after all, he hadn't been giving much thought to them for most of their lives. But every time he saw Franny eating at his table, he saw two dollars a lesson that he wasn't getting and taking down to Barnaby's for a pint. Ma Dewey had made it clear to him that Franny could spend as much time at the house as she wanted. Ma knew that most times, Franny was home alone, and it made good business sense to keep one's best student happy and close by. Besides, she was hoping that Franny could be a good influence on Mary Catherine, who was having some real acting up problems. At least, Franny would answer with a "Yes, Ma'am" or "Please" and "Thank you."

Mary Catherine was most likely to tell you to "shut up" or "stick it up your arse," using one of the colorful phrases of her da. Not that it was the worst of it. After the time that the Sister Mary Celeste of Our Lady of the Assumption called Ma and reported that Mary Catherine was rubbing boy's unmentionables to see them stick up. Well, it was a pretty short hop from there to the city's public school system. The other thing that Ma liked about Franny was that she was helping Jimmy come out of his shell.

Jim had taken to the guitar, but Franny was the only person Ma could remember who Jimmy would actually pay attention to. Ma knew it bothered Jim that Franny had pretty much caught up with his ability on the piano, which had encouraged Jim's concentration on the guitar. Ma liked the way Jim and Franny would sit on the piano bench and play together. It reminded her of her first beau, Thomas Wood. Ma also liked the fact that many times they would gather in the girls' room upstairs and listen to record albums with the other kids until it was time for the little girls to go bed. To Ma Dewey, Franny was always a welcomed guest at the house. After dinner, Franny and Jim crawled onto the floor of the girl's bedroom. Tonight, it was only Jim, Franny, Kathleen, Jim's oldest sister, and the two younger girls, Dorrie and Ann. Kathleen sat on the bed, her hands tucked tightly between her knees, holding her skirt in place. She was the most demur of the Dewey girls, the quiet one, a listener, and the most pragmatic of them all. Dorrie and Ann had one of the kittens that lived in the basement with them.

They knew that they could play with the cat until Ma caught them, and then it would have to go back downstairs, or if their da caught them, the cat would probably be thrown out a window.

Jim and Franny listened intently to the album spinning on the used record player. The voice was ragged; it sang songs of trouble and people struggling, the guitar banged along with the song like it didn't care how it sounded. Franny and Jim had been listening to that record for weeks, ever since Mary Catherine nicked it from the J.C. Penny downtown. Jim had asked her to look for a Gene Vincent album. He really wanted to listen to *Be Bop a Lula*. Later that night, Mary Catherine had left a different album on his bed. The album was by a guy named Woody-- Mary Catherine saw the name Woody and thought it was about Woody Woodpecker, who made her laugh when he was in the movie to come on before the real movie at the Emporium. Of course, she was disappointed when she found out it was some nasally guy with a guitar (Mary Catherine said that she didn't have much time to check names and things when she was busy nicking).

Now stuck with the record, Jim listened to it and liked it. The next time Franny came over, they ran to the record player, and he played the stolen album for her. It had been two weeks since the record arrived in the house, and they hadn't taken it off the record player since. Not even for *Chuck Berry is on Top*. It was an old record, the album cover was worn, and the corners were mashed. It was called *The Live Wire Woody Guthrie*.

Jim and Franny played the record over and over, it was filled with stories about people out west and places that they didn't even know about. They listened to *Pastures of Plenty*, *Grand Coulee Dam,* and *1913 Massacre*. At times, Jim could feel he was about to cry when he listened to Woody talk about the people of Oklahoma losing their homes and having to leave and look for jobs somewhere else. Franny couldn't help but feel for those men who were trapped in the Centralia Mine and wrote their good-byes to their families on the mine's wall in *Good-bye Centralia.* There was also something in the sound of this guy, Woody's voice. It was as if he lived the stories he was singing about.

Between songs, Woody would talk with a woman who was his wife and would ask Woody questions about the song he just played or the song he was about to play. The back of the record album said that it had been recorded in one night at a place called Fuld Hall in Newark, New Jersey. Neither Franny nor Jim had ever heard of Fuld Hall, and only Franny knew where Newark or New Jersey was, but there was a guy singing songs from his life (they guessed), and they were hearing it miles away in Massachusetts, over and over again.

There was something in the songs Woody played, it was just him and his guitar, and you couldn't help but to just listen to every song. Franny and Jim hated when the record ended, they would turn it over and start all over again.

♫♫♫

The girls eventually got tired and took the kitten back down to its ma in the basement. Kathleen fell asleep on her bed, her hands still clenched between her legs. Franny realized that she had to get home. Joanie told her she would be late tonight and not to wait up, but she knew she had better be sleeping on the couch when her mom came home. Franny got up and went to the front door to leave. Ma came out of the kitchen, drying a dish. She smiled at her as Franny opened the big front door and stepped out into the humid summer night. The mosquitoes from the Merrimack River buzzed around her head as she stepped out onto the stoop. Coming up the steps was Da Dewey, reeking of old beer and cigars. He glared at Franny and pushed past her into his house. Franny walked down the steps on her way home. Inside the house, Franny could hear Da's shout, "Is she payin' yet? Toni, is she payin'?" Franny just kept on walking.

♫♫♫

Franny was surprised when she got home; Joanie was home and in her room. Before she knocked on her mother's door, she knew something bad had happened.

Franny walked to the bedroom door and knocked lightly, "Mommy, are you in there?" Suddenly the door swung open, and Joanie stood in her pajamas, her eyes red from crying. It was obvious to Franny that Joanie had broken up with Mutt. In a way, Franny was glad that it was over. She had never trusted Mutt and hoped that at some point, her mom would see through the guy. It always seemed that Franny could recognize the men in her mother's life better than Joanie could. And Mutt was one of the easiest. She wasn't sure if it was the way Mutt talked to her, or the way he looked at her, or just the smell of his aftershave that would linger in the apartment days after he stayed over. Franny didn't like Mutt. When Joanie explained that she and Mutt had a fight earlier that night and that she wasn't going to see him anymore, Franny was relieved. She even looked forward to spending more time with her mom.

To comfort Joanie, Franny slept in her mom's bed with her. Franny couldn't help but notice that the pillow still smelled of Mutt, the last remnants of a lost affair. It was still good to be in bed with Joanie; it felt like those comfy days of being a young child safely wrapped up in her mom's arms. Then there was a loud knocking at the front door.

Franny jumped up, not sure if it was real or a dream. "Don't go," warned Joanie. They both huddled together in the bed while the banging continued at the front door. "Open up, Joanie. I wanna talk to ya, honey," Mutt begged loudly. "Let's call the police," suggested Franny. "Let me in, baby," demanded Mutt through the door. "He'll go away," said Joanie, as she and Franny cowered together in the middle of the double bed that Joanie's mom, Franny's grandmother, had given them when her grandparents got a new one from Jordan Marsh.

The pounding got louder, resonating throughout the apartment. Then it was not loud knocking but the sound of a body throwing its whole weight into the door. "I think we should call the police," Franny again suggested, but it was too late. The sound of the door springing open and slamming against the living room wall was followed by the sound of a man's footsteps pounding towards the bedroom.

Franny and Joanie watched in horror as the bedroom door burst open. Mutt stood in the doorway; his hair was mussed; it was the first time that Franny had ever seen Uncle Mutt's hair out of place. It was usually combed back, in a pompadour, though it was Mutt's eyes that warned the two women of the impending danger. Franny naturally had never seen him like this but it was Joanie who was really scared because she had never seen Mutt look so wild, like a whole different person.

"Get out!" yelled Joanie. Mutt stood in the doorway, sweat and anger dripping off his face. "Don't listen to that cunt!" answered Mutt, trying to control himself. Franny held onto her mother; she had never heard that word "cunt" before. She didn't know who or what Joanie was listening to. "Get out!!!" shouted Joanie, "I'll call the police, Russell." Franny watched Mutt stalk to the bed, suddenly realizing who Russell was. There was a slap of a hand against skin, and Joanie flew off the bed. "I would never do that to ya, baby," reasoned Mutt, even though it had already happened.

Joanie sprung up from the floor as Franny kicked at Mutt, in case he was going to try to hit her. Joanie ran at Mutt, cutting him off from going after Franny. "Get out of here, Russell. I'm gonna call the cops." Mutt wound up and punched Joanie in the stomach, knocking her over the bed. Franny's mind was racing; she shot up from the bed and ran out of the room, yelling, "Help!!! Help!!!"

Mutt stepped to the heap on the floor-Joanie. "Baby, I wouldn't do that. I'd never hurt ya." Mutt caught Joanie in the jaw with a vicious uppercut. After her head snapped back, Joanie slumped over onto the floor; her hair covered her face. "I didn't touch her. I wouldn't fuck that cunt if she was the only whore left on earth," Mutt whispered. Joanie was on her back; she could taste the warm blood in her mouth and tried to raise her legs to push him away. "I told ya I love ya, baby," Mutt reached down and tore at Joanie's pajama pants. Holding Joanie's head with other hand, he ripped and tore at her until he was down to Joanie's underpants. "I love ya, baby," he said, as he tried to pry her legs apart. "I'm gonna show you." Joanie tried to fight back, but Mutt was stronger. The smell of alcohol reeked from him; it wasn't long before he had forced her legs open and ripped her underpants off. "Don't listen to Ginny. I'll show ya how much I love ya," Mutt said, reaching down to undo his pants with his free hand. That's when the keyboard hit him on the left side of the head, from behind.

Mutt staggered onto the bed; when he turned around, the keyboard hit again, violently in the face. Franny couldn't tell whether it was the keyboard, made out of a three-foot-long, 2" X 6" piece of wood, painted white with black keys painted over them, that made the loud crack or whether it was Mutt's nose breaking. Franny was too scared to care. Mutt screamed and fell back onto the bed. Franny stood over him, the rage all placed in her arms and her hands. Raising her fake piano keyboard over her head, Franny aimed at Mutt, who was struggling to stop the flow of blood from his nose while preparing to dodge another swipe of the wooden keys. Suddenly, Franny realized that someone had taken her practice keyboard from her.

The keyboard that Patrick Dewey had made for her from orders of his mother (Ma Dewey thought about having Jimmy make the upgraded keyboard, but Jimmy and any kind of a hand tool besides a guitar wasn't a good idea-- Patrick wouldn't end up in the emergency room at Lawrence General). Joanie stepped to the bed and started beating Mutt with the faux musical instrument. "Fuck you, Mutt. Fuck you!!!" she yelled as she beat her former lover. "Get outta our house!" yelled Franny. Mutt sprang up from the bed and sprinted towards the bedroom door to escape. Unfortunately for Mutt, he had been hit so hard by Franny in the face that everything was a blur. Mutt got a good running start but missed the doorway and ran into the door frame, collapsing into a heap on the floor.

Joanie ran over to him and continued to beat the unconscious Mutt with the keyboard, "Fuck you, Mutt!!!" Franny watched her mother beat her former uncle. Slowly

Joanie started to tire and finally crouched down, still holding the keyboard, ready to use it again if he came to.

"Should I call the police?" Franny asked. Joanie dropped the keyboard, many of the white keys stained with Mutt's blood. Franny looked to her mom, who searched around the room, finally settling on a small space rug. Joanie grabbed the rug and pulled it next to Mutt's unconscious body. "Help me," Joanie ordered. Each took one of Mutt's arms, and they rolled the unconscious man onto the small carpet. "Now what?" asked Franny. "Help me pull," answered Joanie.

She pulled on the carpet while Franny gripped Mutt's torn jacket. Pulling together, they dragged the rug with Mutt's body on it out of the bedroom and through the apartment, towards the front door. "It's a good thing these are wood floors," said Joanie, as they labored dragging him to the building's hall. When they got to the door, Joanie opened it and looked out. "We'll roll him down the stairs," Joanie said with a laugh as she pulled him out the door, "Like a box of trash." Across the hall stood Mrs. Young, with her three young kids, dressed in pajamas, watching them drag the unconscious Mutt out of their apartment.

Once in the hall, Joanie dragged Mutt, still unconscious, down the corridor with Franny pushing him from behind. Finally, they came to the top of the stairs, and with one more hard push, they rolled Mutt down the stairs. When he reached the bottom in the building's vestibule, Joanie instructed Franny to hold the front door open. At this point, Joanie had worked up her understanding of leverage and rolled the unconscious body of her lover out of the front door and onto the front porch of their Marston Street building. Joanie looked to Franny, proud of their little battle together, and led her daughter back into the building. On their way back to their apartment, they passed Mrs. Young standing with her children. Mrs. Young shook her head sadly, "This is what happens when you don't have a husband."

Joanie just kept on walking to their front door, Franny wondered if her mother would say anything to her neighbor's rudeness, but Franny knew her mother wouldn't do that– it wasn't her. Suddenly, Joanie stopped and turned; it was the moment that Franny realized that her mother wasn't wearing any pants, her dark pubic hair showing beneath her pajama tops. Joanie stepped up to Mrs. Young, who recoiled and clutched her children. "The next time Davey comes home drunk and beats you, don't come to my door looking to hide again." Her mom turned around and stalked back into their apartment, followed by Franny– giving Mrs. Young the stink eye. Inside they called the police to report a drunk had passed out on the front stoop of their building.

Lenny and the River Rats

The invitation came in the form of Mary Catherine telling Franny that her "boyfriend" was looking for a piano player for their band…and that they would rather have a girl than a fag. Franny had no idea what that meant, but she thought that it would be fun to be in a band. Mary Catherine had no idea what kind of music they played, except that it was "rock and roll." Franny sat on the bus on Route 114, crossing over the Merrimack River and heading south to a fashionable part of Lawrence, Andover Heights.

Franny had been playing the piano at school for the last few years. If she couldn't do it, Jim would play it in her place. Jim didn't really like to play the piano; he felt that he was more of a guitar player than a piano player, but the Lawrence School system didn't have a big call for guitar players. Franny enjoyed learning all the piano parts for the Lawrence High School production of "Oklahoma" and "Anything Goes." She liked playing for the productions but was always uncomfortable playing in front of people.

She was very self-conscious about wearing her new glasses. Franny had chosen the glasses in tribute to Buddy Holly, but they looked like "boys" glasses. She didn't really like the girl glasses she had been wearing, and when it was time to get a new prescription, she opted for black-rimmed glasses, even though many of the other students called her "His Boy Sherman" in reference to the boy in the Mr. Peabody television show.

Ma Dewey would help her prepare, and then Franny would have to sit through the rehearsals for the production. Most of the other instruments would have to follow her. It was fun and great practice to play with people singing to her accompaniment. Her mom also enjoyed going to the performances and watching the show. Joanie would sing the big songs for months afterward. It also helped Franny to get over her stage fright a bit. The more she played in front of people, the more comfortable she became with glasses or without glasses.

Franny and Joanie had come to grips with what had happened that night. Joanie broke up with Mutt. Franny felt closer to her mom and respected her more for fighting Mutt off, even after he had beaten her like that. Joanie had recovered from Mutt's beating, but she never really got over the attack to her confidence. Joanie had stopped going out with Ginny. Franny hadn't seen Ginny in months. Joanie had stopped going out at night and stopped drinking, except maybe a glass of wine at Aunt Lucy's house or a cocktail at Thanksgiving with Grandma and Grandpa.

Joanie had lost something that night. She no longer talked of men and marriage. She just concentrated on Franny and on being a "better mother." Franny never thought that Joanie was a bad mother. Franny knew that Joanie wanted what everyone else told her she needed, a husband. But it seemed like Joanie was ready to accept not having that necessity. Franny had naturally wondered why Joanie had not married her father, but Joanie would just shake her head and say, "that train's come and gone."

Franny couldn't understand why Joanie wouldn't tell her who her father was and what had happened, but every time she brought up the subject, it got Joanie mad, and she would clam up even more. Franny would lie in bed and wonder at night why her father never tried to contact her. She must have a father somewhere; why wouldn't he be interested in her? As much as she loved her mom, she couldn't really get over the disappointment of her not telling who her father was and why he didn't want to have anything to do with her. Franny always fantasized that the reason her mom wouldn't tell her who her father was because he was famous, and Joanie didn't want to bother him in his busy life.

Once, while sitting out on the Dewey's roof with Jimmy, watching the stars on a crisp autumn night, she mentioned her thoughts of who her father might be. They started imagining all kinds of things; he was a Russian spy, he was a black man (even though Franny was as far from a black man as you could get), he was a priest-- Father Nelson, or an athlete, or maybe he was a musician, Frank Sinatra, Bobby Darin, Elvis (even though Elvis would have been twelve at the time), maybe even the President of the United States (Franny didn't want to be Eisenhower's daughter). Each of them would make up a name and then give the reason why it had been kept secret (because Elvis would have to be single; otherwise, all the girls in the world would kill themselves. Who would want to be responsible for mass suicides?). Franny knew it was only a fun game. Her mother wasn't going to tell her who her father was, and it so disappointed Franny to know that no one had ever come forward and owned up to her. Jim felt sorry for her. He would even offer up his da, but he knew that anyone who had the choice wouldn't take his da, no matter how desperate for a father they were.

Franny enjoyed being with her mom, but she had no real reason to go over to the Dewey house anymore. Ma Dewey and Franny had reached a point where there wasn't much that Ma could teach her. After six years, Franny could keep up with her and with Jim. Most of the times, she would go over to the large house on Haverhill Street to play the piano between Ma's students and listen to nicked records with Jimmy in the girl's room. Da Dewey would come by, look into the room, and grouse directly to Jim, "Turn down that noise, ladies," then leave laughing at the belittling of his son. Jimmy would look at her ashamed, but the music would always pull him back, and the insults that Da tossed were forgotten. Music could do that.

♫♫♫

The bus eventually arrived at the stop that Franny had to get off at, and Franny stepped down to walk the rest of the way. The Andover Heights neighborhood was a lot different than Paddy Hill. The houses were much bigger than where she lived, and you could tell that only one family lived in a house. Most of the houses were on so much land that you couldn't actually see the house from the street. Most of them were hidden by trees and brush. Franny walked up the tree-line lane called Beacon Street to find the sequence in the house numbers. When she came to 1908, she turned up to the long angling driveway and walked to the front porch of a house that reminded her of the White House in Washington, D.C., or the house in the Edgar Allen Poe story, Fall of the House of Usher.

Franny stepped onto the porch and waited to see if the house would collapse into itself. When it didn't, she rang the bell by the front door. An old lady opened the door and smiled at her. "I'm here to see Mary Catherine?" Franny asked the smiling woman. The woman didn't say anything but turned around and led her down a long hallway. Franny noticed that the old woman swayed as she walked down the hall, the way Da Dewey swayed when he came home from Barnaby's, and the rest of the family would hide from him. The old woman walked Franny to what looked like cellar stairs leading down to where she could hear the sound of drums and a high-hat being played.

Franny thanked the old woman and went downstairs alone. She peeked down into the large room in the basement as she carefully walked down the rickety stairs. Mary Catherine ran to the bottom of the stairs and yelled, "Here's your new piano player." Franny smiled awkwardly and looked towards the three boys in a large room, surrounded by musical instruments. She first spotted the tall boy sitting behind the drums, tapping on a high-hat. The other boy was holding a guitar, adjusting the strap so that it would sit comfortably on his shoulder. At first, she thought that he had a sunburn on his face but realized later that he had a bad case of acne. The last boy was just coming out of the small bathroom-- it was him-- Leonard, from Ma Deweys. Franny stopped in her tracks. Lenny smiled at her. Franny thought that she was going to faint.

Franny had kind of forgotten about Lenny. Not really forgotten but had shelved his memory away in some spot in the back of her mind. When she first met Lenny, she couldn't stop thinking about him, but as time went on, Lenny just turned into some young girl's crush that she once heard of… and here he was looking as dreamy as ever. "Everybody, this is Franny," Mary Catherine proudly announced. "She's a chick," said the guitar player with the bad acne. "I told ya she was a girl, you turd," answered Mary Catherine. Lenny walked over to the Franny and dried his hand on the western looking shirt he was wearing. "I know you from Mary Catherine's house," said Lenny, gently but firmly shaking her hand.

Lenny introduced her to the other two guys, "On guitar, Al Gould." Al smiled at her and nodded. "On the drums, Michael Webster…" Michael made a little roll of his drums, ending it with a loud crash of his only cymbal. Franny waved at him; she knew of Michael from school. His family-owned Barnaby's, where Da Dewey drank with the mill men, and Joanie used to go to have a beer and meet people. Michael waved a drum stick at her. Lenny directed her to a spinet piano set against a wall.

Franny removed her coat and took her place on the piano bench. Lenny placed the sheet music to Jerry Lee's *Great Balls of Fire,* which now made all kinds of sense to Franny. "We're working on this," said Lenny, laying out the music in front of her. "Do you know it?" he asked. Franny was disappointed. How many times had she, Jimmy and Lenny listened to Jerry Lee up in the girl's room? "Yeah, I know it," she said half-heartily. "I'm gonna sing, can you follow Mike on the drums?" Lenny asked, innocently. "I'll try," said Franny, setting her hands on the keys for the first time.

Franny started playing. She was glad that Lenny had chosen this song; it was banging on the keys mostly and didn't take too much finesse to get it to sound good. Franny liked the feeling of the piano, it wasn't as big as the piano in the high school gym, but it had a good play within the keys and was really close to being in tune. As she played, she realized that Michael was playing very loud and drowning out her and the guitar player. Franny tried to keep up with Michael's rhythm; eventually, she settled into a somewhat steady beat. Franny looked over her shoulder at Lenny, who was singing into the silver bullet microphone, but she couldn't hear his singing over the banging of Michael's drums. When the song ended, Michael went into a wild flourish and then smashed his cymbal. Everyone stopped and looked around, all asking the same thing in their looks, "How'd we do?"

Mary Catherine jumped up from the couch she was sitting in and clapped happily. "That was great! You sounded just like him." She ran to Lenny and kissed him on the lips. "Thanks, babe," answered Lenny, turning to Franny. "What'd you think?" Franny wanted to say that she was stunned to find out that he was Mary Catherine's boyfriend. She thought he was smarter than that but she hedged; should she give her real feelings about the song or should she lie and tell them it was "great?" "I don't know for sure; I couldn't hear too well." Franny turned to Michael, who was adjusting his cymbal, "I think Michael was over-playing. I couldn't hear anything." Everything was quiet for a minute; finally, Lenny broke the silence, "Mike, muffle the drums a bit. We're not playin' the Paramount, yet." Michael grumbled and hit his bass-drum pedal twice. "Anything else?" Lenny asked. Franny squirmed on her piano bench. "Can we do it again?" she asked, hoping if they got into it again Michael would forget about her critique.

Lenny counted to four, and again, they leaped into the song. This time Michael played softer, and she could hear Lenny singing. Lenny sang into the large microphone with everything he had. He held onto the microphone stand and danced around. She thought that Lenny had a relatively good voice. You could tell that he hadn't worked with Mrs. Ciccorelli, the voice teacher at the school, but he wasn't bad either. Franny could, for the first time, listen to Al's guitar.

She realized quickly that Al wasn't that much of a guitar player. Jimmy had taught her the open chords of a guitar. She had been working with Jim's guitar when it was available (which wasn't often) and felt that she was further along in her guitar than Al was in his. Al did have a very nice looking Gretsch guitar, and it sounded good when Al accidentally (and infrequently) hit a correct chord.

They ran through four more songs, *Great Balls of Fire*, *Blue Suede Shoes*, *Rock Around the Clock*, and *Peggy Sue*. Franny knew most of the songs, the ones she didn't Lenny had sheet music for it. When they finally finished, everyone stopped. Lenny called the guys together, and they huddled in an opposite corner of the cellar. Mary Catherine came over and smiled at her. It was the same smile that Mary Catherine smiled at her when it was her turn to do the dishes at the Haverhill Street house. Usually, Mary Catherine would sweetly remind her that her ma was giving her piano lessons for free, and she was supposed to be working off the payment. At that moment, Ma would step up and remind Mary Catherine that it was her chore, not Franny's. Ma would then assign Franny an easy task like clearing the table.

"I think they like you," Mary Catherine whispered, loud enough so that the guys could hear. "You should play with them if they ask," she prodded. "But if you do," continued Mary Catherine, her green cat eyes poised and serious, "keep your hands off of Lenny. He's mine… and I don't share." Franny nodded in agreement to Mary Catherine's deal-- she knew Mary Catherine didn't share... anything.

The boys turned and walked to Franny, still sitting on the piano bench anxiously. Franny could tell by the smile on Lenny's face and the consternation in Al's body language that she was in the band, but it wasn't unanimous. "You're in," exclaimed Lenny, reaching to give her a hug. Franny looked over at Mary Catherine, who was noting her reaction to Lenny's attempt at a hug. Franny stuck out her hand and waited for Lenny to give her his. Franny and Lenny shook on it as Mary Catherine looked on approvingly. "You're just here to play the piano, no singing or dancing," snarled Al. Franny didn't understand what he was talking about. Why would she be dancing? What did he think she was going to do other than play the piano? "Welcome to Lenny and the River Rats," said Lenny.

"The River Rats?" thought Franny, "Whoa, I just got made a river rat." Even being a River Rat, Franny felt kind of thrilled to become one. "Let's go upstairs and see what we have for a snack," announced Lenny. The guys headed up the stairs. Mary Catherine and Franny followed them. Mary Catherine moved closer to Franny, giving her the woollies. "I'm glad they chose you. It was my idea... but don't tell Jimmy, he'll get all angry and everything if he found out I didn't suggest him. You know how he is," whispered Mary Catherine, "He'll probably throw a hissy-fit." Franny agreed though she wasn't really sure if it would affect Jim like that. In all the time she had known Jimmy, he had never once talked about joining a band. When the school asked him to try out for the school's jazz band, he declined saying that he didn't want to play in front of people.

♫♫♫

Jim looked in the mirror. The shiner around his right eye was going down, and it had started to dissipate into a green color around the edges. Jim had taken to slipping into the upstairs bathroom to stare at himself with his guitar hanging in front of him. He had hoped he looked like Johnny Cash, but he looked more like Buddy Holly holding a very old guitar without the crickets. Jim tried to look cool in the mirror like he was going to fight crime with his trusty guitar. He had read at the library about how Woody Guthrie had scrawled, "This machine kills Fascists" on the front of his guitar. Maybe if he could find some sunglasses, he could cover his black eye.

A week before, Jim was sitting on the mattress that he shared with Kevin, trying to pick out the chords for *Dust Bowl Blue*s when all of a sudden, his da came flying in and socked him right in the eye. Jim fell off the mattress. He made sure he protected his guitar as he fell. Da stood over him and kicked him in the ribs. Jim was able to protect his ribs and his instrument while Da yelled at him. Jim slid his guitar under the bed, that Patrick and Michael slept on, to protect it as his da kicked at him. Jim was later told by Ma that Da had heard from some of the guys at the warehouse where he had been working (for close to nine months, a new record for Da) that they saw Jim down on Essex Street playing the guitar and singing with that Negro Smilin' Leo. Da had stormed home (or stormed home after stopping at Barnaby's to get a head full of steam and belly full of beer) and told Jim in more than words that no son of his was going to play with a nigger or play that nigger-music. Ma finally stepped in front of her husband and got him to go to bed so he could sleep it off, while Jim's brothers and sisters stood and watched.

The unwritten rule in the Dewey house was not to get involved in Da's beatings. It was just as easy for Da to turn and start wailing on you if you stepped in. Since Patrick and Michael had finished school and were working full time now, Da hardly mixed it up with them anymore. It seemed to Jim that Da wanted to beat his bum more now than when he was younger. Whenever he passed Da in the hall or coming out of the bathroom, Da would just grumble, "Pansy" and walk away.

Jim knew his father didn't think much of music; Da would be happier if he was more into playing baseball or boxing. When Patrick and Michael were playing baseball, Da never went to see them play. Jim felt his old man was just angry that he had something he liked to do which didn't involve hurting anyone else. Most of the time, Jim just blamed Da's drinking affected everything. When Da would hit Ma, it was usually because he was drunk and didn't know what he was doing. Whenever Da sobered up, he always felt bad. Da would try to be nice to her (as nice as Da could be); he would bring her flowers or candy (most of the time, Ma would find out he had nicked the stuff). It was different with the kids. Da would always tell them about how tough his father was. Da's father was an organizer in the 1912 Bread and Roses strike. He was one of the first Lawrenconians to join the Wobblies. Jim's grandfather, Pierce Dewey, was a proud IWW member and held out for three months as they walked the picket lines at the Wood Mills. Pierce Dewey was a known trouble-maker before the strike even started and continued to be one until the morning that they found his body floating in the Merrimack.

Da and his two brothers had to be shipped off to New York City till the end of the strike. They lived with a rich family in Murray Hill, who had agreed to take them in for the duration of the strike for their protection and because his parents had no money or job, now. Da said that he never ate better in his life, and it was the first time he ever slept in a bed alone. Many people in Lawrence suffered terribly during the strike while he and his brothers lived high on the hog. Then he had to come back to Lawrence when the strike was settled.

The Lawrence police claimed that Pierce was most likely attacked during a robbery, but everyone (even the family) knew that Pierce had made a lot of enemies over the years and owed most of Lawrence some amount of money. Pierce never ran from a fight or turned his back on a half-full drink. Da had taken up his da's mantle and treated everyone around him as his da did.

What Ma had seen in him when Mick Dewey was younger? Jim could never understand. He had seen the pictures in the old trunk up in the attic of the young couple, and babies, Michael, Patrick, Peggy, and Kathleen, when his da returned from Germany (Da served with Patton in Africa and Italy campaigns. Patton had once singled him out of formations as a "mean son of a bitch." Da had a picture of himself with Old Blood and Guts Patton in front of a jeep. A "mean son of a bitch" usually made a good soldier, but most of the time, an awful parent). Jim recognized his da's smile with his older children, but between then and now, Mick Dewey had become a very hard man. Ma said that the war had changed Da.

It may have been because he couldn't hold a job. Da had a big problem with bosses-- he didn't like them. He felt that he knew better than they did, he could do better than them, and that if they were his boss, it was because they were "arse-kissers." Jim always assumed that Da's bosses became bosses because they didn't fight everyone when they disagreed with them. Jim also thought that Da didn't like being helped by Ma's family.

The Micellis were first-generation Italians from Genoa, Toni Micellis' mother, the gracious Sonia Micelli, was coincidentally the live-in maid for William Wood, the owner, and operator of the Wood Mills, the same mills that Da's pappy organized in 1912. William Wood had been kind to Sonia and young Antoinette and was even paying to give young Toni piano lessons with his son, Thomas. Toni hoped that Thomas would be the one that she would spend her life with, but Master Wood ended that. His son would not marry the guinea daughter of the help

Thomas would go on to Harvard and a profitable Wall Street job far from Toni and that no-good Mick Dewey. Sonia and her husband, Giuseppe, or Gussy, as the people in Lawrence called him when they needed a plumber, saved their money and eventually bought the big house on Haverhill Street, which at that time was in what was called "Little Genoa" and eventually became Paddy Hill. When cancer finally got Gussy, and after Sonia passed, the house went to their only daughter and the drunk she was married to. More kids were born, and the house filled up. No matter how bad times got, Ma fought to keep the house, paying the taxes with the money she made from teaching all the untalented children of Paddy Hill.

Jim decided that he was going to visit Smilin' Leo again; his father wasn't going to stop him from playing the guitar with Leo. Jim decided that he didn't care if his da didn't want him spending time with Negroes. Leo is one of the few adults, other than Ma, who made time to help him. Sometimes, Leo would put a harmonica in a rack and play both the harmonica and the guitar, at the same time, like the hurdy-gurdy man Jim once saw on a downtown corner. Leo could play a song while never using an open chord. He could sing about a rundown roadhouse in the South, and Jim could hear the smoke in Leo's voice. Leo sang songs like Woody did, with pain and experience coming together in every note, every word. Jim would, at times, start playing along with Leo but suddenly lose where he was because he was so caught up in what and the way Leo was singing the song. Jim wanted to do that.

Jim stared at his colorful cheek that his da had given him. He decided his da wasn't going to boss him around. He was going to play music. He didn't care what his da said. The bruises would heal, the bones would mend, but he wasn't sure what would happen without the music. Jim lifted his guitar so that he could see it better and snarled into the mirror. He did look cool snarling.

♫♫♫

The bus ride back home to Tower Hill was a blur. Franny couldn't remember getting on the bus or walking from Lenny's house. She had almost forgotten what Mary Catherine had said, Mary Catherine's threat. She could only remember Lenny's smile as he stepped out of the bathroom and recognized her. The sparkle in his puppy-dog eyes and the excitement that enveloped her heart. She thought that she had gotten over him but realized that it was only asleep inside her like that familiar song that comes to you when you just listen hard enough. She had hoped, and now he had come to her…and then she remembered what Mary Catherine whispered, "He's mine!"

Mary Catherine had already "done it," as the other girls in the eighth grade called it. The rumors had her "doing it" with most of the football team, some of the JV basketball players, the first trumpet player in the band, a wrestler or two, a few hockey players (including the goalie, in his goalie pads), and at least two of the teachers…one of whom was married. A cold shiver ran through Franny when she suddenly thought that Lenny and Mary Catherine were probably "doing it." Knowing

Mary Catherine, they probably were doing it all. Mary Catherine, it seemed, would "do it" with anyone. Franny thought about if she would "do it" with Lenny" She wasn't sure. She wasn't really sure what "doing it" was.

The only real talk she ever had with Joanie about "doing it" was that the girl could get in trouble. Franny wasn't sure if it was the guy going crazy like Mutt or, if it was getting pregnant with a baby that was the trouble. Every time Joanie would try to tell her about the birds and the bees, Joanie would get all flustered and start tripping over what she was saying. Eventually, she would back off and keep her explanation to some other time. For Franny, it was all so confusing and scary, but on that bus, she thought maybe she could… or that maybe she would like to "do it" with Lenny. That's when she remembered Mary Catherine's warning. Maybe she would just play the piano with Lenny and the River Rats… oh, and she was in a band now.

♫♫♫

Lenny danced around the basement; whenever she would have the chance to, Franny would turn and try to watch Lenny perform. Almost every time she turned around, she would catch Mary Catherine sitting on the couch, watching her. Franny would then go back to playing the piano. Lenny and the River Rats were getting better day by day. The songs sounded more fluid and were now resembling the records that they were recorded on. The one thing that wasn't getting any better was the guitar. Al or Alley, as he wanted to be called now that Lenny started to call him that, was still dragging along. Alley was having trouble keeping up with her and Michael's drumming. Lenny would ride Michael's beat very well…almost ignoring whatever Alley was playing. Lenny would sing following Michael and Franny's piano. Most times, the guitar would drag and not being even close to the other three.

Franny wanted to say something, but in the brief talks she had with Alley, it was obvious that he wasn't big on taking criticism. He had no problem doling it out. "Man, wait for me," he would instruct Michael. "It's harder playing chords than just banging drums and piano keys." Franny wanted to argue and tell him that she also played chords and she knew how to play the guitar, so it wasn't that hard to keep up, but she didn't want to fight with him, so she just kept playing her part.

During *Peggy Sue*, Franny looked over at Michael, who seemed bothered that again Alley was dragging behind. She smiled and pretended that it didn't bother her, and Michael quickly looked away. Every once in a while, Franny would look over at Mary Catherine, who continued to stare lovingly at Lenny as he sang to her; the only time she would look away was when Lenny glanced over at Franny. Then Mary Catherine would glare at Franny like the time she took the last hot dog when they were cooking on a burning trash can in the Dewey backyard (Mary Catherine continued to not understand the concept of a "guest").

Franny would smile and look away before Mary Catherine could react to Lenny's attention on anyone else but her. Franny realized that her job was to play the piano and not anger Mary Catherine no matter how much she would like to have Lenny sing to her... no matter how frustrating Alley's playing was. Franny did enjoy being in the band; it was fun playing with other instruments, and looked forward to their rehearsals.

Franny also liked going to Lenny's stepfather's big house. She often would be surprised by how much space they had in the house. Just the formal dining room, with that long wooden table, surrounded by the eight straight-back chairs and the kitchen, with its large stoves and the many cabinets, were much larger than her and Joanie's whole apartment on Marston Street. After the rehearsal, there was always a snack, Oreos and milk or Coca Cola, if Lenny had gone shopping. The new band would sit around the kitchen table and sometimes Grammy Ham would sit and watch them, sipping on her drink. Grammy Ham said that it was lemonade, but she wouldn't let anyone try it (even Lenny, who would usually ask), and it smelled like Franny's Grandpa's after-dinner cocktail. Lenny would usually stand while everyone else sat at the table, and talk about the songs they played, and the way other people played them. Lenny would laugh and eat his cookies with Mary Catherine laughing at everything he said. Lenny was very funny, especially when he was the center of attention.

Franny never realized how well he could handle the group. Franny never really thought that he could have that thing she first saw in Elvis but watching him with Alley, Michael, and even Mary Catherine, Franny could see him play to them. How he could take hold of people and then just grip them in his hands, Franny could see what Mary Catherine saw in him. Franny wished that she could have someone look at her like the way Lenny looked at Mary Catherine.

♫♫♫

Lenny still hadn't figured out Mary Catherine. She wasn't the first girl that he had sex with (she was actually the third), but she was the most intriguing. Lenny had met her at W.T. Grant; he had spotted her going through the records. He recognized her from taking piano lessons at her mother's house on Haverhill Street. He knew she was a Dewey. He also remembered that she had two first names, Mary Beth or Elizabeth Rose, or something like that.

As he watched her, he noticed that she had taken a record album from a storage bin and tucked it into something under her coat. Lenny was surprised that she would steal from this store; it was so openly gutsy. He went over and introduced himself. Mary Catherine told him that she remembered him from his lessons but hoped that he had learned to play the piano better because he stunk. Lenny started laughing. She was so forward he wasn't used to girls talking like that. Suddenly, Mary Catherine grabbed his arm tightly and started to lead him to the door. "Pretend that you're my boyfriend," she whispered as she pushed him to the front of the store. Lenny let her push him. He had gone to Grants looking to see if the new Elvis Presley album had come in. "You've gotten really sexy since I last saw you," injected Mary Catherine as they came nearer to the door.

Lenny took her to the Brigham's Ice Cream Parlor on Merrimack Street. He wanted to get to know her but what he really wanted was to find out what she had taken from the store. Just before entering Brigham's, Lenny grabbed Mary Catherine and pulled her into a small alleyway between Brigham's and the laundromat next door and pressed her against the building's wall. "What did you take from there?" Lenny asked, smiling at her. "Nothin'," she answered. Lenny stared at her, her green cat eyes sparkling back at him. "I wouldn't steal anything; I'm a good Catholic girl," she explained, her eyebrows spreading across her forehead. That's when she touched him. At first, Lenny thought she had accidentally brushed him with her leg, but then he realized that it was her hand that was rubbing on his prick. He realized that he was becoming aroused. Mary Catherine smiled at him and pushed her pink lips closer to his mouth. The next thing he knew was that they were kissing, while Mary Catherine's hand was working up and down his cock like the drunk whore's that he had lost his virginity to. Her tongue was in his mouth, flicking against his.

Suddenly, he realized that they were in an alley. At least the hooker had a room. Then Mary Catherine stopped. "You're gonna buy me a frappe, aren't ya?" She asked as she pulled her mouth away from his. "Sure…" he answered, realizing that there was no way he could go into the ice cream shop with the erection that he had. Mary Catherine smiled at him, "We can wait. I'm not that hungry." That's when she reached into his pants and grabbed his boner. Her cold hands sent a chilling shock throughout his body. Lenny laughed, and Mary Catherine moved her hands down to his balls and held them. "You keep that up, and you're not gonna get your frappe," he explained, grabbing her hand. Mary Catherine removed her hand from his pants and leaned into him-- kissing him again on the lips.

They eventually went into Brigham's, and Mary Catherine got her frappe, and Lenny even ordered French fries and an ice cream cone with jimmies. After the French fries, they walked along the Merrimack River to an abandoned '39 Hudson parked behind the Malden Mills that Mary Catherine knew about. She invited him into the backseat and took him there. Lenny had never felt anything like it before. When he finally came, he was surprised that he didn't shoot Mary Catherine through the roof of the rotting vehicle. Mary Catherine smiled at him as she pulled her cotton panties up under her dress. "You've got a nice prick," she complimented him. "Thanks, I'm very proud of it." She leaned over and kissed him. Then she pulled Elvis Presley's *Elvis is Back* album from inside her coat.

Lenny looked over the stolen record with excitement. It was the album he had gone to buy at Grants. "You stole this?" He asked her, buttoning up his dungarees. "Yeah, it's for my retard brother. He likes his records; I think he's queer," she added. "Is he the one who plays the piano?" asked Lenny, suddenly less interested in Elvis' album. "He's in love with a guitar now," Mary Catherine teased. "I'm starting a band, and we're looking for a piano player," Lenny said, staring into Mary Catherine's eyes. "Do you think he would play in my band?" Mary Catherine laughed, "Not my mongoloid brother. Why don't ya find someone good?" "Do you know someone who would?" Lenny queried. "Is there a student of your mother that you think will want to be in a band?" Mary Catherine stared back at Lenny making it obvious that her mind was working. "Let me check it out."

"I'll walk you home," Lenny offered. "You don't have to," Mary Catherine told him, as she was sliding out the busted-out windshield. Before he slid out of the windshield, Lenny tried to return the Elvis album to her, "Here's your record." "You can keep that if you want it," Mary Catherine said, as she jumped down from the Hudson's hood and into Lenny's waiting arms. "What about your brother?" asked Lenny because he felt he should? "Fuck, my brother-- like anyone would. I'll nick him another." Lenny held his record and grabbed Mary Catherine, pulling her close to him; he had never had any woman ever steal for him. It felt good.

They walked to the Merrimack Street Bridge together, where they kissed and then separated. Mary Catherine walked up the hill, Lenny turned and trudged across the bridge. He looked back at the girl he had just met and had intercourse with. Mary Catherine turned around with her long brown hair blowing in the wind. Lenny waved and kept walking home.

♫♫♫

Mary Catherine never understood what the big thing about sex was. She had been having it for years, soon after she got Eve's drip for the first time. At first, it was a good way to get boys to notice you... at the least, to get them to be nice and pay attention to you for a few minutes. She grew up with pricks always surrounding her. She had four brothers, and she had seen their pricks from the time she first noticed the difference between boys and girls, their first boners before the hair grew around it, getting bigger, boners at breakfast, pricks peeing, and pricks swinging in the wind. Boys don't care if they're naked and walking around in front of girls. Ma cared; she would make the owner of the offending prick go and put some pants on. Sometimes they did, and sometimes they didn't. The girls walking around the house naked was nothing, just the two folds of skin, like the dime-slot of some arcade game.

Mary Catherine looked in Teresa's once, and there wasn't even anything in there. Just the pee hole, and her arse hole. Teresa got all weird about it and said that she'd tell Ma. Mary Catherine had to show the space between her folds to get her to shut up; even little Teresa wasn't too impressed with it. Sure, they got hair down there and boobs, like Peggy and Kathy (after girls get hair down there, they won't let you look at them naked; they're always wearing towels. When they were smooth, they would run around the house like Mary Catherine, Teresa, Dorrie, and Annie. Suddenly they get a pussy, and there's no more looking). But the boys were always different. Even different from each other-- no two were alike.

Jimmy's was the most interesting. When he was born at the hospital, they took off the little sleeve that Patrick, Mike, and Kevin had. Jimmy's looked like a toad stool, like the ones under the back porch. Mary Catherine wondered if his hood would ever grow back? The look of it surprised all the family when Jim came home with Ma from the hospital. Peggy told her that Da was beside himself. He wanted to kick someone, but Jim was too young to kick, and Da said that the delivery was very difficult, as Jim would always be as a child, so Da couldn't kick Ma, either. Da went back to the hospital to see if he could get the hood back, but he seemed happier, or at least not as mad when he found out that the hospital wasn't going to charge Da and social services for the clipping. Da would call Jim "his little Jew-boy" because he was clipped. Mary Catherine had heard that Jewish boys also had their hoods taken off. Da said that it was because their moms like to sew them into sweaters. Da liked to say things like that. Da said that the Jews all ran Lawrence, but to Mary Catherine's knowledge, Da didn't know any Jews.

Mary Catherine had also seen her Da's prick. It was old and wrinkly. It was pretty hard to miss Da's since he would often walk around the house totally naked when he was on a bender and decided that he didn't need pants since he was going to shit anyway. Sometimes, when Da really tied one on, Ma would leave him in the bathtub, so that when he puked, he wouldn't have to get up. Ma would just come by and rinse him off with a pot of water. It wasn't unusual to find Da asleep naked in the bathtub. Once Da passed out on the couch when he came home early from Barnaby's. Kathy was having a Brownie meeting at the house when all of a sudden, Da got up and peed in the corner of the room where the Brownies were painting their faces like the Plymouth Indians. The whole Brownie troupe had a good look at Da's prick. Mary Catherine wasn't sure, but she thought that there should be some kind of a badge for that.

Mary Catherine did think that Lenny had a nice prick. It fit really well into her, not like Mr. Keaton's-- the science teacher. His was really big, and it hurt some– then

Mr. Keaton started crying while doing it. It was uncomfortable in a few ways. But on the other hand, Ma was really happy when she got an A in science. It was the first one she had ever got. It was in Biology, and Mary Catherine thought that it was some kind of joke which she didn't understand.

Mary Catherine liked sex. It felt good, and a lot of times, it could get her out of trouble. She could practically nick anything at Grants since she put Mr. Richard's in her mouth. Mr. Richards, the store's manager, would now almost snap his own neck looking the other way if she was nicking something. Yeah, sure, she had to dodge the fat store guard, but she was sure that Mr. Richards would never say anything about it. Mary Catherine didn't understand what the big deal was; besides, she liked Lenny.

♫♫♫

Lenny stared at Mary Catherine lying next to her. It looked like she was asleep. Lenny liked Mary Catherine-- he really liked having sex with her (Maybe they shouldn't have had sex tonight, she was on her period, and it made a sloppy mess of the sheets). But Lenny wasn't sure of himself. At times, he wondered if he liked it enough. Sometimes, when Lenny was alone and about to go to sleep, he would think of Father Nelson and his last Christmas Eve at Saint Anthony's. After Father Nelson shot on his good pants, Lenny thought a lot about what had happened. Why him? What did Father Nelson mean that he was like him? Did Father Nelson accost every boy who served him, or did Father Nelson see something special in him? Something that maybe even Lenny didn't know about himself? How does a fag know that he's a fag? Lenny was scared, so scared that he lied to Harry about needing a new accordion. He was able to get Harry to lend him twenty bucks for the accordion that Lenny needed for his band.

Lenny went up to Tower Hill and saw the girls standing beside the railroad tracks. He chose a girl, maybe a few years older than him, and very consciously asked her if she would like to walk with him. He and the girl talked. She told him that she knew of a room that he could rent. Lenny and the girl went up to the room. The girl undressed, and so did Lenny. Lenny felt that he should tell her that he never did it before. But he didn't tell her that because he was afraid that she would think he was queer. The hooker took him gently and took his money. After he left her and walked to the bus, Lenny felt excited, but he still wasn't sure that he was supposed to be with women. Even after the senior girl, Barbara, asked him to go to her car after the semi-formal, Lenny still wasn't sure.

When alone, Lenny would think about Father Nelson, tugging his staff, breathing heavily into his neck. And sometimes, Lenny would realize that he had an erection. Then, he would try to quickly think of something else… someone else; the young hooker, Barbara, rumbling around in the back seat of her dad's Buick. Once he got so mad at his prick for getting hard, he actually punched it. Of course, it hurt wicked bad, and he still couldn't stop thinking of Father Nelson. Why? Was Father Nelson really divine? Maybe, he could see that Lenny was different, like him? Maybe God told him that Lenny was a homosexual (he had looked that word up in the encyclopedia), and there was nothing he could do about it but pretend he wasn't. Lenny tried to hold down the fear welling up in his stomach. He unconsciously held Mary Catherine tighter… "Are you crying?" asked Mary Catherine. "No. I've got something in my eye."

She was looking up at him and smiled as her light brown hair spread out over the pillow. Lenny smiled back at her, wiping away the tears. Mary Catherine reached under the covers and grabbed his rock-hard prick. "Looks like you're ready to go again," she announced. Lenny wanted to jump out of bed and run away– to hide in the cellar behind the old coal pile, where he used to hide from his dad when he was drunk. But he knew he couldn't– he wanted to punch his prick again, but he knew that this wouldn't work either. "We should check and see if Grammy Ham is still sleeping," Lenny counseled. "I made her three of those gins tonics, and they're mostly gin." Mary Catherine rolled onto him and massaged his balls.

"Boy, that feels good." "Keep thinkin' that thought," said Mary Catherine as she mounted him. Mary Catherine was the only thing that could get Lenny's mind off of what had happened at Saint Tony's on Christmas Eve.

♫♫♫

Jim played with Smilin' Leo on the corner in front of W.T. Grant on Essex Street. Jim stood with his beat-up, old, 1955 Sears Harmony Supertone acoustic guitar, with its nicked and scratched, rosewood body, wearing his heavy jacket and an old watch cap. It was so cold that Jim's fingers hurt whenever he slid his fingers down the fretboard. Leo stood beside him, a harmonica cupped in his two black weathered hands. Leo played the harmonica with a passion as Jim backed him up on the guitar. They were playing *Malted Milk*, a Robert Johnson song. Leo would bend the notes on his harp (that's what Leo called his harmonica– it wasn't a "Harpo" type of harp) and sang.

Jim wasn't that proficient in this song, so at times he had to wait and catch Leo as the lick came around again. People passed by, on their way home, or on their way to the late shift at the mills. Some were shopping, but most were rushing home with their faces buried in the warmth of their coat collars or a scarf wrapped around their lower faces to keep the evening chill out. When Leo finished the song, he turned to Jim, with his nick-named smile, "Hey Strings, what do ya say if you sing one?" Jim nodded, very unsure if he wanted to. He had come down and played behind Leo three times before, but this would be the first time that he sang alone, not just backing Leo up on *Baby Please Don't Go* or on Leadbelly's *Alberta* (even though Jim didn't really have any idea what the song was about– he thought the woman, Alberta, was like his da and used to disappear for days when she was drinking).

Jim had hoped that Leo would tell some jokes or talk to the people passing by-- anything to delay his singing. Leo liked to yell out to people, "Have you seen Mayor Buckley's new car?" he would wait for a few beats and then add, "Neither have I," and start in on the song. Sometimes, when he knew it was only a single man, or a couple of guys were around him, Leo would ask, "Did ya hear 'bout the blind prostitute?" The guys would stop and wait, wondering what a blind man would know about a blind prostitute, "Ya had to hand it to her." That usually got a small chuckle, and the guys would dig into their pockets for some coins to drop into Leo's guitar case.

Jim had chosen a Woody Guthrie song from the Live Wire album called *Roll on Columbia.* It was a song about a river called the Columbia. Here, in Lawrence, the Merrimack River snaked through the town, west towards Lowell and into New Hampshire. The river was always important to the city of Lawrence. In the days of the great textile mills, the river was the source of how the mills generated the livelihoods of most of the Lawrencioans and the Merrimack Valley. Living in Lawrence was never easy, and the river could be ruthless. Many people would comment on surprisingly that Mick Dewey hadn't fallen in the river yet. Many a drunk had gone to take a walk to sober up and never returned. The winter thaw would always bring the rising river over the banks, onto the Boston and Maine railroad tracks, flooding out Canal Street.

Jim could remember a girl who went to high school with his brother, Michael, Carol Myers, a few years back, had borrowed her parent's car to go to a party with two friends. While driving over the Duck Bridge on South Union Street, they hit a patch of ice, sending the car careening into a snowbank piled on the side of the bridge since the last snowfall. The car hit the snowbank, which had turned to ice, and launched it into the air, like a rocket, diving into the river. It took two days before they found the car with Carol and the two girlfriends in it, fifteen miles away, down at the Pawtucket Falls, in Lowell. The good people of Lawrence were used to living with the river and the danger that came with it. Jim knew that the mighty Columbia was probably mightier than the Merrimack, but maybe the people walking home tonight wouldn't notice.

Jim looked over to Leo, who gave him a smile and played the first chord. He finally threw himself into singing *Roll on Columbia* in public for the first time:

Jim strummed, while Leo smiled and picked notes out in a bass run. Jim sang and tried to make the words as clear as he could. He never really saw himself as a singer, but all the other guitar players sang, so why shouldn't he. He stepped back and let Leo put an old blues lick in as a bridge, and then picked it up at the last verse. Leo stepped in and backed him up with the chorus. It sent shivers up Jim's back when he heard Leo sing along with him. Suddenly, he was like all those guys on his records he and Leo had become a band. Maybe a small one, but it felt like it should be a band.

Jim played, concentrating on the words of the song and the chords, completely immersed, that he spent almost an hour trying to identify by ear. Jim glanced down at the Leo's open guitar case, with the few coins that Leo would drop in, just to make sure that every pedestrian knew what the case was for. Sometimes, Jim would have to chase younger boys away who would try to sneak into Leo's case while Leo was playing and remove as many coins they could grab before Leo realized they were stealing his money. This time he was watching the case for another reason. Jim kept singing his song:

Jim continued to sing and play, but the whole time, he glanced at the guitar case open while waiting for change to be dropped in. Suddenly a man in a long flannel coat walked by and dropped two pennies and a nickel in the case, making a proud but muffled noise in doing so. Jim smiled; he knew now that he was a musician. He was a *paid musician.* Even if he was just busking-- he had been paid to play. Jim kept singing, but he was proud to finally be a real musician. He knew that he couldn't say anything to Leo about his sudden professionalism (Leo considered picking up the instrument for the first time as initiating yourself into musicianship) but deep down in Jim's, just recently turned teenage soul, he had become a musician... and now no one could say that he wasn't. Leo leaned closer to him-- together Jim and Leo sang the chorus together.

Leo played a special lick that he improvised at the end, as Jim finished the song. Leo smiled at Jim, and Jim couldn't help to but to smile back at Leo, not sure if Leo knew he was smiling. No one clapped. People kept walking to work, or home, or to go shopping in J.T. Grant. But no one noticed that Jim had broken his music cherry on Essex Street, in his home-town of Lawrence, Massachusetts, in the United States of America, on the continent of North America, in the Northern Hemisphere, on the planet Earth, in some galaxy (maybe the Milky Way, Jim wasn't really sure)-- tonight. Nobody but Leo knew. "Good job, Strings." Jim was glad that it was a Woody Guthrie song.

♫♫♫

Lenny stood behind the microphone; he turned to his band, Lenny and the River Rats, and The band kicked into *Blue Suede Shoes*. Lenny sang into the microphone with his arms and legs flying behind him. Michael pounded on his drums; Alley strummed his guitar fighting to keep up with Michael and Lenny. Off to the side, against Lenny's basement wall, Franny banged on the piano keys, occasionally twisting around to check out Lenny and their audience. Sitting in front of Lenny was Mary Catherine, who was jumping up and down with excitement on the old couch, and every few bars screaming at the top of her lungs, beside her was the other half of the audience, Grammy Ham. Grammy Ham sat smiling at her step-grandson and never flinched, not even when Mary Catherine would burst out into wild, high-pitched screams.

When the song ended, everyone stopped. Slowly they all turned to Grammy Ham for her opinion. Mary Catherine bounced off the couch and jumped onto Lenny, hanging around his neck. Lenny didn't move; instead, he stared at his step-grandmother. Grammy Ham stood slowly and straightened out her dress. The whole band hung on what Grammy Ham would say next. She took in all the boys and Franny... "It was crap!" she exclaimed. Lenny and the River Rats stood stunned.

Grammy Ham turned and walked to the basement stairs. "What?" asked Mary Catherine, vocalizing what everyone else was thinking. Grammy Ham started to climb the basement stairs. Franny was pretty sure that Grammy Ham hadn't had a gin and tonic yet. It was eleven o'clock on a Saturday morning. The band had hoped to get some idea where they stood since they were going to play their first gig at the high school's annual Sock Hop that night. But Grammy Ham's critique not only being extremely negative was also very lacking in content. Grammy Ham shuffled up the basement stairs carefully, but before disappearing into the kitchen, she turned to the River Rats and repeated, "Crap!!!" Then she closed the basement door.

Lenny turned to his band, "She gets like this in the morning!" Alley looked to Michael and then to Franny. "Do you think they'll like us tonight?" he asked. "Does it really matter?" answered Michael. "We'll just do our music," added Lenny, hoping to buck up his friends. "I don't want to look like an idiot is all I'm saying," explained Alley. "You'll look like an idiot, but it's not the River Rats' fault," injected Mary Catherine in her own way of making something uncomfortable even worse. "My friends will be there," groused Alley. "That's not a lot of people for sure," continued Mary Catherine. "Tell her to shut up, Lenny." Lenny glared at Mary Catherine. He realized that he had to be the leader of the band now. "Babe, c'mon," Lenny coaxed, "We'll be fine; we'll just play our songs and the hell with everyone else." "Yeah," added Franny, "We can only do the act we've been rehearsing." "I just want it to sound good; that's all," explained Alley. "If we wanted it to sound good, we'd get another guitar player," added Mary Catherine. "Lenny!" whined Alley. Lenny smiled and looked at Franny, who shared a smile with him... until Mary Catherine noticed. "CRAP!!!" yelled Grammy Ham from the top of the basement stairs and shut the door again.

♫♫♫

Jim didn't want to be there. He didn't have the good clothes to go to a sock hop (and he had never been to one before), but he promised Franny that he would come and hear her new band. The first thing he noticed when they came out and took the stage was that the kid, Lenny, was the lead singer. When Jim saw Lenny step to the center with a microphone for the first time after Mr. Denson, the music teacher, announced: "Lenny and the River Bats" ("What's a River Bat?" Jim wondered), he recognized Lenny and it all made a lot of sense now.

First, that Lenny wasn't playing the piano because he stunk on the piano. Second, if he couldn't be Jerry Lee, then Elvis would be his back-up plan, and third, if they wanted a piano player, then why didn't he ask him to play. Of course, had he asked Jim to play, he would've declined. The next thing he noticed was that the Webster kid was the drummer. Jim remembered walking in on him at his father's bar, where the big kid was playing the drums, warning him not to tell anyone else and when those kids attacked him on Haverhill Street. Now everyone in the school would know that he played the drums.

But the thing that really surprised Jim was that Franny was in a dress and looked wicked pretty. Jim had never seen Franny in a poodle skirt before; at Saint Tony's, all the girls had to wear uniforms that had skirts, and even at Lawrence High, she would wear skirts and sweaters, but this was the first time Jim saw Franny in a real dress and saddle shoes. She sat down at the piano and pushed the bench closer to the piano. She turned and smiled at the audience. She was not wearing her glasses, flashing one of the most beautiful smiles that Jim had ever seen. He had spent so many hours with Franny, sitting on the floor, watching her twirl a finger full of her blonde curly hair, but never had seen her smile like that... even when Elvis asked to be his "*Teddy Bear*."

Lenny stood in front of the microphone and announced, "We're Lenny and the River Rats!" ("That makes more sense," thought Jim). Lenny counted out the beginning of *Blue Suede Shoes,* and the River Rats kicked into the song. Jim listened to the song from his wall-flower position. He wasn't sure if he could dance if he wanted to. His da had really beaten his bum when he got home from busking with Smilin' Leo.

Jim knew that he was already in trouble when he spotted Plug McHugh making his way, most likely, to Barnaby's. Plug would tell his da as soon as he found him. Since he was prepared for Da's attack, Jim made sure that he snuck into the front door of the house and hid his guitar under the couch in Ma's practice room. After making sure his beloved instrument was safe, Jim went and slammed the front door to announce that he was home. Da shot out of the kitchen and was on him like stink on shit (That was always part of Mary Catherine's threats). Jim was ready to cover up and protect himself, even when Da shoved him into the front stairs. Da had only blackened one eye, but he was lucky since it was the same eye that was swollen in the last attack, so no one who went to school with Jim, noticed that it had been recently re-shined. The rest of the bruises were under his clothes so no one would see the results from Da's kicking (Da had learned early when Patrick's third-grade teacher sent a note home asking if Patrick fell down often-- Da had become really good at not leaving visible bruising on the rest of his kids). Jim touched the sore spot under his left arm; it sometimes hurt when he breathed. Jim was thinking that this might be one of the ways that real musicians suffered for their music, especially if you're making nigger music.

On the stage, Lenny danced around the microphone, singing and looking like he was having fun. Jim didn't really think that they sounded that bad. Lenny seemed to be racing through the song, and it sounded like the Webster kid and Franny were trying to play as loud as they could, but the real problem was the guitar player. The kid seemed less interested in playing the song than where he placed his fingers, which made him drag way behind the other three players. Every once in a while, between verses, Lenny would turn to the gawky guitar player with thick eyebrows, lots of acne, and a wide-eyed look, standing in a too-small suit, with a thin red tie, trying to coax him to keep up.

But it was of no use; the guitar player hadn't got to the point with his instrument where the brain automatically moved the fingers into the correct chords. That was what Jim knew from experience when you have become a player and was not just a student. He knew that he would always be a student, but when he could think of playing a "D" chord and his fingers went directly to the second fret of the "G" string, the ring finger on the third fret of the "B" string, and the middle finger on the high "E" string. Until you can think and make that happen, you're not really playing yet. Then a girl in Jim's Geometry class stood in front of him and gave him a shy wave.

The panic welled up in his chest when Denise Pleshetti asked him to dance. Denise seemed to be nice, but he had never really talked to her unless he needed to know where they were in the book. Jim tried to breathe and mumble something about not needing to know where they were in the book right now. She looked truly disappointed as she slipped away. Jim was sorry, but he didn't think he could dance tonight. His side was hurting, and Franny was on the stage... she might see him. Jim watched Lenny and the River Rats finish their set, which was only three songs.

When the teenage crowd applauded and rooted for an "encore," Lenny and the rest of the band looked lost about what to do next. Finally, Lenny struck up the band, and they played *Blue Suede Shoes* for a second time. Even for the second time, Franny looked beautiful as she added back-up vocals to the song... and the guitarist followed behind the rest of the River Rats. They finished the song with Lenny leaping in the air and swinging the microphone so wildly that Jim was worried about hitting Franny in the back. Lenny stood in the center of the stage, and the rest of the band stood beside him; they bowed slightly to the audience and then rushed off the stage. Mr. Denson stepped up behind them, took the microphone, and said, "Lenny and the River Bats, boys and girls! Lawrence's own!" There was a smattering of applause as the music from a turntable rose, and kids milled around the front of the stage.

Lenny stepped off the stage a hero. Some of the younger girls screamed when he came near them, and he would only offer a slight smile. Mary Catherine threw her arms around his neck and then clutched his waist as they waded through the crowd. Alley and Michael shook hands with some of their fellow students who offered their appreciation for the band's music while Franny followed quietly behind the boys. A couple of the older girls smiled and nodded at her to let her know suddenly that she was on the charts.

Franny couldn't help but cringe a bit at their stares. She didn't really think about what would happen after the show. Now she was stuck wearing the fancy dress that Joanie had bought for her to wear at her Confirmation (Franny wanted to take the Confirmation name, Bessie, for Bessie Smith, but her mom made her take her grandmother's name, Helen--- being named Helen made Frances less painful). While making her way through the crowd, she noticed Jim standing by the boy's locker room door. He smiled at her when she finally spotted him.

Franny walked up to him and smiled back, confident that he was her biggest fan. "You were wicked good!" he gushed. "It was a lot of fun. I was so scared when we went up." Jim wasn't sure if he should touch her or something, but he did come to see her specifically. "You were hep," he assured, "It was like watching Buddy and the Crickets." Franny wished he hadn't said that, she still hadn't gotten over Buddy's death, his poor wife, and the miscarriage of their baby after hearing about her husband's death on the radio (News outlets would change their policy after the incident and not announce the names of victims until the family had been informed first). Jim realized his mistake and quickly looked away at the people slow dancing in bear hugs to *In the Still of the Night* by the Satins.

Jim thought that maybe he should ask Franny to dance. It's what most of the other kids were doing. He could see Lenny and Mary Catherine in a tight embrace on the dance floor; it looked as if they were almost kissing.

Franny also watched Mary Catherine and Lenny dance. She was kind of hoping that Jim would ask her to dance, but then she hoped that he wouldn't. If Jim asked her to dance, then they could dance right next to Lenny and Mary Catherine, and maybe then she could tell Lenny how good he was. She knew that she would have the opportunity to tell him and the band later, but she wanted to go over and say something to him... anything. But it wasn't going to happen with Mary Catherine being there. She realized that the only time she was going to have with Lenny was with the band, but she would have the opportunity to be with him. She looked at Jim, in obviously his good clothes (at least good clothes for the Deweys), she could make out a large stain on one of his older brother's hand-me-down-cardigan sweater. Jim swallowed hard and looked back at the dance floor.

Suddenly, he turned and asked, "Are you going up again?" Franny shook her head, "No, that was it." "I'm going home; you wanna walk with me?" Franny thought about it, "No, thanks. I think I'm going to hang around... maybe get some punch." Jim nodded that he understood, "I'll see ya later then." "Yeah, later," she agreed. Jim waited a minute, trying to decide if he was really going to go, or he should stay with her. He had already said that he was going-- then he should go. Jim smiled awkwardly at her and walked to the exit door of the gym.

Teachers were dispersed throughout the gym, trying to separate the dancing teens, shoving their hands between the tightly clenched bodies, with a close-to-cheerful request, "Leave room for the Holy Ghost." Franny watched Jim walking alone to the exit door and push it open, disappearing into the cold Lawrence night. Franny turned back to the dance floor where Lenny and Mary Catherine were now fast dancing to a recording of Bill Haley's *Rock Around the Clock*. Mary Catherine was wearing the new sweater she had specially nicked from W.T. Grant. Franny spotted Michael and Alley dancing with two girls, who, she was sure, were cheerleaders for the football team.

"Would you like to dance?" came a voice. Franny turned around and noticed Ratsie Murphy standing behind her, in an ill-fitted suit, his horn-rimmed glasses still sporting a fashionable wad of scotch tape holding them together. "Oh, Hi," answered Franny, "I'm really tired-- I think I'm going to get some punch." "You look very pretty tonight," Ratsie felt like he had to say. "Thank you," she said, looking for where the punch was being served, "I'm so thirsty. Playing really builds a thirst." Ratsie adjusted his glasses and watched her leave.

♫♫♫

Jim struggled walking up River Street; he was carrying Leo's guitar case in one hand, while his own guitar was slung over his right shoulder. He held Leo's kit bag in the other hand. Leo gripped his arm, holding his white walking cane as Jim led him up the street. Leo was busy talking while Jim led him home. "Strings, it's a good time to be young; it's a time when the next generation will take over and lead us, as a country and a people, into the next great renaissance." Jim nodded and trudged up the street, leading his blind friend.

Jim was always kind of surprised by Leo because he always said that for someone to sing the blues, he had to live the blues. Listening to Leo talk about his life, after losing his sight at the age of three to scarlet fever and making his living with his guitar and musical ability, he certainly did live the blues, but on the other hand, no one Jim knew had a brighter outlook on life than this man who made his life the blues. "I feel that this could be the beginning of something great... something historical. When this boy from Brookline gets into the White House, who knows what could happen?" Leo was excited because the Senator from Massachusetts was just elected president.

Everyone in the Dewey household was also very excited because not only was the new president from Massachusetts, but he was also to be the first Catholic president. When Mr. Kennedy was running for office, there was a lot of things said about Catholics; lots of people were afraid if they elected Kennedy president, the

Pope would be running the nation. Ma didn't think that would be a bad thing, but Da didn't trust Pope John, the Twenty-Third. Da didn't approve of Italians since coming back from the war (of course, Ma's family was Italian, and that might not have helped either). He felt that the previous Pope, Pius XII, had basically been a collaborator with Hitler and Mussolini to protect his money and the church's property.

Da also wasn't impressed with the fact that Mr. Kennedy was a war hero in the Pacific. He felt that those boys had it easy compared to the guys like him, who had fought in Europe... at least they weren't freezing their arses off'. But Ma was proud that a Catholic could get elected, even if there were rumors that his father bought the presidency. How many men have given their children their businesses when they retired? What's so different if you could just buy a job for your son? In Lawrence, most of the government jobs were bought (Or that's what her pa, Gussy, said. Da wasn't interested in purchasing or even being given a job). Mr. Kennedy's pa had a lot more money than most people, so it was more likely for him to get his son a really good job.

Jim could care less about who the President was. He knew that his da liked Ike, and so he found himself leaning towards the new presidency. "It's a great time to be alive, boy," continued Leo, his head rolling in all different directions. "I think he really likes the colored people, too. Addie told me that she had seen pictures of him talkin' with black folks." Addie was Leo's daughter; she would read *The Boston Globe* to Leo whenever she wasn't busy... and sometimes she would read *The Lawrence Eagle Tribune* to him in the morning if she had some extra time before she went to work at Lawrence General Hospital, where she worked in the laundry. "Great times ahead, Strings," Leo continued, "Good times a-comin'." Suddenly Leo tugged on Jim's arm and said, "Turn here." They then turned up to Everett Street, sometimes Jim wondered if Leo was actually blind. He seemed not to have sight, but at times, he also seemed to know what or where he was going without anyone telling him.

They came upon a darkened building at the end of the street. Jim knew that he was in the Tar Pit section of town. The Tar Pit was always the neighborhood that Da, his brothers, and the rest of Paddy Hill said to avoid. It was supposed to be dangerous to white people and the poor part of town. Of course, to Jim, it looked like most of Lawrence. Jim felt that the people there looked like shadows. Of course, it may have been like that because they had dark skin. Leo stopped at a set of cement steps and lightly tapped them with his walking cane. "This way, Strings. We'll see if my girls are home." Leo led him cautiously up the three stairs to the rundown building. Jim followed Leo to the door, still carrying the bag and the two guitars.

Jim helped Leo through the door and down the dark hall. Leo lightly tapped each door frame as they walked by. Finally, Leo stopped in front of a door and knocked. Jim could hear a television behind the door. A door to another apartment opened, a negro man and woman stepped out and walked down the hall past Jim and Leo. Jim could feel the man's stare as they strolled by, checking out the white boy with the poor blind man from down the hall. The door opened, and a black woman, Addie, in a flowered housecoat and hair done up with pieces of what looked like paper in it, staring at them. "Dad, you can't be bringin' strange white boys home and not tellin' me." Leo shuffled in through the door and pulled Jim behind him, "This is my young friend, Jim. I like to call him, Strings," said Leo, "Jim is a name that needs a nick-name," He then led Jim down a long hall to a comfortable looking living room, and just past that was a small kitchen. "Pappy," cried a young girl, running from the metal kitchen table beside an iron board with a stash of laundry on one end.

"Hey, there, baby. Do you have any sugar for an old man?" Leo asked the little girl. The girl, with her hair in pigtails wearing flowered pajamas, hugged her grandfather and kissed his weathered cheek. Leo smiled and said, "This is my most beautiful baby, Ruby." "You can't see, Pappy," questioned Ruby. "I can see what I need seein'," said Leo, hugging Ruby. Leo pointed at Addie, who had moved to the stove to take some boiling water off the fire. "That's my Addie, my youngest daughter," said Leo. Addie gave Jim a small wave and went back to straining whatever was in the pot on the stove. "Ruby is my big girl--- she's four," Ruby grabbed her grandfather's pants leg and stepped on to the top of his worn shoes.

Jim sat at the table as Addie made a plate for each of them, Jim and Leo. It was chicken with some crunchy bits on top, and something that looked like spinach called collard greens steamed in some spices with some beans that looked like Boston Baked beans, but they were white with black spots on them. Jim watched Leo eating the chicken while holding it with both hands and biting into it like it was corn on the cob. In Jim's house, they never ate with their hands, unless it was a corn on the cob or hot dogs. Da would slap your hand or slap you in the head if you were a boy. He would ask if you were an 'animal' after he hit ya.

Leo ate and continued to talk about the new president and how he could help in bringing new ideas to the country. Addie sat down with Ruby and fed her from her plate. Addie had also made this wonderful cake called cornbread. Jim had two pieces of it. It was very strange for Jim to not to eat fast so that he could get enough to eat. In the Dewey household, the rule was "*Snooze you lose.*" As soon as the food was on the table, you had to grab it as quick as you could, or you would end up eating only bread and vegetables for dinner. The first time Franny came to dinner, she enjoyed half a plate of baked potatoes and a small pile of chopped carrots.

Addie listened to her father talking about the boy from Brookline. "Dad, you're always trustin' them white people," reminded Addie, "You would think you would learn that white people only worry about white people. No white people care about negroes." Addie turned to Jim and said, "No offense." Jim just smiled; he knew he wasn't offended.

"This boy's different. I tell ya, girl," Leo continued, ripping into another piece of "fried" chicken, "This boy is from money; he don't need to make money. He's never known bein' poor." Addie shook her head sadly and said, "If he's never known bein' poor, then why would he want to help colored people?" "Because he's a Catholic, and that's what they have to do if they want to get into heaven," exclaimed Leo, making the point firmly. "Ain't that right, Strings? Strings, is a Catholic, too." Jim kept on eating. He knew a bunch of Catholics that would rather be rich than going to heaven-- they just wouldn't want to tell their ma's. "This boy from Brookline says that he's gonna put a man on the moon," announced Leo. "Sure he is, Dad," agreed Addie sarcastically. Even Jim knew that going to the moon was a crazy thought.

♫♫♫

After dinner, Leo had Jim lead him up to the hall to his bedroom. It was easy to guess that it was Leo's; there were pieces of old guitars laid out all over the floor. On the walls were posters of all the blues artists he played with in Chi-town. There were pictures of Muddy Waters at the Checker Board. Jimmie Rogers, at someplace called the Kingston Mines and B.B. King at the Apollo in Harlem, looking down at Leo, who couldn't look back up at them. Leo took a seat on his bed.

When Leo took his Guild F-20 from the case, with some of the loose change still rolling around inside, Ruby ran into the room and took the special place next to her pappy. Leo smiled, and sensing his girl was next to him; he asked, "You wanna hear a song, baby?" Leo started snapping some of his strings checking to see if the guitar was anywhere near being on key. Leo and Jim could feel the excitement filling Ruby as she bounced happily on the bed beside her grandfather, "See how lucky we are, Strings. We get to bring the music to the people; there's no better job in the world," said Leo. Jim watched as Leo started in a "G" chord, bouncy and bright in tone. Ruby recognized the song and started bouncing even harder on the bed. Leo started singing *The Crawdad Song* to her.

Jim watched Ruby smile while watching Leo sing and play his guitar...only Leo was smiling more. Jim wished that he had that relationship with his da. "Join in whenever you want?" Leo instructed Jim. Jim took up his Harmony Supertone and played along…

♫♫♫

Lenny and the River Rats had been doing well. After the sock hop, they had done a bunch of gigs at kid's houses. This was good because they could basically play and do whatever they wanted since there was hardly ever parents present. The problem with it was that at other people's houses, most didn't have a piano, or at least a piano in the room where they were having the party. So many times, Franny could only sit to the side with Mary Catherine and some of the other girls, left only to cheer the band. The big problem was that when Franny wasn't there with the piano, it became wicked obvious that Alley couldn't keep up on the guitar. At times, Lenny would turn to him and try to coax Alley into staying with Michael. Then, at Sally Sullivan's birthday party, Alley called at the last minute and said that he couldn't come, he had just got braces on his teeth, and they were hurting him so much that he couldn't play.

Michael and Lenny both knew that Franny could play the guitar, but they weren't sure if she could play with them (after all, she was a girl). Now that they were desperate, Lenny asked Franny if she would play the two-tone Gretsch. Franny had messed around with it in Lenny's cellar if Alley was late or if he wasn't there at all. She now had the large instrument slung over her shoulder. The guitar was a lot heavier than she remembered; it made her shoulder ache. Lenny had written down the lyrics of the five songs they had practiced, and Franny had notated the chords and the changes. Occasionally, she would draw the notes in six lines for more complicated chords than she was used to playing. The real problem was that to read the music; she had to wear her "ugly" glasses. Lenny wasn't too crazy about having a girl guitar player (especially one who had to wear dorky glasses), but he had already taken the ten bucks that Sally's mom had offered to pay The

River Rats, and Mary Catherine expected him to take her out for a sub and a tonic after.

When they stepped from the cellar stairs into the room full of kids, everyone stopped. Most had never seen a girl playing a guitar, and many thought that it was a joke. It wasn't until they got to the second song, *Peggy Sue* when the crowd realized that she could actually play the instrument. For Lenny, it wasn't until the third song that he realized he didn't have to wait for the guitar to catch up with him and Michael. Suddenly, he was singing with someone who could keep up, and they could play off of each other... and Lenny didn't feel all that silly dancing with Franny, even though she wasn't too mobile because of the weight and the size of the guitar.

Franny played with the guitar by changing the knob and raising or lowering the volume. She changed the balance and took notice of the changes in the sound of the Brownface Fender amp. At some point, Franny realized that she was having a lot of fun. It was fun to be able to move around the stage area (it was actually the front of Sally's cellar, with a dark sheet hanging behind them). When she was playing the piano, she usually sat with the audience behind her, or at least to her side, but with the guitar, she could face everybody in front of her.

When Lenny kicked into *Tutti Fruitti* as the encore, the audience was dancing and clapping along with the River Rats. Franny bounced on her feet, wearing her Confirmation dress and ugly glasses. Even looking like "His boy Sherman" she was having fun. When Lenny finished singing, he suddenly grabbed Franny and spun her around, with the wire from the amp twisting around her feet. Then, he danced with her as the audience cheered.

Franny looked up into his soft brown eyes-- his hair, all drenched in sweat, flying around on the top of his head. Chills ran down through her body. This is what she had dreamed of for so many nights while lying on the couch. Lenny turned her around again so that the guitar's lead wasn't wrapped around her feet. Then, Lenny turned to Michael and nodded his head, signaling Michael that they were going to end the song. Franny watched Lenny as he stepped close to the kids in front of the audience and threw his arms up, just like Little Richard... then he bowed as deep as he could. Franny looked to Michael, who went into a drum roll and finally ended the song with two cymbal crashes.

The cellar erupted in applause and kids yelling. Michael stepped from behind his 1959 Ludwig New Yorker drum set, in a sparkling red pearl finish, and walked up beside Franny, taking her hand, and then Lenny took hold of her other hand. She looked over at Lenny, who nodded. She turned to Michael, then all three bowed down as the audience cheered. Franny was so excited to stand on the stage with Lenny (oh, and also Michael) in front of all these people. Mary Catherine shot up to the stage and wrapped her arms around Lenny, pushing him away from Franny, who was still holding his hand. The kids continued to cheer and applaud, even as she and Michael bowed again. Franny was out of breath and sweating. Her shoulder was aching from the weight of the guitar and her fingertips were sore from the strings, but she had never felt this exhilarated in her life.

After the gig, Lenny, Mary Catherine, Michael and Franny sat at the table in Sally Sullivan's Mom's kitchen. Sally had given each a Coca Cola in a bottle and some sandwiches that her mom made. Lenny talked of what a good show it was, maybe their best, and how sad it was that Alley couldn't be there. What no one talked about was the fact that maybe the show went so well because Alley wasn't there. The only thing that Franny knew, for sure, was that she hoped Alley wouldn't be back soon.

♫♫♫

When Franny showed up at the Dewey house with her new guitar, Jim couldn't believe it. It was an almost brand new, a Washburn Flat-top J-G Jazz guitar. It was gold and black in a sunburst across the front of the instrument and the bound fingerboard with pearl "split block" inlays, gold Grover tuners, Washburn "Reso-tone" tailpiece, and two Washburn 800 series hum bucking pickups. Jim and Franny ran up to his room to play it.

Franny let Jim play the guitar first. Jim strummed some chord progressions and scales, then played a few of Leo licks that Jim had picked up. It had a beautiful sound and a wicked good tone. Franny looked on as Jim noodled. "Where did ya get it?" Jim finally asked. "It's not mine," admitted Franny, "It belongs to Lenny. His mom got it for him." "And he's just gonna let you keep it?" asked Jim, handing the over-size guitar back to her. "He said that he's not using it and that I could use it if I wanted to." Jim could only shake his head as he added, "Some cat is just giving his guitar away. What a world!" "It's not like that, I'm in his band," explained Franny, now doing the noodling. "The other day, we had a gig over on Riverside and Alley, our guitar player, couldn't show up... so I had to play in his place. Lenny let me borrow his guitar to practice in case it happens again."

"So, you can just take this home with you?" asked Jim, still not able to wrap his head around it. Franny slowly picked out some notes with her fingers, "I can bring it over here, also." Jim reached over and ran his fingers lightly over the front of the Washburn, "It's real nice." "This is only one of two guitars he owns" added Franny, "The other is a Gretsch Duo Jet 6128, 1957, two-tone in lime green, the back is of darker green color with a white pick board, oak fingerboard, and he also has a blonde Brownface Fender Bassma 6G6-B amp," stated Franny, almost remembering the great experience of playing it at Sally Sullivan's party.

"And you get to play that, too?" asked Jim, trying to picture the experience. "I played it at our last gig. It has some wicked nice action to it." Jim smiled and whispered, "... And Lenny doesn't even wanna play it?" "You know Lenny, he likes the songs. He's not that much into playing them," Franny answered. "Hey," Jim chortled, "I've got some new records. My friend Leo let me borrow them." He led Franny out of his room and down the hall to the girl's room where the phonograph was. "Ever since Mary Catherine got this new boyfriend, she hasn't nicked anything at all. Poor Peggy and Kathy need some eye-shadow and they may have to nick it themselves." "That's too bad... Mary Catherine's got a new boyfriend?" pretended Franny, not wanting to expose Mary Catherine and Lenny. "No one can nick things like M.C."

They listened to records until Ma called up and told them that dinner was ready. Jim and Franny took seats at the dinner table; all that was left was on the bench that took up one side of the table. Ma laid out a plate of boiled hot dogs and slices of white Wonder Bread. Franny realized that Mary Catherine wasn't present. She was probably with Lenny-- doing it. She was relieved that Mary Catherine wasn't there it would probably be a very uneventful dinner.

The rest of the Deweys started reaching in and pulling hot dogs off the plate, stacking them on the old mismatched plates placed in front of them. Jim got two dogs and handed Franny two slices of bread to put her hot dogs in. Ma and Dorrie came in with the bowls of spinach and two bottles of milk. The talk at the Dewey dinner table was loud, and there was a small skirmish when Michael stuck a hotdog in Kevin's ear. Kevin, in response, stood up and pushed some spinach up Michael's nose, making him spit milk all over himself and the table. Ma was shouting and trying to get Annie to get up while ordering Dorrie to get a towel to clean up Michael when Da staggered in. It was obvious that he'd been at Barnaby's and had a load on.

Da stood at the door, trying to balance himself. He glanced at his family while Kevin was still trying to dig hot dog out his ear and Michael drying himself, threatening to beat Kevin's bum. "What the feck is going on here?" Da bellowed. "We're fine here," answered Ma, "You go on up to bed, and we'll clean this up." Da lurched at Ma and grabbed her by the hair. "Don't tell me what to do, woman!" Ma screamed as Da pulled her head back. Dorrie screamed, and Annie started crying when Da turned and whipped Ma against the wall with a thump. They fell forward onto the table. Suddenly, Patrick sprung up and tried to pull Da off Ma, as she tried to scratch at Da's eyes with her fingers.

Patrick was taller than Da at the age of twenty and outweighed him by thirty solid pounds, but this was his Da that he was fighting, a particularly difficult position to be in when you're a child. They wrestled around on the table while the other Dewey children were grabbing their hot dogs and trying to save their milk. Da threw some punches at Patrick, but most of them missed him, and the ones that hit barely did any damage. "No more hitting my mother, ya drunk," yelled Patrick when he was on top of Da. Michael and Kevin tried to get Patrick off Da when suddenly Da broke loose and ran into the living room.

Franny stood in the corner, absolutely stunned by what was happening. She felt like she wanted to cry but was too afraid to. Jim stood by her, eating his hot dogs and holding his glass of milk that he was able to save. Ma moved from the wall and started to clean up the table with the younger girls. Michael and Kevin continued to try to hold back Patrick from chasing after their father. Teresa yelled at the door, at her da, telling him to go to bed and sleep it off. Kathy sat in her chair and continued to demurely eat her hot dog. Ma looked up uneasily at Franny and tried to smile with her hair all mussed in clumps, "Sit down, honey. It's all over."

Suddenly horror filled Franny eyes as Da appeared in the doorway waving a baseball bat (it was actually half a bat, an old baseball bat cut in half. Da kept it hidden behind the front door in case someone from Barnaby's would follow him home and want the money that Da owed him. Da called it the "Ol' How-Do-You-Do." Da wasn't shy about using it on his kids if he had to). "You're a big man now," shouted Da, waving the half-bat at Patrick, "How would ya like some of this, boyo?" Teresa turned and ran to the other side of the room.

Ma stepped in front of Da as Patrick leaped at his father. Ma, Kevin, and Michael fought to keep Patrick and Da separated. Finally, Ma was able to push Da out of the dining room. "Go to bed, Mick! None of your children want to see you right now." Da glared at Patrick for a second more and then realized that he had better do as Ma said before the whole family could gang up on him. "Go, Da," warned Michael, holding Patrick with all of his strength, "we can't hold him back all night." Da tossed the Ol' How-Do-You-Do into the front room. Franny stood beside Jim, watching the whole scene, horrified. "Do you want your hot dogs?" asked Jim, finishing his dog. "I'll take one if you don't want it?"

♫♫♫

Jim didn't think this was going to be a good idea at all. Yes, he would like to see Lenny again, and yes, he would like to be in their band, but he really didn't want to do it this way. Franny had talked him into coming with her to band practice to see Lenny and meet the rest of the River Rats. But Jim knew exactly what Franny wanted to do; she wanted Jim to play the guitar in the band and either kick the other kid out or make him play the tambourine or something. Jim sat on the bus beside Franny, taking the Duck Bridge over the North Canal. He looked out at the Malden Mills building, another of the mills that Da worked in and was quickly fired from. Jim couldn't remember why he was let go... there were so many. He glanced over at Franny, who still seemed bothered by the family dinner when they were having hot dogs, and Patrick and Da got into a fight. Franny pulled the case with Lenny's Washburn closer to her. "You'll like them," Franny said, not really looking at him. "Michael, he's the drummer; he's a nice guy." "Yeah," Jim agreed, having met him that night with the Puerto Ricans and at (may be not so nice) Barnaby's."

Franny and Jim got off the bus at the Mount Vernon stop, and they walked from there. Each of them carried a guitar. Franny had Lenny's Washburn in a case, while Jim had his Harmony slung across his back. They walked up the tree-lined lane in the nippy autumn evening.

When they got to the door, Franny rang the bell. "Just be yourself," she counseled Jim, who was looking a bit anxious. They waited for Grammy Ham to arrive and let them in. Finally, when the door did open, it was by Mary Catherine and her friend, Bridie, both of them wearing dungarees and t-shirts, just like boys. "Oh, you brought the retard," Mary Catherine said, as she let them into the house. Mary Catherine and Bridie led them to the cellar stairs. Jim couldn't stop craning his neck, looking at the large house and into the many different rooms. They followed the girls down the rickety stairs and into the cellar where Lenny, Alley, and Michael were waiting.

"You remember Jim, don't you?" Franny re-introduced Jim to Lenny. Jim nodded to Lenny, who nodded back, then Franny pointed to Alley and introduced him, "This is Alley, our *guitar player."* Jim nodded to him, but Alley didn't nod back; he just stared at the guitar that Jim was carrying on his shoulder. It didn't take a great schemer to see what was happening here. "And you know, Michael?" Jim smiled and nodded to Michael, who was sitting behind his drums. Michael knew that his drums weren't in jeopardy; he could be as nice to Jim as he pleased. "This is my mongoloid brother," added Mary Catherine, "even though he really can play the guitar," she added, if only to gut Alley.

Lenny clapped his hands together and said, "Let's get going. My mom and Harry are coming home tonight, so we've gotta get some time in before they get here." Lenny took his place behind the microphone while Michael turned in his seat (drummers call it a "throne"--just like the throne in the small bathroom they use) and pounded on the bass drum twice and let his sticks piddle on one of the cymbals.

Franny walked to the upright piano and lifted the keyboard cover. She took her place on the piano bench and noodled a few keys. Jim stepped over to the couch that Mary Catherine and Bridie were sitting on. He was about to sit until he got a good look at the expression on Mary Catherine's face. Any other person would not understand Mary Catherine's expression, but Jim, having spent most of his life being aware of that expression, decided he would stand, closer to the Franny and the piano.

Lenny counted off Michael, and they kicked into Fats Domino's *Blueberry Hill.* Jim listened as Lenny told of finding his thrill on said hill, but he was really watching Alley and the beautiful two-tone Gretsch. Jim confirmed that Franny was right; Alley hadn't gotten too far in his understanding of how a guitar was to be played. He played mostly open chords and didn't play any leads, which was almost a shame with the instrument he was using. Jim knew, as did Franny, that there is a maturation as a musician. At first, he starts learning his instrument, no matter which it is, and then he begins to learn how to play the instrument. Jim knew that Alley hadn't got there yet. Alley had to look at the neck of the guitar and make sure he had the right fingers in the right frets on the correct strings.

Occasionally, Alley would look up at Jim and then look away quickly. Jim couldn't help staring at the guitar that Alley was holding. It was one of the most beautiful things he had ever seen. Jim didn't know how long Lenny had had the instrument but he could tell that it wasn't new. It was an older guitar but the sound was very good-- Jim couldn't wait to try it. If Alley would let him-- or maybe Lenny, whoever's call it was.

Lenny finished the song and turned towards Jim, obviously looking for his opinion. Jim was willing to give it to him, but he'd rather Alley not be there, so he said, "It was good." "Wicked good?" asked Lenny, giving him that smile that made the girls melt. Alley stared at him; Jim could feel the daggers shooting out of his eyes. "Yeah, sure it was..." "Of course, it was," shouted Mary Catherine, bouncing off the couch, "Don't listen to him; he's a retard." But Lenny wasn't really listening to Mary Catherine, "Do you wanna give it a try?"

Boy, did Jim want to give it a try. He glanced at Franny, twisting around on the piano bench. Franny gave him a nod to take Alley's place. "Sure," Jim indicated to Alley, "if he doesn't mind." Alley was trapped; he could say no, but it was Lenny's guitar, and he had the ability to over-rule him, or he could relent and then have to sit through the agony of listening to someone else playing his guitar. Alley looked like he was going to say something but then stopped... he had to do something. "No, problem," Alley lifted the guitar strap from his shoulder, "Knock yourself out" (which is exactly what he hoped would happen).

Jim took the guitar from Alley, who looked like he was having his new braces tightened. Jim draped the leather guitar strap over his left shoulder and strummed once with his hand, listening to the sound it made. He was impressed by how much the amplification brought the highlights out in the sound. Jim looked up at Alley and stuck out his hand. At first, Alley didn't understand what he wanted, but slowly, it dawned upon him. "But it's mine..." he said plaintively. "Can I just use it? I didn't bring one?" Alley reached his hand out and dropped *his* guitar pick into Jim's palm.

Jim took the pick from Alley and turned to face the Fender Brownface amp. Jim ran through a series of scales that he used to warm up (of course, if you busked in Massachusetts, you had to learn how to warm up your fingers). Michael banged around on his drums, while Lenny smiled and laughed about something that Mary Catherine had whispered to him. Franny watched Jim warming up and then looked at Alley, who stood on the side, poking his new braces with his index finger. Franny and Joanie were told by her dentist that she would need braces sometime in the future, and that was about four years ago, but Joanie had said that they didn't have any money for braces, so she should better get used to having an over-bite. Watching Alley standing alone and poking his braces, Franny thought that maybe buck teeth weren't that bad.

Jim started to run through some of Leo's blues licks. He played the lick that went with *Alberta* and the lick that went in *Walking Blues*. Lenny was so impressed that he stopped flirting with Mary Catherine and listened to Jim run through the chord progressions. As Jim was running through a lick, he realized that Mary Catherine had that "I'm gonna kill you, you dink" look on her face. The great sound of the guitar coming out of the Bownface Fender amp was the only thing that could and did quell the fear of his sister. Lenny listened and started to tap his foot,looked over at Michael, and both boys smiled. Lenny glanced over at Franny, and he smiled at her-- she had to grab the edge of the piano so that she wouldn't slide off the piano bench. Lenny looked over at Bridie and Mary Catherine, who was sulking on the couch now. Then, Lenny smiled over at Alley, who forced his best fake-smile back and controlled the impulse to scream and run home, crying.

Jim tried a few slides on the neck of the Gretsch. He was gone completely into the world of sound, into the sound that was coming out of the amp, into the action of the strings under the fingertips of his left hand, under the spell of the magic that kept on coming back at him as he ran his right hand across the strings. There was a part of him that wished for Leo to be here with him so that Leo could have a chance to play an instrument like this. Leo had once told him about playing B.B. King's Gibson *Lucille*, how B.B. let him play it, and how beautiful it sounded. But he wanted Leo to be here and hear what he would say about this instrument. How did it compare to *Lucille*? Was it the most beautiful instrument he ever tried? This was the only electric guitar that Jim ever played. Jim had been to Chuckie's Secondhand Store and held the '57 Rickenbacker Combo 450, but Chuckie wouldn't let him plug it in. This was the first time he played a hot guitar. Jim slid his fingers up past the octave and bent the strings.

"Let's play something?" yelled Lenny over Jim's noodling. Jim stopped and looked up at everyone waiting for him. He suddenly had that same feeling after he was jerking off in the bathroom when his father made him stop and get out because he wanted to take a piss. Because his da was banging on the door, everyone knew what he was doing in there, defiling himself (It was a wicked good defiling). He had the same feeling as he walked back to his room. Jim stood holding the guitar; Lenny inquired, "You know *Blue Suede Shoes*?" Jim nodded and asked, "What key?"

Lenny looked at him, not understanding the question. "In A," replied Franny. Lenny took his place behind the microphone and counted down. Jim waited for Michael and his drums to kick in before he started playing. It was a bit difficult for Jim because he wasn't used to playing with a drumbeat behind him. He found himself having to turn to Michael to follow his beat. Jim was used to accompanying Franny on the piano, but it was unsettling to stay with Michael and still support Lenny. Lenny sang the song while turning to watch Jim while watching Michael. As Jim watched Michael, he strained to hear what was coming from the amp. Jim tried to stay with Michael and not to really pay attention to Lenny. Somewhere in the middle of the second verse Lenny started yelling, "Whoa, whoa, let's do that again."

Jim stopped and looked around. He was glad that they stopped because he was lost in where they were in the song, but he was afraid that they weren't happy and why they had to stop. Jim checked the faces of Lenny, Michael, and Franny, and it didn't look like they were upset; on the other hand, Alley, still standing off to the side of the piano, looked like he had won the Irish Lottery.

They played the song again, and it sounded a bit better this time. When they finished, Lenny went over to a pile of papers on a side table. Jim looked over at Franny, sitting in front of the piano. Franny smiled reassuringly. “It seemed to be going pretty good,” thought Jim. "Here, I wrote this song. Let's see how it sounds?" asked Lenny, holding some of the papers in his hand. Jim and Franny swooped in and looked at the song on the pages. It was called, “Here I Come.”

Jim and Franny read the words that Lenny had written on the page. "Ooo, baby, you really wrote a song?" cooed Mary Catherine, pushing past Franny to read over what, she was sure, was going to be quickly a number one record in the country. "I just knocked it out one night," answered Lenny, trying to sound modest. "It's great!" announced Mary Catherine, not really reading it. Jim read the song, then glanced at Franny, who had also realized that Lenny hadn't written any chord notations on it. They were going to have come up with the melody. "Do you have an idea what you want it to sound like?" asked Franny. "I want it to sound cool," was Lenny's answer. "it will sound cool, you'll be singing it, baby," announced Mary Catherine.

She and Lenny calling each other "Baby and Babe" were starting to wear on Franny. Franny had promised herself that she would never call Lenny "Baby." Mary Catherine looked up from the pages and glared at her, giving Franny the feeling that Mary Catherine could read her thoughts. Franny promised herself not to make promises to herself concerning Lenny when Mary Catherine was around.

"Let's try it," urged Jim. Jim stepped back and started to noodle again on the beautiful guitar. Alley sidled up to him and said, "Let me try it?" Jim turned away from him quickly. "I think it would sound a little like *Jailhouse Rock,"* suggested Lenny, taking his place behind the microphone. "Yeah, great idea," lied Jim, but he felt as if he was going to play the guitar with them; he had better agree with Lenny. Michael pounded out a beat on the tom-tom as Lenny jumped into the lyrics from the page:

> *You're trapped in the tower, held by the king with all the power, the army had all started to cower...*

As Jim played, he also kept turning away from Alley, who was trying to pursue him for a chance to get back on the guitar. Jim ignored Alley, pretending to get something from Michael, or he was following Franny or just digging what Lenny was saying. Jim had no idea where this song was going, the only one who seem to know was Mary Catherine, who was making large gestures with her hands like she was a conductor:

> *Here I come, to save you from your tears, here I come, you're the hero for the coming years, here I come, I'll show you how it's done.*

Jim stepped up and played a lick that he had heard Leo play when doing *Born Under a Bad Sign.* Lenny stepped away from the microphone to watch Jim play, while Michael kept time. Lenny kicked into the last verse:

So, here I come, to see you undone, here I come, looking for nothing but fun, what have you done, sugar, what have you done.

They finished the song in a big flourish, and then looked at each other approvingly. "That was good," answered Lenny, sounding pleased with the results of their improvisation. "It was wicked good," ejaculated Mary Catherine, bouncing over to Lenny. "Yeah, wicked good," agreed Jim. "Really good," agreed Franny. "Beautiful," said Alley, waiting to get the guitar back. "I think I screwed it up," admitted Michael, standing and stretching, "I'm sorry about that." "No, man. No problem," said Lenny, the leader of the group, "It's coming along." Finally, Jim couldn't ignore him anymore. He took the Gretsch off his shoulder and handed it to Alley, who put it on with an "its rightful place" attitude.

The practice continued for another hour or so. Jim would sit in with his acoustic or playing Lenny's Washburn. At the end of the practice, Jim took over the piano so that Franny could have a turn on the Gretsch. Franny, on the guitar, always surprised Jim. He knew that she didn't play all that often, but yet she was good at it in such a short time. Franny was miles ahead of Alley already, and she didn't play all that much. Every time Jim heard Franny play the guitar, he got the feeling that she was gaining on him, as if he took any time away from his instrument, she would pass him, and then he would have no idea what he would do. He certainly didn't hate Franny, but if he could, it would be because she connected to music so much faster than him. It took him weeks to learn how to play a song good, Franny just needed to play it through a few times, and she would have it down.

♫♫♫

"We need to write our own songs like 'Here I Come,'" said Lenny, with a mouth full of Oreos. He swilled some milk to wash it down as Lenny and the River Rats, Mary Catherine, Bridie, and Jim were joining him for a post-practice snack. "You should handle all the song writin', Babe," confirmed Mary Catherine, as she stuffed a handful of cookies into her coat pocket. "No, if we're gonna do something, we have to write our own songs," said Professor Lenny. "But the people we play for want covers. I think writing a song is all well and good, but the people only want to hear what they've already heard before," stated Franny, also noticing that Mary Catherine nicked a good half dozen Oreos. "But we don't wanna be the band that everyone knows for the one song that they're playing," reasoned Lenny, "we want to be the band that knocks them out with something new." "Yeah, I agree with Lenny," said the *now* very agreeable Alley, "We should write songs like the one Lenny wrote." Jim looked over at Franny, who gave a bit of a shrug with her shoulders.

♫♫♫

Riding home on the bus that night, Jim and Franny were quiet. Jim couldn't stop hearing the sound of the Gretsch ringing in his ears. Franny spoke up first, "That song was terrible." "Yeah," Jim agreed. He stared down at the end of the bus, where Michael was sitting with Bridie and Mary Catherine (Lenny's ma and Harry were coming home that night, and Mary Catherine hadn't been introduced as the "Babe" yet). "Maybe you should try to write a song?" Franny asked.

Jim had thought about writing a song-- he even tried once, but it sounded stupid, and then when he tried to put it to music, it sounded worse... like Lenny's song. "I don't know," replied Jim, "I like playin' the blues." "Can you write a blues song?" asked Franny. "I don't know, probably not. Leo says that you have to live the blues to be able to sing the blues. I guess you would have to live the blues to write a song about the blues, too." "I don't think all songs are about the blues. Maybe you could write Lenny a song to sing?" suggested Franny, snapping the clasp of the guitar case. Jim didn't answer; he was watching Merrimack flow under the Duck Bridge.

"Maybe if you wrote a song, Lenny would let you in the band?" Jim still wasn't sure if he wanted to be in the band. He was sure that he liked playing the two-tone Gretsch guitar, but he wasn't sure if he wanted to play with a bunch of people. He liked playing the blues with Leo while people dropped money into Leo's guitar case. "I don't think that kid, Alley, wants me to be in the band." "It's not up to Alley," replied Franny, "it's Lenny's band, and it's also Lenny's guitar. He makes the decisions."

"I think Lenny wants to write the songs," said Jim, "why would he want me to write one?" "Because it wasn't any good." Jim thought about it. "Why don't you write a song?" he asked Franny. "I'm a girl; I've never heard of a girl writing a song." Jim spotted his stop coming up next, "I don't see why that should matter. A song's a song. If girls can sing 'em, I can't see why they can't write to 'em."

The bus slowed down and prepared to stop on Haverhill Street. "Think about it?" she asked Jim as he swung out of their seat and carried his guitar to the front of the bus. Just before stepping down the stairs to get off, Jim looked to the back of the bus, where Michael was sitting. Bridie and Mary Catherine pushed their way to the front of the bus. Michael gave him a nod, telling Jim that he could step down now. Jim would think about writing a song, but for now, he had to think about sneaking his guitar into the house so Da wouldn't see it. There was a lot of sneaking around for music.

♫♫♫

Lenny handed Franny a tonic. Lenny's mom and Harry had left for Europe earlier that day. Lenny and Grammy Ham had the whole house to themselves for the next few months. Harry had some business buying hardware products in London, somewhere in Germany and maybe even the Soviet Union; that's what they call Russia now. Lenny asked Franny to come over early, before anyone else arrived, to ask her a question. Franny got nervous when she realized that none of the other bandmates were there. Could Lenny be telling her that they didn't want her in the band-- they didn't want to have a girl in the band? She took the bottle of Coke he offered; after popping the cap off, she waited to see what he was going to do.

"I've been thinking about changing guitar players," Lenny said, "maybe bringing in your friend, Jim." "Finally," Franny thought. "What about Alley?" she asked, trying to sound surprised. "Maybe he would like to play the bass?" answered Lenny, though he was pretty sure that Alley wouldn't want to play the bass. "Does Jim want to be in my band?" "Tell him that he can play the Gretsch," Franny instructed, being pretty sure of that. "Where are we going to find a bass?" asked Franny, just so that she could hear the answer. "My mom and step-dad left me some pocket money for while they're gone." "Wow, pocket money that will buy a bass," she was thrilled; she asked the question because the answer was so cool. "You should ask Jim to play some of the songs he wrote. Maybe we could use one of them?" offered Franny. "We don't need his songs," grumbled Lenny, finishing his tonic, "We're gonna play my songs." Franny smiled at him but cringed inside.

♫♫♫

Jim sat on his mattress as he noodled a few strings on his guitar, running scales that Leo had taught him. Beside him, on the bed, was a pad of yellow paper that he had nicked from Kathy. Kathy liked to draw, mostly pictures of horses, which was strange since she had probably seen four live horses in her life and had never ridden one as far as Jim knew but she could draw horses for days. Jim tried to think of words for a song but he couldn't find the chords to match them or he couldn't find the words to match the chords he found. He would just play the scales and some of Leo's licks but nothing was coming out that sounded like a song. It all sounded like he was just noodling.

Jim wondered if it was possible to just will something into being. Like, if he tried long enough, could he find a song in there somewhere? That, maybe, if he kept noodling, suddenly a song would spring out and stand in front of him with a look of "Here I am-- I'm your song." But at the moment, he couldn't get any ideas. Franny had told him that if he could come up with two new songs, he could be in the band and play the Gretsch. Jim wasn't too sure if he wanted to be in the band, but he did realize that if he was going to be in a band, he would like to be in one with Franny. But he wasn't really sure if he could come up with two songs just like that and have them ready by Monday for their next band practice. It was like willing yourself into finishing homework, and yet you didn't know what subject it was about.

Jim had talked to Leo about playing in the band, and Leo was all for it. He said that the times that he really enjoyed the music was when he was playing with other people. Leo once told him that when he plays with other musicians, he doesn't feel blind anymore. That he can almost see people by the music they make. He didn't have to see their faces; all he had to do was listen to the music they made. Leo said that every band he was in, as soon as the music started, it was like having a conversation with those people, but he wasn’t using words anymore; he was using music and sound. And since it was music and sound, he didn't need to see anyone. Leo used to tell Jim all kinds of wild stuff. But Leo said that when he was playing in a band, he felt like he could see again.

Now, Jim wasn't blind, but he did like to play with Franny. He liked to watch her when she was playing. The way she would stare down at her hands on the keyboard, her wrists raised just as Ma always said. Jim liked the way that Franny would concentrate on the keys she was hitting. Her blue eyes staring intently at the keys, occasionally she would toss her head back to get the curly blonde bangs out of her face. Then, she would go back to concentrating on what she was doing, like she was listening to the music in her head, just knowing where to pedal and where to hold it down. Sometimes, lately, since they both had guitars now, they would sit facing each other learning a new song. If Jim was teaching her a Blues song or something that Leo taught him, she would stare at his fingers as he went through the song. But when he was watching her hands, at times, he would look up at her face and it would be so beautiful that it would throw him. He would have to stop and they had to start all over again.

Jim would never tell Franny what threw him, but he couldn't help staring at her. Her eyes were sometimes like pools, like they were filled with water, but the water was blue and these water pools were floating in freckles that seemed to float all around her eyes and her light eyebrows, moving under her glasses. Then, she might smile with her lips pulling back and her slightly bucked front teeth slipping out of her mouth. Jim wondered what she thought about all the time. Did she always think about music? Did she always think about the piano? Did she ever think about him? Jim wanted to be in a band with Franny, he wanted to do everything with her. He wished that he could write a song.

♫♫♫

Jim came down the cellar stairs with Franny. From the first minute, he recognized the new guitar as a bass. He also realized that they had just told Alley that he was going to be playing the new bass from now on and Jim would be playing the Gretsch. Lenny had found the old two-tone sunburst Epiphone Viola bass at a secondhand shop, up on Riverside. The guy there thought that it was a factory reject because it only had four strings on it. Lenny paid him fifteen dollars for it and the guy was glad to get it. Unfortunately, Alley was not so glad to get the bass. Alley took it for what it was, a demotion from first chair to the rhythm section. Alley had played the trumpet in junior high school and he had lost his seat on that instrument, also.

Alley had heard that guitar players got laid a lot more than trumpet players, and he was hoping to someday get laid... with a girl. Now that he had lost his guitar (just when he was starting to get the hang of it) and was going to have to learn to play a whole other instrument. And he wasn't even sure if bass players ever got laid, since he wasn't sure what a bass was. Alley had put the bass on when Lenny showed it to him and that's when he realized that he was the new bass player, sort of like, "bass meet Alley, Alley meet your new bass."

Lenny had shown him how to bat the strings rather than strumming like a guitar, but after that, Alley was totally lost. For one thing, the bass didn't really use a pick, so it was a lot more specific on which string you are hitting. The other thing was that the instrument was a lot lighter than the Gretsch, which made it easier to handle-- of course, he couldn't tell that to the other guys. He was at a point now where he was going to have decide how much he wanted to be in this band. And if he wasn't going to be in the band, how was he going to get laid.

Jim and Franny entered the cellar, and Franny took her place on the piano bench. Jim took from his pocket the songs that he wrote the night before. They were written on the yellow paper from Kathy's pad, spaced out in verses. Jim showed the songs to Lenny and the others, all of the kids were impressed with the songs. Lenny even acted surprised that Jim had actually written the songs. After all, he was only joining the band because he could write songs...that's what Franny said.

Jim took up his Sears Harmony guitar and prepared to play. He wanted to use his guitar because he wanted to use an instrument that he was comfortable with. Jim stood in front of Lenny, Franny, Alley, Michael and Mary Catherine, who was smirking on the couch. "Let's see what the dink-weed wrote," hollered Mary Catherine, preparing herself to despise whatever Jimmy had written on those pages. Jim looked down at his paper and started to sing his song, “The Mighty Merrimack.”

Of course, no one but Franny was familiar with Woody's *Roll on Columbia* so no one but Franny knew he was blatantly ripping off the great Woody Guthrie. When he finished everyone agreed that Jim's song was a lot better than Lenny's song. No one seemed to pick up the fact that many of the landmarks in the song were not even in Massachusetts and if they looked on a map, they would find them way across the country in the Pacific Northwest. But they weren't really listening to the words-- they were listening to the song.

Lenny listened to it thinking whether or not he could sing it, Michael listened to it thinking whether he could play it, Franny didn't really listen; she was busy deciding whether she should expose Jim as a plagiarist.

Alley was deciding whether he still wanted to stay in the band.

Mary Catherine thought that it was a whole lot of hooey-- first off, the Merrimack was not so great. The mighty Merrimack was nothing but the natural sewer of the Merrimack Valley, the way old car bodies and the sludge from textiles was washed away in it. It was too large to be a stream and that's why they called it a river but it certainly wasn't great and she'd never seen it roll on in her life. Sometimes, in the spring, it was deeper than the rest of the year but you couldn't say it was rolling. It was pretty much just a piss-stream of a river and it didn't deserve a song.

Jim played his other song next, "The Streets of Lawrence." Again, no one noticed that there wasn't any seaman's mission, teacups or all-night cafes in Lawrence but who was really listening to the words. It didn't matter, and the way Jim sang it, he made the song about the problems that most cities have, big or small. Franny, of course, knew he didn't write this one also, she couldn't place it, but she did have to tip her hat to the fact that he tried to pass it off (and pretty much did) as his.

After Jim finished, he turned to the rest of the group, and Lenny shook his head in appreciation. "That was really good. I dunno know if I could sing it, but I can sure try to sing both of 'em." It was determined that they would all learn both songs and add them to their short repertoire. Jim spent the rest of the afternoon teaching the two songs to his new band. Alley sulked, holding the Epiphone bass all afternoon.

"It took a lot of guts to do that?" exclaimed Franny as they walked to the bus. "I tried to write a song but I couldn't. They all sounded dumb," replied Jim, honestly. "We've got to do something about that. Maybe, there's a book or something we can find to help us?" reasoned Franny.

The October wind, blowing through their coats. Jim was carrying both guitars, he thought that it was what Ma would want him to do. "We could go to the library. Maybe, they have one there." Franny reached over and took her guitar from him, "You don't have to carry both."

"No, I want to," Jim argued, but she still took it. "If I'm going to play it, I should carry it," reasoned Franny, " Yeah, let's go to the library and see what we can find." They had to start running, the bus was rumbling up the road, to the bus stop. "Yeah," agreed Jim, "And I've got a book report to turn in."

♫♫♫

Jim was nervous; this was gonna be the first time he gigged with Lenny and the River Rats. He wore his brother, Michael's, old suit coat and clip-on tie. The clasp on his church pants was broken and kept opening every time he moved his legs. Franny was in her Confirmation dress, wearing a light sweater and a thin necklace holding a small crucifix that belonged to Joanie. Alley paced up down the hallway where they were waiting, while Michael tapped the cement wall with his drumsticks. Everyone was nervous but no one looked as nervous as Lenny, when he arrived with Mary Catherine, Bridie and some other girls. Lenny looked like he was sneaking into the gym of Saint Anthony's. He kept glancing around the hall, acting startled every time there was a sound in the hallway.

"Look, everyone, let's do our set and then get the hell out of here," instructed Lenny, holding the list of songs they were planning to play-- they were up to eight songs, now. No one disagreed with Lenny, though they didn't realize how much Lenny didn't want to be there.

Alley's mom was on Saint Tony's Community Association. When she heard that Allan was in a band, she knew that he had to play at the parish's Advent Extravaganza. The Advent Extravaganza was a festival of sorts, with games, food booths, Catholic remembrances and a raffle of a Christmas turkey... they also had an open bar. It was the only church celebration that Da attended.

It was Mary Catherine's job to make sure that Da didn't go to the Extravaganza this year. Mary Catherine had a well worked-out plan, she wrote in the celebration on the Dewey calendar, taped to the refrigerator in the kitchen. Three days after the actual event and she also reminded Da of the changed date, one afternoon before he had gone off to Barnaby's, to ensure he would remember. Jim hoped Mary Catherine's plan would work but he still wasn't as nervous as Lenny.

Lenny stood waiting. He took some deep breaths and made some strange noises that he saw the Von Trapp family use when they were going to sing in front of the Germans. Lenny wasn't going to sing in front of Germans but if Father Nelson was in that auditorium, it was almost the next closest thing.

Lenny hadn't been back to Saint Tony's since his last Midnight Mass. He hadn't seen Father Nelson since that night when the priest anointed his corduroys. Now, he was going to go up there and sing "rock and roll" to the Advent Extravaganza. That's when it hit Lenny, he was going to sing "the devil's music" to the whole Saint Anthony's congregation. If he wanted to really get back at Father Nelson, this was his chance. He could go out on that stage and strut his stuff in front of the priest and everything that is holy.

"Let's go out there and show 'em what we've got," said Lenny, leading his River Rats to the stage. When they got out to the stage, there wasn't anyone there to introduce them. Lenny, Alley, Franny, Michael and Jim just came walking to an empty stage (except for the preset drums, microphones and piano). Jim looked over at Lenny, who just shrugged and stepped to the microphone on a stand in the center of the stage. Jim attached the lead, or the chord, from the Gretsch to the Brownface amp. Franny walked to the piano on the other side of the stage, she looked out over the crowd who were mostly shopping for Christmas gifts and playing the games in the booths set up along the other three walls.

In the center of the gym, where a large group of men and some boys were gathered, Sister Mary Celeste was serving beer and whiskey; this was the only way to get most of the menfolk of the parish to attend. Sister Mary Celeste, or Sister Scary Celeste as she was known to most of Saint Tony's elementary schoolers, was the most gregarious of the nuns, occasionally making pilgrimages to Barnaby's to save souls and drink for free on Friday nights... especially when the Bruins played (Saint Tony's rectory didn't own a television). Franny took her seat at the piano, gently feeling the keys under her fingers.

"We're Lenny and the River Rats," Lenny announced, even though the hum of the crowd didn't change. Franny looked out across the audience and saw her mom and Aunt Lucy standing at her side of the stage. They both had a glass of punch in their hands. Suddenly, Lenny counted off, the band kicked into the song.

Jim looked out over the crowd; he thought the guitar sounded good. They had come in earlier, before the festival started and checked to see how the sound was. It was good then and Jim was pleased with how it sounded now. He concentrated on what he was doing, going from chord to chord, waiting for his turn to back up Lenny singing.

Lenny looked out from the front of the stage; it was hard to see who was in the crowd. Most everyone was busy doing something else. Lenny sang and stared out, looking for one person in the crowd. Somewhere in the second song, *Peggy Sue,* Lenny spotted a dark figure at the back of the crowd. He wasn't sure if the figure was watching or ordering a hot dog from Mrs. Dunphy. Then the figure moved, and Lenny was able to spot Father Nelson's profile in the red and green colors that were reflected from the Christmas tree in the corner. The thing was that Lenny couldn't be sure if Father Nelson was watching-- it looked like he was talking to someone with his back to them. Lenny knew that he had to do something to get Father Nelson's attention so that Lenny could be sure that the priest knew he was there in front of his people, in front of his parish... bringing them a different message. He wasn't sure what that message was but he was sure that it was different.

In the middle eight, Jim went into his solo. While Jim was playing, Lenny danced at the edge of the stage. He stood in front of everyone and felt it coming on. It was the only way in which he could think of getting Father Nelson's attention... the best way of getting anyone's attention. He gave them what they wanted. Lenny danced at the edge of the stage his legs wide apart and swaying his hips to the music. He stared out into the audience watching the figure that he thought was Father Nelson. He swung his hips and suddenly there was a reaction from the audience. The reaction didn't come from the Father Nelson but a group of young women in the front of the crowd. The girls pushed each other towards the stage, some screaming and most dancing and waving to Lenny.

When Lenny realized that Father Nelson wasn't going to react, he turned to the girls and swung his hips towards them. Grabbing the microphone stand, he swung it in front of him and straddled it like a cowboy riding bucking bronco. There was a loud yell that went up from the girls and it seemed that the crowd in front started to grow. Lenny took up the song from Jim but continued to target the girls with his gyrations and pleading to be true.

Franny heard the reaction and turned to see what was happening. She spotted the group of girls in the front and recognized many. She continued to play and then looked to her mom and aunt in the far corner. Joanie was almost blushing, watching Lenny bouncing on the microphone stand. Aunt Lucy covered her face, with just enough space for her eyes to see out between her fingers. Lenny danced over to Franny and started to do gyrations in front of her waving the microphone stand at her, wantonly. Franny smiled at him and then looked down back at her hands on the piano keyboard. Lenny bounced over to Jim and gyrated in front of him.

Jim could feel the energy of the crowd changing; he wondered why Lenny had added this extra musical break. When he looked up and saw Lenny dancing with his stand in front of him, it caught him off guard. Jim couldn't help but to laugh and keep playing. He looked out over the crowd and noticed how all the activity that greeted them when they stepped on the stage had seemed to be stopped, and the front of the stage was now filled with people, mostly young girls; some were yelling and reaching out for Lenny, but most looked like they were having fun. Lenny discarded the stand, ran to the lip of the stage and continued gyrating in front of the swelling crowd.

The next time Jim looked up from his guitar, Lenny was again dancing at the lip of the stage. He could make out some kind of disturbance at the very front of the crowd-- it looked like someone pushing girls back away from the stage. At first, he thought it was probably some aldermen of the church trying to control the frenzied young girls, but at second look, he realized that it was Mary Catherine, pushing the teeny-boppers away from her boyfriend. Jim also noticed some men running, back and forth, from the bar to a man in the corner. It was too dark to know who the man was, but he hoped that it wasn't his da.

Lenny danced in front of the crowd full of screaming girls. His shirt was sopping with sweat, and his hair hung down in front of his eyes. He felt so free that he couldn't really think of anything but how free he was. He danced making sure that Father Nelson was staring at him, making sure that Father Nelson was hating him, making sure that Father Nelson felt that he, Lenny Hamilton, was corrupting all the youth at the Advent Extravaganza, just days before Christmas. He was making these girls scream, jump, and making them trying to get closer to him. They pressed against the edge of the stage, trying to touch and feel him. Lenny knew he was pissing off the priest and all those smug adults, who thought they were so above everyone else by being there in some form of the church's supporters, deserved extra privileges and tokens for the gates of heaven. Lenny wanted to show them that their days would be over and there would be a different order, one judged by those who had the courage to stand out in front, not those who hid behind clergy robes to get what they wanted. Lenny stood in the center of the stage, in dramatic effect, he whipped his hair back from his face. He looked down at his yelling fans and realized that they were watching something else. Lenny turned to the side of the stage and suddenly he was there.

Father Nelson strutted across the stage-- straight to Lenny's microphone. Lenny stopped short confused about what was happening. Father Nelson waved his arms to Franny and Michael. Alley stepped backward, trying to disappear into the dark wings of the stage. "Stop it! Stop it, right now!" yelled the priest. He turned to Jim, who was the only one still playing at the moment, "Mister Dewey, please!" Jim looked up and was surprised to see Father Nelson on stage with them. The parish curate stood a few feet from him. Jim was stunned that the priest even knew his name.

They stopped playing with the slap-back of the amplifier still echoing throughout the gym. Men, from the back of the arena, surged forward and started pushing the girls away from the stage. Sister Mary Celeste had two girls by the hair and was pulling them to the exit. Grown men and mothers were pushing young girls towards the doors trying to save their young souls. Father Nelson turned to Lenny with the disgust of a man who could jack-off on a twelve-year-old, and said, "Leonard, this has to stop. You're making an ass out of yourself." Lenny looked at Father Nelson and didn't say anything.

The crowd looked at Lenny and his reaction. Slowly, a smile spread across Lenny's face. Jim looked at Franny to see if she knew what was going to happen (this was Jim's first gig with the River Rats). Franny looked to be just as in the dark as he was. Jim next looked over at Michael, who was still seated behind his drums but watching Lenny for some hint of what was to come. Jim could also glimpse Alley back by the exit in the wings, he clearly looked ready to run if needed.

A calm look came across Lenny's face as he looked down at Father Nelson's hand, reaching out to take the microphone from him. Lenny gently handed the microphone to the rector. Father Nelson took the microphone, sealing the end of the show. When suddenly, Lenny turned and ran with every ounce energy he had left he leaped off the front of the stage, body-slamming a group of the men busy clearing out the young girls from the hideous music that was happening at the Advent Extravaganza. When Lenny hit the mahogany gym floor a group of men and boys rushed on him.

From the stage, Franny, Michael, and Jim watched fists fly in the pile over Lenny. Mary Catherine, followed by Bridie and Sister Scary Celeste began pummeling the backs and asses of the men on top of Lenny. Michael looked over at Jim and Franny, then he jumped off the stage and ran to the pile to start pulling parishioners off his lead singer. Franny looked to her mom and her aunt. Joanie glared at her daughter on the stage, "Is this really what you want to do?"

♫♫♫

As bad as the Advent Extravaganza went, it was like hell-fire on the streets of Lawrence and the halls of Lawrence High School. Parent meetings were held to denounce Lenny and the River Rats. There was talk of expelling all five children from any further church functions (this would've have been a great penalty if Alley wasn't the only regular church-goer-- Joanie Walsh stopped attending, having tired of the whispers and stink-eyes from the upstanding Saint Anthony parishioners, Michael and Lenny's family were not even members of the parish and the Deweys were of course the Deweys, what did you expect). There was talk about black-balling Alley's parents, Jack and Gilda Gould, but they were always generous at the donation plate, so just wishing them to Purgatory or at least holding some pity for their sinning son was all that could be done.

Most of Lawrence High was now referring to the performance as the Adventaganza and the band as Lenny and the Eternally Damned (In later years, the Advent Extravaganza would be re-titled "Advent-apalooza") and was a hot topic, everyone wanted to be in on it or least see them in person.

Parents tried to talk their kids out of wanting to have Lenny and the River Rats play their birthday parties and sock hops. But kids being kids and having nothing else to really do in life in 1961 but to bug their folks, who eventually would give in and have the River Rats play their parties.

The River Rats themselves had survived fairly well. Lenny did receive a nice shiner after his leap of faith (it was nothing compared with to the way Da decorated Jim's face) but other than a few bruises he was ready to rock. Michael had his shirt ripped and lost a drum stick somewhere. Alley was getting the cold shoulder from both his parents but they were kind of proud of his playing in the band, even if they were a bunch of godless thugs (it was really just Lenny-- they all agreed to pray for him). Jim was worried that his da would hear about it and feel that he had disrespected the church.

Jim was interested to learn that Da felt that the church and that "snooty" Father Nelson got what they deserved, always pretending to be all high-flutin' and not talking to him except only about the new program the church was involved in called "Alcoholic's Unanimous," where guys went to talk about drinking. Da had lost interest when he found out there wasn't any real drinking done there.

Joanie had a heart-to-heart talk with Franny about the associations you make and how in life you're judged by that. Franny told her mother that she didn't want to be judged and anyone who judged her wasn't a friend. Joanie couldn't help to be impressed that Franny was considered to be part of the group and the people who were in the group were men, and none of those men seemed to care that she was a woman playing the piano. Joanie could only wish what Alley's parents were wishing, that it was a phase and they would grow out it (Though Joanie was aware that Franny had been going through this phase for the last five years or so).

Lenny and the River Rats took the incident in stride and worked out more songs in the show that catered to Lenny's newly discovered talent and his dancing. They added Elvis' *Don't Be Cruel* and Gary U.S. Bonds *Quarter to Three*. Most parents would spend the first few songs hanging around the audience of the show but after realizing that there wasn't anything they could do but to pray, they would retreat to the back of the room, or upstairs. The other thing that would assure them was Mary Catherine would usually maul any girl who got too close to Lenny. Unless the child was their daughter, they usually felt better to have Mary Catherine there.

Lenny was enjoying his new-found fame after the Adventaganza. He would walk down the hallway of Lawrence High School, and young girls would scream, just seeing him and finding themselves in his presence. Lenny realized that it was beneficial to be recognized as a celebrity. Many times, students would offer him their lunch if the school's cafeteria had run out of any food he liked, and he was always offered a seat he wanted to eat at, even if the kid sitting in the seat had to sit at another table. The thing that he didn't understand was the reaction to his singing that night. Of course, he liked it, but he never really thought he had that attraction that could make girls scream like that or make men and boys dislike him so.

He had never been very athletic, which in Lawrence High School was almost essential for being in the limelight but now everyone, even the boys, knew who he was. Lenny always sensed that it wasn't because of his singing but the threat he was to their sexuality and the girls they liked. This way, they thought, Lenny would be romancing every girl in school, but in real truth, Mary Catherine would never allow that.

Lenny was still attracted to Mary Catherine, but her constant hovering over him as he attended school, rehearsed with the band, went to Brigham's with Michael, Alley and Franny was starting to bug him. He liked Mary Catherine a lot, but he wished she would ease up, especially during the shows. Mary Catherine actually punched Debbie Mulcahey at Debbie's sweet sixteen, which made it wicked uncomfortable to collect the money from Debbie's dad as Debbie stood there, holding a piece of rib steak over her eye.

When they were alone, Lenny would try to reassure Mary Catherine that he liked her and her only, that the flirting was part of the act and how it had raised their recognition as a band. But Mary Catherine was a Dewey, and there ain't much talking to a Dewey if he/she thinks you're lying to them. The Deweys were introduced to lying long before they even started talking (as it happens with most children of drunks). So, Lenny would try to be nice to her and occasionally counsel her on how to treat the screaming girls. It was also in Lenny's best interest not to get Mary Catherine too riled up, whether it was for patrolling the girls at their show or in bed.

Mary Catherine was insatiable when it came to sex. If her body didn't have to force her to sleep, Lenny was afraid that she wouldn't stop. Even her being only fourteen, she still had no problems with any kind of sex; it doesn't matter what Lenny wanted. She was similar to her brother in that he could learn quickly whatever song they were playing. All Lenny had to do was tell Mary Catherine what felt good, and she would repeat it almost every time. A part of Lenny knew he was very lucky to have Mary Catherine, but on the other hand, it bothered him more that sometimes he couldn't stop thinking about boys and even that Christmas Eve.

One time, when he was chatting up Susie O'Sullivan in front of the gym, her boyfriend, Mike Shaunnessy, the captain of the hockey team, ran up to him and tried to punch him. Lenny was able to tie up Mike's arms, and they ended up wrestling on the floor, like how most high school fights end but out of nowhere, Lenny realized that he had a full-on boner. All he could do was to pretend to be hurt and lay flat on his stomach until the incriminating erection deflated when he let Mr. Andruzzi drag him and Mike down to the principal's office.

When Harry and his mom were home from their trip, Lenny approached his ma and sat with her while she watched "Father's Knows Best" one night. It still bothered him about Father Nelson and what had happened in Saint Tony's sacristy. He sat next to his mom and blurted out, "Father Nelson masturbated on me." He just didn't know how to broach it, but he also felt he had to tell all of this to someone; otherwise, it would burn a hole inside him. At first, he really wasn't sure if she heard him. They both stared at the television as Robert Young gave his oldest daughter some sage life advice. Lenny was about to say it again when his mom shook her head and said, "No, that's not right."

Lenny looked to his mom, not sure if she was talking to him or to the television. "A priest would never do that," she added. Lenny wanted to argue, but the way she said it, she was so sure, and he knew he couldn't convince her. Lenny just turned to the tv and continued to watch the show.

He wondered if Bud had said to Robert Young that the parish priest had jerked off on him, would Robert Young had done anything, but Lenny was sure that Robert Young probably would've told Bud that he was wrong... that a priest would never do that. Days later, Lenny decided that he was going to take a stage name, Lenny Suggs. Suggs was his birth name-- Monty's name. Lenny wanted to think that Monty would do something about Father Nelson-- he really wanted to believe that, even though he didn't.

♫♫♫

One of the great benefits that Michael Webster brought to Lenny and the River Rats was that his family business was a bar that hired bands to play on the weekend nights. After the Adventaganza and the word on the streets from it, Michael's father, Paul Webster, or Pudge, as he was known for all his life, invited the River Rats to participate in its semi-annual "Battle of the Bands." Pudge didn't really think that the band could actually win since many of the other bands would bring their followings (and hopefully they would come thirsty). Because the River Rats following were mostly under eighteen years old, their following couldn't come and root on their band at Barnaby's. But for Lenny and River Rats, this was a great opportunity to see where they rated in the real world of gigs.

The first thing that Franny realized after entering Barnaby's was that the drums, and even the Gretsch, and the Brownface amp were not Lenny's. They actually belonged to Michael's family. Both of which once belonged to a band from Atlanta, Georgia, called the Meloncollies. A few of the Meloncollies got drunk and, when it came time to settle upon the bar bill, they realized that they were flat broke. Michael, who at six feet and two inches, was the runt of the brood, and his four brothers and dad, asked the Meloncollies how they planned to settle their bill; that's how the drums, Gretsch, and amp become part of the Webster family.

Michael was the only Webster interested in trying to learn the instruments, taking to the drums almost immediately. Pudge was glad to see the drum kit and guitar back in his establishment. When Michael wasn't using the drums or the guitar, the instruments were loaned out to any band who didn't have most of their equipment, or something was broken. Lenny and the River Rats showed up early to try out the room and set up their equipment. Franny was thrilled to see that they did have a piano so that she could play that night and not just back up Jim on the acoustic guitar. When Pudge spotted Franny, he had to make his way to his son, drumming lightly on the snare drum between his legs. "You didn't tell me you had a girl in the band?" he asked. Michael looked up at his father, his relationship being a bit more open than Jim and his da. "Franny just plays the piano; she doesn't dance or anything," he answered, trying to read his father's concern for having a girl in the band. "I don't know how people are going to take that," humphed Pudge, "This isn't really a place for girls."

Michael looked at his father. He was as practical of a businessman as they came. At times, Pudge would guide Michael on how the bar business ran, in case Michael had any desire to take up the business when Pudge decided to retire (and after any of his four sons didn't want it first). Michael couldn't understand why having Franny in the band would bother someone. She was a very good piano player, and she added a little bit of sweetness that the boys couldn't bring to the show. Michael suspected the whole shebang at Saint Tony's would have been a lot worse if Franny wasn't on stage with them. She gave the band a bit more legitimacy because of her presence.

Lenny stood at the microphone, repeating "Test, test, test," Jim stood off to the side, giving the Gretsch a good last-minute tuning. They all stopped and watched as the T-Birds entered. Each man was carrying their instrument in hard-shell cases. They wore white shirts, ties, and black tuxedo pants. Each musician carried a powder blue tuxedo jacket, wrapped in plastic on a hanger. The T-Birds walked through the table area of the bar, checking out the River Rats on stage. "How're you boys doin?'" asked Lenny from the stage. A few men nodded while they made their way to the one green room behind the bar.

♫♫♫

"Ladies and Gentlemen, welcome Lenny and the River Rats to Barnaby's Big Battle of the Bands," Announced Beef Stew, one time Hot 88 Deejay, now full-time Barnaby's regular. Beef Stew was dressed in a loud jacket, sporting a pink pocket square that he would never use even if you did sneeze. This was a big night for Beef Stew. He was trying to make his comeback in the hosting world. He had combed over his bald spot and was wearing a thin electric blue tie that hanged just a few inches above his belly-button. Stew smiled and waited as the band came on stage, lifting one of the free beers that he was being paid up to his mouth. When Beef Stew spotted Franny, he quickly scooted to the piano and pulled the bench out for her. Franny thanked him and took her place. Lenny stepped up to the microphone and announced, "We don't have any fancy tuxedos to play in. All we brought was rock and roll."

Michael quickly jumped into the thumping introduction of *Streets of Lawrence.* Jim stood in his usual place, to the left of Lenny and played the speeded-up version of the song he supposedly wrote about his home town filled with all-night cafes. Because of the battle aspect of the evening, the bands were only allowed to play two songs. Lenny had decided that they should use two of their most powerful selections, *Streets of Lawrence* and *Quarter to Three. Quarter to Three* was a real barn-burner, written by Gary U.S. Bonds, about staying up all night, singing and dancing to the music of Daddy Gee, that Franny had found and felt it to be a good song to learn.

Lenny enjoyed it because he could rip up on stage as the band tried to play as fast as they could.

While dancing, Lenny had noticed a guy in a neat suit, who was also wearing a pair of dark glasses (sunglasses inside at night). "That was so wild," Lenny thought, sitting alone at a table, sipping a single beer but still watching Lenny perform. Lenny couldn't stop going back and checking this guy's reaction to everything he did. He didn't know the man, but something about him made Lenny constantly check him and his expressionless sunglasses (indoors, at night).

While playing, Jim kept an eye on one of the open windows in the back of the audience. Jim had hoped his da wouldn't go to the show, deciding to drink down at O'Herlihy's or the Green Barrel, because "The Battle of the Bands" had a cover charge and Jim figured Da wasn't about to pay a cover charge when he could use that money for real beer. But there he was, with his friends.

Jim watched his da sitting at the bar with his buddies, Plug and Raymie Farrell, talking and just generally screwing around. What Jim didn't know was that Da had been supplying Frenchy, Barnaby's doorman, with cigarettes that Mary Catherine had been nicking from the Rexall. The thing that comforted Jim was that it didn't appear that Da had noticed him on stage, just a beer-bottles throw from him. Every once in a while, Jim would glance over to the open window at the back of the audience. Once, he thought he saw a dark shadow of a face on the window- - but only for a second.

♫♫♫

Outside of Barnaby's, Addie stood with her father. Leo smiled as he listened to the band on stage that his friend Strings was in. Strings have been that young white boy who sometimes played beside him in front of the W.T. Grant on Essex Street. "Hey boy, are ya lost?" asked Frenchy, from his post in front of the door. Frenchy was there to make sure everyone had paid and at least looked like they were close to the eighteen years old (legal drinking age).

The band in the bar now was underage, but the owner, Pudge, had told Frenchy that they could come in, but they couldn't drink. They could only have tonics (and only one of them). Frenchy had to keep his eyes open for a crazy little girl who kept trying to tell him that she was with the River Rats. But Frenchy knew that she wasn't. The band had been there most of the afternoon, and she showed up just as the battle had started. Frenchy also knew she was a Dewey. Other guys had said that she was fast and you could have your way if you bought her lunch at Brigham's.

"We're fine, boss," answered Smilin' Leo. Leo always thought the "boy" label was funny. He, being at least fifty years older than the little shit at the door, who sounded like he was in his late twenties, and his only real accomplishment other than being kicked out of the Satan's Sons Motor Cycle gang was lucky enough to be born with white skin. Leo could feel Addie cringe, "Let's go, Dad." "Let's wait," suggested Leo, "It's so beautiful a night," Leo pretended to look at the stars and moon above him. "There is nothing like marveling at God's creations." Frenchy turned away from the two harmless Negroes; the old one looked like that blind guy who played in front of the Grants. He wondered if he let that Dewey girl in would she blow him in his pickup truck.

♫♫♫

Inside Barnaby's, Lenny was dancing up a storm on the stage. Many women in the audience were standing and clapping along as Lenny promised to dance with them to *Daddy Gee* and his *swinging ax*. Even the guy on the side of the stage, wearing the dark glasses, was clapping along. Whenever he said "swingin' ax," Lenny would turn to Jim and let him run a couple of riffs on his guitar, then Lenny would go into a gyrating strut across the stage. Every time Jim looked up from his guitar or from the window in the back of the room, he couldn't help but smile at Lenny as he took the audience further with the story the song was telling.

Franny pounded on the piano keys, it was really hot in the bar, and she knew that her mom was going to have to have the dress washed since she was sweating so much and Barnaby's reeked of cigarette smoke and the smell of old beer. Alley played the Epiphone Viola bass, hoping that God wasn't watching him because this was surely a den of inequity, and some wanton women were staring at him from the side of the stage.

Michael pounded his drums. This would show his dad that he wasn't wasting his time with the music, which was useful, and maybe at some point, he could play for a band that only played the bar. Michael also spotted a figure of a woman at the door to the kitchen, where the glasses were washed (Barnaby's didn't actually serve food, which usually stifled the effects of the liquor) and was sure it was his mom. Pudge wouldn't let Donna into the bar. To him, it wasn't a place that a lady wouldn't be seen in. That was why he was alarmed when he found that Michael's band had a girl in it until he found out it was Franny.

Bar owners are like priests. They see and know a lot more than people would like others to know about them. Pudge wasn't so surprised about Franny because Joanie Walsh used to come to Barnaby's often with her friend, Ginny, to meet men and take them home. Why shouldn't her daughter do the same-- he hoped that Joanie's daughter hadn't enticed his son, Michael, who was a good kid but had the sense of a doorknob.

♫♫♫

"We should get a saxophone," suggested Lenny. He, Alley, and Franny stood by the back door of Barnaby's, sipping their tonics and watching the T-Birds play on stage. All the T-Birds wore their powder blue tuxedo jackets and a smart ruffled tuxedo shirt underneath them. One of the T-Birds stood at the center of the stage, blowing a shiny saxophone, burning up the night with its screaming sound. The band was playing a song called, *We're Having a Party,* it was a Sam Cooke song, but the musicianship of the T-Birds, and especially the cookin' sax, just stopped the show and brought everyone to their feet cheering. It was one of the most exciting things that Franny had ever seen in person. The way the band played together and the excitement in the sound had Franny dancing in place and clapping, even when Lenny gave her the stink-eye. She stopped for a minute until Lenny looked away, and then she started swaying to the music again.

Lenny glanced at the table where the guy with the sunglasses was sitting. He was gone. The table had been taken over by four mill men, two pitchers of beer, and a bunch of beer mugs.

Franny looked for Jim but couldn't see him. She did spot Michael behind the bar, stocking clean glasses for the draft beer. She figured out that Jim had probably gone off by himself as he usually did, and she would see him some other time. Stumbling from the bar, Franny spotted Da being led out by the big doorman, Da's two friends following him. Da was arguing with Frenchy, who pushed Da roughly to the front door.

♫♫♫

"What did ya think?" asked Jim. Leo leaned against the front of the building. Addie stood in the corner, smoking a cigarette. "You were cookin', Strings," answered Leo, smiling and staring up at the stars. "A little more seasoning and some more practice, and I think you cats might have sumptin'." "We were outta key a few times," Jim quizzed the blind man. "Yeah, but who isn't," counseled Leo, "Tell your boy, there... the singer, to stay consistent when counting you in. It will help in the long run when you start to get on your game." Suddenly, the doors of Barnaby's flew open, and a person was pushed out. As soon as Jim recognized the familiar figure, he ducked into the shadows of the corner of the Barnaby's, hiding behind Addie.

"Frenchy, Frenchy, my boyo, what about those smokes I've been givin' ya?" asked the figure, as he got his balance back. "Smokes or no smokes, that was the boss' wife you offered to give a ride," yelled Frenchy, threateningly. "How am I supposed to know?" answered Da, with Plug and Raymie taking their places beside him. "I meant to give her a ride in my *car*." "Everyone knows Mick Dewey doesn't own a car and never has," replied

Frenchy, blocking the front door, "Why don't you see if that girl of your's will give you a ride?" added Frenchy, watching the three men leave.

Da looked over at the blind Negro leaning against the building, which was odd. Barnaby's was always off - limits to the niggers, then he saw the negress smoking on the side of the building and also made out a figure cowering beyond her in the dark-- they were always so hard to see at night. Then Da thought about Frenchy's comment about his girl, "Which girl are ya talkin' about?" he yelled to Frenchy. Plug and Raymie led him away so as he wouldn't get kicked out permanently.

Jim slipped around the building to the back door where Franny, Lenny, and Alley were just about to leave. Franny had his guitar (just in case they needed it), and he offered to carry her guitar case when the musicians of the T-Birds exited to go out to the parking lot for a smoke after their set. "You cats are really good," tossed Lenny, trying to sound as honest as possible. "Thanks, you guys aren't bad yourselves," answered the sax player. Lenny stood there and let them all pass, "Thanks, cool."

Jim walked Franny home while Franny excitedly talked about playing at Barnaby's. Her mom would be waiting up for her to hear how it went. They, of course, didn't win but that wasn't why they were there, they played with real bands. Bands with real musicians in them, and they weren't that bad themselves, either. Jim only thought of one thing; he hoped his da hadn't seen him with Leo and Addie.

♫♫♫

Lenny watched the T-Birds move to a beautiful powder blue Thunderbird in the parking lot of Barnaby's. Four of the T-Birds got in the boat of a car, and the other two got in an old Edsel, and they started the automobiles up. "You guys have something," a voice announced. Jim turned and realized that the guy from the side of the stage was right there, still wearing his sunglasses. "My name is Rickie Rooney," he said, holding his hand out. Lenny reached over and shook Rickie's hand. "I'm Lenny Suggs, and this is Alley." The "Suggs" had caught Alley by surprise. He knew him as Hamilton, of Hamilton

Hardware. Lenny would tell the rest of the River Rats later that his real name was Suggs. Hamilton was the hardware store. Alley shook Rickie's hand. "I was wondering if you boys would be interested in a steady gig this summer. Maybe we can go inside and talk about it," suggested Rickie, finally removing his glasses. "We can't go inside," said Alley, realizing maybe he should have let Lenny speak. Lenny was always better at this, whether it was getting money from parents after playing a party or even bargaining with Eddy at Eddy's Second-hand Shop.

Rickie led them to a brand new 1962 Oldsmobile Cutlass, with a red interior. Rickie opened a door, "How about if you boys climb in, and I'll buy you a hamburger?" Lenny went to the passenger side of the car and climbed into the front, and Alley followed him. "My parents don't want me to take rides with strangers," Alley whispered to Lenny, as he took the front seat. "He's not a stranger," Lenny replied, smiling at Rickie, who was slipping into the driver's seat, "That's Rickie." Alley thought about it and finally decided to get in.

♫♫♫

Rickie drove them to the Friendly's on Route 114. Inside the red and white decorated restaurant, Rickie told them that he was a booker for many of the clubs on the coast. He worked for clubs and bars all along the seacoast from Rye Beach to Revere Beach. Rickie let Alley and Lenny order anything on the menu, and he even let them each have a *Fribble.* Rickie then told them about some of the groups that he booked into his clubs. Most of the bands they had never heard of, but they both nodded like they recognized the names and were impressed. What Rickie wanted to do was book Lenny and the River Rats into some of his clubs. He promised that he would book them at first in clubs that were close, like the Casino in Hampton Beach and The Frolics at Salisbury Beach. This sounded really good, even though neither boy had been to either one of those beaches and had no idea where they were. They just had to take Rickie's word for them being close.

Rickie told them that he wanted to sign them to dates. Lenny took a long sip of his straw that was in his chocolate Fribble. For a moment, Alley thought that Lenny had an ice cream headache because he thought so long about it, but finally, he said, "Will we get paid for these gigs?" Rickie smiled with bright white teeth and a gleam in his eye. He stared deeply into Lenny's caramel eyes and said, "Of course, who would ask you to do it for free?" Lenny looked to Alley, who was sipping on his vanilla Fribble (he wanted a chocolate Fribble but his mom had told him to stay away from chocolate, which made his acne flare-up), and Alley looked back at Lenny. Alley couldn't believe that someone was offering to pay them, and it wasn't even for their kid's party. This would be like a real job. Alley's dad couldn't say that he was wasting his time and paving his way to hell with this devil music-- now he was getting paid.

"I don't know," said Lenny, staring into his glass, stirring his straw. "It will be good exposure for your band. You could build a following." "What kind of people go to these clubs?" asked Alley, suddenly afraid of the kind of company he was being led into. "You know, beach people. People on vacation. Some students, adults who want to be entertained," assured Rickie, stealing a crinkle-cut French fry from Lenny's plate. "Will we be able to drink at these bars?" asked Lenny, teasingly swiping at Rickie's hand and his French fry. Rickie smiled and dipped the fry into Lenny's dab of ketchup. "We'll see what we can do." Rickie slipped the French fry into his mouth, between his perfectly white teeth. "Can you get us phony I.D.s?" asked Lenny. "We'll see. I can't make promises about that." "We're all underage, ya know," assisted Alley. Lenny turned quickly towards him and glared. "We are," confirmed Alley to Lenny's glare. "Don't worry, I'll take care of that," assured Rickie.

Lenny thought some more. "We're interested," he said, sounding uncommitted. "I need to know soon," said Rickie, "We need to nail down dates for the summer." Lenny looked over at Alley, who didn't know what to do. He wanted to be in the band, but he wasn't really sure of what his parents would say if he told them that he was going to play at the beach... wherever that was. His Dad had taken him, his mom, and little brother to Revere Beach when he was younger, but he didn't remember all that much about it except that there were a lot of black people there, and they had to leave. Alley's family used to go to his grandmother's cottage on Mousam Lake, in Maine. He had never swum in the ocean.

"I have to talk to the rest of the band," answered Lenny. Rickie changed his position in the booth they were sitting in. He leaned closer to them. "One thing," he went on, "You're going to have to get rid of the little girl on the piano." Lenny pulled back from the table. "But Franny is in the band." "I know she's in the band now," continued Rickie, almost in a whisper, "But she can't be in the band at the beach. They're not going to let her play with you." "What kind of places are these clubs?" Alley asked again. "I said, they're adult clubs, they don't want to have little girls there." Lenny looked to Alley and then back to Rickie, "All right, Franny's out." Rickie smiled big so that those pearly-whites gleamed.

When they were walking out to the car, Alley grabbed Lenny's arm and stopped him. "We're going to take this gig, but Franny's out?" Lenny nodded, "Yeah, it's a gig...a bunch of gigs. She'll understand." "Come on, guys. I'll drop you off," coaxed Rickie. "I don't think she's going to understand," said Alley, following Lenny. Rickie opened the driver's door and announced, "We'll work on another name for the band, too." Alley looked to Lenny, who was sliding into the front seat beside Rickie, "A new name?"

♫♫♫

Jim and Franny were walking up Haverhill Street towards Jim's house. He wasn't really sure where he was on Haverhill Street, but it looked like Haverhill Street. They were just walking, Jim had his guitar slung over his shoulder, and he was carrying Lenny's acoustic guitar that Franny was using. They walked together, it seemed to be a dark night, but it wasn't cold. He reached over to take

Franny's hand, and she looked up at him. He was filled with fear but took her hand...

Suddenly, she grabbed his right wrist and pulled on his arm. Jim was confused. He could feel himself being dragged. Dragged across the mattress, he reached out and tried to grab for Kevin, who he was sure was asleep beside him.

Jim woke up as his da pulled him off the mattress. Da dragged Jim by the wrist onto the floor of the bedroom. Jim tried kicking at Da to get free, but he accidentally kicked Kevin, who shared the bed with him. "Cut it out, dink-weed," yelled Kevin, startled. "Da? Da? Whatta ya doin'?" asked Jim desperately. "I told ya, I feckin' told ya..." Da pressed Jim's hand to the floor and reached back. Jim glanced up and saw the hammer above Da's shoulder, lit up by the moonlight flooding the shade-less bedroom. Da brought the hammer down with all his might. It crashed into the floor, missing Jim's right hand by inches, making his three older brothers jump awake in their beds.

Jim wiggled away from his father, who was lifting the heavy machinist's mallet over his head again. Da had that crazy look that Da would get when he had too much whiskey. He swung down again, but this time Jim was able to roll away. Again, the hammer pounded the floor, making a sickening sound that reverberated throughout the sleeping house. "I told ya to stay away from that nigger," hollered Da, the room filling with the smell of the old whiskey wafting out of his breath and his pores. Jim backed away, sliding under the double mattress that Patrick and Michael shared. Jim pushed himself under the bed so that most of his body was out of reach, and only his head was sticking out. Da swung the hammer wildly at him. The heavy head of the hammer whizzing by his face, just missing him.

Michael and Patrick jumped up and pushed against the far wall, trying to avoid Da's swings at Jim on the floor. "Da, whatta ya doin'?" screamed Michael, thinking it was all a dream. "Da, go to bed. You can beat his balls tomorrow," suggested Patrick, the older brother, who was more used to these invasions at night. "No one is going to be a nigger-lover in this house," yelled Da.

Patrick reached out, catching the head of the hammer, and snatched the tool from his father's hand. He took the hammer and quickly opened the window on the other side of the bed. "Don't drop that, you son-of-a-bitch," warned Da. But Patrick just let the weapon fall from his hand, and they could hear it bounce a couple of times off the roof and hit the asphalt in the alley behind the house. Da stood in front of his boys, slightly swaying, and said, "Ya could've hurt someone droppin' that outta the window."

Patrick stood up on the bed and walked to his father, "You're going to bed, now." "You want another go, boyo?" challenged Da, putting his dukes up. Patrick pushed his father backward towards the bedroom door. Da tried to push back, but he was too off-balance to make headway. "Let's do this tomorrow when you can stand, you old drunk." Da swung at Patrick, but it was so telegraphed that Patty just danced out of the way.

Ma appeared in the door to the bedroom, pulling her thread-bare robe closed. "Come on, Mick. You can yell at the boys in the morning." "There'll be no nigger-loving in this house!" he exclaimed. "Not tonight, Da," confirmed Michael as he stepped down from his bed. "They'll be no playin' with niggers, either," yelled Da, as Ma pushed him out of the bedroom. "...From anyone!" he added as he got in the hallway. "Go, Mick. Go to bed!" Ma pushed Da down the hall to their room. Most likely, Da would be sleeping in the bathtub tonight, so if he pukes, Ma will just wash him down like the front walk in the summer.

Jim slid out from under the mattress. Kevin pulled an opening in the blankets and let his little brother crawl in, "You okay?" Jim looked up at Kathy, Teresa, Dorrie, Mary Catherine, and Annie standing in the doorway, staring at him. Jim nodded; he was all right. Jim realized that all the girls slept in pajamas, except for Mary Catherine, who was wearing only a bra and underpants. Jim slipped into the bed, as his brothers, all of whom were wearing just their boxing shorts, climbed back into theirs.

"Mary Catherine, put some clothes on," yelled Ma, from down the hall, "What if there was a fire or somethin'?" Mary Catherine stalked back to bed in her Maiden Form bra and high-waisted panties, "Who do ya think the firemen are gonna save first, me or that cow?" Jim lay down in his bed, not knowing which sister Mary Catherine was comparing herself to (most likely it was Kathy, Mary Catherine's usually victim). "Are we gonna have a fire, Ma?" asked Teresa. Jim tried to fall asleep but couldn't. For some reason, he realized at that moment that Mary Catherine and Lenny were "doing it." Jim stared at his hand in the moonlight, the hand that he strummed the guitar with, the hand he needed to play with.

♫♫♫

Franny felt terrible. As soon as she came home from school, she climbed into her mother's bed and had lay there, heart-broken. She felt like someone had died. She had gone through the school day like it all was a bad dream, and it was even a gym day. Franny liked gym and looked forward to the days that it was scheduled. She enjoyed running, and if it didn't conflict with band practice, she even thought about going out for the Freshmen Girls' Basketball team. Now that she didn't have band practice, maybe she could go out for the team. She was so disappointed she was thinking about joining the girls basketball team.

When Lenny called her and asked her to meet him at Brigham's, for a moment, she thought that it would be a date, but since there hadn't been any news burning through the school, most likely, Lenny hadn't broken up with Mary Catherine. On her way there, she thought maybe he had some ideas about the band and wanted to see what she thought-- like that time in the kitchen when he decided that Alley should become the bass-player.

When she finally got to the restaurant, she never thought that it was to tell her that she was out of the band. Franny couldn't really understand why Lenny said she couldn't play with them anymore. He said it had something to do with some guy he and Alley met at Barnaby's and some gigs at the beach. Franny wasn't sure if she was totally out of the band or that she just couldn't play with them at these gigs. Lenny said that it was because she was a girl and was too young to play these clubs because people drank there. But she was less than a year younger than Jim (and she even had gotten him in the band), and she'd been around a lot of people who drank booze-- she grew up in Lawrence, for God's sake.

She had come home from school and just crawled into bed, not even having dinner with Joanie. She lay in the bed, listening to cars go by on Marston Street, their light-beams swooping across the far wall. She couldn't understand what she did wrong. There was a knock on the door, "Fran, there's someone here for you," her mother whispered. "Tell them I don't feel good," Franny moaned through the door. "It's a boy," choked Joanie, a bit too excited.

Franny got out of bed. She was still wearing the sweater and skirt she wore to school that day. She checked her hair in the mirror over Joanie's dresser and hoped that it was Lenny visiting to tell her he was kidding her and not to get all upset over what he said at Brigham's. She really liked that restaurant. It was where Joanie took her for good grades and Confirmation. Now it will be the place that she was kicked out of the band. She took a deep breath and opened the door.

Jim stood by the front door of the apartment, holding his guitar. He immediately detected Franny's disappointment. He smiled uneasily, "You don't mind if I came over to see if you're okay?" Joanie led Jim to the couch, "No, that's very kind of you." Jim followed her as Franny sat down at the other end. "Can I get you something to drink?" Joanie asked, trying to be the good host. "No, thanks, Ma'am," answered Jim, in his best Eddie Haskell, even though he had never seen Leave It to Beaver. Jim set his guitar down and sat on the couch.

"Lenny told me that we couldn't have you play with us at the beach gigs," Jim stated, as comfortingly as he could. "It's not fair," complained Franny. Jim agreed, but what could they do. Franny tried to hold it in, but the next moment she realized that she was crying. Jim sat uncomfortably on the opposite end of the couch. He didn't know what to do. Franny put her hand to her face to cover her eyes. She felt so much like a girl, she wanted to do something else, but she couldn't think of anything else to do, and she couldn't stop crying. Jim looked for Franny's mother, who must have disappeared into the bedroom to leave them alone.

Jim slowly moved down the couch and gently took Franny in his arms. He couldn't stop thinking about what had happened the last time he did this when Franny had told him of Buddy Holly's plane crash. This wasn't as sad, but Jim knew how he would feel if they told him he couldn't be part of the band up at the beach. He hadn't been all that thrilled to be invited in the band, but now that he had played a few gigs, he knew he would miss not doing it anymore.

Franny continued to cry, eventually resting her head on his shoulder. Jim patted her on the back as she cried. "I'm gonna miss you," is the only thing he could come up with that he thought didn't sound stupid... or at least, not as stupid.

Jim could feel how comfortable it was holding her. It felt like the way his ma held him when he was little; he felt safe, even if Da was around, he knew that no one could hurt him when he was with his ma like this. The weight of her head on his shoulder, the feeling of warmth on his neck, the moistness of her tears. He took in the feeling of her arms around his shoulders and the motion of her body as she breathed. This was nice. This was very nice. He was pretty sure that Franny couldn't feel the bulge in his pants that was starting to gather.

Franny hugged Jim. She could feel the itchy sweater he was wearing. She hated herself for crying. She also realized that Jimmy Dewey was holding her. They had known each other for over six years (a long time for kids), and he had never held her before except for that time at Saint Tony's. She could feel herself become more comfortable with his arms around her and gently patting her on the back. For a minute, she wondered if she could ever like him-- like that. She thought about it, but the only thing that kept on coming back to her was watching him cry that time in church with his family. The older brother that was crying for no reason or because of something his little sister had said. No matter how Franny tried to view Jim as a boyfriend, she could only see him crying in Saint Tony's, his face red with pain.

Suddenly, Franny pulled back and wiped her eyes. She was so disappointed in herself and the way she had behaved to the news that she couldn't play up at the beach. "Just because you can't play the gigs at the beach doesn't mean you're not in the band anymore," Jim reasoned. "I hope that's what Lenny's thinking," Franny said, wiping her eyes with a tissue she was holding. "Who really knows what Lenny's thinkin'," replied Jim, smiling at his joke.

Franny smiled back, getting Jim's dig at the boy who had hurt her. "I'll make sure he takes you back after the beach gigs," assured Jim, now reaching for his guitar. Jim hung the guitar on his shoulder and ran his thumb down across the strings. "You wanna play some?" he asked, "It's what always makes me feel better." Franny got up and ran to Lenny's Washburn, leaning against the wall to the bedroom.

She put her head through the guitar strap and thumbed across the strings. "I've got a new song, it's called *Crying* by a guy named Roy Orbison," said Jim, "He has a great voice. Listen to this." Jim started singing…

Franny sat and listened to Jim sing to her. It was a sad song about someone who realizes that the person they love doesn't love them... that they love someone else. Hearing Jim sing and play, Joanie came out of the bedroom and sat down next to her daughter. Franny leaned over and rested her head on her mom's shoulder. Joanie thought it was a beautiful song-- commenting that Jim had a "lovely" voice. Franny thought that it was very inappropriate since the song basically described her situation... almost rubbing her "crying" in her face. But of course, Jim had no idea how on the nose he and the song was. After they played a few songs together, Jim went home. Jim was right about one thing-- it did make her feel better. She hoped that one day she could come back to play with Lenny and the River Rats.

Spindal

Spindal made the ride from Lawrence to Hampton Beach, New Hampshire, in two cars. Spindal was the new name that Rickie had given the band. Lenny wasn't too happy about dropping the Lenny and the River Rats name, but if it meant that they were going to gig somewhere, Lenny would change his own name (again). Alley wanted to point out to Rickie that Spindal was misspelled, but he thought if no one else cared, he didn't want to look like a know-it-all. Jim was never really big on The River Rats name, even though it was Lenny's idea, he wanted something that seemed more like the Crickets or the Four Seasons. But Spindal was fine with him. He figured that Rickie probably had a better idea of what a good name was.

Rickie, Lenny, and Alley rode up in Rickie's Cutlass with Jim and Michael riding in Michael's father's pickup truck, carrying the drums and other equipment in the back. Though the trip was only thirty miles from Lawrence to Hampton Beach, it was probably the longest trip that Jim had ever taken. He and Michael listened to a pop station on the truck's radio. It was an old truck that smelled like old beer. Jim hadn't any real relationship with

Michael and wondered if he should mention the night Michael saved him and his guitar from those Puerto Ricans. "You're a good guitar player," Michael started from out of nowhere. "Thanks, I haven't been playin' long," replied Jim. "I've been playing the drums for a few years now." "I know," said Jim, "I saw you one night playing at Barnaby's. You were good then." "Do you think this guy Rickie is on the up and up?" Michael asked. "I don't know, he seems kind of slick to me," observed Jim. "Me, too," agreed Michael. "He has a nice car," added Jim. "I think he's queer," added Michael. "He seems kind of strange to me, too," confirmed Jim. Michael glanced over at Jim in the passenger seat, then he smiled. Jim got an uneasy feeling that wasn't what Michael meant.

The Casino at Hampton Beach was a large hall with a small stage in the center. When Spindal showed up at the establishment, the place was empty. Rickie, Lenny, Alley, Michael, and Jim walked in through the back door. Jim was filled with excitement. This was the biggest room he had ever been in-- it was like Saint Tony's, but with two bars. Lenny led the band through the tables to the front. The four boys walked up on the stage and almost by impulse went to their places, even though they didn't have their instruments. Rickie stood in front, taking in the reactions from his new friends. Rickie was dressed in a suit, with a tie under a V-neck sweater, argyle socks, penny loafers, and a pork pie hat. The guys stood in front of him and looked out over the cavernous hall.

"Here you are, fellas. Now knock 'em dead tonight," coached Rickie. They moved their equipment in from the truck, and Rickie took them out, across the street to Hampton Beach. They passed a large bandstand shaped like a seashell that was being finished. A large sign announced, "*First concert, July Fourth-- Fireworks to follow.*" It was the first time Jim had ever been to the shore. He found that he had a hard time walking on the sand. They looked strange, a man and four boys, all dressed in suits, walking across the beach to the Atlantic Ocean on a June day. Everyone else on the beach was in bathing suits and large, floppy hats. Some families huddled under large beach umbrellas, stuck in the sand.

Most of the Easterners were very pale, and some were already sunburned. They stood at the water edge and looked out to the horizon.

The ocean was a lot like Lenny's future. It was all there in front of him. He turned and looked back at the Hampton Ballroom and the surrounding shops and stores on Ocean Avenue. To the north, he could see the Ashworth Hotel and where the beach ended and more rocky terrain started. To the south was Hampton Beach State Park and Hampton Harbor Inlet, flowing under the bridge they had come over. On the other side of the inlet was Seabrook, New Hampshire, and Beckman's Point. Lenny stood with his friends, realizing that this was the first moment of the rest his life, the life he wanted and wasn't given to him by his mother or even Harry. He had worked hard to get here, and it was all in front of him, just like the inviting ocean. All he had to do was just step forward and start on the way to what he was supposed to do.

"What are you doing," yelled Alley, "You're getting all wet?" as Lenny walked out into the easy waves rolling into the shore. Lenny walked until the ocean was just above his knees, the surface of the water cutting a dark line at mid-thigh in his suit pants. Lenny stopped and turned to his friends. He raised his hands over his head and yelled, "We're here!" Alley looked over at Michael, and Michael looked to Alley. They both quickly flung off their suit jackets and ran into the water. Jim watched the boys splashing around in the waves, kicking water onto Lenny. Rickie looked over at Jim and asked, "Are you going to go in?" Jim smiled, embarrassed, "I can't swim." Rickie smiled back at him, and they watched the other boys cavort in the ocean.

♫♫♫

The Hampton Casino Ballroom had a large dance floor in the center in front of the stage, surrounded by tables and chairs spread out along the edges. Two large bars functioned in the back of the room, pouring draft beers, whiskey, and vodka drinks. It was early when

Spindal made their way to the stage. The room wasn't more than a quarter full, mostly men and women dressed for a night out. Many were sunburned and not yet drunk. They waded near the tables, waiting to see who was going to open for Tim Flynn and the Senders. Before the lights went up, Michael pounded on the pedal of the bass drum, making some muffled thumps; Jim ran his pick down the strings of the Gretsch, making sure it was on, and no one had changed the settings since their sound check before dinner. Lenny looked at all three of his bandmates and nodded.

They kicked hard into *Blue Suede Shoes.* As the song went on, Lenny would go into his gyrations during the musical breaks. He danced around the stage until he eventually realized that he wasn't having the same effect that he had always had on the kids in Lawrence. This made Lenny try harder, dancing around as he sang into the microphone like his lips were stuck in the mouthpiece, his feet and hands were waving around, almost out of control. This didn't work either... unless, of course, having people look up at you and laugh was what you were after. Lenny was waiting for the moment when the audience would suddenly realize what a special band Spindal (he still wasn't used to that name) was. The more the people talked and laughed, the harder Lenny tried.

At one point during "The Streets of Lawrence," Lenny spotted Rickie at a table on the side of the dance floor. Rickie was dressed up as he always was, even with a flower in his lapel. Sitting with Rickie was the owner of The Hampton Casino Ballroom, John Dineen. Lenny and the boys had been introduced to Dineen earlier in the evening before they went on. A dapper man, who wore a white suit and wingtip shoes, he was known around Hampton as "The Baron of the Boardwalk."

Jim played and watched Lenny, recognizing how much more Lenny was giving to this audience, and it seemed like the audience wasn't really interested. It reminded Jim of the Adventaganza, and he was hoping that wasn't going to happen again. Then in the middle of *The Wanderer,* Lenny set the microphone on its stand and walked off the stage into the wings. Jim looked to Alley, who kind of shrugged, and then looked to Michael, who continued to play. Without unplugging his guitar, Jim hurried out to the wings, following Lenny where he had exited.

Jim was able to get to the back of the stage where Lenny was sitting and pouting on some black wooden platforms. Still playing, Jim yelled, "Hey, you've got to get back out there." Lenny didn't say anything. He just grumbled and shook some sand out of his pants cuffs.

Alley and Michael, still onstage, had no idea what was happening or if they should stop playing. But Jim's guitar was still playing, so they figured it was probably best to keep going. Alley started backstage to see what was happening. When he got back there, he realized that Jim had gone as far as he could without the cord to his guitar becoming unplugged and was yelling to Lenny to come back to finish the set. But it didn't look like Lenny was coming back. He had his shirt off and was shaking more sand out of it.

Since Alley, Lenny and Michael had gone swimming earlier in the day, and they had no change of clothes, they could only wear the wet ones they had on. Alley had noticed that his clothes had become itchy also, and the salt from the ocean made the acne on his face sting, but he knew that he couldn't stop playing. "What's going on?" asked Alley, pretty aware of what was really happening. "He won't come back," reported Jim, yelling over his guitar.

Back on the stage, Michael didn't have the luxury of moving around, so he started to drum in flourishes. He did rolls and many cymbal crashes, hoping to get his band-mates back on stage. Michael started nine and ten beat rudiments to fill the empty stage. At times he felt like his idol Buddy Rich, rolling and banging the drums. He was also starting to get tired. Michael looked out into the audience and realized that for the first time that night, people were on their feet. The audience was watching the near-empty stage except for Michael and his drum kit. There was the sound of the guitar and bass but no players.

Michael played faster and as loud as he could. Some people in the audience would cheer when he ran a particularly long drum roll and cymbal crashes.

Alley and Jim were pretty yelled out. Lenny rushed to Jim, looking angry. "Fuck them!!" he screamed, "Fuck them, we can't do everything." "Fuck 'em," Jim replied, feeling very grownup because he had said "fuck." "But we've gotta finish this song. And we can't do it without you. Michael's out there all alone." "Fuck 'em," Lenny repeated. "We're going back out," warned Jim, "If you don't come, I'll finish the fuckin' song." He turned, feeling victorious that he said "fuckin" again and walked back to the stage. Alley looked, begging Lenny to come back out, but even he turned and walked back out to the audience.

Jim passed Michael as he strolled back to his place on the stage. Suddenly the audience started applauding. The applause got even louder when Alley appeared and walked past Michael, who looked relieved that they had actually come back. Alley and Jim took their places and waited for one more pass through the song. When Lenny didn't appear, Jim walked up to the microphone and looked at it like it was about to punch him in the mouth and prepared to sing to finish the song.

When the audience screamed their approval. Jim turned, and Lenny bounced up behind him and took the microphone in his hand, "I'm sorry, I was wandering through your pretty town, and I just love it here," he said with a smile. Lenny sang as the audience stood and applauded. When the song ended, Lenny made sure to look over at the Casino's owner, Dineen, the Baron of the Boardwalk, and Rickie, who both were standing and applauding. Rickie gave them a big smile of approval.

♫♫♫

When Spindal finished *Quarter to Three,* and while the audience applauded, the boys took a bow, turned, and walked back into the backstage, Jim and Alley carrying their instruments. Lenny had recovered and was feeling good about how the performance ended. When they got off the stage, Michael pulled up next to Lenny and poked a drumstick under his jaw, "If you do that again,

I'm gonna come off stage and give you a fat lip. Do you understand me?" Lenny tried to push Michael away, but Michael was a good three inches taller than him. "I was coming back," assured Lenny, "I just needed a break." Michael pulled his drumstick away, "No more unscheduled breaks. There are other people in this band, and we need to know what you're doing." Michael stalked away to get the road boxes for his drums. Lenny looked over at Alley and Jim, who didn't argue with Michael. "Great set, you cats really ripped it," said Tim Flynn, a Bill Haley look-alike, as he and the rest of the Senders prepared to take the stage. "Thanks," said Lenny, straightening his rumpled shirt, "I hope you guys rip it up."

They packed up their equipment and loaded it into the back of Barnaby's Ford pickup truck. On the way back home, Rickie stopped at an A&W and bought all four guys a hamburger, and a root beer. They sat in the cars and ate. It was all so exciting for Jim. He had never eaten in a drive-in restaurant before. He watched some guys, smooth-talking some of the waitresses, who were on roller skates, and in short skirts, taking orders and rolling around while balancing trays with food on it. He had played music in a real club, where people had to pay to get in. Spindal had opened for a real band. "That was great tonight," Lenny proclaimed between bites of his hamburger. Jim couldn't help but ponder if it was so great, why were you sitting in the wings. But he figured he wouldn't bring it up. It was great. It felt great to be in a band, at the beach, in the summer.

♫♫♫

The next day, they drove to the beach again, this time to Salisbury, a small town in Massachusetts, but only twenty minutes down the road from Hampton. When they pulled up in Salisbury Center, the boys realized that it would be a lot different here. Salisbury center was at the end of Broadway Avenue, which made a U-turn when it reached the boardwalk. On the right was Shaheen's Fun-O-Rama Park, an amusement park with a large roller coaster, a Ferris wheel, and even an old-style carousal.

Past Shaheen's mid-way was a large club abutting the boardwalk and towering over the beach, called The Frolics. Making the left and going around the hairpin turn on the other side of the street were the bumper cars, Tripoli Pizza and Christy's Fried Dough, The Kon Tiki Lounge, and on the corner a Howard Johnson's restaurant. Michael followed Rickie's Olds Cutlass in the pickup truck. This time Alley got a ride with Michael. Alley talked about the importance of religion in his life and how Michael should go back to the church and become a better Catholic. Michael wished that Jim had jumped in the truck rather than Alley. At least, Jim didn't talk a lot.

Jim liked Rickie's car. They listened to the radio all the way from Lawrence. Rickie and Lenny talked and laughed in the front seat; Jim couldn't really hear them since he had the window down and could only hear the music coming from the small radio in the dashboard and the wind blowing through the car. When they pulled into Salisbury Center, it was very crowded, many of the people going into the Fun-O-Rama Park. Jim stared at the beach-goers walking around in bathing suits, bathrobes, sandals, and large, floppy hats. Finally, when the car stopped in front of the Kon Tiki, the boys all got out.

Rickie pointed out The Frolic's Club at the end of the street. They were to open for the headliner that night, Mac's Mob. But first, Spindal was going to play a set at the Kon Tiki Room. When they entered the bar, Jim was almost blinded for a few minutes because it was light outside and so dark in the club. It was a small joint, what some people would call a shot and beer bar, with just a small crowd at three in the afternoon. Rickie led them to the back, behind the bar. The boys carried their equipment, Lenny helping Michael carry his drums in. Rickie introduced the band to the manager, Big Karl, a big man (of course) with a nasty scar running down the side of his face. Karl led them to the stage, which was elevated above the bar that skirted in front of the stage. Lenny led the guys up onto the stage, and they started to set up their equipment. Besides being elevated above the bartenders, the stage felt kind of rickety. Like a good jolt could collapse the whole thing. Cautiously, they set up their stuff and tried to get use to the Kon Tiki.

Jim set up his brownface amp and plugged in. When he finally got some sound out of his guitar, he quietly tuned it the best he could. The bar had a jukebox, so it was hard to get everything right, as The Kingston Trio sang about *The Man Who Never Returned.* Michael got the drums set up the way he liked them and set out the cymbal. Another thing about the stage was that it was very small, and once they got all their equipment set up, there was very little space for the guys to stand. Lenny had almost no room to dance. Jim and Alley couldn't really move without fearing of falling off the sides.

Jim and Alley noodled their guitars, checking the volume and the sound. Michael banged on his drums and then hit the bass drum twice that shook the stage. Lenny, Alley, Jim, and Michael looked at each other with concern. Lenny just shrugged and said, "Let's try it."

Spindal kicked into their set. Lenny could only stand behind the microphone, waving his hands. Any other movement gave everyone on the stage the feeling that they could be dumped into the bar soon. Like the Casino show in Hampton, no one in the audience acknowledged them, even in their death-defying occupation of the unsettling stage. Lenny and Rickie had had a long talk on the way up from Lawrence about what Lenny could do if the audience wasn't paying attention. Rickie stressed that he couldn't do what he did at the Casino. Rickie encouraged him to work at getting the audience on his side.

Lenny spent a lot of time making jokes and addressing the audience. He even did the bit about wanting to go wandering during *The Wanderer.* It was made even tougher by the fact that it was in the afternoon, and most of the audience had stopped in to slip away from the family who were still at the beach or the Fun-O-Rama. But Lenny worked at it, every once in a while, asking the bartenders below if he could have a glass of water... with a lot of vodka in it. Of course, the bartenders had been told that the boys couldn't drink there. They finished off the set with *Quarter to Three* and quickly broke down their equipment so that the next band could come on.

♫♫♫

Rickie led them, carrying their equipment, down the street to The Frolics Club. A massive building, they hoped that the stage would be roomier than Kon Tiki Room. When they walked in, they were assured it was. It was twice the size of the Hampton Casino. This would be the biggest room they've played yet. Rickie led them backstage, and they stored their equipment.

Rickie took the guys outside, telling them that they had the rest of the afternoon to themselves and had to be backstage by seven-thirty. They walked down Broadway and got a slice of pizza at Tripoli's. After the pizza, they continued to Shaheen's Fun-O-Rama. They had a little money from the show at The Casino the day before, but Rickie hadn't given them much, not enough to go on any rides. The mid-way was very exciting. There were games to play, balls to throw at milk bottles, plastic clowns to shoot with water guns. Barkers called out to them to try their strength, try their skill, or just try their luck. They joked, laughed, and ogled girls who walked by.

When Lenny spotted a very attractive girl, about eighteen, he slipped over and told her that she and her friends had to go to the... (Alley reminded him of the name) The Frolic's Club at seven-thirty and watch the best band at the beach, Lenny and the.... oh, yeah, Spindal (he was never going to get used to that name). Everyone was gonna be there. "Can I get in for free?" the attractive girl asked, smiling sweetly at Lenny. "Ah, I don't think so," replied Lenny, not sure if he got to bring anyone in for free. "How 'bout my friends," the girl asked, acting more glamorous. "Probably not," mumbled Lenny, as Michael pushed him down the mid-way, so as not to get in any trouble before they actually played at The Frolics. Lenny turned back and yelled, "You're the one who is gonna have to tell your friends you didn't see Spindal when you were invited."

When they finished with the Fun-O-Rama, Spindal strolled down the boardwalk that abutted the beach. This time they stayed on the boardwalk so as not to have to play in wet clothes again. Jim stood looking out over the sand and out at the horizon, as the sun was going down, "I never thought that there was a place that looked like this." The other guys laughed, and Lenny pushed him towards the beach playfully. "We were supposed to not tell ya," joked Lenny. "Yeah, this was all a secret, and now we've ruined it," laughed Alley, helping Lenny push Jim to the wooden stairs that led to the beach. Jim broke away and ran back towards The Frolics. "I just like it," replied Jim, "That's all."

♫♫♫

When Spindal took the stage that night, it wasn't even a quarter of a full house. Rickie had explained that the season hadn't started yet, and the real summer people wouldn't come up to the beach till the Fourth of July. That during the summer, it was going to be a lot more packed and that the boys should get their act down now before the real crowds came. Lenny strutted up to the microphone and started to sing. Jim realized playing in such a large and almost empty hall, that the band sounded very thin without Franny and her piano. It also stuck out that Alley was still learning his instrument. But since Michael had no problem beating the rhythm out on the drums, you had to really listen to know it. It was a great time for Jim to just mess around with the songs as Lenny sang. He played mostly rhythm guitar, only trying any soloing when Lenny would step back from the microphone and turn to him.

Rickie was waiting for them after the set. They loaded the equipment in the truck and Rickie's car and headed back to Lawrence. Spindal came back the next day, Sunday, to play another afternoon gig at Pete's Blue Whale on Central Avenue, just behind the Kon Tiki. Pete's was a small bar, with a small stage in the corner. There couldn't be more than a half dozen people drinking and half-listening to Spindal's show. When they finished, the boys packed up their instruments and equipment and headed back to Lawrence. As great of a weekend it was, they had to get back to school for the last two weeks of the semester. Jim had finals in a week, and he hadn't even studied.

"How did you like it?" asked Rickie, driving. Michael was in the pickup truck all alone. He looked very happy every time Jim turned to look back at him. "Because this is what you're going to be doing all summer," he added. The guys looked at each other. This was maybe the first time that they really understood that they would have to do this every weekend. "I'll try to get some gigs around Lawrence during the week. But you know how it is, don't count on it."

♫♫♫

Rickie dropped Jim off in front of his house. Jim took his paper bag of a change of clothes and waved good-bye to Rickie, Alley, and Lenny. Jim watched the Cutlass leave, with Lenny in the passenger seat, laughing. He climbed the cement steps to his front door and entered. As always, the house was alive with his family. His ma swept down the stairs and took him up in her arms. "How was it today?" she asked as if he were playing in a symphony. "It was good, wasn't too crowded," he answered, realizing how tired he was. It seemed like the air at the beach took the energy out of him. "How did you sound?" she asked, not like his ma but like his piano teacher. "It sounded good-- I love that guitar." Jim looked down at his Harmony, resting safely under the sofa in the piano room. He felt bad mentioning the Gretsch, with his own acoustic guitar just a few feet away. He tried to smile at it and gave it a "nothing-personal" wink.

Ma walked him upstairs to his room. She asked if he was hungry and would he like a sandwich before bed. Jim told her that they had stopped at Atomic Subs. Ma helped him to bed. He was asleep before anyone else in the house that night.

♫♫♫

Rickie was right-- that was how the summer was going to go. Michael didn't have any problems getting the truck for the weekend. They would pay Pudge ten dollars and fill the tank on Sunday. Since Barnaby's did most of their business on the weekend, the pickup usually just sat in the Webster's driveway until Monday when Pudge would start stocking for the next weekend. Michael's brothers all worked at the bar, so none of them needed the truck because they had to work. Rickie would only show up at the shows when he could, and most times, the guys would have to find their own ride up to the beach. If it was possible, Lenny and Alley would try to get their parent's car. Alley's family had an old Edsel, but it was the only car the family owned, and so it was rare to actually get it. Lenny's step-dad, Harry, had a beast of a Lincoln Continental that drove like a boat.

Big Karl at the Kon Tiki saw them pull up in the Lincoln once and got the idea that they were rich kids, doing this just to kill time while waiting for college to start. Lenny tried to tell him that it was his step-father's and that he used it mostly for business to visit other stores. Karl wasn't buying it-- he enjoyed the idea that they were some rich college kids from Lawrence (Karl, obviously had never been to Lawrence... ever). But to most of the gigs, they took the pickup truck with Lenny in front with Michael and Alley, and Jim crouched in the back with the equipment (Lenny complained that it wasn't good for his vocal cords to be in the wind). This was how the summer went along.

Being in Hampton and Salisbury was fun. It was like a party almost every weekend. On the Fourth of July, Lenny got the Lincoln (Lenny's mom & Harry had gone to Nantucket), and the boys took Franny, Mary Catherine, and Bridie up with them. Mary Catherine, Bridie, and Franny sat outside of the Casino Ballroom, in the back parking lot and listened to Spindal, as the sound pounded out of the stage door. They went to Shaheen's Fun-O-Rama, and all rode on the Himalaya roller coaster. Bridie had just finished a Dairy Queen Frosty and threw up on Alley, who was sitting next to her in the car. After Alley had washed up in the soft waves, they sat on the beach in Salisbury and watched the fireworks explode over the Atlantic Ocean.

Mary Catherine noticed couples would walk down into the shadows of the boardwalk and suddenly disappeared underneath, into the dark. Just before the fireworks hit their crescendo, Mary Catherine grabbed Lenny's hand and dragged him into the darkness of the boardwalk. "Hey, where are we going?" joked Lenny. Franny and Jim watched as they disappeared into the dark shadows under the boardwalk. Franny looked at Jim, unable to hide her disappointment. Jim smiled and pretended to watch the exploding rockets above him. Both Jim and Franny were sure that Lenny and Mary Catherine were "doing it"-- and they were probably doing it under the boardwalk right now. Bridie laid on her back in the cool sand and said, "I think I'm going to be sick again." Alley moved a safe distance away from her.

♫♫♫

After school ended, Jim had a lot of time on his hands (though he did have to go to summer school for six weeks). He decided he was going to write a song this summer. He had tried before school ended, but he couldn't come up with anything he wanted to present to the band-- or even to Leo. When Jim got home from summer school, he would take his guitar and go over to Franny's apartment. Franny's mom had been very welcoming to Jim since the night he dropped by when Franny was told she couldn't play up at the beach. Franny and Jim would usually watch American Bandstand from 4:00 to 5:00. Sometimes they would take their guitars and try to play along with the songs. Jim was always surprised at how fast Franny could pick up a song. Sometimes, she could get most of the song in just one hearing of it.

One day while watching Bandstand, Jim started finger-picking a lick that he had been repeating to practice his technique. Jim hadn't finger-picked long. He was working on getting his coordination of fingers picking the strings with one hand and the other hand forming the chords on the neck of the guitar. Jim had, like most guitar players, just strummed, so the finger-picking was a whole new thing for him. The best way to practice this new technique was to just continue picking the lick while doing something else, like watching Bandstand. Franny took up the sequence of picking and followed along with him (damn, she could keep up with him already). Then she started, "I'm right here, but you can't see me." Jim turned to her and added, "I'm not hiding. It can only be me." They continued to finger-pick until finally, Franny sang, "I want to know if you really care?" Then from nowhere, Jim sang, "But how could you, because I'm not here."

Suddenly, Franny stopped and grabbed a notepad off the kitchen table. Jim kept finger-picking as she scribbled on the pad with a pencil. "What are you doing?" asked Jim, still finger-picking, kind of knowing what she was doing. "I'm writing it down. I always forget if I wait," said Franny, finishing her writing. She scurried back to the sofa with her pad and pencil. Franny took up her guitar, waited until she could jump in with Jim's finger-picking. They spent the next two hours until Joanie arrived home from her night class, where she was taking Elementary Accounting at Merrimack College and made them all a dinner of warmed-over meatloaf.

Franny and Jim kept working on the song every time Jim came over. After a few weeks, both of them thought it sounded pretty good. It was a song about someone who was in love with someone else, and that person didn't even know that they existed. They called the new song "I'm Not Here."

Before a Friday night show, Jim and Franny sat on the edge of the stage at The Hampton Casino Ballroom and finger-picked their new song to Lenny and the rest of Spindal. They played the whole song, singing together. Lenny sat listening intensely with Alley and Michael. When Franny and Jim finished, everyone turned to Lenny, who looked deep in thought. Finally, he shook his head and looked up at them, "I couldn't sing that. It's kind of sissy." It was obviously disappointing to Franny and Jim.

Jim tried to console Franny, but if Lenny wasn't going to sing the song, there was nothing they could do. Franny sat through the show and after Jim took her out to Connie's Cones for an ice cream. After they got their cones, they walked to the Casino's parking lot and waited in the pickup truck for the other guys. Alley and Michael came out a few minutes later, and they packed their equipment into the back of the pickup. But they couldn't leave because no one knew where Lenny was. Eventually, a car a few rows over from them opened their passenger door, and Lenny climbed out. His hair was all mussed, and his shirt was undone, hanging out of his trousers. Michael, Alley, Jim, and Franny watched him make his way to them, buttoning his shirt and smiling like the cat that ate the canary. When he got a few yards away, a woman climbed out of the car and yelled to Lenny, "When are ya gonna be back here, baby?" Lenny turned and yelled back, "...Appearing every Friday night until Labor Day." "I'll see ya later then," assured the woman, straightening out her skirt and adjusting her hair.

Lenny sauntered over to Alley's dad's car, still wearing his self-satisfied smile. "See ya later, baby," smirked Michael as Lenny passed him. Jim watched Franny's reaction as Lenny slid into Alley's front seat. "Hey, why don't we ride with Mike?" suggested Jim to Franny. Franny looked at him. It looked like she was about to cry or at least say, "I'm not here." Franny agreed, and they got into the cab of Michael's truck. Alley pulled out of the parking lot, followed by Michael, Franny, and Jim in the truck. It would be a long trip home.

♫♫♫

The guys kept making the trek up to the beach every weekend. The more they played, the better they got, and the audience grew. Spindal still wasn't the marquee act, but it was getting a small following from the Hampton and Salisbury townfolk and summer visitors. The boys also got to enjoy some of the benefits of being an act at the beach. They got to know many of the people who worked the Fun-O-Rama. Many times, they were allowed to go without a ticket on the Dodge 'em Cars, The Broadway Flying Horses, the Round-Up or Himalaya Roller Coaster, where John Salter held court. Every Friday night, there were fireworks on the beach, and sometimes they could go to Tripoli's Pizza, and maybe one of the girls there would sneak them a slice... and if they didn't, you could always go to Christy's Fried Dough and get some of their sugary pastry. Jim especially like the Fried Dough at Christy's, Michael was more partial to the onion rings from Seals. If they had any money, they could go to Playland and play the games of skill there.

Every Friday night, before they played at the Casino, Spindal would have to play three songs at the Hampton band-shell on the beach. Rickie and John Dineen had set up this quick set to advertise their playing at the Casino later that night. It was a difficult place to play since you were not only competing with the traffic on Ocean Boulevard but if the waves were pounding on the beach, it could throw the whole rhythm section off. Though, Lenny liked this venue because he found it as a big challenge to get the pedestrians of Hampton Beach to stop and listen to them. Lenny would stop a whole song just to beg a few people dressed in swimsuits and Bermuda shorts to come and listen to them. After the quick set at the band-shell, they would move across the street to the Casino, have a quick dinner, and play their set there.

One weekend, The Blandini Circus arrived in Salisbury. They held a parade that marched down Main Street, with real live elephants, one who was named Jules, who shat all over the street. Unfortunately, Spindal never actually got the chance to go to the Circus, but it was exciting to watch the parade before their show.

Every few weeks in Salisbury, there were wrestling matches in the center of the Broadway U-turn. A ring was set up, and wrestlers would spar while crowds would watch and cheer on their favorites. One Saturday afternoon before their set at The Kon Tiki, Spindal found themselves watching two women wrestle, Dynamo Deb versus Irene the Siren. The guys watched and cheered. After Deb was ruled the winner by unanimous decision, the master of ceremonies asked for volunteers. Dynamo Deb would take on all comers. The guys tried to push Lenny in the ring, but he had decided that if he was going to be abused by a woman, it might as well be under the boardwalk. Michael surprised his friends by volunteering to wrestle Dynamo Deb. Dynamo Deb was a sturdy woman, dressed in a red, white, and blue leotard, her blonde hair cut short and bobbed. Michael removed his shoes, shirt, and socks and climbed into the ring. Michael was about two Debs taller than Dynamo Deb.

The Referee informed Michael and Deb about the rules, and the two combatants squared off. Michael had been a secret fan of "Big Time Wrestling" that was on television on Saturday afternoons. Michael squared up like his favorite wrestler, Bruno Sammartino, watching Deb circle him. Deb stalked around the ring, occasionally jumping at Michael and retreating. They circled each other a bit, and then Deb made her move. She shot out at Michael's left ankle and pulled his foot with all her might. Michael grabbed Deb by placing his arms around her waist and raised her over his head. Deb fought to get loose, but Michael held her up for everyone to see. The crowd in the center cheered. That's when Deb reached back and grabbed a handful of Michael's hair and pulled-- hard. Michael screamed and started to twirl around, hoping to get Deb to let go of his hair. Suddenly, Michael lost his footing and stumbled, dropping Dynamo Deb.

Deb sprung up, ready for round two. She shot again at Michael's ankles. This time Michael hadn't gotten his balance and fell back. Dynamo Deb leaped on Michael in an ankle lock and wrestled him into a Boston Crab lock in the center of the ring. Lenny, Alley, and Jim were going crazy cheering their friend wrestling this spunky little woman.

Even though Dynamo Deb was on top of Michael, she still couldn't control him. Michael rolled onto his stomach and tried to get to his knees. Deb was working on a hammerlock into an arm drag but realized that she couldn't get enough leverage to control Michael. Michael quickly grabbed Deb's arm and rolled over into a shoulder block, pinning Dynamo Deb to the mat. Deb laid on the mat, with the giant Michael on top of her, clutching her left arm. The referee got down and started slapping the mat, counting Deb out. The guys cheered their drummer, who looked like he was going to pin the great Dynamo Deb. When suddenly a large man rushed out of the audience, dressed like some weird super-hero, in a yellow and red leotard, it was Gorgeous George Gant, the champ of the men wrestlers.

George climbed through the ropes and body-slammed on top of Michael and Deb. He and Michael wrestled around as Deb curled up into a ball, moaning like a wounded seal. George was able to roll Michael over and get one of his arms in a sleeper hold. That's when Lenny climbed onto the top turnbuckle of the ring and dived at Gorgeous George Gant, climbing on his back, putting him in a bear hug. Alley turned to Jim to see what he was doing, as they stood outside of the ring. They realized that they were a band, they were brothers now, they had each other's backs. Alley jumped in the ring, followed by Jim, and leaped on George and Michael.

The referee blew his whistle, trying to break up the melee which had gotten out of control. George stood up with Lenny, Jim, and Alley hanging on his back. George whipped the boys around, shaking Alley and Jim off. When Alley hit the mat, Deb shot up and jumped on top of him, putting a tilt-a-whirl body press on him. Michael, Lenny, and Jim surrounded George, who stood and roared. The crowd loved it. George grabbed Lenny and was about to put Lenny in a Canadian Backbreaker.

Alley was pinned by Deb with a nasty face-lock. The referee was finally able to get between Gorgeous George Gant and Lenny before George could actually break Lenny's back. Michael and Jim explained to the referee that they had to work for Big Karl at the Kon Tiki, and Lenny couldn't get hurt. The referee was familiar with Big Karl (as was most people in Salisbury) and realized that if Lenny got hurt, others could get really hurt by Big Karl and his friends, so he called the match a no-decision. Spindal was able to walk back to The Kon Tiki as a band. They had stood up for each other against the superpowers of Dynamo Deb and Gorgeous George Gant.

♫♫♫

Big Karl was a tough boss to work for. He never took to Spindal, and every chance he could, he would make comments about them being rich college kids (even though they kept telling him they were still in high school-- and only Alley had any real chance of getting into a college) and how this was just a summer job. Whenever Lenny would pull up in front of the club in his step-father's Continental, Big Karl would ask them where their chauffeur was. When they were onstage, Karl would turn off the lights or turn on the jukebox, blasting some another song. Lenny then would pretend to piss on the bartenders below him, in front of the stage, making Karl bellow from wherever he was in the club. Lenny would just turn and pretend to take a dump on the bartenders, angering Big Karl more.

Playing the Kon Tiki was different than playing at any of the other clubs since it was a biker bar and there were a number of fights during the show. At first, Spindal was frozen in their places as a bunch of real college students got their bums beaten by Karl and the bikers. After a few more fights during their sets, Spindal learned to pull in close to Michael's drum kit until the fight was over or the Salisbury Police told them to stop playing. Big Karl had yelled at them the first time they stopped playing during a fight. After that, whenever a fight broke out, they would just step back next to the drums and play quietly until the fight ended. Lenny liked to announce that that's what usually happened when someone criticized the band, "*they had that kind of following.*"

Alley and Jim tried to talk to Lenny about pissing Karl off more. They didn't want to anger Rickie by getting themselves fired. The other clubs were strict, but they didn't have the animosity that Big Karl carried toward every act. After the clubs closed, the bands would sometimes meet at the Howard Johnson's on the corner of Broadway and Ocean Boulevard. The musicians would gripe and bad mouth the club owners and management, but everyone, including Tim Flynn and the Senders, Mac's Mob, Strutter, agreed that Big Karl at The Kon Tiki was the worst. Everyone also agreed that he was probably most dangerous to piss off.

♫♫♫

Jim felt sorry for Franny. He tried to make time when he was home to go and visit her or have her come over to his house so that they could play together and work on their song; "I'm Not Here."

Franny liked going over to the Dewey's house. It always felt good to see Ma Dewey and get one of Ma's firm hugs when she would enter the front hall. Franny was still Ma's favorite student, even if she didn't really take lessons with her anymore. Franny would wait until the front room was free and take her place on the piano bench that always felt like home to her. She would play for an hour or so, or until the next student arrived, or it was time to have dinner, and then she would eat with the Deweys, catching up with what the younger girls were doing at school and Dorrie in the Girl Scouts or Teresa's softball team. Franny would listen to Kevin and his preparation for the forthcoming football season. Kevin was going to be a senior and a starting linebacker. Peggy would make a plate for Franny and always ask if she wanted more. The older boys, Patrick and Michael, would come home from work tired and hungry. After dinner, before she and Jim would go to the front room and play guitar, or Franny would get a look at whatever Kathy was working on, a sketch of Ma or a poem.

Da would come home and announce himself to his family. The kids would look up and continue whatever they were doing. Ma or Peggy would make him a plate of food, and after he wolfed it down, he would take himself to bed to sleep it off. Patrick, Michael, and even Jim pooled their money and giving it to Da, "To help you and Ma with the bills." Of course, the contributions never saw Ma's underwear draw where all the house money was usually kept. Da would take it and spread it around Barnaby's and the bars along Merrimack Street. But it kept Da in a good mood, and he didn't want to stupidly cut off his drinking money, so for everyone in the house, it was money well spent. Jim was making a little money now, Rickie wasn't giving them enough to buy a new guitar or anything, but he could actually buy a few records at W.T. Grant or take Franny to Brighams for a burger and a frappe.

Franny and Jim had been working on "I'm Not Here" and two other songs, Orbison's *Crying* and The Everly Brothers' *Wake Up Little Susie.* Jim had learned the songs to do something with Franny, but he never thought that anything would come of it. Until one night after dinner when, while they were tuning their guitars, Franny just tossed out, "You want to play a gig with me?" Jim said, "Sure," just so that he didn't seem like a jerk who played all the time and didn't have any time to play with her. "There's a coffeehouse in Cambridge that has an open microphone night where you can play two songs." Jim listened to Franny pluck her strings slowly so that he could tune his guitar off hers (She did have perfect-pitch if he knew what that meant). "Yeah, sure, we can play *Crying* and *Susie*," he said, confident in his selections. Of course, he knew that Rickie had warned him about playing other gigs. Rickie wanted Spindal only playing as a band, not gigging with other people-- even Franny. Jim agreed to do it, hoping it would never actually happen. He still busked with Leo on Essex Street but that wasn't gigging in Jim's opinion.

Dick and Jane

Club 47 was in Harvard Square in Cambridge. Franny and Jim had taken the train from Lawrence. They carried their guitars with them and descended down the steps into the coffee house, which was mostly open space with a stage and tables. Club 47 was opened by Joyce Kalina and Paula Kelley. When Franny and Jim entered, they were greeted by Paula, who said that they could play two songs between the sets of other musicians. Jim and Franny agreed. While they waited, Franny and Jim decided to try out "I'm Not Here" and *Wake Up Little Susie.* Paula told them that they would be recording the act after them and asked if it was all right if they were recorded by the engineer to get the levels right on the sound. They, of course, agreed. They were just happy to get a chance to play that night.

When they sat down to watch the opening act, the waitress informed them that they were there on a good night, Joan Baez was going to play that night, and they were going to record it. Franny had bought *Joan Baez Greatest Hits, Vol. 2* earlier that year and was very familiar with her music. Jim had listened to the album and liked some of the songs, but he was interested in her guitar playing style. It was a bit of picking and a bit of strumming. They ordered two coffees and waited for Paula's signal to get ready to go on.

The opening act was a young man, who looked like he was in college (to Jim, he was the college boy that Big Karl at The Kon Tiki kept accusing Spindal of being) and sang with a very high-pitched voice. The college boy would occasionally make a joke, and no one would laugh. As the college boy's set went on, Jim got more and more concerned. This was definitely not the same crowd that came to see them at the beach. Even when the crowds at The Kon Tiki Room and Pete's Blue Whale were not paying attention, at least they were talking to each other. Club 47's crowd just sat and listened quietly. When the college boy's set was over, they clapped politely. To Jim, this wasn't the kind of audience he wanted to introduce his original song to. When the college boy finished bowing and stepped from the cane chair he was sitting on, Paula came to Jim and Franny's table to tell them they were up next.

Franny and Jim stepped up onto the low stage and took up their guitars. Jim ran his fingers down the strings of his Sears Harmony Supertone. Franny slung Lenny's Washburn over her shoulder and looked over at Jim. They made sure their guitars were in tune while the engineer set the levels on their guitars and the single microphone. Paula Kelley stepped to the microphone wearing a fashionable black sweater, stirrup pants, and some fuzzy shoes. "Ladies and gentleman, please give a warm Club 47 and Cambridge welcome to Dick and Jane." Many of the people in the audience laughed, knowing that Dick and Jane were not their real names. Everyone had read the Dick and Jane books, but they probably didn't know that they were folk singers. Jim thought it was the best way of making sure Rickie didn't find out he was moon-lighting on his real gigs. When the engineer was ready, Paula told them that they could start.

Jim looked over at Franny and counted off, one, two three... "*I'm right here, but you can't see me*," Franny started to sing. *"I'm not hiding. It can only be me,"* sang Jim, trying to match her pitch. *"I want to know if you really care?"* sang Franny, sounding like she really wanted to know. Together they sang, *"But how could you because I'm not here."*

Franny and Jim stood facing each other, singing their song, the song they wrote... together. Jim stared into Franny's limpid blue eyes. Her blonde curly hair pulled back. He realized it was the first time that that he could remember her wearing make-up and eye-liner. He watched as her lips formed the gentle, soft words of the song they had written together. He worked hard to concentrate on the words and his finger-picking. One time he could feel that he was falling behind and had to speed up to catch her. They played the whole song through. Franny only wondered how wonderful it would be to sing this with Lenny.

Jim couldn't believe how beautiful her eyes were when she wasn't wearing her glasses. They were magnificent, in his opinion. Suddenly the audience was applauding Franny's eyes, as well as they should. That's when Jim realized that they had stopped playing-- the song had ended. Franny looked away from him and bowed. Jim awkwardly followed suit. When the applause stopped, they kicked into a lively version *Wake Up Little Susie.*

The gig at Club 47 went well, better than either he or Franny thought it would. When they finished Little Susie, the audience kept applauding and wanted another one, so they played *Crying*, again rotating verses, and it also went over successfully.

After they had packed up their guitars and took their seats, Joan Baez walked from the back and took the stage. Franny was captured by the young lady in a peasant dress and bare feet, standing on the stage alone, singing beautiful songs. Most of them were old and familiar. Franny had never really seen a woman do this before. Sure, she had seen women singers on television, but Joan was different. It was like she had this big voice fighting to get out of her small body. A voice calling to all women, come, sing your song, sing my song, we're here to sing together. In a way, it was like the night with Donna and Elvis. It all seemed to be right there, everything she wanted. It was that lady on the stage with her guitar and her pretty voice, with something to say. Franny wasn't sure whether she was ever going to get there, but she knew where she wanted to be, there-- up on that stage... like Joan Baez.

Franny and Jim sat through the whole of Joan's set. Jim was very impressed with her guitar work, and she even played one of Jim's favorite Woody songs, "*Pretty Boy Floyd.*" When the show was over, Franny and Jim crept over to Joan, who was packing up her guitar and talking to Paula, Joyce, and a few friends on the side of the stage. Franny went over and introduced herself, making sure that Joan knew her name wasn't really Jane. She told Joan how much she liked her set and how she thought her songs were so moving. Joan was very kind, thanking Franny and mentioning that she really liked their set and especially the opening number. Jim introduced himself to Joan, making sure she knew his name wasn't really Dick and complimented her set. Franny couldn't remember anything after that. She felt so thrilled that this lady had complimented her and Jim on their own song. It was a very happy train ride back to Lawrence and then the bus to Haverhill Street. Dick and Jane had hit it big.

♫♫♫

Jim had asked Lenny if Smilin' Leo could come to one of the gigs at the beach. Lenny was intrigued. He had heard Jim talk of Leo and how most of Jim's knowledge of the blues had come down from Leo. Lenny was just getting into the blues. He had bought some records at W.T. Grant and was really hooked on B.B. King. He loved the sound of his guitar and his rich playing. Lenny was also starting to play the harmonic (both Jim and Franny had called divs on the harp when Lenny tired of it-- like the guitar and piano), and Jim had told him that Leo was very good on the blues harp. It was decided that they would pick Leo up at his daughter's apartment and take him to the beach so that he could be at The Kon Tiki and The Frolic's shows.

On the way to the show inside the Continental, Lenny came up with a plan that would really stick it to Big Karl at The Kon Tiki. Lenny drove up to the beach with Leo in the front with him and Jim, Michael, and Alley in the back seat. On their way up Broadway, Lenny noticed that Big Karl was holding court in front of his club. A bunch of bikers sat in some chairs at the front door, watching the tourists (and especially the women tourists) walk by. Lenny drove the monster car to the top of the hairpin turn that dumped out in front of The Kon Tiki, where he stopped and threw it into park. Lenny slid over on the front seat and hopped over Leo, exchanging seats with him.

Leaving Leo in place at the steering wheel, Lenny reached over and put the car in drive, instructing Leo from the passenger seat. "There is a good reason I don't have a driver's license," Leo reminded Lenny. It didn't matter to Lenny, who had Leo maneuver the Continental blindly down Broadway. Leo gripped the steering wheel straight, as Lenny had instructed him, while Lenny stretched over and pressed the gas pedal with his foot. Leo would have to use the brake.

Big Karl was sitting in his chair, taking in the tourists and listening to Dumpy Magee talk about his old lady, when that college kid's Continental pulled up in front. The Continental came to an abrupt stop, tossing everyone inside forward. Then an older Negro man, in a black suit and the tell-tale dark glasses, climbed out of the driver's seat and closed the door. The Negro patted the side of the car, looking for the backdoor handle (if you asked Leo, he would've told you he was playing it up for the guys). Finally, he found the door handle and opened the door for the college kids inside. Then the Negro patted the side of the car and made his way around to the other passenger door in the back seat and opened that door. The Negro then continued to the front passenger seat and opened the door so that the wise-assed singer could get out.

The black chauffeur, who was obviously blind, then hand-patted his way to the front of the car and around to the driver's door. He got into the car and eased the car into gear. He drove and halted-- drove and halted-- drove and halted, till he finally stopped, parked, still in the middle of Broadway, got out and carrying his white cane, hobbled into the club. Karl even directed Leo to the door himself. The bikers were so scared, they ran to their motorcycles and prepared to leave if the blind chauffeur came anywhere near them with the Continental. Lenny came back out a short time later and parked the car himself. As he was walking past Big Karl and the bikers, he mumbled loud enough to hear, "Damn, the help these days. Ya can't even find a blind chauffeur who knows how to park."

♫♫♫

Spindal prepared for their set at The Kon Tiki, Smilin' Leo sat at the end of the bar nursing a beer and very much playing that he was blind. Every once in a while, he would turn quickly with his cane, knocking everything that was on the bar to the floor in a crash of glass. One time he got up and asked to be directed to the men's room, then made his way there by swinging the white cane wildly. When he came back, he asked the bartender loudly, "Hey, what did the blind man say when he pass the fish market?" Everything in the bar stopped. Even the bikers playing eight ball in the back stopped at the table and turned. "Good morning, ladies," answered Leo, breaking up in a fit of laughter, clapping his hands together. Even the leather-clad greasers had to laugh at that. Spindal started their set, and Leo just sat and smiled, occasionally snapping his fingers to a song and shaking his head with pleasure.

After the gig at The Kon Tiki Room, while the other guys broke down their equipment and moved everything up Broadway to The Frolics Club, Jim took Leo to the beach. Leo clutched Jim's arm as they strolled to the boardwalk. Leo went on and on about how good the band sounded and how it seemed that Jim's guitar had improved "ten times over." Leo then went on about what a great opportunity it was to play every week. When they got to the boardwalk, they walked to the edge, where they could hear the waves tumbling into the sand.

Leo held Jim's arm as Jim looked out over the ocean, "I played some gigs in Atlantic City years back... decades, I guess," Leo started, "In those days a black man couldn't play the white clubs-- you had to play your own color's clubs. We were at the Harlem Club, where black folks came from all over the east coast. It was a good club, but it paid like shit. Not like those white clubs. I always wanted to go back and go into one of those clubs down there, but I never did make it. I bet it would smell just like this." Leo stood smelling the ocean, still holding Jim's arm. "Ya know, I don't see a man's color," said Leo, with a big grin on his face-- even Jim got that one.

♫♫♫

Spindal was getting more attendance at their early shows. Mostly it was young girls who liked to have Lenny sing to them. Once in a while, some jealous boyfriend would be waiting for him after the show and threaten Lenny to lay off his girl until Michael appeared, and suddenly it wasn't so important. Lenny opened the show with *Blue Suede Shoes* and continued with the usual setlist that they had been using for the last year, but tonight, after *The Wanderer,* he stopped the show and stepped to the microphone, "Who would like to hear some real Chicago blues tonight?" he asked. The audience responded with enthusiasm, and Lenny turned to where Leo was sitting, at the side of the stage. "Then let's call up Smilin' Leo."

Leo was genuinely surprised and waited as Jim removed his guitar and made his way to Leo's table. The audience waited with a murmur running through it while Jim led Leo to the stage, instructing him where each step was and when to lift his foot. Lenny stood on stage at the microphone, watching Leo being led by Jim. He got a tightness in his stomach. Suddenly he wasn't so sure if this was a good idea. Sure, Jim told him that Leo was great, but when did he start listening to Jim or his opinions. If this Negro sucked, this could be bad for the band. Lenny was starting to regret his invitation as Leo hobbled up to him, still hanging on Jim's arm, like a nervous prom date.

Jim got Leo to the microphone and placed one of Leo's hands on the stand that held it. Jim turned to Lenny and said, "Wait for me." Jim got the Gretsch and slung it over his shoulder, then nodded to Lenny to continue. "What do you do you wanna play, Leo?" asked Lenny, hoping that Leo had a song handy. Leo turned to where he thought Jim was, "How about that Albert King song, Strings?" Jim nodded and turned to Michael, and Alley yelled, "In C, a driving blues beat." Michael kicked up his drums and ran a driving rhythm; Alley, having gotten better on the Epiphone, followed suit. Jim played the lick that Leo would usually play on Essex Street in front of W.T. Grant.

Lenny stepped back to listen to Leo sing when all of a sudden Leo pulled out his old Kohner Marine Band harmonica from his coat pocket and blew a screeching note, bending the end. He then did some quick slides and bends, waking everyone in the Salisbury. Then Leo started to sing, *Born Under a Bad Sign.*

Leo again went to his harp, blowing loud and quick notes. The audience rushed forward, pushing up against each other. Leo went on with the song.

Leo went back to his harp for a short burst. Lenny was dancing on stage, as the crowd was now bouncing up and down in front of them. Leo yelled into the microphone, "Strings, show 'em what ya got." Jim picked up Leo's lick and ran with it for a few bars. Then Leo growled *Born Under a Bad* into the microphone again.

It was obvious to the audience that they were watching a real show biz veteran now. Leo barked into the microphone, "Take it down, let's hear just the drums now. Take it, drummer." Michael stepped in with his rolls, using the cymbals freely. After a bit, Leo leaned into the microphone and purred, "I could use some bass right about now..." Alley picked it up and pulsed a beat through, as Jim and Michael pulled back on their instruments. Lenny and Jim watched Leo as he danced in place. Both were worried that he would take several steps forward and tumble off the stage. But Leo never left his microphone stand. Still, every time Leo took a step, Jim or Lenny would make a sudden movement in case they had to sprint to save Leo. But Leo had stage presence from long ago and was never in danger of falling or leaving the microphone stand. Alley finished his lick. Then Leo stepped up to the microphone again and sang,

Leo turned to where he felt Lenny was, "Lenny, my boy, help me finish this." Lenny bounced up next to him, and together they sang together. The kids on the floor were wildly bouncing up and down as Leo pulled his harp out one more time and blew the roof off of the Frolics. No one in the joint would have been surprised to see smoke coming from the harmonica as it slid between Leo's lips and blasted all of Salisbury away.

When the song ended, everyone in Spindal looked at each other as the crowd screamed for more. Lenny looked back at his friends and immediately kicked the band into *Quarter to Three.* Not to be outdone, Leo pulled out his harp and added some harmonica licks that The Frolics have probably never heard since. They ended the show all sweaty and smiling. The crowd screamed for more and chanted, "LEE-O, LEEE-O." Jim helped Leo backstage, still carrying his guitar as Lenny, Michael and Alley broke down their equipment, Tim Flynn and the Senders were set to come out.

Tim stopped Jim backstage and asked if the Negro would come on at the end of their set? Jim turned to Leo, who was batting his head around wildly. "Well?" asked Jim, knowing that Leo had heard Tim. "The Negro would love to come on for their set," answered Leo. And he was; Leo came out at the end of Tim Flynn and the Senders set and sang Blind Lemon Jefferson's *Black Snake Moan* with Tim. What neither band had known was when Leo stepped out on stage with Tim, the word went out onto the Shaheen's midway and the boardwalk that the Negro had come out again at The Frolics, most of the kids already have heard about the set with Spindal, rushed for The Frolics and pushed their way in, past the bouncers.

By the time that Tim had called Spindal out to join them on stage, The Frolics ballroom floor was packed with people, all dancing and bouncing up and down. Tim and Lenny chose Sam Cooke's *We're Having a Party* and roared into it. By the end, Jim was trading licks with Tim's guitar player, Tim's sax player was trading licks with Leo's harp, and most people in the joint couldn't wait to tell their friends about what happened at The Frolics that night.

After the show was over and most of the audience had filed out Spindal, Tim Flynn, and some of the Senders huddled backstage with their instruments and played songs, many of them the blues. Tim and Lenny would ask Leo to play some song, say, like *Key to the Highway,* and after the first refrain, everyone would jump in. Michael and the Senders' drummer banged on over-turned trash cans. The group was boisterous. Some of the guys in the Senders talked the bartenders into letting them have a few beers. Many of the players would ask Leo about playing with B.B. King and Buddy Guy. Leo told all the stories he loved and laughed and slapped his leg, happily. Jim had never seen Leo like this, bathing in the adulation of other musicians. It made Jim feel good to know that his friends and band appreciated Leo and the talent that Jim had always talked about.

♫♫♫

It was well after two in the morning when the bands broke up and headed home. Lenny drove the Continental back to Lawrence while Leo sat in the front seat, telling his stories of the old days and laughing. When they pulled up in front of Leo's daughter's building, Jim got out with Leo and helped him to Addie's door. On the way to Jim's house, Lenny told him it was great to have Leo play with them and did he think that Leo would play with them again. Jim said he didn't know. He promised to ask some other time. It probably wouldn't be up at the beach. They only had two more weeks until Labor Day, and then their clubbing would be over. Jim said good-bye to Lenny, Michael, and Alley (who was asleep in the back seat) and started up the stairs to his parent's house. It had been a good night.

♫♫♫

Lenny was excited when Rickie called him and asked him to lunch. Lenny wasn't sure what it was that got him so anxious when Rickie picked him up from his house and took him to Doc's Pizza on Elm Street. Rickie and Lenny ordered a large pepperoni and a pitcher of Coca Cola. "You boys are a big hit up there," Rickie informed him, wiping his lips with a napkin. "Would you guys want to play some of the other clubs around?" Lenny was excited and a bit disappointed with Rickie's question. He had hoped that this was more than a business meeting.

Lenny looked forward to spending time with Rickie. He had hoped that it would be more personal and less about the band. Recently, the dreams that Lenny had been having that usually involved Father Nelson now contained Rickie in the role of the priest. It was never as cold as the dreams when Father Nelson was there. Rickie was always kind and listened to Lenny, sometimes touching his face and giving him a back rub... then the person behind him who was rubbing his back so gently and sensuously would suddenly be Father Nelson pounding on his back as the rector rubbed his staff. Rickie was always kind to Lenny. He wanted the band to do well and for Lenny to do well, also.

"Sure, where do you want us to go?" asked Lenny, shoving a large piece of pizza, dripping pepperoni, into ho his mouth. "The South Shore, Connecticut, Manchester, New Hampshire, maybe even Boston." Lenny finished his pizza slice and washed it down with a mouth full of Coke. "Boston, you think we're good enough?" asked Lenny, wiping his mouth with a paper napkin-- a first. "Maybe not right now, but with some more experience. I can't see why you couldn't play The Pepsi Dance Party or even the Paramount Theatre." Rickie took a big sip from his straw of Coke, just to piss Pepsi off. "The Paramount would be wicked cool," answered Lenny, now looking deep into Rickie's caramel-colored eyes for some hint of how much Rickie liked him. "But I've talked with the other guys, and we'd like to have the piano back in the band?" asked

Lenny, testing to see how far he could go with Rickie. Jim had talked to him about trying to get Franny back in the band. Jim felt that the sound was thin without the piano.

Lenny felt that "his sound" had piano in it-- even if they were well-liked up at the beach, it sure wouldn't hurt to get the piano back into the band. "Are you asking to bring the girl back?" Something happened in Rickie's smiling brown eyes. When he asked, Lenny could see it. "Yeah, we need the piano. It's part of our sound." Rickie looked deep into Lenny's eyes and asked, "Are you hung up on that girl? Is this what it's all about?" Lenny leaned back against the seat of the booth they were sitting in. "No, I've got nothing for Franny. It's just that she's the best piano player we've had, and she's also a good guitar player if we need one." Rickie looked at him and finally smiled, apologetically.

"Sorry, I can't have a girl playing to those clubs. I don't want to be responsible if something happened. Besides, you guys are not famous enough to try to change any club rules," even after Rickie laid down the law, Lenny didn't look all that disappointed. "We're gonna keep looking for a guy piano player," assured Lenny, but even he knew he was lying. Franny was out of the band until they could think of something.

Rickie paid for the pizza and tonics. When they got in Rickie's white Oldsmobile and arrived at Lenny's house, Rickie told him he would call, and they would work out where they would play next. Rickie again told him that Spindal had done a very good job in Hampton and Salisbury this summer and that these upcoming gigs could be a big step forward for them. Just as Lenny was getting out of the car, Rickie offered Lenny his hand to shake. Lenny reached over and took Rickie's hand. For a moment, a very quick moment, they shared a look, it didn't take any words, there was no knowing wink, no whispered invitation, but Lenny knew then, he and Rickie would share something, someday. He didn't know when or where, or what it would be. He just knew that it was bound to happen. It was bound by that handshake. Lenny knew it. He had shared a moment just like that with Mary Catherine in the Grants record section. It, too, had come to be. Actually, it came to be a lot quicker than he thought it would-- but that was mostly because it was Mary Catherine Dewey.

♫♫♫

Spindal stood in the wings of the stage, it was just another gig, but all five members of the band looked nervous. This would be the first show with their new piano player, Frankie, who looked a lot like Franny but with her hair cut short in a boy's cut (now very much resembling His Boy Sherman), her thick Buddy Holly black-framed glasses, pants, shirt and tie with a sweater over it. Jim could see little beads of sweat over Frankie's lip. Jim had thought the idea was crazy when Lenny brought it up to the band, and now he was sure it was crazy. Though, he also thought Franny, I mean Frankie, was even cuter than before. There was something about how his Sunday pants hung on her hips that got him excited, and he had to force himself not to think about who was in his pants.

Lenny was sure no one would notice. Rickie hadn't been at the show since they stopped playing the beach. They had played two South Shore gigs at the Teen Scene in Hyannis and The A-Go-Go in West Yarmouth, and Rickie didn't come to those. When Lenny called Rickie and told him that they had found a decent pianist, he didn't seem to be too interested. Everyone decided that the Surf Nantasket Ballroom in Hull would be the best place to try Frankie out.

"Please welcome, from Lawrence, Massachusetts, Spindal," announced the master of ceremonies. Lenny led the band out to the stage, bouncing happily. The band members ran to their places. Frankie took her place on the piano bench, with the back of the piano facing the audience. All anyone could see of him (her) from the front was the top of his (her) head. Lenny grabbed the microphone and yelled into it, "Hey there, surfers!" A loud yell came back to him. "Let's go, boys," coaxed Lenny. The band kicked into *Blue Suede Shoes*.

♫♫♫

Jim was glad that Franny was back in the band, even though it probably meant that Rickie was going to get pissed and they won't be able to play the beach next year. The summer was over, and as Mary Catherine would tell anyone that would listen, "I've almost got all the sand out of my crack." School had started. It was Jim's junior year at Lawrence High School. Lenny, Alley, and Michael were all seniors and would be graduating this year. Jim was never really that concerned with whether or not he would be promoted into his next year. With Mary Catherine a year behind him, the school found it in their best interest to promote the Dewey kids and get them through the system as fast as they could. One Dewey a year was a whole lot better than trying to make some ridiculous point about the integrity of the Lawrence education system. Franny was a year behind him, but she was practically taking the same classes he was in (they were actually in the same science class). Franny wasn't only smart on the piano and the guitar; she was also smart in school.

Franny had encouraged Jim to read more. Jim had been (like all the Dewey children, except for Kathy) a pretty weak reader. Franny had given him a book early in the summer called "Catcher in the Rye," and Jim had read the book twice already. There was something about the guy, Holden, that really connected with Jim. He understood how Holden felt and how no one understood him. Franny read a lot of books (Jim was surprised that Michael was also a reader. He also had read "Catchah in the Rye)." When Jim was at Lenny's, he used to like to go and read the covers on the bookshelf in the living room.

♫♫♫

In November, there was a lot of talk about Cuba and the atomic bomb. Cuba had got missiles from Russia, and President Kennedy was worried that Fidel Castro would launch the missiles at the United States.

Lawrence High School went into full nuclear alert, holding mock attacks with drills and sirens. All students were instructed to crawl under their desks and cover their heads when they heard the alarm. Most of the boys thought it was exciting, and you could get a good gander of underwear when girls were crouching under their desks in a skirt. Franny was very concerned, checking the Boston Globe whenever she could and watching the news on television, which would sometimes interrupt American Bandstand. Jim, Lenny, Michael, and Alley all stood with most of the other boys in school-- if the Russians drop the bomb, do you think they will let us go home early. No one wanted to waste another minute in school during a nuclear annihilation. Of course, nothing came of it-- Kennedy told the Russians to cut the crap, and they did.

As much as Jim and Lenny were glad to get Franny back in the band, Alley still wanted to play the guitar. When Lenny had mentioned that he wanted to bring the piano back into the band, Alley suggested that Jim play the piano, and he could play the guitar, and maybe Lenny could learn to play the bass. Lenny never took the suggestion seriously. Since the night at The Frolics with Leo, Lenny had gotten serious to learn the harmonica. He was only using it now to open songs and to close *The Wanderer*.

But Jim had to give Lenny credit; he was learning fast and was starting to get pretty good at it. Jim also noticed that Lenny had picked up much of Leo's patter during the songs, asking for some drums or more bass. Lenny had also taken to calling Jim "Strings," which bugged Jim every time he used it. To Lenny, it was just a cool sounding musician nick-name. To Jim, it was a reminder of when he couldn't even tune his own guitar himself. Besides, the way Lenny said it was a lot different than how Leo said it. Lenny's version sounded like he was mocking Jim, whereas Leo's was just a name. "Let's hear it, Strings!" Jim grimaced in Franny's direction and went through the lick he was using for *Blue Suede Shoes*. Franny smiled back at him, her blue eyes flashing in the light behind the heavy glasses. Boy, she was a cute boy.

♫♫♫

Dick and Jane sat at the table in Club 47 when the owner, Joyce Kalina, came over and sat with them. She said how happy she was to have them back. Joyce said that they had a lot of people compliment their performance from the summer. Joyce asked them what they had been doing-- Were they touring? Franny glanced over at Jim with a "What?" look. Jim replied that they hadn't, that they were in a band and had been working with them (he didn't want to admit to her that they had to finish high school before they could think of doing any real touring). "You must be so happy?" asked Joyce. "I guess," replied Franny hoping that Joyce would give them some hint of what she was talking about. "You guess, listen to you two," Joyce smiled happily at them, bursting with pride. "You are one of the few acts to play here and then get air time on WMEX at their first open mike."

Franny turned and looked at Jim, who looked back at her. Franny adjusted the red beret on her head that was hiding her boy's cut. "Air time on WMEX?" she asked, with a bit of a quiver in her voice. "Yes, you didn't know. Woo-Woo Ginsburg played it on his Night Train Show," "Woo-Woo Ginsburg?" asked Jim, still trying to understand what they were talking about. "Yeah, Woo-Woo played it on Night Train," Joyce confirmed, "They recorded it that night the Joan was here." Joyce leaned down and gave Franny a hug, almost knocking her beret off. "Are you going to do 'I'm Not Here' tonight?" Franny sat back down, "Yeah, yeah, sure, if you want us to..." "Of course, we do. You're up next."

Joyce smiled again and then headed to the front door to greet some more patrons entering the small coffee house. Jim turned to Franny with urgency, "I'm not supposed to playing outside the band." Franny took a deep breath, "I didn't know they recorded it." Jim looked around, hoping that Rickie wasn't around for some reason, "It must've been when they were recording the levels. What are we gonna do?" "I don't know," said Franny, watching the previous act, a duo, pack up their equipment to leave, "They won't know it's you." Jim leaned over and reached for her arm, "Maybe we should take off before we have to go up?"

Franny spotted Joyce signaling to her that it was their turn to go. "Too late," said Franny, standing and leading Jim to the stage. They carried their guitars to the stage and slung them over their shoulders. Jim and Franny stood at the back of the stage, tuning their strings with the pegs on the top of the neck. "Everyone, welcome back two young artists, who the last time they visited us played their new song, 'I'm Not Here'." Jim glanced over at Franny, who was picking a string with her plectrum; she gave him an uneasy smile. "Let's give a big Club 47 welcome to Dick and Jane," introduced Joyce, helping Franny to the microphone. "Thanks, everyone," said Franny, "We're wicked happy to be here again." They started playing, staring at each other-- they went into "I'm Not Here."

♫♫♫

It was a long trip back to Lawrence. The last time they made it, they were both very happy. Tonight, they were quiet. Finally, Franny broke their silence, "Do you think anyone else knows?" Jim thought about it before answering, "I don't know who Woo-Woo is on WMEX, if he plays mostly pop and it's on late at night-- maybe not." Franny stared at the dark towns passing them on the train to Lawrence, "I think we shouldn't play it anymore," suggested Franny. "Maybe we could get a record deal out of it?" asked Jim, kind of day-dreaming. "Do you want to take that chance?" asked Franny, turning to him, "Will Rickie let us record on our own and still be part of Spindal?" "Probably not," answered Jim, "But we don't have a contract with him." "Do you want to record without the band?" asked Franny. "I've never really thought about it before. I don't know if I want to be a folk musician?" "You could be Woody Guthrie," injected Franny, laughing. Jim also laughed, "No, I don't think anyone could be Woody. There's only one Woody." They rode in silence until they came to the Lawrence station. "We should stay with the band," suggested Jim, picking up his guitar. Franny agreed. They at least had dates lined up for Spindal.

♫♫♫

The next night Jim and Franny sat next to Joanie's radio in her bedroom. They laid on the bed, waiting and listening to Woo-Woo Ginsburg's WMEX AM Night Train show. They had been lying there for a few hours before Franny abruptly woke Jim up; he had fallen asleep about a half-hour earlier, "Here it is." Jim and Franny listened intently to their voices coming over the small Phillips transistor radio on the bedside table. At one point, Jim looked over at Franny, who gave him a salacious smile and shrug. The song sounded wicked good, each person feeling that their voice or their guitar playing was the only problem, but the rest of the song sounded good, and it was so cool to hear your song on the radio, even if it was on very late at night. Jim could feel a shot of pain every time his fingerpicking hit a clunky note, but all in all, it was pretty good. When the song ended, there was applause, "That was new artists named Dick and Jane, and their song, 'I'm Not Here'."

"I don't want you two in here alone," growled Joanie, still wearing her coat and scarf. Jim and Franny sat up quick, looking more than caught. "We weren't doing anything!" squealed Franny. "This is no place for children to be," scolded Joanie, relieved that it looked innocent. "We weren't listening to the radio," said Jim, obviously lying since the radio was still on. "We were only listening to the radio," confessed Franny, sitting up. "Yeah, we were only listening to the radio-- that's all." Franny glared at Jim. He wasn't helping the situation. Franny turned off the radio. "You were listening to Woo-Woo?" asked Joanie, changing her tone, "I listen to WMEX all day at work." Franny and Jim shared a look of concealed panic.

♫♫♫

"Are you two going steady?" asked Joanie as Franny climbed into the double bed with her mother. Franny tried not to laugh, "Ma, please. No one goes steady anymore. He's not even my boyfriend." Joanie looked at her daughter. Franny was in her pajamas; they were flannel with small guitars and cowboys on them. "Are you still a virgin, Frances?" "Ma, why are you asking that?" complained Franny. "Because you go out all the time--with those boys." "They're not boys, Ma. They're in my band." "Are you having sex?" again asked Joanie. "No, Ma. I'm not having sex," confirmed Franny. "I don't like it that you're the only girl going with all those guys," hounded Joanie. "I'm not the only girl. Mary Catherine Dewey comes with us sometimes."

Joanie groaned, "That doesn't make me feel any better." "Ma, you have to trust me. I'm not having sex. I'm not dating anyone, especially Jimmy. I'm just playing in a band." Franny pulled her pillow over her head. "I just don't want you to do something you will regret," scolded Joanie. Franny whipped the pillow from her head, "Like what you did?" Joanie pushed at her daughter, "What's that supposed to mean?" "You know what I'm talking about," scolded Franny, right back. "You are not to talk about that," warned Joanie, turning over quickly, facing away from Franny. "Don't like to talk about your mistakes, do ya?" Franny shot back. Joanie rolled over to face her, "That's not what I mean. I've always considered you a blessing." "Then don't assume that I'm going to make the same mistakes you made. I promise you I won't do that!" This time Franny rolled over so that her mom could talk to her back. Joanie rolled over and looked sadly at the radio. "Did Jim like your new hair-do?" Franny groaned and placed the pillow over her face again. "I still think it's too tom-boyish," Joanie said, as critically as any mother would.

♫♫♫

Frank Conley walked into the Hilltop Steakhouse, on Route One, in Saugus, past the giant plastic cows, posed munching grass as you walk to the front door. He slid into a booth with a western motif, joining Lenny, Alley, and Michael. Lenny introduced Alley and Michael to Mr. Conley. Conley was one of the biggest promoters in the Boston area. Mr. Conley had met the boys once, at The Brockton A-Go-Go, after their gig there. He and Lenny had talked, and a few days later, Mr. Conley called

Lenny to set up this meeting at The Hilltop. Set back from the street, this was one of the best restaurants that Michael had ever been in. The boys sat, anxiously drinking their tonics. Mr. Conley told the boys to order whatever they wanted. All three got the strip steak and French fries.

"Where's your guitar player and the little guy who plays the piano?" "They couldn't make it. They have school," answered Lenny (even though they were actually skipping school to make this meeting), trying not to sound rehearsed, even if it was. "Well," began Mr. Conley, taking out a large cigar, "I liked what I saw the other night. I understand that Rooney isn't representing you, so I want to know if you would like to play some Boston gigs?" Lenny looked to the other two boys. Each looked impressed with the offer. "What kind of money are we talkin' about here?" asked Lenny, trying to sound experienced (he had asked his step-father, Harry, what to do in the meeting when his mother called two days ago). "We can start you at thirty-five dollars a gig, eighty dollars if you do a double."

They looked at each other again. Thirty-five dollars would be the most that they had ever made in one night-- eighty dollars, get out of here. Alley had prayed before he came, and even he didn't expect this much money. "I think we could do better," said Lenny, stirring his Coke. "If you're getting more than that with Rooney, then go with him, but I don't have a problem of sharing you with Rickie. But if I do represent you, I expect you to be there for me." Conley lit his cigar and took a deep drag on it, whitening the end in ash. "We could do that-- we love to play," replied Lenny. "Yeah, we love to play," parroted Alley, quickly regretting he said anything. "But if I schedule you, you had better be there, be on time and ready play," warned Conley, as he blew a wisp of smoke into the restaurant's air. Lenny promised that they would if Conley took them on.

When the food arrived, the boys dug in heartily. Conley drank his Jack Daniels and smoked his stogie, "I liked that 'Streets of Lawrence' song. You wrote that?" Lenny stopped wolfing down his steak to answer, "Yep, me and Jim, the guitar player, we wrote it together." Alley stopped eating for a minute to look over at Michael, who was savoring the steak. Michael gave a shrug and cut into another piece of meat. "I also like 'Roll On Mighty Merrimack'," added Lenny, never one to give just enough, "That's one of my favorites." "Yeah," agreed Conley, "But the Streets of Lawrence song sounds familiar. That's how I know a good song." All three boys stopped to listen to the big man in Boston music, "If the song sounds familiar." They all agreed and had ice cream for dessert.

♫♫♫

Christmas Eve was always a special night in the Dewey home. First, there was the anticipation that Santa Claus was going to come. Secondly, Ma Dewey always made a large pot of spaghetti and meatballs for dinner... and finally, but most importantly, Da usually wasn't home for it. Most of the mills closed early on Christmas Eve, and the mill men would take their paychecks and any Christmas bonuses to the bars along Merrimack Street. If there was ever a night that a good Christian man would buy another hearty gentleman a drink, it was on Christmas Eve. Da was at Barnaby's, ready to receive as many Christmas spirits that he could suck out of the holiday revelers. Da knew that on Christmas Day, he would have to accompany Ma and the kids to church, no matter how hung-over he was. So, it was his holiday duty to get as drunk as he could in the name of the birth of our savior.

Ma invited Franny to Christmas Eve dinner and also invited Joanie. Joanie and Franny sat uncomfortably at the end of the table, with Jim and Teresa. Teresa was trying to be a good hostess by talking to Joanie as Ma and the other girls got dinner together. The problem was that Teresa kept asking personal questions. "Are you seeing anyone, now?" "Not at the moment," answered Joanie. "Do you like being single? I don't really like boys all that much; they're stupid. Do you think I would like being single?" Joanie cringed, almost regretting coming.

When Franny had invited her, she thought that it would be a good way of getting closer to her daughter, who was spending more time away from home because of the band. "Boys are kind of jerks, aren't they?" Teresa confessed. "Only to you, with good reason," added Kevin sitting across from Jim, who was sitting next to Franny munching on a slice of Wonder Bread. "Shut up, poop-poo-head," shouted Teresa. Joanie looked over at Franny, who was trying not to laugh. "Franny, what does your mom do?" asked Michael, sitting down and getting comfortable. "I work for Malden Mills, in the Accounting Department," Joanie answered. "Michael works at the Everett Mills, on the loading dock," informed Kevin, ripping a slice of bread apart. "He's a dock-head," giggled Teresa, "That's what Da calls him." "He's a dock-hand. Da call's him a dick-head," added Kevin slinging a piece of the bread at his older brother. "Our Da calls everyone a dick-head," corrected Michael, throwing the slice of bread back at Kevin but hitting Teresa by accident. "Let's watch our language at the table," warned Ma.

Ma appeared in the doorway, followed by Dorrie, Peggy, and Kathy, all carrying plates filled with spaghetti and meatballs sauce. Ma smiled uneasily. She had invited Franny's mom, thinking that a single woman would have a lot more to do than coming to Christmas Eve dinner at her house. She was surprised when Jimmy had told her that Franny's mom would come. Now, if only her family could act normal for about three hours, just while Joan Walsh was here. Ma laid down the two plates she was carrying in front of Joan and Franny. "Guests first," she announced. "It looks wonderful," Joanie complimented. "It's an old family recipe," added Ma, trying to sound mysterious. "Yeah, it's old," announced Kevin, "We have it almost every other day." Ma shot him a look. "Mary Catherine, dinner!" Ma screamed to the upstairs. "I'm not hungry," came Mary Catherine's voice back. "Get down here, Missy. We have guests." Ma smiled sweetly at Joan, "Kids, it gets so much more difficult when they get older."

Joanie agreed, smiling just as sweetly at Franny. There was only the sound of food being munched by the family as all the Dewey children, but Mary Catherine ate. "Mary Catherine, get down here-- now!" Ma shouted. There was the sound of Mary Catherine stamping down the stairs and through the hall to the dining room. Mary

Catherine appeared in the doorway, wearing a very attractive, tight, bright red dress (that she had nicked just for the occasion) and looking very festive. "I'm supposed to go to dinner with Leonard," shouted Mary Catherine, pulling her hair back and inserting a decorative flower over her ear. "Sit down," instructed Ma, now taking her place at the table. "Didn't you hear me? I'm going out," replied Mary Catherine, "I'm not hungry." "Sit down, Missy," bellowed a familiar voice from the doorway.

Everyone turned to Da, swaying in the doorway of the front hall. It was very obvious that Da had more than his share of holiday cheer. Joanie openly cringed. She had heard about Mick Dewey and was relieved when Franny and Jim told her that his Da wasn't going to be there. Now he was.

"What are ya all dressed up for, sellin' meat?" asked Da, holding onto the door frame to steady himself. "Mick, go upstairs," instructed Ma, "We have guests." Da haltingly walked to Joanie and Franny, with a crooked smile running over his lips. "I see," he said, offering Joanie his hand, "And she's very pretty, too." Joanie gave him her hand and smiled uneasily. "It's nice to meet you," Joanie said as sweetly as she could muster. "You too, malady," answered Da. Without missing a beat, he turned to Mary Catherine, who had taken her chair but hadn't touched her meal. "Where do ya plan on goin'?" asked Da threateningly. Mary Catherine looked up at him and, almost in a whisper, said, "Over to my boyfriend's." Da reeled on her, "Your boyfriend? You're just a child!" Mary Catherine looked away and didn't answer. "Answer me, girl? Is that hardware guy you're boyfriend?" Mary Catherine again didn't answer. "Answer me, girl. Is that queer singer, your boyfriend?" "He isn't a queer!"

The slap caught everyone by surprise, causing all to jump in their seats. The whole table had been watching, but no one expected Da to hit Mary Catherine across the face with his open hand. "I won't stand for a slag in this house!" Mary Catherine held her face in surprise. Da stood over her and yelled, "I will not have a slut for a daughter," he continued. Mary Catherine jumped up and ran out of the room, looking like she was going to cry. Da staggered to the head of the table and took a chair. He smiled at Joanie one more time, but he didn't understand what the surprised look on Joanie and Franny's faces meant.

After Da was seated and had helped himself to a bowl of spaghetti and meatballs, he set in to enjoy his Christmas Eve dinner. Suddenly, Mary Catherine ran up behind Da from the living room and swung the ol'-how-do-you-do directly to the back of his head. The half-bat hit Da with a crack, sounding like a Ted Williams homer or a dog getting hit by a speeding car out on Haverhill Street (Da actually yelped inadvertently when the bat made contact).

Da's head slammed forward into the plate of pasta that he was about to eat. "Don't ever touch me, old man!" yelled Mary Catherine, taking aim at his head again. "Don't ever raise your hand to me again. You can do what you wanna do to the boys, but keep your fuckin' hands off me, or I'll kill you." Ma stood, she wanted to do something but couldn't because she was so horrified. She just stood at the end of the table, her mouth moving but nothing coming out.

She smiled awkwardly at Joan and Franny, who were stunned. The mother and daughter sat staring at Da, his face in his spaghetti and meatballs, while the rest of the Deweys, except for Ma, went back to eating.

"I'm goin' out," yelled Mary Catherine, storming out the room and tossing the ol'-how-do-you-do into the front room. The front door slammed, and Ma walked slowly to Da, who was starting to stir in the spaghetti. Da sat up with his face covered in spaghetti and sauce. Franny thought that his eyeballs had popped out his eye-sockets but quickly realized it was just two meatballs that had stuck to his head, dropping off his face. "Mick, let's go upstairs. I'll clean you up," consoled Ma, helping Da to stand. "That girl is feckin' crazy," reasoned Da, missing the family resemblance, "What's got into her?" Just before they reached the door to the front room, there was a snicker at the table.

Da stopped and gripped the door frame. Ma was still holding his arm to steady him. Da looked over his family at the table, trying to determine if that was an actual snicker. "I'm going to..." he abruptly stopped, unable to remember what he was going to say. "Come on, Mick. I'll put you in the bathtub tonight." Ma and Da left the room, Da staggering towards the stairs.

It started with Kevin, who may have been the one to originally snicker. Then Michael, Teresa, Dorrie, Kathy, Patrick, and Jim started laughing. It wasn't a belly laugh. It was more like a group laugh that was trying to be stifled. They looked over at each other and laughed more until all the Dewey kids were laughing so hard they couldn't eat. Franny looked to each Dewey; Jim was laughing so hard that tears were running down his cheeks. Franny looked over at her mom, who was appalled by what she had just witnessed. The Deweys continued to laugh at their father. Franny smiled at her ma, who tried to suppress the smile that she felt coming on. "Fuckin' Mary Catherine," said Patrick, still laughing. It would become one of their fondest Christmas memories.

♫♫♫

"That fuckin' dink," complained Mary Catherine, sitting in the backseat of Frenchy Fritzgerald's station wagon. Michael had enlisted Frenchy to be their roadie; he had told Frenchy about the women at their gigs and how they were crazy for the bands (he probably didn't mention that only the most desperate of groupies would consider the roadies as a member of the band) but Frenchy had a 1953 Buick Roadmaster Estate. In California, they were called Woodys. In Massachusetts, they were called a station wagon. The Buick Roadmaster may have been coveted by surfers at Muscle Beach, but in Massachusetts, it was a great car to haul a band in.

"He's been out stuffin' the pork into any drunken bar mop he can find," continued Mary Catherine, sitting between Lenny and Michael in the backseat, "and he's gonna call me a slag!" No one really wanted to get involved in this, not even Jim, who was sitting in the front seat with Franny and Frenchy, listening to Peter, Paul, and Mary sing about *If I had a Hammer* and it was his da, too. "I mean, what a dink," Mary Catherine went on, as she had been going on the last few weeks since Christmas Eve, "he has that bullshit brogue. Where do you think he got that?" she asked. "In Ireland," answered Jim, meekly. "Really, stupid? When has our da been to Ireland?" Jim thought about it for a minute, mostly because he couldn't run away, "During the war." "The war was in Germany, Rand McNally," shouted Mary Catherine from the backseat, "not in Ireland… because he's never been to Ireland."

Mary Catherine looked around the car, waiting for the answer. "Then how did he get his accent?" asked Alley, saying a prayer, silently in his head. "He didn't," she yelled, "he made the whole thing up. He was born and raised in Lawrence, like the rest of us." No one answered her. "It's all made up. He's never been to Ireland. He doesn't really have an Irish accent. He only has it because the stupid mill men get all weepy over the old shamrock. He talks with his bullshit brogue so that they will buy him drinks and sing Danny Boy with him," Mary Catherine groused. "Where would he get it?" she angrily asked. "At Barnaby's," suggested Frenchy, laughing at his own joke. "It's on the menu," added Michael, also cracking up at his joke.

It had never occurred to Jim before that his da had made up his accent. Jim had figured he'd picked up from his grandfather, who actually did come to America from the old country. Jim remembered asking his grandpa about Ireland when he was alive; all his grandpa said about Ireland was that it was "*a shit-hole, a land that never loved anyone back*". His da always talked of Ireland like it was a slice of heaven (Jim could remember one of Da's record albums had a song about Ireland being a little bit of heaven sung by Gerry Flanagan), but he never had actually been there... and Grandpa called it a shit-hole.

They were driving to The Cotillion in Taunton. Lenny had met with another promoter and had gotten this gig. Jim was kind of surprised when Lenny told him about Mr. Conley; he had thought that Lenny was good friends with Rickie. At least, they looked like they liked each other. But he had no problem with more gigs. The band had been doing well. Tonight, they would be opening for The Ramrods. Jim didn't actually know who the Ramrods were, but he didn't know who Tim Flynn and the Senders were, and he liked them. Mary Catherine was bitching about Da in the back seat

That's when "*I'm right here, but you can't see me, I'm not hiding, it can only be me,"* played on the radio. Jim turned to Franny, and both held their breath. "*I want to know if you really care?"* sang Franny, sounding like she really wanted to know. Together they sang, *"But how could you because I'm not here."* Suddenly, all the talking in the car stopped. It was quiet, except for the song coming from the radio. Lenny leaned forward and instructed, "Hey, turn that up?" Jim and Franny pretended not to hear him. "Frenchy, can you turn that up?" Frenchy glanced over at Jim and Franny, then reached over himself and turned up the radio. "Isn't that the song you said you wrote?" asked Alley, realizing that this might be his chance to become the guitar player. "No, ours was a different song," Jim weakly answered, feeling like he was caught with another band by his angry husband, Lenny, and looking to Franny to see if she felt the same way.

"No," Lenny said, leaning in close to Jim and Franny in the front seat, "That's the same song." Jim kept looking to Franny for an answer, but Franny didn't seem to have one. "I knew it," exclaimed Alley, slapping the back of the front seat, "That wasn't your song. You stole it." "We didn't really steal it," answered Franny, "We just wanted to see if Lenny would sing it. We thought it was a good song for him." Lenny leaned back into his seat, "Well, I still don't like it. I don't care who wrote it." "It sounds like some fag wrote it," Mary Catherine said just as Woo-Woo Ginsburg came on after the song finished. "That was Dick and Jane with 'I Not Here,' recorded live at the Club 47," Woo-Woo informed everyone before going into The Miracles *You Really Got a Hold on Me.* "Dick and Jane… what an original name! I bet they're some old beatniks!" proclaimed Mary Catherine. "I think the song sounds okay," said Michael, squished into the back seat. Jim glanced over at Franny, who was very relieved that their secret was safe and that someone besides her and Jim thought the song was okay.

♫♫♫

Franny placed the forty-five-record onto Lenny's portable record player. The record spun around, the record's label spinning in circles, **King Records, Athens, GA**, going around and around. The name of the record was *Last Kiss*. "I found this in Kirby's Record Store, downtown." said Franny, as the song started, "It's by a guy named Wayne Cochran." They were in Lenny's basement listening to the forty-five play out.

Lenny started to snap his fingers to the song; Michael tapped his foot. Then the chorus kicked in. By the end of the song, everyone was singing it. Alley liked it because it mentioned heaven, and he had always wanted more religious songs, like the ones they do in church. But there was no talking about the church in front of Lenny. He was what his parents call a *godless Atheist*. Alley was kind of surprised that Lenny would snap his fingers to the song.

It's not really what Lenny heard in the song that got him to like it. It's what he thought he could do with the song. "It's good. Do you think we could do it?" Jim reached over and lifted the record player's plastic arm to start the record over. He listened; it was a little schmaltzy (a word that Mary Catherine used when a movie or television show got too sentimental like Father Knows Best), but the real thing that caught Jim was the refrain. "I think we could do a real good job with this one," Franny added, to see if she had some sort of consensus. Franny chose the song because it was a song she would like to hear Lenny sing to her if he would sing a song to her. "Yeah, we should try to learn it," agreed Lenny. So, it was settled, they would learn *Last Kiss*.

Each player played the song on their instrument, trying to figure out what the chords were and the beat. Lenny sat down and wrote down the words, listening to the song a dozen times. Jim and Franny worked out the song-- G, E-minor, C, D. Jim worked out a strumming pattern that sounded like it matched Franny's record. Franny worked on an introduction to the song, and Jim added a short bridge to the last refrain. Michael and Alley worked out the rhythm pattern on the drums and the bass. Within two weeks, they had put the song together well enough to try it out at a live gig.

♫♫♫

The club was called "The Where's It At" on Commonwealth Avenue, in Boston. It was a large venue, part of it was formerly a warehouse in the Back Bay. The stage was raised about three feet, and every time someone took a step, it would creak and shake like a good bass drum beat could bring the whole thing down. Also, Franny, or Frankie, found that the piano that the venue owned was very old and out of tune and wouldn't be playable for that night. Frankie took up her Washburn and decided that she would play that rather than just playing the tambourine (since on a few of the songs, it was the instrument that Lenny used).

Spindal was opening the show for Argonauts and The Pilgrims, the headliners. When the band came out, it was the usual small group of early drinkers, but Lenny went right into his romancing of the audience. Lenny had worked up a lot of things that would get the attention of the audience, no matter what was going on in front of him. Some of it was just yelling into the microphone at odd times about odd things. Other times, it would be pointing out attractive women (the women loved the attention, and it helped the guys looking for a lay to know where to shop) to gushing about the venue or the city or the town they playing in ("Cambridge has the prettiest women... and they're smart, too." They had been in Cambridge for all of an hour before the show and only in the club, but someone had told Lenny that there was a bunch of colleges around) to dancing like he was swinging his prick at them (this was referred to as the Adventaganza, referencing the Saint Tony's gig). Spindal was a good opening act because Lenny and Jim would work at getting the audience to pay attention to the band, even if they were not the headliners.

Jim had been working more on trying to move around the stage and not getting in Lenny's way. Jim would've liked to have just stood in one place and played, but he felt like he wasn't helping Lenny in bringing the audience in if he just stood there like a statue. On the other hand, when he moved around the stage, he had to be always aware of where Lenny was. Once at The Casino Ballroom, Lenny was dancing around crazily, and Jim walked into him, not seeing Lenny, and they both fell over, ruining the song. They had to start over-- Michael glaring over the drums at Jim. As much as Jim wanted to move, it was hard to play and keep his awareness of where Lenny was on the stage; Lenny danced and bounded around as he liked.

Now, with Frankie walking around behind him, it was even more difficult to play. Though, it was fun to occasionally play to Frankie and her acoustic guitar. Jim thought that Frankie was wicked cute in Alley's little brother's pants, white collared shirt, and armless sweater vest. One thing he noticed with the guitar was how her right tit would rest on the guitar body. At one point in *Rock Around the Clock,* he went over and whispered in Franny's ear to tuck her boob in. Frankie shot him a sour look and turned her back to him and the audience. When she turned around, she had adjusted the guitar to make her look like a boy again, a wicked cute boy, in Alley's little brother's clothes.

When it was time to do the *Last Kiss,* Spindal stopped, and everyone looked at each other. Spindal had about twelve songs they all knew, but they almost always played the same songs in the same order every show. Even the weekly shows at the beach had all been the same setlist, so when they had a new song, it was a big deal, and *Last Kiss* was a different song than anything they had ever done. It couldn't be done fast to make it rock; the song had to be handled-- it had to be told like a story.

Jim started with his opening in bar chords. Frankie laid down the rhythm with the acoustic guitar, followed by Alley and Michael coming in lightly behind them. Lenny started telling of the fatal car crash, how he found his lover and held her in his arms. Frankie couldn't help but be pleased with her choice for Lenny. Hopefully, he would like it and hold it special that she chose it for him to sing. Of course, she knew he probably wouldn't, but a girl dressed like a boy, could hope. By the time they had gotten to the refrain, Frankie could see young girls in the front of the audience with tears in their eyes and holding handkerchiefs, waving them at Lenny, begging to tell him that his baby was right where they were.

Lenny loved it. This is what he wanted to do from the first time he had seen Elvis on Ed Sullivan, that Sunday night. He dragged the emotion from the audience singing about this tragedy of young lovers and the vow to be good so they could be together forever. When the song finished, there was a quiet moment of the crowd recognizing that the song was over, then there was an explosion of applause and girls screaming. Spindal walked to the front of the stage, Michael rushing up from behind the drums, and together, they took a bow.

The audience continued to applaud. Spindal went back and took their places. When it was quiet enough, Lenny turned to Michael, "Mister Mike-- let's go!!" Michael kicked the drums into the beat, and Spindal rolled into *Quarter of Three* and dancing to Daddy G.

After Spindal finished their set, an attractive woman named Ruth Clemens stopped Lenny and said it was one of the most moving songs she had ever heard. Lenny realizing that Jim was standing next to him, grabbed Jim by the shoulders and said, "Strings and I wrote it. Do you really like it?" Miss Clemens told him that she did. It was a very *moving* song. Jim wanted to say something about it belonging to some cat named Wayne Cochran, but who was he to start owning up to plagiarism, since they were still playing two songs that he had ripped off of Woody Guthrie and some guy named Ralph McTell, who wrote *Streets of London*, maybe he shouldn't be the one calling out Lenny (Let alone the one song he wrote that was getting airplay that he couldn't own up to). "Yeah, we wrote it," added Jim, with Lenny squeezing his shoulders.

Miss Clemens told the boys that she worked for a show on television called "Community Auditions." Lenny knew the show. He had watched it a few times. The tv show had live musicians, dancers, singers, and some novelty acts perform. Miss Clemens gave Lenny her phone number and told him that they would like to have Spindal play that song on the show. Lenny took the number, but he wasn't sure if he wanted his band to go on television and play for the chance to win a brand-new hairdryer or something.

♫♫♫

Lenny told the rest of the band on the way back to Lawrence in Frenchy's station wagon. Alley and Franny were thrilled with the idea of playing on television. Alley thought it would impress his parents if he played a song on television that mentioned heaven and people looking forward to going there when their time on earth was done. He was also hoping some of the people at Saint Tony's would be impressed with the song and stop treating him like he was possessed by the devil whenever they saw him.

Franny thought that it would be a good way of getting their band out into the public, and if she was in on television, most people would expect a five-piece band rather than the group that played the beach this summer. Franny also thought it was a great opportunity to show Lenny at his best, talking romantically about love and loyalty to the one he loved. Of course, Franny had no illusions about Lenny's loyalty. Jim had told her about the girls up at the beach, and Franny had even walked in on Lenny and some fan in the backstage ladies' room after the gig at The Teen Scene in Hyannis.

Franny was also aware that Mary Catherine wasn't all that loyal to Lenny either. Most recently, she had asked Franny and Bridie about offering Rocco Riccoli a blow job if he would break one of her da's arms. The offer was even too crazy for Rocco, who decided to pass on the offered blow job-- which should have been a good reminder to Franny to keep her distance from Mary Catherine. When she was on stage with Lenny, Franny would sometimes catch a glimpse of Mary Catherine in the audience or in the wings of the stage, with a threatening look on her face if Lenny was singing or dancing with her.

The Bridge

The band went back to Lenny's basement and rehearsed *Last Kiss* to compete in Community Auditions. Community Auditions was a game show shot in Cambridge on channel 5. The host was Gene Burns, an older guy who had a syrupy sweet way about him. No matter how bad the act was, he was always complimentary and positive that the crash and burn act would get a good score. The viewing audience was encouraged to mail in their votes for the winner, and the next week the winning act would be announced. The winners got bragging rights, a trophy, and something like a brand-new television set or a washing machine (Everyone in the band was pulling for the tv).

There were only two real reasons not to do Community auditions. The first was that you had to share the stage with many different acts, and only a few were musical acts, so the sound was never really mixed well, and the technicians were not that adroit in shooting a band. The second was at the end of the show, everyone participating had to sing the show's theme song, which was kind of stupid. Paulie in the Argonauts told Jim and Michael that they had been asked to be on Community Auditions, and their manager, Stewie, had told them to pass.

♫♫♫

When Spindal made their way up to Brighton, Jim felt that maybe this was a big mistake. He knew that Lenny was excited about the chance to play in front of television cameras, and Franny thought that it would be good exposure for the band, but Jim wanted it to be like a gig, and he wasn't all that thrilled about being on tv (his family still didn't own one).

When they got to the studio, they realized how bleak the Public Broadcasting set at WBZ-TV was. It was just a basic stage with a blank background, lights, and two large cameras. The stage manager led them to the upright piano, then instructed them and Frenchy where to set up the drums. Michael's drums and the piano would be rolled onto the set when it was Spindal's turn to perform. The band waited in the "green" room, though it was more of a dusty office with two couches (and not even painted green).

Jim and Alley tuned their guitars, while Michael and Franny exercised their hands, loosening up their fingers. Michael tapped on the couch with his sticks while Lenny paced back and forth, waiting to go on. Alley had hoped that there would be a make-up lady to put some make-up on his acne-filled face, but he was told that they didn't do make-up there and if he wanted make-up, he should have put it on at home. Alley wanted to put it on but didn't want it enough to give the other guys a chance to know that he had it on. He decided not to push the matter. Also, he didn't need his dad seeing him with make-up on, playing in the band already had his old man suspecting sexuality (it was common knowledge in 1962 that all musicians were queer-- see Liberace-- not Frank Sinatra, he was the exception).

They waited with the other acts for the show to start. There was Linda, a thirteen year old, who was going to twirl her baton to a John Phillip Sousa song and Karen, Janet and Mary, high school juniors, who were going to Irish step dance (they had on these large blond wigs that they kept having to adjust on their heads), Robert who was nine, he was going to play *The Flight of the Bumble Bee* on his kazoo, Lewis was an older black man, who was going to sing *old Man River* from Porgy and Bess, and Jeffrey, who was in sixth grade, was going to spin six plates on tall stands. Spindal was going to close the show.

They waited patiently for their turn, watching what was happening on a closed-circuit television, mounted on the wall in the corner. Linda had to do her baton-twirling twice because the first time, she threw her baton too high, and it hit something in the ceiling of the studio, and she couldn't catch it coming down. The director told her to toss it lower, and it worked the second time. The step dancing girls were still having trouble with their wigs (they kept falling off), and then the record they were dancing to kept skipping (uh-oh), but they were able to finally get through it. Robert buzzed through the Bumble Bee on his first try, but really can you have sound problems with a kazoo? Lewis had a really good voice and could sing the crap out of the song.

Then they had to pause so that Jeffrey could set up his stands for his plates to twirl on. This took some time, and Spindal sat anxiously in the green room, now starting to regret to have taken up the invitation to perform. Finally, Jeffrey got all the sticks upright the way he wanted them, and the music started. Jeffrey started spinning the plates on the ends of the sticks, first one, then two, then three. As he set the plate on the stick and started to spin it to get it going, he also had to keep an eye on the plates already spinning and make sure they had enough speed on them to keep up till he could get all six plates spinning. Jeffrey was doing fine until he got the fourth plate, where he had to rush back to the first plate and spin it more. Jeffrey went to start five when two started to spin awkwardly and lose momentum. While getting two, three started to die, and one was wobbling on its stick. Jeffrey got those going again, but now plate four was wobbling, and he hadn't even made it over to six yet. Jeffrey got his plates spinning and went to start six when three started to wobble.

Jeffrey made the decision to get three, but he hadn't started six strong enough, and already it was wobbling. Jeffrey darted to six when one and two wobbled. He ran back to one and two, but it was too late. Six fell to the floor, smashing into pieces. Jeffrey got one and two together, but four and five wobbled and fell. Jeffrey ran to catch them, but he was too late. They crashed to the cement studio floor. Jeffrey dashed back to three and four, but they too fell and smashed on the floor; Jeffrey could only watch as one and two followed them to the floor and into pieces. Jeffrey looked up at the camera and shrugged his shoulders.

Gene Burns entered the frame, clutching his microphone, "You had them going there for a minute, Jeff," he said, resting a friendly hand on the eleven-year old's shoulder, "I'm sure you deserve a good score."

The show paused, and the stage manager came in to tell Spindal that it was their turn to perform. The boys followed the stage manager to the studio, where some men were sweeping up Jeffrey's broken dishes. Some other men pushed the piano out to where they would be playing, while Frenchy and Michael got the drums into position. As soon as she could get to the piano, Frankie started banging on the keys to see how it sounded. It was good enough, the piano sounded in tune, and the play in the keys was pretty easy, which was important since Franny didn't have long fingers; she needed a piano with easy play.

Jim and Alley pulled out their amplifiers and plugged their guitars in, running through some scales and bass runs to hear how they sounded. Jim went back to the brown face and shifted some of the dials, trying to get something that sounded clear, but not as loud as they would play it at a club. Jim turned to the director and asked, "Do you want to do levels on the guitars?" "What?" answered the director, “They sound fine.” Which isn't what Jim wanted to hear. "Okay," retorted Jim, lying to the director.

When Lenny took his place in front of the band, he immediately realized there was gonna be a problem. They had swept the studio floor, but there was residual dust left from Jeffrey's broken plates. He stood on top of the X marked on the floor and slid his feet back and forth. The dust had made the cement floor very slippery. "Can they sweep here some more?" asked Lenny, trying to sound nice about it, "I can't really move around." "You shouldn't move," instructed the director, from the darkness beyond the cameras, "We need you to stay in one place." Lenny slid his feet around some more but said, "Okay." He lied also.

Jim realized that he also couldn't move and that Jeffrey's plate dust was also making his steps perilous, and that he was also going to have to stay in one place. The good thing was that if Lenny wasn't moving, there wouldn't be much chance of them smashing into each other. "Places," called the director.

Jim looked back at Franny, who was standing at the piano rather than sitting. The show had supplied the piano but didn't supply a piano bench for her. She looked back at him, wearing her large, black framed glasses and Alley's little brother's clothes. Michael banged his snare drum and then rolled through the other drums to let everyone know he was ready. Jim was hoping that they would sound check each instrument first, but it became clear that that wasn't going to happen.

"Three, two, one," the director counted down. Lenny looked at Frankie, and the director shouted, "Go." Michael started with the beat, as Frankie followed him and then Alley and Jim following with their guitars. The stage manager had instructed Lenny to sing to the camera that had the red light on it. Lenny was surprised the first time the red light came on, but he went right into the song ready to make New England girls weep.

♫♫♫

Mitch sat on his couch, watching Community Auditions. He was waiting for the announcement of the winner from the previous week in the hope that the girl singer on that show would win and he could get her name; he was sure it was Carol or Caroline or maybe even

Carolyn-- it was something like that. If she won the competition, they would say her name, and maybe Mitch could find her in a talent directory and call her to see if he could do some recording tests with her. But then those boys came on.

It was your usual five-piece rock band, but it was really the singer that interested Mitch the most. He was a gangly guy, with wavy brown hair, in a shirt and tie, that looked as if he hadn't really cared how he tied it on, but when he sang, Mitch couldn't help but think of Jerry Lee Lewis without the manic piano playing. This kid seemed in control. Though he wasn't polished, he seemed to be able to see how other people saw him, which in Mitch's business was rear, if not impossible. Mitch listened as the singer told his tragic story-- he wasn't familiar with the song, it could be an original, which would be even better than just finding the singer, but he was more impressed with the way this boy could draw a person in.

The television cut to the other players in the band, the rhythm guitarist, who looked competent but was way too involved in his own playing, the piano player, who looked very effeminate, the drummer, a big kid in the back, who obviously followed in the Buddy Rich mode of drumming the hell out of the song, the tall bass player, who kept on looking at the guitar player, like he was hoping the kid would fall over (it looked like the guitar player was also afraid of falling over) so that he could take his position. But the real star was the singer. Mitch hadn't seen anyone like him since Gene Vincent in Liverpool.

Mitch sat up on the Naugahyde sofa, in the fashionable den that his wife, Ellen, had decorated after they moved into the Beacon Street townhouse, right after they had got married. He made it a point to get the name of the band so that he wouldn't have the Carol, Caroline, Carolyn problem. He was sure he could find them through the name. They looked a bit seasoned, so someone must know how to get in touch with them.

♫♫♫

Jim realized that he couldn't really worry about anything but what he was playing now. All they could hope for was that the sound would come out reasonably well. He just wanted to get this gig over and prepare for their show in Burlington that night. Lenny sang into the cameras as the red lights instructed him, all the time trying not to move or slip and fall in Jeffrey's plate dust. When they reached the final refrain, Jim, Franny and Alley sang the chorus, even though none of them were miked up.

When the song was finished, Gene Burns came out with his microphone and exclaimed, "Wow, Spindal, what a song!" The band stood together, "Who are the others in the band?" Gene asked, sticking the thin microphone in Lenny's face. "I'm Lenny, that's Jim, on the guitar." Jim was relieved that Lenny hadn't called him Strings, "That's Alley on the bass, Michael on the drums, Frann..." Lenny had caught himself just in time, "Frankie on the piano, and we're Spindal," He announced for anyone to hear. "If you liked Spindal's song, please send a postcard to the address at the bottom of the screen," coaxed Gene to the viewing audience, "And maybe they could be the big winner of a Kenmore clothes dryer."

Mitch watched the end of the show, his girl singer, Carol, Caroline, Carolyn didn't win that week, and to the relief of the band, they didn't win the next week-- Lewis won, he had a great voice and sang the crap out of that song. But they all had to sing with Gene, and the other contestants the show's theme song.

They may not have become the star of the day, but back in Lawrence and up on Paddy Hill, they had become celebrities. Ma, Peggy, Kathy, Kevin, and Teresa went to Uncle Anthony and Aunt Maria's house to watch it on their new black and white television. Ma was very proud to see three of her former students were on tv (She counted Lenny as a former student, even though it was a short time).

Joanie Walsh watched it at home with her sister, Lucy. They were both delighted and mailed over a dozen ballots voting for Spindal to win. Alley's parents didn't watch the show because there was a bake sale for Saint

Tony's CYO basketball team, also because Alley didn't tell them they were on the show-- he had changed his mind, why re-enforce the sons of Satan image that his parents already had of his friends. Leo told Jim that he couldn't see it, "I'm blind, ya know." But he did hear it and thought it was wonderful. Grammy Ham caught the show-- she thought they were "Crap."

♫♫♫

Lenny was nervous going to the gig. He had spoken to that guy Mitch over the phone. Frank Conley had given the manager his phone number. Lenny wasn't sure if Spindal needed a manager. He was doing a good job. They were playing all the time-- all over the Boston area.

Tonight, they were taking Frenchy's woody to Lowell to play a gig. This was one of the short trips, straight down Route 495, in less than twenty minutes. If Spindal had a boat, they could take the Merrimack River down to the club. But Lenny wasn't sure if they wanted a manager-- all the other groups he talked to who had a manager were unhappy with him. Some thought the manager was stealing from them. Others thought that the manager was more concerned with their other groups and not them. None of them seemed happy with their managers, not Tim Flynn and the Senders, not The Remains, not even The Barbarians (And who would rip off a barbarian?). Michael was the only one with any kind of business background in the group, and he considered everyone in the music business a crook, and they would be best off to consider any manager a crook, also. But if he could get them some big gigs in Boston that would really help.

Franny was nervous about going to the gig-- and not because of the manager (Lenny had only told the real members, Alley and Michael) but because they were going to play at The Commodore Ballroom on Thorndyke Street, the club where Mutt McCarthy was the manager. It had been about six years since the last time Franny saw Mutt, trying to rape her mother, and a lot of things could happen in six years, and knowing Mutt, most likely they got wise to him and fired him. For all Franny knew, Mutt was probably in jail. As comforting as that thought was, it still didn't help her forget what had happened that night.

When they pulled up in the back of The Commodore Ballroom, a large club with a vast parking lot, everyone got out and started inside. Franny made sure her glasses were on and buttoned up the large trench coat she was wearing. As they made their way into the club, Mutt was there to meet them, looking older and more washed-out, his hair was starting to grey and thinning out on top of his head, he had his dress shirt opened and his tie hanging about his collar.

"I'm Mutt McCarthy, the boss of this joint," he said, a cigarette hanging out of the side of his mouth, "Which one of yas is Suggs?" Lenny stopped and shook hands with Mutt. Franny pretended to cough and covered her face with the guitar case that the Washburn was in (they brought it to every gig now in case there wasn't a piano) as she walked by Lenny and Mutt. "I'll show you where to set your stuff up," Mutt led Lenny and the band to the stage while Franny kept her distance from her mother's attempted rapist.

Once inside, it got easier. Mutt went about his business, and the band set up their equipment. Spindal waited backstage for their cue. Jim quietly ran scales on his unplugged guitar, loosening up his fingers, Michael tapped his drum sticks on the wall. Alley said a quiet prayer, while Franny kept an eye out for Mutt.

Lenny kept staring out from behind the stage curtain, looking for someone. It couldn't be Mary Catherine, because she was standing next to him, looking very curious and very jealous at the same time. Lenny hadn't thought to mention the manager to her. The last thing Mary Catherine wanted was to split the money another way, and she felt that Lenny was getting the short end of the shit-stick anyway. He was doing all the work but only getting an even share of the thirty-five dollars (and now they were paying Frenchy Fitzpatrick for the use of his car and gas-- and Frenchy wasn't even French. He was Irish like the rest of Paddy Hill). Fortunately, it was time to start the show, and Mary Catherine could only stew and stare down every woman in the audience that Lenny was singing to.

♫♫♫

Mitch sat in the back, with just a beer, watching the show. He was right. The singer had a way about him. By the second number, *Peggy Sue,* he had all the women eating out of his hand. Mitch could tell that some of the guys in the audience were a bit miffed that they had lost their date's attention, but he knew they weren't going anywhere as long as Spindal, or more specifically, Lenny Suggs, the singer, kept playing. The kid had a way about himself. He was very confident, but not off-putting. He sang, danced, on a couple of the blues numbers, he added a decent harmonica.

Mitch could tell that Lenny studied other singers; he had a lot of Jerry Lee Lewis. What Mitch had noticed from the Community Auditions performance, there was some Little Richard in there, and at times, he moved like young Elvis or even James Brown. The rest of the band looked competent, the guitar player tried to interact with the singer, but he seemed nervous about bumping into him. The drummer had no problem with making himself known, and it almost looked like the bass player, who had a real good case of acne (that he would hopefully grow out of), was either singing or praying as he played. The piano player was the hardest to judge. It looked as if he was trying to hide. Mitch was told by Lenny that the piano player was the newest addition to the band, so maybe that's why he looked so shy.

When the show ended, the audience of The Commodore sprang up to applaud Spindal. Most of the members came out to take a bow after *Last Kiss*, even though the still nervous looking piano player stayed at his instrument, tapping lightly on a few indiscriminate keys.

A woman appeared at one side of the stage and glared menacingly at a few of the more excitable women in the front. Taking their cue from the audience, they went back to their instruments and went into a rollicking version of *Quarter of Three,* a real barn-burner of a song. What the singer hadn't dragged out of the audience already, and especially the women in the audience, he came back to take what was left. Mitch knew he had to sign these guys, if not just the singer, then the whole band. It was then that Mitch's grand plan started to grow in his mind. This was going to be the band that was going to take on America... before the Beatles got here... even if God-damned Epstein would be bringing those boys to America soon.

When the band ran off the stage, Mitch had planned his next move. Mitch hoped that these kids were the kind of kids that America wanted to see. Kids like them that were respectful to their parents, sober, good citizens, proud Americans. Mitch would wait for them to come out from backstage.

♫♫♫

Spindal strolled off the stage, leaving the audience behind them, cheering and applauding. Franny followed the other guys when suddenly she felt an intense pain clutching her right breast, then she looked up and saw Mutt. "I thought it was you," he hissed, squeezing her breast harder with his hand, "I wanted to go back there and show that cunt of a mother of yours..." Mutt had to stop talking because Michael's drumstick was threateningly pressing into the bottom of his jaw. "If you have a problem with Frankie, you have a problem with all of us," growled Michael. Mutt squeezed Franny's tit harder.

Jim was walking off the stage, preparing to remove the lead from his guitar, when he noticed the distressed and pained look on Franny's face. That's when he saw where the manager's hand was. Realizing that he didn't have access to the ol'-how-do-you-do, he knew he would have to improvise.

Mutt was trying to back away from Michael and the drum-stick sticking in his throat when the Gretsch hit him directly on the crown of his head, knocking him onto the stage. There was a loud POING of the guitar striking Mutt's skull, followed by a screeching of the strings as the still-plugged in instrument fell to the stage. Jim was following right behind it, leaving Franny to hold her injured boob. Michael asked her up, "Are you okay?"

♫♫♫

There was a loud PONG that echoed throughout the club, and all of a sudden, a man in a suit stumbled out onto the stage. The crowd stopped and watched as the guitar player dove out of the wings and onto the fallen man. Jim got on top of the man and started to pummel him with his fists. Mitch watched, repulsed at what might happen to the guitarist's hands in the middle of a fight. Also, he was re-thinking his "proud American boys" assumption when the drummer ran out onto the stage and jumped on the guitarist and the man, who was trying to fight back now.

Club bouncers rushed to the stage and tried to peel the guitarist and drummer off the man, only to be jumped on by the singer, another man, and the angry woman. The pianist stepped out of the wings, holding his left pectoral muscle, and was joined by the bass player, who seemed concerned with what had happened. Mitch was now trying to decide if he should sign these guys or get the hell out of before it the cops got there. They had to delay the next act until they could sort out the fight at center stage.

♫♫♫

The woody sped up Route 495 to Lawrence. Inside, Spindal was celebrating their fight with the manager of The Commodore Ballroom and his bouncer minions. Jim's shirt had been ripped open, exposing his white under-shirt, Michael had a mouse under his eye from when someone kicked him in the pile, everyone else was a bit rumpled, except for Frenchy, who actually had a bloody wound on the side of the head.

One reason that Michael had taken Frenchy on as a roadie was because of his prowess with his hands. Frenchy still worked Barnaby's door, but when he wasn't helping to set up Spindal's equipment, this was exactly what he hoped would happen-- getting into a fight in someone else's bar and kicking some ass. Frenchy had held off four of the club's bouncers himself.

What surprised everyone was Jim going after that asshole manager. No one thought for a second that Jim would be the one to end up in a fight. They all had gone to school together, but nobody could ever remember Jim fighting anyone. Even Mary Catherine was surprised. She couldn't ever remember Jim fighting back in any family disagreement. Usually, it was someone beating upon him. She couldn't imagine what could have set him off like that.

Jim sat in the front seat beside Franny and Frenchy, bathing in the spotlight of his first fight. Jim glanced over at Franny, who gave him a thin "thank you" smile. He still didn't know really know what was going on with Franny and that guy, but when Jim saw him hurting her, his deep dark Dewey side leaped out. After Frenchy and Alley had gathered up his guitar and amp, Jim checked and didn't notice any real damage done to the instrument when it hit Mutt's head.

Franny's boob was still sore. She had checked in the backseat of the woody when no one was looking, it looked like she was going to have a bruise, but Mutt didn't do any real damage. She smiled to herself with the thought of telling her mother about Jim's guitar smashing into Mutt's head. Mutt had been smacked in the face with a practice keyboard, nearly gored by a drumstick, and had a Gretsch guitar bounced off his noggin-- he was getting some hard music lessons. On second thought, Franny decided not to tell her mom-- maybe she would lobby to move to another apartment. Lenny sat with Mary Catherine on his lap, in the tightly filled back seat. Mary Catherine kissed his knuckles gently, cooing at times, "Poor hands, hitting that bad man." Lenny stared out the window, wondering if that Sutherland guy was at the show. If he was, do they need a manager-- or not need a manager question, wasn't even a decision anymore. "I kicked that fat guy in the balls," added Mary Catherine.

♫♫♫

"Let's try this?" Jim asked, playing a fast group of chords. Franny picked up the progression and played along with Jim. Both were sitting uncomfortably on the slanted kitchen roof outside of Jim's bedroom window. It was hard to play here, but it was pretty much the only place where they could play and not be interrupted by anyone. The songwriting wasn't going well. Jim and Franny had continued to write songs, but they never could get all the way through. They had taken to trying to just play some chords and makeup words as they went along. Both had been working from the words first but then could never find the chord progressions and rhythm that went along with it.

Jim got confused and missed some chords, sending Franny's part reeling, and they both stopped playing. "That sounded good," Jim said, hopefully, "Until I messed it up." "I don't know," said Franny, "I think it was too fast." Jim picked some notes, thinking. Finally, he decided to ask, "What happened at The Commodore the other night?" Franny stopped picking and looked at him, deciding if she should tell him or not... and how would she tell him. Franny was always cautious about her mother's dating life and the men she saw. She knew that most people thought that Joanie deserved being single because she had Franny out of wedlock. But Franny never felt that way. She was always puzzled why her mother couldn't find a man-- sometimes she was actually afraid to ask herself if it was because of her that Joanie couldn't meet a husband.

"That guy was an ex-boyfriend of my mom's," Franny declared, pretending to tune her already tuned guitar. "He hurt her-- he wanted to hurt her bad," she added, turning a guitar knob of the Washburn J-G Jazz guitar. "I'm sorry," apologized Jim. "No, it was probably her own fault," Franny said, working on another knob, "But you don't like seeing it happen to your mother." "I know," confessed Jim, still picking at strings. Franny had forgotten the violence in Jim's parent's relationship. "No one should treat you like that," said Jim, with all the courage he could muster, "You deserve better than that." Franny stopped frigging with the knobs and looked over at Jim. Jim could see that her eyes were watering. Franny wiped her eyes with the sleeve of her heavy knit sweater. "No one does," she added.

Jim started playing a bouncy tune, trying to brighten up the subject, "No one should be treated like that," he sang. Franny picked up the rhythm and sang, "Baby, that's a fact." They both sang, "No one should be treated like that." They continued to play along with the words and the rhythm, making things up and trying different strumming patterns. It may not have been a song in the making, but it felt better than thinking about their problems in the middle of the night, playing guitars on the roof.

♫♫♫

Lenny sat in the passenger seat of Rickie's Oldsmobile Cutlass. Rickie looked over at him and smiled. It was a comforting smile, a smile that said, "It's been a while-- good to see ya." Lenny had been looking forward to this night since Rickie had called him and said he wanted to take Lenny to dinner. Rickie drove up Route 114 towards Peabody. They talked about the group and what was happening with the band. Rickie had shown up at the Pepsi Dance Party in Porter Square, hosted by WCOP-AM D.J. Ken Karter. The show had gone well, and Lenny was hoping that Rickie was pleased.

They arrived at the Daniel Fuller House and went inside. Lenny got the feeling that the house hadn't changed much since Daniel Fuller owned it (during the Revolutionary War). They were led to a table in a quiet corner. Both men took their seats, Rickie ordered two Cokes, and they looked over the menu. Lenny felt strange. It felt like a date, but they were both guys, and no one had to push in the seat for the other. "You're looking good," observed Rickie, taking a sip out of his tonic. Lenny just smiled. He was very interested in where this was going. "When are you turning eighteen?" asked Rickie, "For tax records." Lenny got the feeling that Rickie was taking the piss out of him. "August 29th," replied Lenny, waiting to see where this was going. "A summer baby, huh?" observed Rickie, staring into Lenny's eyes. Finally, Rickie leaned forward and asked, "Does Spindal want to play the beach again this year?" he waited for Lenny's answer.

"Sure, we like to play, and we had a good time last year," answered Lenny, trying to sound professional but not too anxious to get back to the beach. "Good," said Rickie, reaching under the table to pat Lenny's hand, which was resting on his knee. Lenny jumped, unconsciously. "I think I can get you some headlining gigs this year." Lenny was excited to hear that, "At The Frolics?" asked Lenny. "Yeah, that and at the Casino--Tim Flynn and the Senders are going to play the south shore this summer. I figured I would try you guys headlining." "Will we still have the gigs at the Kon Tiki and Pete's Blue Whale?" "We'll see about those, but I'm talking about playing every night this summer." Lenny had to stop to think about that. That would be a lot of traveling from Lawrence to Salisbury and Hampton.

"We'll have to drive up every night?" Lenny asked after a moment. Rickie smiled. That smile comforted Lenny. "No, we'll find you all a place to stay for the summer. Usually, it's in Seabrook, halfway between each town," Rickie assured him. Lenny was thrilled. It would be like being a grown-up. Living at the beach, the girls, fun... Rickie. "That sounds wicked good," answered Lenny.

Their food arrived. Rickie cut into his steak and said, "You can keep the girl in the band..." Lenny stopped eating his pot roast in mid-bite; he had thought that they had pulled it over on Rickie with Franny and Frankie. "She can stay?" confirmed Lenny. "She can stay as long as I don't hear from any of the booking agents. They want her out. After that, you'll have to find another piano player." Rickie took a careful bite of steak, savoring it in his mouth for a second. Lenny nodded in agreement. After Rickie finished swallowing the piece of steak, he added, "She's a very competent piano player. I hope we don't have any problems." "Me too," agreed Lenny.

They had a nice meal together and shared the apple pie a la mode for dessert. Driving Lenny home to his house, Rickie stopped just before turning into Lenny's road. When Lenny realized that the car had parked, he turned to Rickie to see if there was a problem, when suddenly Rickie leaned forward and kissed him. A warm kiss, softer than the way Mary Catherine ever kissed him. Rickie gently rested his hand on Lenny's shoulder. When they touched tongues, Lenny thought that he was going to explode in his pants. Rickie withdrew from the kiss, suddenly, the fear took over Lenny's body. He had never felt anything like it before. Not with Mary Catherine, not with Father Nelson, not with the hooker. As much as the fear knotted in his stomach, the rest of him loved it, and he wanted to be kissed by Rickie again.

Rickie threw the car into gear and pulled up Lenny's street. Just before pulling into Harry's driveway, Rickie smiled at him and said, "That was nice." Lenny didn't know how to respond to that-- he just smiled-- it was. Rickie pulled the Cutlass up in front of Lenny's house. Lenny didn't know what to do next. Should he shake his hand, try to kiss him again (he didn't want to do it in front of his house. His mom and Harry had just got back from Denver). Lenny thanked him for dinner and said he would tell the band about going to the beach again. Rickie told him that he would let him know about the housing arrangements when he knew more. Lenny got out of the car and gave Rickie a smile before he closed the Olds' door.

Lenny lay in his bed, thinking about Rickie and what had happened earlier that evening. He wasn't sure if he was ready for something with Rickie, and he was deathly scared of Mary Catherine finding out about it. She was very threatening to other women, and he couldn't imagine how she would be towards a guy. There was something very scary about it, but there was also something that was very exciting about it. Lenny couldn't help but wonder if this is what Father Nelson meant when he said, "We're alike." Was he like Father Nelson? He hoped not.

♫♫♫

When Franny heard that they were going to stay up at the beach this summer, she was very excited, but then the thought of telling her mom was another story. Her mom wasn't going to be thrilled with her living with four guys for the summer. She thought about lying to her and telling her that she was going to stay with some girls, but that would blow up as soon as Joanie came to visit her at the beach, and Franny knew that her mom would come to visit-- it wasn't that far away. The only reasonable thing to try was to beg her to let her go, no matter how bad of an idea it sounded.

They were watching The Andy Griffith Show on the television one night when Franny figured now was better than never, "The band is gonna play the beach again this year." Joanie looked up at her, knowing well enough that there was something coming behind it, "Are you going with them?" "I want to," confirmed Franny, "But Rickie's getting us a place to stay up there," Joanie didn't say anything-- she didn't move. "We're going to be playing ten shows a week-- as the headliners. We can't keep coming home and driving back up every day." Still, Joanie didn't say a word. "Mom, I really want to go with them. But I'm not going to lie to you. I will be the only girl there. Even Mary Catherine won't be there." Joanie was still quiet. "I really want to go. This is a big chance. I want to see if I could be a musician. A working musician. This is what I want to do." Still no reaction from Joanie. "I'm going to have to learn to be the only woman in the room. That's what being a woman and a musician usually is. But I still want this chance." Joanie stared at Barney, just after Thelma Lou slapped him for getting fresh in the backseat of Andy's car. "I want to do this, Mom."

Joanie slowly nodded, "If that's what you want." Suddenly, Franny realized that she was crying. "Thank you, Mom. Thank you, I'll never forget this. I won't," she promised. Joanie reached over and gave her daughter a hug. "You do this. Just be careful." "I will," she promised again. They sat and made plans for Franny to go and spend the summer up at the beach, being a musician.

♫♫♫

The ride to the beach was exciting. The house that Rickie had rented for them was a disappointment. It was a remodeled garage on Ashworth Avenue, in Hampton

Beach, behind a house that had been rented to a bunch of girls from the University of Massachusetts in Amherst. The garage was one room, with two bunk beds facing each other, two couches, a kitchen area, a very small bathroom, and a shower that was outside, on the back wall of the garage. It was obvious that it wasn't even a two-car garage-- it was more of a shed. Everyone brought their luggage in (Alley, Lenny, and Franny actually had suitcases, Jim and Michael just had brown paper bags with their clothes in them) and started to get used to their new home.

What Franny hadn't realized was that this would be her summer of being a boy. Because they were playing every day at both Hampton and Salisbury, she was going to have to dress as a boy all the time. Now being the headliners at both the Hampton Casino and The Frolics Club, after a few weeks, everyone working and living at the beach knew them as almost local celebrities. She could only go to the beach in her new one-piece bathing suit if she wore a large brimmed hat and hoped that no one would recognize her as the piano man for Spindal at The Frolics.

Rickie Rooney arrived, and everyone crammed in his car so that he could take them to dinner at Brown's Lobster Pound on the New Hampshire - Massachusetts border. The band sat at one of the picnic tables, and Rickie ordered six lobsters. Lobster wasn't a common meal for any of the kids, but it was the first time that Jim had ever tried one. The way it looked when it arrived like it was alive and as red as the cherry bomb Strat that Jim saw in a second-hand store on Market Street. It had long antennas, claws that were already cracked, and butter to dip it in.

Rickie helped the guys (and Franny) crack and pull the meat out of the lobsters. Each band member wore a plastic bib with a picture of a red lobster on it. When Franny cracked her lobster claw, some juice shot out and hit Jim in the kisser. Everyone laughed as Jim wiped the juice from his face. He had decided that he didn't like lobster; it was too much work. After dinner, they went to Creamy Cone for an ice cream. The musicians of Spindal sat in the new pavilion and watched the people preparing for summer.

♫♫♫

They played The Hampton Casino Ballroom the next night for the first time as the headliner. It was very exciting for Franny to perform as Frankie, Spindal's piano player. Lenny was happy to find out that many people, not only at The Hampton Casino but also at The Frolics, The Kon Tiki and Pete's Blue Whale, remembered them from the summer before and welcomed them as conquering heroes. The band didn't have to work as hard at the beginning of the show; the audience would be more intense as the show went on. What they also realized was that they needed to change their setlist of songs. They had been playing almost the same songs now for more than a year, and with the exception of *Last Kiss* and Jack Lawrence's *Beyond the Sea* (it sounded like a beach song-- they "rocked" it up a bit), it was almost the same show as last summer.

Big Karl was still at The Kon Tiki; he welcomed the guys back and asked them how college was going. Lenny told him that they would be graduating soon and were going to buy the joint just to be his boss. He didn't mention that he, Alley and Michael had just graduated from Lawrence High School; it was better that Karl didn't know. After arriving at the club, they realized that there wasn't a piano in the club anymore (some drunk had got on the stage over the winter and pushed it off, directing it to land behind the bar. Besides almost killing the bartenders, it destroyed much of the alcohol stock, let alone the physical bar itself) so Frankie had to play the acoustic Washburn Flat-top when they played there. The first time Frankie took the stage, she realized she didn't like heights and that this stage didn't have a lot of room to move around in.

The crowds at The Frolics Club were just as big and just as raucous as the year before. Being the headliner was a lot better than being the opening act. No one really cared when you came out. There was no house manager yelling at you to get out there before the audience tore the place down. Actually, the more time you spent hanging out backstage, the more beer and booze they could serve to the waiting crowd. Also, the headliners got the big dressing room, and since they were staying in the shed, it was nice to have some space to hang out in. The other thing was that as the headliners, you got some free drinks-- it depended on what house manager was on that night that determined how much beer you got. Most of the time, it was Carling Black Label, but it was still free.

This was the summer that Spindal discovered drinking. It was usually just beer and occasionally whiskey, but there was a lot more than last summer, which only consisted of what they could sneak from the bartenders. Both Alley and Michael were eighteen and able to legally buy beer. Alley didn't like beer or whiskey, but he liked Lenny more and would buy him beer whenever Mary Catherine came up to visit. Jim, unlike Mary Catherine, who enjoyed drinking, didn't drink to excess. His experience with Da had soured him on drinking and the kind of behavior that came of it.

Franny had never been a drinker. After what had happened with Mutt that night on Marston Street, Joanie had cut the booze out and only had an occasional beer or glass of wine when she was over at Lucy's or her parent's house. On the Fourth of July, the band went down to the beach in Salisbury and watched the fireworks after the show at the Frolics. Lenny had brought a fifth of Jim Beam with him, and when he and Mary Catherine slipped under the boardwalk, Franny took the whiskey and started slugging it back almost in rhythm with the exploding rockets above her. When the fireworks ended, she wanted to go swimming, but everyone else was beat and knew that they had two shows the next day and wanted to go. But before they could leave, Franny sprinted into the ocean, wearing the only suit she had on loan from Alley's little brother.

Jim and Michael had to go in and drag her out. Then they had to help her back to the shed. She was staggering so bad. After throwing up a few times in the backyard, she ended up sitting in the outdoor shower until she fell asleep. Jim dragged her out, soaking wet and set her in an Adirondack chair, and stayed up with her all night. When she threw up, he would help her and then set her in the chair again.

Franny awoke with the first and the worst hang-over she would ever experience. The light would jab into her brain every time she opened her eyes. Jim took her to Connie's Cozy Kitchen and ordered a large meal for Franny. She said she wasn't hungry, but Jim got her to eat most of her breakfast. Being a Dewey had the advantage of knowing what to do for a hang-over. When Da came down still drunk in the morning (almost every morning), you had to know how to make him comfortable, or he was going to make you wicked uncomfortable pretty quick-- getting food in him was a good first step.

Jim tried to play the "Franny's father is..." game. Suggesting that maybe Gorgeous George Gant was her father and was saving her from the public humiliation of having a professional wrestler as a dad or Mr. Dineen, the Baron of the Boardwalk and owner of the Hampton Casino, or maybe even Big Karl. After breakfast, they walked to the laundry mat in Hampton to wash and dry their show clothes. Franny still looked miserable when they arrived at The Frolics that night, but she was able to go on. That night Jim and Fanny walked down to the beach, alone.

Jim helped her sit in the sand and was silent as she looked out into the blackness of the Atlantic Ocean. "Why do you do this to yourself?" He asked, pretending he couldn't understand. "I don't know, I like him, I guess," Franny said sadly, thinking that no one knew what was happening in her heart. "Why?" asked Jim. "I dunno-- I just do." "You can't have him, you know," Jim pointed out, "Mary Catherine will fight you for him... and you don't want to do that." Franny started crying, covering her face with her hand, "I know." Jim slipped closer to her and held her in his arms-- he was getting good at this. They sat in the sand for a while longer, and then Jim took her to Christy's for some fried dough, and they got their instruments from the Frolics, taking the shuttle bus back to Hampton and the shed.

♫♫♫

Not only was Franny learning to play with Spindal at the beach, but she was also learning how to live with boys for the first time. The guys slept in the four bunk beds, while Franny slept on one of the couches. As hard as it was to play music with Lenny right there, it was even harder having to live with him. Alley, Jim, and Michael wore pajamas to bed, but Lenny slept in his underwear or in nothing at all. It was nothing to see him getting up in the middle of the night, his sheet wrapped around him as he stumbled over clothes and books to the bathroom. In the morning, he would get up and make coffee with his morning wood pressing through his boxer shorts.

After the second week, the shed started to smell like sweat and then cigarettes when everyone started smoking. With the raise in salary that they were being paid and no parents looking over their shoulders, all four guys took up the habit; at first, it was a few cigarettes after the show ended, and then it was packs of ciggies or butts. Franny tried it, but between the taste and the sense memory of the whiskey of the Fourth, she couldn't do more than a few puffs. The shed became a tangle of old clothes, left-over food, empty beer bottles, guitar strings, harmonicas, records, drum-sticks, musty towels, and bathing suits. Let alone the individual personal habits she had to learn to live with.

Michael, even at eighteen years old, had a heavy beard, and whenever he shaved before a show, it would always linger in the sink, fighting to not be sucked down the drain. Alley continued to pick at the acne on his face, making them more red and more irritated than before (Franny kept warning him to stay away from chocolate, but he wouldn't listen). Mary Catherine harped on him-- if he kept picking at them, he would have craters on his face for the rest of life and be even uglier. This usually would put Alley in a bad mood for the rest of the day. And then the farting and the smell in the bathroom, boys missing the toilet, leaving the door open when they were peeing-- Franny refused to even think about it.

Jim, Franny, and Michael went to the beach once, and Jim got badly sunburned. Unlike Michael and Franny, he had the Irish skin like Mary Catherine. The Dewey children were a mixture of the fair Da line and the dark, hard to burn Italian complexion. Jim found it very uncomfortable playing that night. The guitar strap painfully irritated his shoulder every time it moved. He knew from past experiences that it would eventually blister and peel. Jim's darker siblings would always tell him that he didn't try to tan correctly. They said what he should do is go out for five minutes on the first day, go out for ten minutes the second day, go out for a half-hour the next day. Jim would do it and get five minutes of sunburn on the first day, ten minutes of burn on the second day, a half-hour of sunburn on the third, and it never turned into tan; the closest it got was more freckles.

♫♫♫

Lenny strutted across the stage at the Hampton Casino Ballroom, holding the beach crowd in the palm of his hand. Mitch had seen performances like this before, but they were usually by much more seasoned performers-- Gene Vincent, Johnny Cash, Buddy Holly, Johnny Ace, and of course, Elvis. But this guy was still a kid. It was obvious that he knew what he had but did he know what it could do once he knew how to use it?

Mitch had decided after the melee at the club in Lowell to pass on Spindal, but since then, he had revisited the idea to represent them. Finally, he broke down and called that fag, Rickie Rooney, and asked him if he knew where to find Spindal. Rickie had told him that they were playing up at Hampton and Salisbury. Mitch had made the trip with the idea that if he liked them, he would think about talking to them; now, after watching half of their set, he was sure he was going to talk to them after they finished.

There was so much that could go wrong with a band-- even Mitch was never sure. It could be the level of commitment, the parents, inner-band politics, a drinking problem; one girl could set off the destruction of a whole band and the loss of any investment that he put in them. Mitch knew if he was going to represent Spindal and make them the "ones," he had to find out what perils were in store... and even then, something else could come out of nowhere and sink the whole thing. But the more he watched Lenny Suggs dance and cajole up on the stage, the more he felt that maybe these boys were the ones who could do it-- who could compete. There was just something different, something strange up on the stage. Maybe it was the little piano player; it was the way he moved, or it was the way he was on stage but still hiding... something.

♫♫♫

"Yeah, I'm sorry," Mitch started off, "I couldn't make the Lowell show, and I should have called, but I got busy..." Mitch lied; he was standing in Spindal's dressing room, Lenny, Michael, Alley, Jim, and Frankie were surrounding him. Lenny was sitting on a folding chair, with a towel over his shoulders, drying the sweat off his forehead and listening to the visitor. "You guys put on quite show," he added, trying to sound a not as excited as he really was. Mitch looked over at Michael, who had removed his shirt and was drying his armpits with another towel. Jim was bent over his hard-shell guitar case putting his instrument away; the skin on his neck was fiery red from sunburn.

The way the guitarist put his instrument in the case was like a mother putting her child to bed. "I've heard a lot of good things about you boys," Mitch added, noticing the bass player trying to comb out the cowlick in a mirror he had sported all through the show. "I would like to take you guys out sometime, and we could talk about what you want to do in the future."

The piano player kept his back to Mitch. It was obvious that he was listening intently, but he didn't seem to want to turn around. "We don't need a manager," replied Lenny as he lit a cigarette. "I'm not saying you do," replied Mitch, trying not to sound hurt, "But could I tell you what I could do for you?" "We would have to have a manager who shows up when he calls and tells me he's going to show up," said Suggs, after exhaling a plume of smoke.

The rest of the band, except for the piano player, turned and glared at Suggs, like they didn't know that he was going to be at the Lowell gig.

Mitch took a folding chair and sat down across from Lenny. "Look, you can do these gigs if you want, go from hick Massachusetts town to hick Massachusetts town, maybe travel to Manchester, New Hampshire or Hartford. You can come here every summer and play the Boston clubs a couple of times a year," Mitch explained. "Maybe even get on Community Auditions again in the next few years." All five guys cringed-- that hit home. "But you're all going to have to get day jobs. You can't support yourselves playing for a living." Mitch paused. He waited and let it sink in.

He watched the piano player walk to the bathroom and go in. "Unless you go national. Now, I'm not saying you can be successful, but I am willing to promise to help you make that step," Mitch looked around the room at the four boys left. "But you will have to listen to me and know that I'm in charge. You may have to change your act some, you might have to play some songs you don't want to play, but you still have to learn them and play them and sing them like you mean it. Like you played those songs tonight."

The guys all looked at each other, trying to read each other's thoughts. "You can do this for us?" asked Lenny, still smoking and holding the towel, "Why should we believe you?" Mitch noticed that no one requested that they wait till the piano player had come back; either he was a minor member or he was a sideman they had hired. "You shouldn't believe me. But what's your alternative? Let Rickie Rooney and Frank Conley book your shows and do the same gigs year after year, or try to go bigger?"

The guys continued to look at each other-- they had never really talked about making it a full-time job. After all, they were still in high school. Who thought of a full-time job at eighteen? "Do you think we could make a record?" asked the drummer, saying something for the first time. "Of course," replied Mitch, matter-of-factly,

"We're going to have to record something if you're going to go anywhere." This got a new round of sharing looks from the band (except for the piano player, who was still in the bathroom). Finally, Suggs had looked around enough to say, "Leave your card, and we'll talk about it, Mr. Sutherland."

Mitch stood and removed the card that he had set in his jacket pocket before entering the dressing room. "Let me know quickly. It's all going to change soon, and we're going to need to be ready," "What's gonna change soon?" asked Lenny, standing. "The music industry, it's all going to become a money-making machine, and we want to be a big part of it." Mitch noticed that the bass player was waiting outside of the bathroom for the piano player to exit. There was something wrong there. When the piano player went in, it was obvious that there was more than one stall in that bathroom. Why wouldn't the bass player enter?

Lenny extended his hand to Mitch and took his card. Once he pocketed the card, he again extended his hand. "We appreciate you comin' to the show tonight. We'll talk about it and then let you know what our answer is," said Lenny, shaking Mitch's hand. Mitch walked around the room and shook hands with all four of the guys present. He thought about waiting for the piano player to come out of the bathroom but decided he should just leave. It was strange.

♫♫♫

Joanie had driven up from Lawrence with her sister, Lucy, in Lucy's 1958 Chevy Belair, to Hampton Beach and came to the Casino Ballroom show. Since it was Wednesday, Spindal played its quick weekly gig at the Hampton Beach bandshell. Lucy and Joanie enjoyed the Casino show after Franny and Jim took them down the boardwalk for some fried clams and ice cream. While walking on the boardwalk, they ran into John Dineen, who owned The Casino Ballroom. Mr. Dineen exhorted the musical deftness of Frankie and Jimmy. Mr. Dineen looked very spiffy in his wing-tipped shoes and white striped seersucker suit topped off with a Pismo pink tie. Lucy and Joanie were very impressed with the Baron of the Boardwalk, but it also convinced Jim and Franny that Mr. Dineen wasn't her long-lost father.

It was difficult for Joanie to get over the fact that most people up at the beach thought that her beautiful daughter was a boy. The long pants and fishnet sweater and the Hush Puppy shoes made her wonder where the girl she lived with had gone while this boy was playing music at the shore? But Franny did seem to be very happy, as opposed to how heart-broken she was all last summer when she was told she couldn't join the band up here. It was an odd sort of way to get what she wanted, but neither Joanie nor Lucy could argue it didn't look like a lot of fun.

It was hard for Franny to watch Joanie and her Aunt Lucy pull out of the pebble driveway of the shed. She was still just a child, and watching her mom leave wasn't easy. But she had decided that this is what she was going to do even if it meant that she had to live at the beach with the band. Franny would call her mom every Sunday, just before they would prepare to play at the Blue Whale. Franny realized that if she was ever going to do this full time, like the way Mr. Sutherland was talking about, she was going to be leaving her mom often. Like most musicians, in a short time, she had learned to live for the hour that she and the band were on stage. All the rehearsing, setting up and tearing down of equipment, walking or taking the beach bus to gigs, hanging out with everyone at the shed was for that one hour on stage, when it all paid off. Having money was fun, but to Franny, it was all about playing music in front of the people in the audience.

The downtime at the shed could be boring. Michael had turned Franny onto J.R.R. Tolkien's "Lord of the Rings" and "The Hobbit," helping her to past some of the free time (Jim started "The Hobbit" and Alley read only the bible and Sad Sack comics). Jim and Franny had been spending a lot of time trying to write new songs. They had come up with two new ones that they played for the band. The first was called "Let's Go All Night," with the retort of "*All Right*," being the big hook. The second was called "Feel My Heart," which was pretty much Franny bidding Lenny to recognize her and Jim bidding Franny to recognize him. The band listened intently to the songs, and Lenny agreed to try them out, but he needed to make some changes first.

Jim and Franny agreed to the changes because they were not huge and were mostly just changes so that Lenny could say that all three of them wrote the song. At this point, Jim and Franny agreed to any chance of playing them so that they would have something new in the show. Unfortunately, the first time they tried them at The Frolics, Lenny (intentionally or unintentionally, who really knew with Lenny) screwed up the title and called "Feel My Heart", Smell My Fart. It broke up Lenny and the audience so that Lenny would call the song Smell My Fart for the rest of the summer. Both Jim and Franny thought it was a good song that accidentally (or not so accidentally) got a bad name.

Sometimes they would go to the Rialto in Hampton and watch movies. Usually, it would have to be the first showing of the day where they watched Elvis in It *Happened at the World's Fair*, *The Great Escape* with Steve McQueen, *Hud*, with Paul Newman, who Franny loved, and *P.T 109*, about the president, John F. Kennedy, in the war (in the Pacific, where he wasn't freezing his arse off like Da). After seeing *The Birds*, Alley would duck whenever he heard a seagull scream overhead at the beach (that film scared everyone).

The shows were good, Lenny wanted to bring Smilin' Leo up for a show, but Big Karl at the Kon Tiki made it clear that their blind chauffer could stay with the car, and the management of The Frolics also made it clear that the "Negro" bluesman could also stay with the car. Though Leo had a big reception from the kids in the audience, the adults in town also had their own reaction, and since The Frolics had to continue to carry a liquor license, they chose the license over the black harmonica player.

What the band was learning this summer was living together. It is always difficult to learn to first live with people who are not your family, but it is even harder when you know that you have to work together. At first, there had always been a politeness in the room when Franny was present, but as the summer wore on, the fellows became much more casual with their language. When there was a time that the masturbation jokes and woman jokes would be kept between the boys, now it was tossed off at dinner without a thought. Franny looked to Mary Catherine, who had been brought up with boys all her life and always held her own in their company.

Mary Catherine had the crazy unpredictability factor on her side, which Franny could never hope to have. You could say or do anything in front of Mary Catherine, but be prepared for some over-the-top response, like the Christmas Da beating, if she disagreed with your point. Franny found that boys tended to fart a lot more than girls, or at the least, enjoy it more. All bodily functions were much more entertaining for boys than for girls. Yes, when Michael used the bathroom, you would probably be smart if you could wait ten minutes before going in. Franny learned to ignore the bunk bed shaking on any given night and just pretended it wasn't happening, even if Lenny asked the bed's occupant what's he was doing down there. Franny tried to encourage daily showers in the outdoor shower stall to keep the B.O. stink down, especially after shows. She cleaned and made some meals and was surprised to find that Michael was much more house-helpful than any of the other boys. His mom was demanding that her boys help out in the house as they had to help out at the bar.

On the weekends there were always many guests. It wasn't unusual to come back from a Friday night or Saturday night show and find people scattered across the floor, sleeping. House rule: The band members got the beds-- no arguments. Michael's brothers visited during the week most of the time since Barnaby's big days were on the weekends, and they were working a man short. What Michael had realized to his amazement was that his dad, Pudge, wished that his kids would do better than him and find a real career rather than being a bar owner. As long as Michael made a living making music, he could get out of his family bar commitments. Pudge had always been so proud of the business he built himself; Michael had always contended that it was his destiny to follow in his father's footsteps. Michael was very surprised after his dad attended a few of their shows and how he was very easily letting his son step away from the family business.

Bridie and other girlfriends of Mary Catherine would usually visit and stay the night with her and Lenny. Lenny and Mary Catherine kept most of their love-making to under the boardwalk in Salisbury or occasionally in the backseat of someone's car. One night, after a Friday night show, when the beach was hit with a downpour rain, she stayed in the shed with the band, in Lenny's bed. Everyone had bunked down for the night when the sounds of Lenny and Mary Catherine's lovemaking competed with the gentle tapping of the rain outside.

At first, it was muffled and just some rustling of covers, but quickly it picked up to a storm of passion. To add to the rhythmic bed-shaking was that Mary Catherine, as it was written on the locker doors and the walls of the boy's bathroom stalls of Lawrence High School, was a *moaner,* a loud moaner. Now everyone in the shed was pretty sure that Mary Catherine and Lenny were doing it... and they wished that they would do it more quietly.

Jim leaned down from his bed on the top bunk over Alley and watched Franny's reaction, who was nestled in a blanket on the couch where she slept. He knew how she felt about Lenny and how this scene must be ripping into her heart. "Oh, Oh, Oh," moaned his little sister. Franny kept her eyes closed and pretended it wasn't happening, that it wasn't Lenny who was making love to Mary Catherine Dewey.

She tried to pretend that she was somewhere else, somewhere peaceful, somewhere where Mary Catherine wasn't moaning loudly, and the sound of Mary Catherine's head wasn't gently banging off of the bed's headboard, it wasn't echoing over the falling rain outside. Jim tried to put out of his mind that the moaning was his sister's and that it was giving him a boner. Alley pretended to be disgusted in the animal act, as much as he was fascinated by what was happening in the bed across from him and what was happening in his mind-- Alley was also kind of thrilled when Mary Catherine had added a bunch of "Oh God, oh God, " as she came closer to climax. It was only the only time that "God" was mentioned in the shed all summer. Michael tried his best not to laugh out loud.

The next day a new house rule was made that there was to be no co-sleeping when the band was trying to get some shut-eye. This, of course, didn't stop the fornicating in the shed. Once, after coming back from breakfast at Connie's Cozy Kitchen, Franny, Alley, and Jim walked in on Michael and Bridie in the middle of the act. When Alley tried to establish a new house rule about no fornicating in the shed all summer, Michael threw a shoe at him, and they left, waiting outside until Michael and Bridie had finished.

Jim had tried to make some girls that summer. He had talked a little to one of the waitresses at Connie's Cozy Kitchen, an older woman of twenty-seven, named Patty. Patty was aware of the band and actually had seen them play a couple of times over the last two summers. Jim invited her to a Saturday night show at The Frolics and told her that she should come backstage after. Patty did attend the show but arrived with her boyfriend, Ross. Jim pretended to greet them warmly, but he and Ross knew exactly why Jim had invited her backstage... and Patty probably was aware of Jim's intentions, also.

There was also Sandra, a shy seeming, bat-faced girl, who came to a lot of the shows at Pete's Blue Whale and would stand at Jim's side of the stage. Sandra would smile at Jim whenever he looked out at the crowd, and unlike most of the girls at the shows, she didn't scream for Lenny. After a Sunday night show, Sandra was waiting outside of the club, at the back door.

Jim took Sandra out for a slice of pizza at Tripoli and then a Frosty ice cream cone. Sandra suggested that they go down to the beach and listen to the waves roll in; eventually, they ended up under the boardwalk. Jim looked for his sister and Lenny, when he convinced himself that they weren't screwing down there, he found himself kissing Sandra. It was the first time that he had kissed a girl other than his sisters and his mom. Sandra stuck her tongue in his mouth, and it surprised him, but it did feel good, and he let himself enjoy the warmth of her mouth. As she kissed him more, Sandra took his hand and placed it on her firm, left breast. Jim squeezed and rubbed her breast, making Sandra moan. Not a Mary Catherine moan, but a small, muffled moan.

Jim continued to kiss Sandra in the dark but maybe because she had small breasts like Franny or maybe because it was so dark in the sand, and he couldn't see her face, she became Franny in his imagination, even being aroused, he suddenly felt that he had to leave. That it wasn't fair to Sandra to kiss her and be thinking of Franny even if it was Franny he wanted to be kissing. Jim knew he wanted to kiss Franny and that kissing Sandra or whatever this was going to lead to in the darkness under the Salisbury boardwalk wasn't going to be kissing Franny. It wasn't going to be anything, but lust, and Jim realized that that wasn't going fulfill him in any way.

"I'm sorry," he said when he stopped kissing Sandra. Her face, what he could see in the dark, looked devastated, like this wasn't what she expected to happen when they went under the boardwalk. He stood up and made his way through the sand, to the beach, and then back up onto the boardwalk and fast-walked all the way back to the shuttle bus to Hampton and the shed. Franny was there, reading a paperback copy of "To Kill a Mocking Bird," alone in her bed on one of the couches. Franny had already read the book a couple of times, but she liked to go back and read of Scout and her honest pa, Atticus Finch. They stayed up and played guitars together, trying to work out a new song. They didn't find a song that night, but Jim enjoyed playing and singing with Franny. It was even better than kissing Sandra.

Sandra stopped coming to the shows after the boardwalk rejection. Then suddenly, just before Labor Day, she appeared in the audience again-- this time standing on the other side of Lenny, in front of Alley and his Epiphone bass. One night after coming home from riding the Himalaya at Shaheen's Fun-O-Rama, Jim, Michael, and Franny walked in on a couple screwing in the shed. Thinking that it was Mary Catherine and Lenny, they turned the light on (Mary Catherine would still sleepover with Lenny and was very casual about walking around naked in front of her brother, Franny, and the other boys) to find Alley in the middle of copulating with Sandra, who screamed and ran into the bathroom. It took Alley, Franny, and Michael ten minutes to get her out of the bathroom. Jim needed to use it and had to pee against the side of the shed as the others coaxed Sandra out of the can. Alley promised everyone he would go to confession the next day. The others suggested that he go and help Sandra get dressed and do what he wanted to on Sunday. As bad as Alley felt about getting caught with Sandra, it's not like he stopped seeing her. He did like most Catholics do and went to confession-- in fact, he became a regular at Saint Elizabeth's.

♫♫♫

Tuesdays were special for Lenny. Almost every Tuesday, Rickie would pick him up in his Cutlass, and they would go to the beach, or to a movie at the Rialto, or on the rides at Fun-O-Rama. Then Rickie would take Lenny to a late lunch at Howard Johnson's or Sam's Steak Out, and after they would find a quiet place to park the car, and they would kiss. Lenny hoped that it would go farther than that, but when he reached for Rickie, Rickie would stop him and eventually take him to The Frolics at Salisbury Beach to join the band for their show that night.

The Tuesday night shows became more distracted and detached. Lenny was singing the songs as they had all summer, but there was something missing in the show. Mostly, he was just going through the actions. He seemed to be thinking of something else. What the other members of the band didn't know was that he was thinking about Rickie and their afternoon together. Lenny couldn't understand why Rickie wouldn't allow him to go further with a physical relationship. Mary Catherine was easy…easy in giving sex, easy in getting sex.

Rickie didn't seem interested in anything but kissing. Granted, the kissing was wonderful, but Lenny wanted to take it further. He was anxious to see what a relationship with another man would be like, what the sex would be like, but it didn't seem that Rickie wanted to do it with him. It was the only time that Lenny could remember where he was refused sex, where he felt frustrated. Most times, he was the victim of unwanted advances (like Father Nelson). This one time, he wanted something to happen, and he was rebuffed.

Lenny asked Franny to go for a walk with him on the beach after one of their Tuesday shows, so they could talk. Franny jumped at the chance. It being the middle of the week, and Mary Catherine had to be back in Lawrence to work at W.T. Grant where she was hired in the woman's clothes department (the store taking the "keep your friends close but keep your suspects closer" approach with her. She was mostly there to identify and scare less-accomplished shoplifters), and so Franny wasn't in any real danger till Thursday. Lenny and Franny walked along the shoreline, the waves lapping at their bare feet. Jim watched them from the boardwalk until Michael coaxed him to go to Christy's for a fried dough.

They walked and talked, eventually ending up back at the boardwalk, where Lenny grabbed Franny by the hands and dragged her into the dark. He pulled her to him and, in a complete re-enactment of her many dreams and fantasies, kissed her passionately. Lenny pulled her deeper under the wooden walkway and continued to kiss her like she had seen him kiss Mary Catherine. He pulled her down to the cool sand, and they continued to make-out. Franny reveled in the warmth of his tongue in her mouth, his hands moving up and down her body. She could feel him unbuttoning her shirt, and she pulled away so that she could pull her sweater over her head. Once off, Franny smiled, and they kissed passionately again.

Lenny ran his hands into her shirt, under the t-shirt, and then under her bra, the one that pushed her boobs tightly against her chest. Franny could feel her bra and t-shirt being pushed up over her breasts, and Lenny leaned down and kissed her left nipple. The thrill ripped through her body. She had never felt anything like this before. Suddenly, Lenny's hands were in her pants and rubbing her lubricated privates. She closed her eyes and started to help him pull down her pants and underpants. "Wait, wait," whispered Lenny, removing his hands from her. "Here, this would be better," he murmured, as he undid his belt and unsnapped his own pants.

Lenny pulled his pants down, his erection standing out in the moonlight drifting through the cracks in the boardwalk overhead. Franny was surprised. She had never seen a penis this fully erect. She had seen Slim's that night at her house, the bulge of the morning wood from the boys in the band, but this seemed to be a whole other appendage.

Franny looked at Lenny's erection, not really sure what he wanted to do. She had heard about intercourse, but she thought it just happened. Naturally, you weren't left looking at this thing like some monster out of a science fiction movie. Lenny grabbed the back of her head and said, "Blow me." Franny was confused and disoriented; this being her first sexual experience, her pants and underpants were half-way down her legs, gathering sand in them. Lenny was pulling her head to his penis. Franny recognized the phrase, "Blow me," but it was something that guys usually said to other guys. She wasn't sure what it meant when a guy said it to a girl; she had some vague idea about puffing on him. "Put your mouth on it," instructed Lenny harshly.

"Put my mouth on what?" thought Franny, the movie monster? Lenny pulled her head to his prick as she tried to push away. "Please," moaned Lenny, still pulling her head to the head of his penis. Slowly, Franny relented and let it slide into her mouth like a rocket-pop.

"Suck on it," Lenny instructed, "Up and down, up and down." Franny raised and lowered her head, feeling the stiff skin in her mouth. "Watch your teeth," warned Lenny, realizing that Franny had never done this, "Up and down, let your tongue run over it." Franny continued until suddenly something flowed out of the erect cock and into her mouth. Franny stopped and looked up at Lenny, hoping it was over. "Don't stop, don't stop. I'm almost there," coaxed Lenny, sounding urgent. Franny spit some of the pre-cum out of her mouth, and Lenny pushed her head down to continue. Franny went up and down on Lenny's stiff organ when suddenly an explosion went off in her mouth, leaving her choking on his orgasm. Lenny withered, climaxing. Franny raised her head and spat out what shot into her mouth into the sand. She looked at him, lying in the sand, with a look of complete exaltation.

"Come here," he said. Lenny pulled Franny to him. Franny spit some of the remains of Lenny's load out into the sand and decided that if she got anything out of this, it would be to lie with him now. She rested her head on his chest as he breathed deeply and enjoyed the post-ejaculation. Franny laid in the sand. Her pants and underpants were down around her ankles, her white button-down shirt open, and her repudiated bra was pushed up over her exposed breasts. "Thank you," whispered Lenny, kissing her forehead. Franny waited in anticipation for her first time to arrive. It didn't happen that night.

♫♫♫

The summer started to drag on. They played their shows at night and in the afternoons on the weekends. The sorority girls from U-Mass Amherst pretty much kept to themselves. At first, the guys thought it might be a goldmine but, unfortunately, after Alley confessed that three of them had just graduated from high school and the other two were under-classmen. When they realized the boys of Spindal were younger than they were, they lost interest, and none of the girls ever came to a show. Once, they invited Jim and Frankie over to play their guitars for them, but beyond that, they hardly saw each other. The other thing was that Spindal played most nights and the girls went to the beach most of the time, so it was just a passing acquaintance as most sorority girls would be.

Lenny kept meeting Rickie every Tuesday, and then he would play a detached show and meet Franny under the boardwalk for some inter-band head. For Franny, the thrill started to wear off when she realized that it probably wasn't going any further than fellatio when Mary Catherine wasn't available. A couple of times, she tried to avoid Lenny after the show but would find herself waiting on the boardwalk until Lenny showed up.

Jim was aware that Franny was meeting Lenny after the show. It stabbed at him, but what could he do? The real problem was that Franny couldn't concentrate on anything else but Lenny, so the songwriting was going to waste. It was a shame because they had so much extra time on their hands, but Jim could see her watching Lenny or concerned about where Lenny and Mary Catherine, or Michael, or Alley, or Rickie had gone with him. Lenny had said that he had spoken a couple of times with the manager, and he was going to get them some work after the summer was over. Jim really wanted to go and talk to Leo. He had so much on his mind, but it didn't seem like anyone he was living with would be interested.

On Thursday, Michael, Alley, and Jim decided to go to an afternoon showing "It's a *Mad, Mad, Mad, World* at the Rialto." At first, Franny was going to go with them until she realized that Lenny was going to be home alone in the shed. Lenny said that he had to go make a phone call to his mom to see if Mitch had called, looking for him. Lenny would have to walk to the payphone in the Ashworth Hotel lobby to make his call.

Lenny was laying on his bed in only in his boxer shorts after the other guys left for the movies, reading the liner notes to an album of a new record that Mary Catherine had nicked (It was one of the few things that she had nicked from W.T. Grant since she started working there), called *Live At The Apollo*, *James Brown and the Famous Flames*. Franny got up and went into the bathroom. Once inside, she decided that this was it; she was going to do it.

When she stepped out of the bathroom naked, Lenny didn't even look up. She walked to him, trying not to look embarrassed. "I want to make love to you," she said. Lenny lowered his album, and his eyes grew wide. "I don't think it's a good idea to do this here." Franny slid in beside him on the bed. "It's better than under the boardwalk. Or am I your stand-in for Mary Catherine?" Lenny smiled at her sweetly, the way she hoped he would. "No, of course, you're not. It's just that it can be really messy for us if anyone else found out." She reached down for his prick, and she could feel that it was becoming hard, "Do it now, or I'll never go under there again with you." This was a complete, if not weak, lie. She hoped that he would do it now because there was no way that she wouldn't meet him under the Salisbury boardwalk if he asked her. Franny suddenly realized how pathetically deep she was in.

Lenny looked at her, those blue eyes looking close to crying if he didn't fuck her. He leaned over and kissed her. She grabbed at his prick. He reached between her legs.

♫♫♫

Lenny turned away from the audience at the Hampton Casino and turned to Frankie, who was smiling at him, enjoying his singing and his showmanship. Lenny had also like to think that she enjoyed his cocksmanship earlier in the day. He smiled at Frankie, and she almost lost her place in the song. She knew she couldn't stop smiling, even knowing that tomorrow night Mary Catherine would be back and there would be no way their lovemaking could happen again until Monday. But whenever Franny thought of that, she would think about that wonderful afternoon when they made love-- twice.

It was pretty obvious to Jim that Franny and Lenny had finally done it. He wasn't sure when, but he was pretty sure (as he was with Mary Catherine) that they had screwed. As much as it hurt Jim, he was glad that she finally had the man she wanted. How could you not want a friend to be loved by the one she loved? Maybe now they could get back to songwriting?

♫♫♫

The end of the summer was near, it was Labor Day, and the sorority girls from U-Mass were preparing for a large end-of-the-summer bash. The guys had gone to the State Line package store to help the girls get two kegs of Narragansett beer and ice, leaving Franny alone with Mary Catherine and Bridie. Franny decided that she would take her shower now, and that way, when the guys came back, they could use the outside shower before they would go to the show that night at the Casino.

Franny removed her clothes in the bathroom and only wore a towel out to the shower stall in the back of the shed. She turned the shower on and thought about how it made her anxious having Mary Catherine in the shed. It made her skin crawl thinking about what would happen if Mary Catherine found out that she was seeing Lenny, also. Lenny and Franny had only been together another time since the shed tryst. It was under the boardwalk, and it was really uncomfortable-- the sand got in everywhere. Franny couldn't stop thinking about the first time until she heard the half-door of the shower open and shut behind her.

Franny turned to see Mary Catherine in front of her, in one of Lenny's undershirts. "You don't mind if I shower with ya?" asked Mary Catherine, so innocently, "I wanna get the sand out of my crack." Mary Catherine quickly pulled the undershirt over her head. "I'm in here," Franny murmured. Mary Catherine swung the undershirt over the side of the shower. "Come on, Frankie? It's just us two girls," she said, stepping under the shower stream. Franny pushed away from her, stepping into a corner. Mary Catherine let the water run down over her face and naked body. Franny realized that Mary Catherine's breasts were much fuller than she had noticed. "You are a true blonde? I would never guess you were," commented Mary Catherine, stepping closer to Franny. Franny didn't know what to do... or what to say. She just kept backing up against the wall of the shower. Mary Catherine blocked her into the corner, "Have ya ever thought about kissing a girl, Frankie?"

Franny pushed up against the side of the shower. She could feel the green scum on the wood rub against the back of her leg. Mary Catherine moved closer to her, with her heavy pink-tipped tits resting on Franny's. "No," answered Franny, stuck between Mary Catherine and the wall. "It could be nice, don't ya think?" she asked, more as a threat than a seduction. Mary Catherine began soaping

Franny's breasts with a bar of soap, rubbing her thumbs gently around Franny's areolas. "I don't think so," said Franny, feeling Mary Catherine's hand going between her legs. "Does this feel good?" "Please-- I'm going to scream," whimpered Franny. "No, you're not," whispered Mary Catherine, "You're supposed to be a guy. You're not gonna tell people I was fingerin' your twat?" That was when Mary Catherine slipped her soapy finger up Franny's vagina.

Franny's eyes bugged out, she wanted to scream, but she knew she could never explain what was happening and what she had been doing all summer dressed as a boy. She held her breath as Mary Catherine moved her finger in and out of Franny's vagina. "This is strange. I've never done this before," whispered Mary Catherine. The shower water ran over her shoulders, splashing Franny in the face.

"Please," Franny begged. "I thought maybe I could tell if you were a virgin or not?" Mary Catherine pulled her hand from Franny's loins and checked her fingers. "I don't see any blood. There's supposed to be blood, isn't there?" "I don't know," moaned Franny, trying to push Mary Catherine off her. "Who took your cherry, Frankie?" "No one," replied Franny, pushing as hard as she could to get Mary Catherine off her. "Was it my retard brother? No, it couldn't be him-- He would be fuckin' you right now if he could." Franny was able to push her off, Mary Catherine's feet sliding on the wet boards of the shower floor. Mary Catherine reached up and grabbed the door to the shower to hold it closed.

"It had better be one of the other guys," she warned, "I find out your spendin' time with Leonard, my finger will probably be the smallest thing going up your cunt." Mary Catherine glared at Franny, burning fear into her brain. Franny turned quickly and pushed the door to the shower open and ran, covering her breasts and blond pubic patch the best she could with her hands. Fortunately, most of the sorority girls were with the boys at the packie. Franny ran naked into the shed and directly into the bathroom, slamming the door behind her. "I thought M.C. was taking a shower?" asked Bridie, looking up from the movie magazine she was reading. Franny didn't answer. She sat on the toilet and cried silently into her hand.

♫♫♫

"On the piano, Frankie Walsh," announced Lenny to the crowd of The Frolics. "On the drums," Michael did some quick rolls, followed by cymbal crashes, "Mister Michael Webster." "On the bass, the one, the only, Alley Gould," Alley slapped out a bass scale as the crowd applauded (which he screwed up mid-way through). "To my left, on the gee-tar, we call him Strings, but his mom calls him, Jim Dewey," followed by another round of loud applause, as Jim made the Gretsch squeal. Jim stepped to the microphone, as he had done all summer long, and announced, "Your host tonight, Lenny Suggs." A much louder ovation rattled through the club. Lenny smiled sweetly and said into the microphone, "Thank you, Hampton. We've had a wonderful summer in your town. We all thank you for having us." The band stopped playing and walked to the front of the stage, taking a final bow together. That was it, it was over. They would break down their equipment and go back to the shed for one last night and then head back to Lawrence tomorrow.

The ride back to Lawrence in Frenchy's woody was quiet, as everyone reflected on the summer and how the band performed. Alley had to start classes at the University of Lowell in a few days (he also had to see a doctor about the burning feeling he when he peed), Michael knew he was going back to picking up beer and liquor for Barnaby's (and had to find some way to avoid Bridie whenever he saw her), Jim wanted to see Leo and tell him about the summer and their shows (he knew he had to buckle down and do better in school since he skipped summer school. If he did as poorly as he did last year, he might not graduate), Franny was determined to never see Mary Catherine again (It was going to be hard because Mary Catherine had shown her the schedule of classes for this term and she and Franny shared more than a few classes-- one of which was gym).

Lenny sat in front with Frenchy, but he wasn't thinking about what was going to happen; he was remembering what had happened a few days before. It was his eighteenth birthday; during the show at Pete's Blue Whale, Lenny noticed Rickie sitting in the back (who could miss that smile?), nursing his drink. Rickie came backstage after the show and waited for Lenny to finish dressing. Rickie had told the other boys that he had promised to take Lenny back to Lawrence so that Lenny could apply to Northern Essex Community College (this kind of caught everyone off guard since Lenny had never mentioned going back to school, in fact, he was desperate in making the band his career so he wouldn't have to go back to school).

They didn't go back to Lawrence in the Cutlass, they went straight back to Medford and to Rickie's apartment. Rickie had left a casserole in the oven and opened a bottle of Pinot Grigio. After dinner there was cake, with eighteen candles and after that was the real dessert.

Lenny realized that Rickie wasn't toying with him. He was just waiting for him to become legal. What happened in Rickie's bedroom that night would always be the gold standard of lovemaking to Lenny? Where Mary Catherine plowed through sex like a spider monkey on fire, Rickie was in control, measured but with a quiet, sincere passion. Lenny was left drained and fulfilled; it was like when the band was cookin', and even the audience had hopped on the vibe. Rickie cooked him eggs for breakfast and took him back to the beach in time for the show at the Kon Tiki. Lenny learned things that night that Northern Essex Community College would never teach him.

♫♫♫

Jim was kind of relieved to get back home. At the same time, he was surprised that home had not changed all that much while he was gone for three months. Mary Catherine was again "almost getting the sand out her crack." His Ma said he had grown and was starting to get the first hairs of a beard, but the rest of the family seemed the same.

Jim took his Sears Harmony Supertone to Essex Street in front of the W.T. Grant, where Smilin' Leo was playing his old Guild T-50, a harmonica rack hanging off his neck. "Hey Strings," Leo yelled when he recognized Jim's footsteps. Jim had to chase away a few pre-adolescent boys who were trying to silently scoop some of Leo's earnings. Jim tuned up his acoustic, and they began to play a few Woody, B.B., Howlin' Wolf and Chuck Berry songs, while pedestrians dropped more coins into Leo's battered guitar case. "Strings, watch me play this one with my eyes closed-- let me know if ya catch me peeking." It felt good to be home.

During a break, Jim wanted to tell Leo all about the summer and playing every single night and how good the band had got, but all Leo wanted to do was tell Jim about his trip to Washington. He, Addie, and some of the parishioners of the Third Baptist Church, on Warren Street, that they attended, traveled to Washington D.C. for "The March on Washington for Jobs and Freedom." They had taken buses and joined over two hundred thousand other people at the Lincoln Memorial.

Leo told him of the many different kinds of people he and Addie had talked to that day and the music that was played by Mahalia Jackson, who had a beautiful voice and sang the old spiritual, *How I Got Over*. There was this young girl, Joan Baez, and how wonderful voice her was (Jim wanted to tell him that he and Franny had met Joan at the Club 47, but it was wicked hard, almost impossible, to interrupt Leo when he got going) and this young man, who sounded like just Woody Guthrie. The young man's name was Bob Dylan. Jim knew this was just Leo getting carried away, and no one sounded like Woody.

Leo told Jim of the speeches by John Lewis and Roy Wilkins and many others whose names he couldn't remember, how Rosa Parks herself was standing up on the steps of the Lincoln Memorial and how Doctor Martin Luther King junior gave a rousing speech about a dream he had where his children were judged on the measure of their character and not the color of their skin. Leo hopped up and down, and there was a light sheen of spit on his lips as Leo spoke with jubilant enthusiasm, remembering this monumental trip.

After Leo finished his story about his trip to Washington, Jim was left with empty answers to his questions about the band and the gigs at the beach. He had so wanted Leo to come back up to the beach, but Lenny and Rickie didn't think it was a good idea that they bring him on again, and Jim certainly didn't want anything bad to happen to Leo when he was visiting him. Jim was somewhat oblivious to the world around him (he still didn't understand that whole Cuba/Russia thing), but he wasn't totally unaware that Leo was a black man in a white man's world (and if he did, Da was there to remind him that none of his kids would be "nigger-lovers" with the ol' how-do-you-do) and there were places where Leo was allowed and not allowed. There might not have been any signs about no colored in Massachusetts, but the signs were there; even Leo could see them. They played for a few hours, and Leo took Jim home to Addie and Ruby for some down-home cookin'.

♫♫♫

Franny was glad to be back from the beach. It was a little difficult getting used to sleeping next to her mom again, but her absence had made Joanie a little more appreciative of having her around. Franny was very disappointed with how the summer ended. She wanted to talk to Lenny, to see if Mary Catherine had said anything to him about their time together. She figured that since Mary Catherine hadn't attacked her since the day in the shower, that Mary Catherine wasn't totally convinced she and Lenny had been together. If Lenny had told Mary Catherine, she certainly would have been in trouble, and she didn't want to approach Lenny taking a chance that that would raise Mary Catherine's suspicions. Lenny hadn't made any attempts to get together with her since the time under the boardwalk, and that wasn't even memorable. The only thing that she could do was get ready for a new year of school.

One night when they were watching The Patty Duke Show, Joanie asked if she was still a virgin. Feeling trapped and not wanting to own up to her illicit affair with Lenny, she lied and said she was. She hoped her mom wouldn't use Mary Catherine's method of confirming whether she was or she was not. They watched the end of the show and went to bed. Franny worried about becoming pregnant; they had used what Lenny called "skins" that Mary Catherine nicked from Rexall (Rexall was still on the table since she didn't work there), but Franny wasn't sure that the balloon-like things would make sure she wouldn't have a baby. A baby could really screw up the band.

♫♫♫

The Town Line House is on the line of Alston and Lynnfield, on Route One. A large white colonial house with plantation columns. Mitch huddled with his new clients, Lenny, Alley, and Michael, at a table. They had just finished lunch when Mitch cleared his throat, "I need to know who writes your songs?" The guys looked at each other anxiously. Alley injected, "Jim.... and..." he glanced over at Lenny, who gave him a nod. "Jim," he continued, "And Lenny. They wrote the songs." "Do you have these songs written down?" Mitch asked Lenny. "Yeah, we've got them. But most of them aren't that good."

Mitch took a sip of his second martini and replied, "You've got more songs than the ones you played up at the beach?" "We've got a few more," answered Lenny, sipping on a large beer in a mug, "They're hard to write." "I know, but it would be good to have an original song. Rather than just doing someone else's songs." "We've got no problems with covers," said Lenny, self-assuredly. "Oh, and one more thing," offered Mitch, "You've got to get rid of the girl." Lenny started coughing. The beer having gone up inside his nose.

"What, girl?" Lenny asked after he recovered from his choking. "The piano player. You have to get rid of her. You're a boy band... and if you haven't noticed, she's not a boy." The guys looked at each other, realizing that they've been caught. "We really like having Franny. She's a wicked good piano player," offered Lenny, weakly. "I don't care. I can't sell a group with a girl in it. It has to be all boys. If you want a piano player, get a piano player; just make sure he has a dick." Their food arrived, the waiter placed a plate in front of each member of Spindal and Mitch. "Jim's not going to be happy," added Alley, a bit happy that Jim wouldn't be. "Where is your guitar player?" asked Mitch, cutting into his white fish. "He's in school," answered Alley, "He's in high school still."

Mitch stopped eating and looked at the other boys. "You mean he's not of legal age?" "No, I guess not," answered Alley, realizing that he may have made a mistake. "His parents are cool," assured Lenny, hoping that this wasn't the end of lunch. "Yeah, cool," seconded Michael, suspiciously so. "If I need to have his parents sign this contract. Is there going to be a problem?" Mitch asked. "No, problem. Jim's parents are really easy," continued Lenny, as the spokesman. "Yeah, wicked easy," added Michael, following it by laughing into his beer mug. Alley couldn't help laughing at Michael's crack at Da.

"Is this going to be a problem?" probed Mitch. "No, it won't be a problem. Believe me, Jim's dad doesn't care," replied Lenny, trying to calm any fears that Mitch may have had. Mitch looked to Alley and Michael, who were trying hard not to laugh. "Am I going to have trouble getting Jim's father to sign the contract?" asked Mitch, sounding very serious. "Buy him a few drinks, and he'll sign anything," Alley spitted out, busting up in laughter. "Yeah, he'll love signing his name," added Michael, also laughing, "X."

Lenny reached over and touched Mitch's hand, comforting and friendly, "Mr. Sutherland, Jim's dad will sign the papers. Don't worry-- I'm sure of it." Mitch looked at the boys, trying to determine how difficult this chore will be. Finally, he went back to his meal. "I've got you a gig at the Paramount Theatre in November." The boys stopped eating and smiled. "The Paramount in Boston," confirmed Alley, knowing that this was the top of the mountain of Boston's live clubs. "That's right, we've got to get ready. It will be right before Thanksgiving. We've got to get to work." Lenny glanced over at the two guys and smiled-- it looked like they had a deal. "Get rid of the piano player. You're a boy's band," instructed Mitch Sutherland, their new manager.

♫♫♫

Lenny felt terrible about meeting with Mitch, so much so that he talked with Rickie about Mitch representing them. Rickie had congratulated him on Mitch taking them on. Rickie was only a booking agent and really didn't have any ambition to be a manager. He liked getting gigs for his bands, but he wasn't comfortable in the career planning end of the business. When he told bands that he had a job for them, they were always happy, but he never had to tell a band that they had gone to the apex of where they could go. Rickie hated being the bearer of bad news to his clients. He liked being the hero. Spindal's meeting with Mitch was good news to Rickie.

Rickie was familiar with Mitch, and he had told Lenny that Mitch's family owned a successful jazz record store in Harvard Square called "Dizzy's." Mitch had branched out and signed some jazz artists who got deals, some on Blue Note Records.

Rickie had heard that Mitch had gone to London to check out some of their groups and had traveled up and down the English coast for a bit looking for talent. Rickie had also heard that Mitch had been involved with some artists in England, from Liverpool. Lenny was relieved to find out that Rickie was actually happy for him and the band. Rickie had also warned him to be careful, maybe, have an attorney look over the contract before they signed anything. Lenny didn't know any attorneys, or lawyers, that didn't go to court with you when you got arrested.

♫♫♫

Jim felt sick to his stomach, walking down the hall to Franny and Joanie's apartment. He still didn't know why he had to tell Franny that she was out of the band again. Lenny had said that he was her best friend and that she would take it best from her friend, Jim. Jim didn't think she was going to take any better from him than she would take it from Lenny. Actually, she would probably be honored that Lenny came all the way over to her house to tell her that the new manager didn't want her in the band. Well, maybe not honored.

It went just as he remembered it went the first time. She cried, she swore, she kicked things, she cried some more. The only good thing that came out of it was that he got to hold and comfort her when she was crying. Poor Franny-- she loved playing live so much and added so much to the sound of the band, whether she was playing the guitar or the piano, or even just backing up the vocalist. She was so talented and so good, but there seemed to be no place for her in the group. Jim sat with her, and they watched American Bandstand. When he left her, she was still crying and deeply disappointed.

♫♫♫

Franny laid in the double bed with her mom asleep next to her. She wished she could get up and beat herself with the practice keyboard. Franny didn't believe that Mitch didn't want her in the band. She was sure that Lenny had asked Jim to tell her that they couldn't have her in the group because he was afraid of Mary Catherine finding out about them, and so it was safer to just fire her. It was all her fault that they kicked her out. She felt so stupid. What was she going to do now?

♫♫♫

This was the first band practice that Mitch, their new manager, was at. Mitch had been given copies of the songs that Jim and Franny had written, including "I'm Not Here." Mitch had gone through the songs looking for one that they could record as a demonstration record. He would take one song at a time and have Lenny sing it, while Jim accompanied him on the piano. Mitch wanted to hear the songs with just the melody and the words. Jim still played the piano every once in a while, really not wanting to forget how. He thought he sounded a little rusty, but then, on the other hand, Mitch is the one who fired Franny. They went through the songs, and finally, Mitch decided to use "Let's Go All Night."

Lenny agreed with Mitch, and so they played it through a few times with the whole band. Jim played it as he usually played it, but he didn't really feel that "Let's Go All Night" was a good song for a record. It was a good song for a show like *Last Kiss, We're Having a Party,* and *Quarter to Three,* but it wasn't a song that Jim thought would sound good on a record. After they finished, Mitch asked Jim and Lenny if they could come up with another song-- at least try to. This sounded like a good idea, but Jim hadn't really written any of the songs with Lenny. He had written them all with Franny, but Franny wasn't in the band anymore, and Jim was pretty sure she wasn't going to help write any more songs.

After the rehearsal, the guys went upstairs and had a tonic and Oreos. Mitch got to meet Lenny's mom, Louise, who, ever since Lenny returned from the beach, had been spending more time at home, even when Harry went out of town on business. Lenny was somewhat bitter that he spent most of his teen years alone, and now when he could use some time to himself, his mom wanted to hang around the house. After leaving the band at Lenny's, Mitch had understood how the writing worked with the band. The songs they had were adequate, but it was obvious that Jim was the writer and that Lenny added whatever he needed to feel comfortable singing the song. Mitch knew he had work something out with Jim as far as publishing rights and song credits. He had a good idea of where to start.

♫♫♫

Da sat at the bar of The Toiler's Club. Da usually wasn't encouraged to patronize The Toiler's Club, but this evening he had entered with an unknown man, who incidentally was wearing a suit and tie. Da was here because this guy, Mitchell, offered to buy him dinner (and of course, dinner usually included drinks-- if you're invited) because he wanted to talk to him about his boy, Jim.

Da was trying to figure out this guy's angle while Mitchell was in the bathroom. The beer at The Toiler's (or The Toilet Club, as it was known to most of the mill men) tasted good. It tasted expensive, even though it was just Schlitz on tap. It had been tough on Da since his Little Jew Boy came back from the beach, Jimmy had money, but he wasn't giving Da anymore since he wasn't working regularly. Patrick had a girlfriend, and so he wasn't dropping any bills in his father's lap, either. Michael was doing the best he could, and Kevin had just started working for the city, that could be good money there. Mary Catherine was working at Grants, but he wasn't asking that crazy bitch for anything (too much of her mother in her). Da considered himself lucky to have run into Mr. Sutherland. He could use the meal (and the drink that went with it, naturally).

"Sorry about that. I had to shake out the pants-snake," joked Mitch. "Thankee, Mr. Sutherland," said Da, raising his beer mug to him, "Slainte." Mitch tapped his glass with Da, "Slainte." Mitch had no idea what "Slainte" meant, but who was he to argue with a real Irishman. "So what I can do for ya?" asked Da, leaning closer to Mitch. "Let's order something to eat first," offered Mitch. "Don't mind if I do," agreed Da.

They ordered two steaks. Da liked sitting at the bar, so they didn't move down to a table. Da always felt more comfortable at the bar-- he felt he would be a good barman if there was such an establishment that would trust him with all their alcohol. After some small talk about how Jimmy looked like him and how proud he should be of his son-- what a good guitar player he was (Da didn't think it was the time to tell him that he would've busted that guitar up into kindling if his wife hadn't stop him).

"What's the boy done? I'll beat his balls for ya if need be," offered Da. "No, it's nothing like that," then Mitch made his play, "Your son Jim is still a minor, isn't he?" "A miner?" injected Da, wondering about this man," I'd doubt he would make a decent mill man. I can't see that lad going down in any mine." "No, no, sir," clarified Mitch, "I mean, he's under the legal age to sign a contract?" Da didn't really know what this beatnik looking guy was talking about. "Is Jimmy under eighteen years old?" asked Mitch, realizing he was going to have to be very clear with Da, and there was still a great chance that he wasn't going to understand anyway.

Da started counting on his fingers, "The oldest, the second oldest, the oldest girl, the second oldest girl..." Mitch realized he had to take another tact. "Is Jim still in high school?" Da thought about it. Yeah, he remembered that he was going to school, that's why he couldn't give him money anymore. "Yeah, I think so," replied Da, not really sure. "Well, I'm going to need you to sign a contract between myself and your son," informed Mitch. "Sure," said Da, but not so sure. "It's a contract, Mr. Dewey, stating that Jimmy is my client as part of the band, The Weavils." "The Weavils, who came up with that cockamamie name?" asked Da. "I did," informed Mitch, "It's the name of Jimmy's band."

After a bit of a go about how good of name it was and what exactly was a weevil anyway, Mitch was able to make Da understand that he had to have a contract with Jim about representing him and the band, and most importantly, an agreement about how the royalties and rights to the publishing of the songs that Jimmy and some other guy (Da suspected it was crazy Mary Catherine's hardware boy) would write. Da looked at him, pretending to think. He needed a few minutes... and another beer to think about it. That's when Mitch dropped the bomb, and he would pay Da ten thousand dollars to sign the contract for Jim.

Da was no fool. If he was going to offer ten thousand dollars for the contract, Da was sure he could get fifteen. "I couldn't do that to poor, Jimmy," confessed Da, "I'm sure it's hard to write those contracts..." Mitch interrupted him, "He doesn't have to write the contract--you just have to sign it." "I know that," corrected Da, "I meant what he had to sign." "No, you have to sign it. He's not of legal age. He has to have a parent sign the contract because he's a minor." “It’s a contract to be a miner?” asked Da.

Their steaks came, and they started to eat, mostly because Mitch didn't want to go through the whole thing again. "All I need you to do is just sign the bottom of the contract," Mitch said simply. "I won't be able to do that, Mr. Sutherland," argued Da, ordering another beer to wash down the delicious steak (even though he had only taken one bite of the T-bone).

"What will it take to get you to sign the paper?" asked Mitch, discarding any attempt of trying to out-maneuver him. "It will cost you fifteen thousand for me to sign your paper," stated Da, very business-like. "Twelve," countered Mitch. "Fourteen," countered Da. "Twelve, take it or leave it. I'll have the Suggs kid do all the writing. Your boy will only get a quarter of what they're paid for a gig... or he could share the royalties and rights with Suggs and me and also get the twelve grand," stated Mitch, finishing his New York sirloin, "I'll make the check out to you, and you can give it to him."

It didn't take Da too long to realize that this was the deal of his lifetime. Not every day some beatnik-looking guy comes and takes you to dinner, offers you twelve thousand bucks to just sign a piece of paper. Da had three more beers to think about it and a whiskey for dessert, but finally, he agreed to the twelve thousand dollars for all Jim's rights to the publishing and royalties of the songs he's written and was going to write.

Wouldn't you know it, but Mitch had the contract in his fancy coat's pocket. Da signed it, *Michael Seamus Dewey*, just like he did whenever he had a job and got paid in a check. Mitch shook his hand and dropped him off in front of Barnaby's. Da showed Frenchy doorman the check, just so that he would know that Da had money to pay with.

♫♫♫

Franny hadn't really gotten over being kicked out of the band, but she realized that she should do something other than feel sorry for herself (this is what her mom did every time she broke up with a guy). She had decided that she was going to put together an act and contact Joyce Kalina at the Club 47 to see if they would let her do a set there solo. Franny decided that she wasn't going to sit and wait feeling sorry for herself. She could play rock and roll or, she could play folk. It didn't matter to her.

The Weavils

Jim sat at the piano in Lenny's basement fingering keys, trying to come up with a song. It was different trying to write with Lenny than writing with Franny. He and Franny would just play their guitars, working off of phrases that one of them would throw out. If it didn't work, they would stop, noodle around a bit, and try another set of chords, strumming, finger-picking, or hand-slapping, until something fun or interesting came up. Lenny had given Jim a list of song names, first lines, and cool lyrics that didn't go together. Some of them were interesting, but they never really could get beyond the original thought.

Jim was fine with playing "Let's Go All Night" if that's what Mitch wanted, but Lenny wanted something better to sing for their first record, and a cover was absolutely out of the question. They were going to play their original song even if it killed Jim to write it. Most of their writing sessions were Jim either on his Harmony Supertone acoustic or sitting at the piano playing while Lenny either paced or lay on the couch, trying to think of a line or some lyrics that he wanted to sing. It was getting wicked frustrating to keep working this way. Jim would come up with a lick and play it-- trying to put some words to the sound coming out of his guitar, but Lenny wouldn't be happy and complain that the song was too slow or too fast, not enough melody or kind of boring.

Jim wanted to go over to Franny's and try to write with her, but he knew that she wasn't going to help them write songs for The Weavils anymore or anything else that Jim was doing (Mitch had just informed them that their new name was “The Weavils.” Alley looked up the name in the encyclopedia of Britannica and found it was a small beetle that attacked mainly wheat. Alley also pointed out that their new name was again misspelled-- *weevil*. This was the second misspelled band name that someone else had given them. He suggested that they should be called “Mispeled").

The other problem with writing with Lenny was that he seemed to be very distracted. He could lie on the couch for a long time just thinking. Lenny couldn't stop thinking about Rickie. He was very happy when he spent time with Rickie, whether it was Rickie making dinner for him or when they were fooling around. Lenny wasn't sure if he was a homosexual. He didn't like all boys. He just liked Rickie. Lenny still liked Mary Catherine, and he still liked having sex with her, but he liked having sex with Rickie, also. He felt so confused. The other thing about being with Rickie was that maybe he was a homosexual, and he knew that was bad.

He had listened to other men for most of his life talk down to and disgustedly about "queers" and "fags." He also got that feeling again that the reason why Father Nelson did what he did was because he recognized the fact the Lenny was a homosexual, and that might have been Father Nelson's way of teaching him a lesson. Of course, if Father Nelson's plan was to stop him from having relationships with men, it certainly didn't work. But Lenny didn't like all men-- he just liked Rickie. He and Jim worked on the song ideas that Lenny had, but nothing came of it. It's too bad that Franny wasn't still in the band. She and Jim wrote best together.

♫♫♫

It was the day before they were going to play the Paramount Theatre in Boston, and Jim found that he was very excited about this show. Mitch was going to take them to the club. This was a big show for them. The Paramount Theatre was the premier club in Boston, and they were going to be the opening act. Mitch told them that since New England was a big college town and this was the Friday before Thanksgiving, it would be the last day of classes before the holiday and that the club could be very crowded. Jim couldn't wait for school to end.

Just after lunch, people started gathering in groups, and they all seemed to have this look of shock, like the look on Da's face the moment after Mary Catherine walloped him with the ol'-how-do-you-do. Then Jim heard from some other kids that school was going to end soon, and they were going to send everyone home. Jim asked the kid sitting next to him at lunch, who happened to be Ratsie, what was happening.

"Dewey, didn't ya hear?" Ratsie whined, "The president was shot." Jim couldn't believe what he had heard. "Shot where?" Jim asked. "In the head," answered Ratsie, after drinking out of a small milk container. "No," countered Jim, "Where was he when he was shot?" "Dallas or Denver or maybe Danvers," answered Ratsie, not seeming all that bothered by the news. "Is he okay?" asked Jim, trying to put together what he had just heard. "Of course he's not okay," said Ratsie, Jim realized that he had new glasses, which made him look like Mr. Peepers. "I told ya he was shot in the head. If I shot you in the head, would you be okay?"

Jim decided he would ask someone else, but he still couldn't get more than the president was shot in Dallas (Jim was pretty sure that he wasn't shot in Danvers since it was a town about ten miles south of them). Jim was finally able to chase down Franny, who had lost a lot of the color in her face. When Franny spotted him, she ran into his arms and started to cry. Once again, Jim was surprised how much he liked holding her (even if she did seem to cry a lot).

Jim tried to comfort her, and he walked Franny home after school was abruptly dismissed. It was very difficult for Franny to understand who would do this to the young man from Brookline. When they arrived at Franny's apartment, Joanie was there, and she was also crying. All three sat on the couch and watched Walter Cronkite on the television. Mr. Cronkite seemed very upset about the shooting. It was heartbreaking to watch Mrs. Kennedy getting on that plane with her husband's body, still wearing that pink dress that had her husband's blood on it. Joanie and Franny were weeping when the plane took off from Texas.

When Jim got home that night, his ma and his sisters were all crying and grief-stricken. His ma was almost distraught, and she just kept repeating, "He was the first Catholic president, and they shot him" as she fingered her rosary. Even Da seemed moved by the news of the Brookline boy's death, commenting that the boys in the Pacific had it almost as bad as the boys in Europe, even if they weren't freezing their arses off. Lenny called him and told him that the Paramount show was called off because of the president's death. Mitch didn't know when they would get to play there, but he thought that the death of the president would blow over soon, and hopefully, they would be able to be booked there before Christmas.

♫♫♫

The postponement of the Paramount show was a blow for Mitch. Epstein's boys had released two albums this year and had four singles on the top ten lists. It was only a matter of time before the Beatles came to America, and he had to get the Weavils going before then. Everyone remembers who came first, but no one remembers who showed up second. Mitch had hoped to make the Paramount Theatre debut a big moment in the Boston music scene, but the death of the president had closed everything down at least until the funeral was over. All he could do now was try to re-book the Paramount show and keep Suggs and Dewey trying to come up with a number one single to record. It was a very sad time, and the president dying wasn't consoling either (his wife and friends were very distraught).

Jim went over to Franny's to watch the state funeral of John F. Kennedy. They sat on the couch. Franny and Joanie cried, watching the caisson being led to

Arlington National Cemetery. Franny and Jim had played the "Franny's father game" with John Kennedy-- he was one of the few people Franny didn't mind imagining he was her long-lost father. Kennedy's real son, John-John, saluted his father's casket as it went by on television, sending everyone into heavy sobbing. Jim was unsure of his feelings for the fallen president.

Kennedy to Jim was just something that happened in the world. People were born, people died, people lost their jobs, men got drunk, they beat their wives and their children, some people became the president, and some presidents got shot. But this was a boy who grew up and lived in the same state that Jim did. Maybe John Kennedy lived a much different life than Jim. He still felt that they were alike. They were both of Irish descent, both raised Catholic (though Jim hadn't been to church in a while), and they both were from big families. But the other thing was the way Leo and Franny would talk about him, like with him running things, the world would change everybody's minds about blacks and whites, about taking care of the poor and how to treat each other.

Franny watched the rider-less horse, Black Jack-- they called him, with the boots in the stirrups, being led down Pennsylvania Avenue. Franny had believed that John F. Kennedy would lead this country into the future as he promised and fight against injustice and help all people be free. There was something about the violence of his assassination that felt like it brought the world crashing down. That the young, handsome, president had promised to lead the country into a new age and someone, someplace, had said "no," we need it to stay the same.

For Franny, the killing of this president was like the crushing of the hope that all young people feel. Franny knew that when the war ended, her mother and the adults of that generation had felt that they had changed the world and would steer it into a better future for their children, a better place to be, and a world without the mistakes of the past. But now, after the death of the president, it felt like there was no change coming, just the same mistakes to be made by the same people.

When Jim walked home that cold night, it felt as though the whole country was sobbing. A great sadness had fallen on Lawrence, on his street, and in his house. People went about their business, but you could tell that the thought that that young man from Brookline had been gunned down before he could bring any of his ideas to reality had left people shocked and grief-stricken. He seemed to be the chance to change the world, and now it laid in a grave in the National Cemetery, with a flame burning above him to say all hope is not lost but won't be done by this man. Even with the knowledge of recording a record, Jim was also wounded by what had happened in Dallas, as most of the nation had been.

♫♫♫

Jim returned to the place where he always went when he felt down. He went down to Essex Street with his guitar and found Smilin' Leo on the sidewalk singing his blues. Jim didn't say anything to Leo. He knew he didn't have to. Leo was busking because the only time he was felt alive was when he was playing for the people.

Jim tuned his own guitar and joined Leo in playing Blind Lemon Jefferson's *Black Snake Moan*, Howlin' Wolf's *How Many More Years*, Bo Diddley's *I'm a Man,* and Roy Hawkins *The Thrill is Gone.* It amazed Jim how quick playing those old songs turned him around, even if they had to compete with a man dressed as a Santa Claus, ringing a bell for the Salvation Army in front of W.T. Grant's doors. To play and sing with his friend Leo had changed his mood and his belief that something good would come out of this tragedy. That maybe the change could come from him, and Franny, and Lenny and The Weavils... that maybe the change could come from the music. From the music of the south, the music of Chicago, the music of Essex Street in Lawrence, Massachusetts. That the music of the blind Negro man beside him could change the world. That the music from Elvis and Jerry Lee and Little Richard and Chuck Berry and the great Woody Guthrie could set the world on fire with hope once again.

When it got dark, Jim led Leo home to the Tar Pit and to Addie and Ruby, who were waiting for him. On the way, Leo spoke of his grief for the fallen man from Brookline. He also talked about how once the change is in motion, it can't be stopped or turned around. It was like a wave; you couldn't stop it no matter who died or was leading. It was just the initial impulse to start the wave that was important.

"Life is like music," professed Leo, holding his walking cane and the crook of Jim's arm, "It goes on, no matter who lives or dies, no matter who plays it or sings it. Take it from someone who's known a lot of life." Jim had his guitar slung over his shoulder and carried Leo's beautiful Guild F-20 inside its worn case, leading his friend home. "No matter what happens in life, a musician has to keep doing his job." Jim knew what the next thought was, and Jim chimed in along with his friend, "...Giving the music to the people." Leo laughed and slapped his hands together. Leo knew that he had taught his student the most important lesson in music-- it was for the people.

Jim went home with new hope and the first understanding of the opportunity that he and The Weavils had laid out in front of them. He was determined to become the musician that Leo wanted him to be. He would become the person who would bring the music to the people as Leo wanted. Jim was determined to write those songs that could change a person's life.

♫♫♫

Franny had called Joyce Kalina and identified herself as Jane of Dick and Jane. She told Joyce that she would like to play Club 47 but that she would have to be a solo, Dick couldn't make it. Joyce told her to come down when she wanted, and she would be able to play a few songs between other performer's sets. Franny put a bunch of songs together, including "I'm Not Here, "Feel My Heart," Woody's *Plane Wreck at Los Gatos,* and a song she found in the library. She wanted some song that was connected to Lawrence, so she went to the Lawrence Library and asked the librarian, who helped her find a song she had heard about that was sung by the picketers at the 1912 mill workers strike in Lawrence. The name of the song was *Bread and Roses.* It was a pretty easy song to learn, and it had some good lyrics that were very pro-union, so Franny thought that the hipsters at Club 47 would appreciate it.

♫♫♫

Mitch took the band to lunch at The Ship Restaurant in Danvers (Where obviously, Kennedy wasn't shot, even if Ratsie thought it was), which was a restaurant designed like a ship that was floating down Route One. After ordering their food, Mitch told the Weavils that he had booked a recording studio in New York City (There wasn't an adequate recording studio in the Boston area) and that they would all drive there. He also told them that while they were in New York, they were going to audition for a few record companies that he had lined up. He also told them that they would be going to New York over the Christmas vacation so that Jim wouldn't have to miss any school. Jim was embarrassed that he would tell everyone that, even though everyone was aware that he was still in high school.

Mitch also announced that he was going to take them all shopping for new clothes and haircuts. This made Jim nervous since only his ma had ever cut his hair before. He wasn't sure about having some stranger cut it. Lenny told Mitch that he and Jim had been working on some songs and that they had some good ones coming. Jim couldn't understand what songs that Lenny was promising were "good ones." Actually, Jim couldn't understand how come Lenny had taken such an interest in songwriting all of a sudden. He hadn't really worked at any songs since the “Here I Come” attempt. But now, all of a sudden, he wanted to help Jim write songs even though Franny was the one who wrote the others.

After signing the contract with Mitch, Lenny realized that he was going to have to write the songs with Jim. He knew that they needed original songs, and if he wanted to have any say in what he sang, he had to be there when the song was being written, and if he wasn't, there was gonna be a good chance he would sound like a pansy.

Lenny felt that Jim got too corny in most of the songs, and then he had to sing them, making him feel corny. Besides, it said in the contract that if they published any of the songs, Lenny would get a third of what the song made. He wasn't sure of what that would be, but it had to be better than nothing.

Mitch ended the meeting by telling them when they would leave for New York and what they would need to bring, and before that, they were to play the Paramount Theatre a few days before Christmas. They would be staying in a hotel for a week while they recorded in New York, and that Mitch would pay for whatever they needed there. The news about staying in the hotel was almost the most exciting thing for Jim. He had never stayed in a hotel, and when Lenny said that they could just call and get lunch and dinner, well, that was too much. Jim knew he was going to call.

♫♫♫

Franny's Aunt Lucy drove her Chevy Belair with Joanie and Franny into Cambridge so that Franny could play at Club 47. They entered and sat at a table. Joyce Kalina came over and told Franny when she could get up and play two songs while the other act prepared to play their set. Franny told Joyce that she wanted to be introduced as "Frankie Walsh" in sort of a protest of being expelled from Spindal for being a girl. Franny had decided that she would take her band name instead of her real name. She also decided to grow out her hair and to get rid of those heavy framed glasses and wear glasses that looked more girlish and less Buddy Holly. She wasn't pretending who she was anymore; if the Boston rock scene wouldn't have her, then she would be a Folk artist. It didn't matter what she had to play, she was going to do it.

Franny got up on the small stage when it was her turn and played "I'm Not Here" and "Feel My Heart." Joanie watched her daughter sing and play her guitar (she had bought the Washburn from Lenny with some of the money she had made at the beach). Her Aunt Lucy and Joanie were very proud of her playing and singing. She got a nice round of applause when she finished.

The boy who came on after she was very strange. He wore a brakeman's cap (like they wear on a train), baggy clothes that probably came out of a second-hand store, his hair was unkempt, and he was unshaven, but he wasn't old enough yet to grow a full beard. He had sad puppy-dog eyes and wore a rack for his harmonica around his neck. The boy came on and talked a bit. Franny couldn't help but think how much he sounded and looked like Woody Guthrie. Suddenly, Franny became very anxious about playing a Woody song. The boy started playing, and the way he sang his songs and the way he played them were really different. At first, she was kind of surprised by his voice. It was gravely and nasally sounding, but after a few stanzas, it became much more listenable.

The boy sang his songs, and the patrons of Club 47 listened intently. Many of the songs sounded like poems put to music, without any real hook lines in them. She knew he was using words and sentences put in stanzas, but it was the way he used the imagery of the words, like he was painting the song. He was a small kid, standing on a small stage singing big songs. Songs that were about people and about thoughts, but they were big thoughts, thoughts that covered a world, that covered a life, songs painted so well you could see them, even though you knew you heard them, painted by a brilliant artist-- with one hand waving-free.

When the boy finished his set, Kelly came on and announced that the boy had released two albums on the Columbia label. Franny really liked his songs, and especially one called *Blowin' in the Wind*; Franny made a note to herself to buy one of Bob Dylan's albums.

It wasn't until she played in front of the last set that she played *Plane Wreck at Los Gatos* and then *Bread and Roses.* As she played, she realized that many in the audience had become attached to the words in the song and the message of the people coming together to protect each other and stand up to the injustice of the dangerous and low paying millwork. After she finished, many of the performers came over and complimented her songs and her playing. She was very happy to be thought of as a performer and told her aunt and her mom that she wanted to come back soon.

Franny wanted to go over and tell the boy that she liked his songs, but there were a lot of people around him, and it looked like he just wanted to leave. Franny, Joanie, and Lucy drove back to Lawrence. Franny really wanted to hear some more songs of that boy in the brakeman's cap.

♫♫♫

Mitch picked up The Weavils at Lenny's house. Lenny's mom watched them load their equipment into the large station wagon. Mitch had a friend with him, Bork, a large man who looked like Red Skelton's Freddie the Freeloader, with wilder hair. Bork helped Michael load his drums in the back of the station wagon, beside the two amps and Alley and Jim's guitars. It was December in Massachusetts, but Bork was only wearing a suit jacket and a large flowing scarf. When everything was packed into the car, Bork climbed into the driver's seat, and they left for New York City and The Weavil's first record.

The Paramount Theatre show went well. The theater was in the middle of *The Combat Zone,* in downtown Boston, a very dangerous area even though it didn't look that much different than Merrimack Street back in Lawrence, it was famous for its crime and prostitutes. The Paramount was a large venue, and it was packed that night. The location didn't seem to be much of a deterrent, given its reputation (also, like the postponed show, it was on the last day of school for most colleges before the Christmas break). At the end of the show, just before *Quarter to Three,* Lenny announced to the audience that they were going to make a record and it would be out soon. Jim hoped that everyone in the club that night would buy the record. At least then, it wouldn't seem that bad if no one else bought it. When they were leaving, Lenny saw some hookers hanging out on the corner. "Boston hookers didn't look that much different than Lawrence hookers," he said to himself as they drove off.

The drive from Lawrence to New York City is about six hours, and most of it was through western Massachusetts and Connecticut, not too much local color. The boys sat and talked about what they should do in New York City. Jim wanted to go to some record stores, Mitch had said they had some really good stores there, and since Mitch's family owned a record store in Boston, Jim wanted to see what he considered to be a good store. Michael wanted to go to Forty-Eighth Street, where there was a whole row of music stores. He wanted to check out the drums that they carried there (Jim wanted to go there too after he had heard about them).

Lenny and Alley wanted to do some sight-seeing. Alley wanted to go up the Empire State Building, but Lenny had already been up there and said it was no big whoop. Lenny did want to go to the Statue of Liberty. Alley agreed that he wanted to go there, too. Then Lenny said he wanted to go to Radio City and see the Rockettes. Michael agreed that he wanted to go there, also (Jim was going to agree but thought maybe he shouldn't in front of Mitch).

Lenny then suggested that they should pick up some hookers, which got Mitch to spin around quickly in his front seat and warn them that there would be none of that happening on this trip. Lenny and Michael had to laugh at that one-- Mitch had suddenly become their scout leader. "We should go to Saint Patrick's. I hear it's beautiful," suggested Alley. "We'll do that after the hookers," joked Lenny, leading Mitch to spin around again. "Let's go dancing," suggested Lenny. "Boys, this a business trip," warned Mitch, trying to take the scout leader role again, "We've got the studio for three hours, and then we have meetings scheduled, that's what we're going to be doing on this trip." Lenny and Michael were openly disappointed. "Then can we go tonight?" asked Lenny, hoping scoutmaster Mitch would cut them a break. "All right, you can go dancing tonight," compromised Mitch, "But not Jim. I promised his father that I would look after him."

"Let's go dancing tonight," sang Lenny, happily, followed by Alley and Michael, "Let's go dancing tonight." Jim sat unhappily, listening to his older bandmates sing about going without him. "Come on, baby," sang Lenny, mockingly dancing with Alley, still sitting in their seats. Jim turned away bitterly but still found himself singing with Lenny and Alley, "Let's go dancing tonight -- Let's go dancing tonight." That's when it hit him.

♫♫♫

Bork pulled the station wagon up in front of the Hotel Edison, on West 48th Street, an older hotel in a rundown neighborhood called Hell's Kitchen, though, to the guys, it looked better than the Tar Pit and maybe the Paddy Hill sections of Lawrence. They went into the hotel and were led to their rooms by a bellman, who looked like he had just woke up. He also smelled of gin and sweat. They carried their instruments and equipment up with them because Mitch said it wasn't a safe neighborhood. Like at the beach, Jim and Michael had only paper bags for their clothes (Mitch had promised to take them to Gimbels to buy them each a suit). When they got everything in their room (which smelled like sweat and cigarette smoke), Alley, Michael, and Lenny got dressed in their best clothes that they brought and happily went out for a night on the town. Mitch had told them that he was going downtown to visit a friend and that they shouldn't stay out late...or get in any trouble.

Mitch and Bork had another room down the hall. As soon as the older Weavils left, Jim took out his Harmony Supertone and tuned it. He had to call down to the front desk to find out how to call back to Lawrence. The guy at the front desk was gruff and asked him how he ever got by without knowing how to use a telephone. Finally, he put Jim through so that the phone was ringing at Franny's apartment.

Franny answered it since Joanie was working late again. "How does this sound?" was the question on the other end of the phone, "Come on, baby, don't be hazy, let's go crazy. Let's go dancing tonight," sang Jim. "Who is this?" Franny asked, pretending not to know who would call her like this. "What do you think?" asked Jim, not caring about when he called her. "I don't like the word "hazy," it's really vague. Are you drunk, dizzy?" "I'll try something else," he answered, trying different chords for the song.

"I think you should start in a "G." Jim went to a barred G chord and strummed, "That's better." "Try a G, then an A," suggested Franny. "Yeah, that's good," answered Jim. "Where're the other guys?" asked Franny. "They've gone dancing," answered Jim, strumming the G and the C. "Try, 'don't be lazy,' instead of hazy," suggested Franny.

♫♫♫

Lenny, Alley, and Michael came back after midnight. When they walked into the room, Jim was asleep on the bed. His guitar was still slung over his shoulder. Alley was bothered because he had to share a double bed with Jim, and now he was going to have to wake up Jim to get his side of the bed back. Alley shook Jim to wake him. "Jimmy, it's your ma," said Lenny, taking his voice an octave higher, "You have to get up and go to school." Alley kept shaking Jim to wake him while Lenny and Michael laughed at him.

Finally, Jim stirred and sat up. "Sleep on your side," scolded Alley, "And don't kick me." Jim rubbed his eyes, "Hey, I've got something," he said. "Yeah, you've got a new boyfriend to sleep with tonight," continued Lenny. "He's a cutie," joked Michael. "No, I've written a new song," said Jim sleepily.

"Look at him," laughed Lenny, "We go out dancing with some pretty girls, and he stays home and writes a song." "You wanna hear it?" asked Jim, slipping his guitar into place to play. "Sure, knock our socks off," offered Alley, taking a comfortable place on his side of the bed. Jim sat with his legs open and the guitar resting between them. He played a quick introduction that he and

Franny had worked on;

Come on, baby, don't be lazy, let's go crazy -- Let's go dancin' tonight, come on brother, grab another, you don't have to love her, Let's go dancing tonight. We're dancin' all around the room, the band's all beat, playing out of tune, everyone knows morning coming soon. Come on, Eddie, rock her steady, are you ready, let's go dancin' tonight, come on, Flo, there ya go, don't you know, let's go dancin' tonight. Yeah, we're dancing all around the room, the band's all beat, playing out of tune, everyone knows morning's coming soon.

"We do a small bridge here," Jim added, doing a quick bass run on the 5th and 6th string.

Come on Fred; it's like ya said, we'll sleep when we're dead -- let's go dancin' tonight.

Jim did a couple of quick slides and pounded the ending chords. He stopped and raised his hands so that everyone in the room knew he was finished.

Lenny, Alley, and Michael looked at each other; finally, everyone turned to Lenny. "I like it. It had a groove and a nice beat." "Can you do something with that, Mike?" asked Jim, realizing that he had gotten some interest in this song, rather than usual, "I don't know" reaction. "I could do something with that!" Everyone turned to Alley, "I guess I could come up with something for it." Jim smiled-- now they were getting somewhere.

♫♫♫

Mitch sat in a chair of the room he was sharing with Bork. "I like it," remarked Mitch, waiting to see what the other boys had to say. "Me, too," added Bork, though no one was really paying attention. "Can we use it?" asked Lenny, like a boy who is begging to have his school work hung on the refrigerator. "We can try it," said Mitch, "but I don't think we should use it at the meetings." "I think it's stronger than "All Night Long," coaxed Lenny. "Well, let's take it to the studio and see how it sounds on tape." Mitch had the boys get their instruments and head down to the car.

Mitch stopped at the front desk to get the mail and check what the bill was. He stormed over to Jim, displaying a charge of $12.46 for a phone call to Lawrence, Massachusetts. "I'm sorry," apologized Jim, "I got lonely last night and called my ma." The other guys chuckled; Jim was such a baby. "A four-hour phone call?" asked Mitch, trying to be sympathetic but really. "I won't do it again," promised Jim, lying. "Let's go record our song," ordered Mitch. The boys followed him, still laughing at Jim's phone call.

♫♫♫

The Weavils walked into the Dick Charles Demo Studio at The Brill Building on Broadway and 49th Street, with their mouths agape, like contest winners on television. "You got the big one," Lenny observed, sarcastically. The room was actually a small office with the furniture removed. Jim strolled to the small closet that was now a control room and looked over the small control board and a reel-to-reel tape machine. Lenny, Alley, and Michael stared at the small room with just a few microphones and some rugs on the floor. They stood in the middle of the tight space and turned around, trying to decide where they could place Michael's drums and still have enough room for the other three boys. Bork and Mitch stood in the doorway, staring into the small studio. "You boys ready to make some magic in here?" asked Mitch, not actually expecting an answer.

They set up their equipment, with Jim and Alley crowded next to Michael's Ludwig New Yorker drums, their amps tucked behind Michael's drummer's throne. Lenny was stationed by the doorway to the closet (or the control room), facing a large microphone on a stand. While a tall man named Scottie, with flaming red hair and beard, wearing dungarees, a white shirt, and a tie under a white lab coat, set up a large microphone hanging from the ceiling and the one for Lenny to sing into. When he was ready, Scottie stood behind the small soundboard in the cramped control room, in the closet. Scottie had large black glasses that made him look like the Lone Ranger.

"You cats ready out there?" Scottie asked, adjusting some of his knobs on the dual-track tape machine. Mitch and Bork had to settle for standing in the hallway.

Mitch had them run through the two songs that they had planned to play, "Let's Go All Night" and "Feel My Heart." Scottie only had a two-track recorder; one track was for the instruments, and the second track held Lenny's vocals. After they played the songs, twice each, the guys listened to the recorded tape played back. All the guys were disappointed in the way the songs sounded. The drums weren't loud enough for Michael at times, and at other times, it was too loud. To Jim, the guitar wasn't loud enough and sounded behind the beat or ahead of the beat; he could hear every mistake he made. Lenny felt that many of the words were slurred or, at the least, not clear. He also wasn't happy with the harmonica on the bridge of "Let's Go All Night." Alley thought the guitar playing was awful, but he didn't say anything.

Mitch wasn't happy with the songs either. It was just as Jim thought, "Let's Go All Night" didn't carry well on a recording. It was written to be played live and didn't sound all that great recorded. Mitch thought a moment after Scottie turned off the playback. The guys waited-- all hoping he would come to one conclusion. "Let's try the new song," he suggested. Lenny clapped his hands and led the guys back into the studio.

The Weavils took their places. Scottie recorded, "The Weavils, 'Let's Go Dancin',' take one," and gave them a nod to let them know they were rolling tape. Michael tapped his drum sticks together four times, and they went into the song, with Lenny reading from the piece of paper that Jim had written up for him. They played the song twice. Since they only had the two tracks, they had to play the song all the way through or start all over-- there was no editing or dubbing of anything after the song was put on the tape.

Again, they listened to the tape of themselves singing the song that Jim had just written. This time there wasn't the sour looks like the last song. They listened to what they recorded. Actually, Michael was tapping his fingers on the edge of his snare drum. Lenny tapped his thigh lightly, keeping beat with the song. Then Mitch started nodding his head. Jim watched his bandmates follow along with the song and realized that they liked it. The more they listened to it, the more they liked it.

When the song finished, Mitch looked up at the guys and said, "It's coming along. Let's keep working on this one." The other guys agreed. It looked like "Let's Go Dancin'" was going to be their record. They got the demo done in a day. They also recorded "Feel My Heart" in three takes. Jim was relieved that Lenny never once slipped in a "Smell my fart" during the whole recording. He was afraid that Lenny couldn't help himself, and then Mitch wouldn't want to put it on the "B" side of "Let's Go Dancin'. " Recording was pretty straight forward in those days. You just played it and recorded it-- if you make a mistake, then do it again and it was all monophonic sound recording. There wasn't much sweetening of the sound or the effects. Just play and record. Plus, Mitch had only rented the studio for three hours, so everything had to be done in that time slot.

Mitch took the boys to a nice restaurant to celebrate after they finished recording. Lindys was in Times Square, and at the window booth, they could watch everyone walk by. They all ordered their dinners, and Mitch even let them have some of Lindy's world-famous cheesecake. They all agreed-- it didn't look like a cake, and it didn't taste like cheese.

♫♫♫

The next day Mitch was going to make some office visits with the new demos that they had made at the Brill Building. He instructed Bork to take the boys downtown and let them go record shopping in Greenwich Village. The guys went from store to store, checking out different albums and artists. When they finished, they had bought a bunch of albums, Johnny Cash's *Blood, Sweat, and Tears,* The Miracles *The Fabulous Miracles,* The Beach Boys, *Surfin' USA,* Del Shannon's *Little Town Flirt, Heat Wave* by Martha and the Vandellas. Jim picked up the two albums that Franny had asked for, Bob Dylan's self-titled and *Freewheelin' Bob Dylan.* Michael also got The Surfaris' *Wipe Out*-- a good record for a drummer.

They walked around the Village like school kids while Bork watched over them. They went by Gerde's Folk City, The Bottom Line, Kettle of Fish, Cafe Wha. They tried to recognize the musicians' names that were playing there. They even hung out in Washington Square Park for a while, feeding the pigeons. Then Bork piled them back into the station wagon and took them back to the hotel.

♫♫♫

The next two days were made up of visits to record company offices. Mitch would introduce the boys, and the record company guys would listen to the demo, shrug their shoulders, nod their heads, close their eyes and look like they were sleeping; some smiled, most didn't, they would ask who had written the song, the boys would tell them it was Jim and Lenny (Lenny had added a new line at the end during the recording of the demo), they would say that they liked it and then everyone shook hands and left.

When they went to Reprise Records, two executives there, Sandy Solomon, a man with a cheap haircut and heavy framed glasses, and Vernon Desiletz, a large man in a crew cut, asked them to play their song rather than listen to the demo. Mitch looked uneasily at the guys, who just shrugged. Jim and Alley took up their instruments that had to be played unplugged (which they had brought with them so as not to have them nicked from their hotel room or the car) and Michael tapped on the bottom of an up-turned wastebasket to simulate a drum, while Lenny sang, emphatically punching the words he wrote, *" So don't disappoint, we're at a boiling point, come on,"* Lenny stood and shouted, "*Let's rock this joint."* Solomon and Desiletz seemed impressed that the boys didn't let their request to play it live soften their performance.

Lenny offered to do "Feel My Heart" for them. As soon as Jim realized what Lenny was about to offer, panic raced through his limbs until Lenny finished saying the correct song title. Sandy and Vernon, as they wanted to be called (at least right now), declined the second song. Everyone shook hands, but it seemed warmer this time, more genuinely friendly, as they left.

The next day they went to Gimbels to have their suits made. It was weird having someone measure you all over, but Mitch had told them how important it was for them to look right. The suits were black, with white dress shirts, with stiff French collars and thin black ties. The jackets and pants were tailored to each boy, so there would be no swapping like up at the beach. Each boy got a new pair of shoes; they were Florishiem loafers and had no laces. This was good for Jim since his shoes always seemed to be untied. Lenny had them all stand in front of a mirror and smile to see if they looked like a band (a young band-- but a band just the same). Mitch seemed pleased. They made a few more record label visits and then went back to the hotel. For their last night in New York City, Mitch took them and Bork to Mulligan's Irish Pub on Eighth Avenue. They all got steaks, mashed potatoes, and a beer (except for Jim, who had a tonic).

The next morning, they packed the car with their equipment and headed back to Lawrence. Jim watched the Empire State Building slowly disappear from sight as the car made its departure from the city. He realized that he had been there but had never made it to the top of the tallest building in the world. The next time he came, he promised himself, he would go to the top.

♫♫♫

As soon as Jim walked into Franny's apartment, they opened the two albums that Jim had bought in Manhattan. Jim wasn't familiar with Mr. Die-lan (Franny corrected him, it was Dil-lan), but Franny had heard him at Club 47 and told him how much Bob Dylan reminded her of Woody. They took the record out of the album, making sure they didn't touch the surface, by holding it by its edges. Franny laid the disk of *Freewheelin' Bob Dylan* on the turntable, set the arm down on the record's grooves, and listened.

It started with the usual crackle and pop of a record before the strumming, a bass run, and then Bob Dylan's voice singing *Blowing in The Wind.* Jim had been taken even before the first harmonica interlude. Of course, Franny was already on board. They spent the night just spinning those two records. Joanie came home around nine from business class. She sat through the albums for two cycles but then decided that she had to go to work the next morning and went to bed. Jim and Franny stayed up until after midnight listening to the new albums.

Jim was very taken by the second track on Freewheelin' called *Girl from the North Country*; he wondered who Dylan was singing it to, what was she like, and why was he leaving her if he loved her so much. Franny's favorite was *A Hard Rain's A-Gonna Fall*; to her, it was almost a prophecy of coming times, after what had happened with Cuba and the Russian missiles and then the march in Washington and President Kennedy's assassination. It sounded like this guy she had seen at Club 47, with just a guitar and harmonica, was going to change the world alone. Bob Dylan knew what was coming and that this song was telling everyone to prepare themselves for tough times. When school started after the New Year, Jim and Franny would run home and spend the rest of the night listening to Dylan-- which would almost become a trend in the coming years.

♫♫♫

Vernon called Mitch and said they were on board, but they wanted to see what The Weavils could do in front of an audience. Mitch said he would set it up. He would find a venue for his boys, and Vernon and Sandy could come to Boston and see them in action. It was decided-- now Mitch just had to find someplace to play.

One of the benefits that Mitch had managing The Weavils was that one of The Weavils had a dad who owned a bar called Barnaby's. Mitch called Michael, who talked to Pudge, who said "Okay" to The Weavils playing a set. Mitch and Pudge set up the night they would play and called Vernon and Sandy. It was all set; Pudge even put a big sign by the door, announcing "Recording Artists, The Weavils" playing on Friday night.

Jim was hesitant in playing at Barnaby's at first, but then he realized that Da hadn't been around for a few weeks (It was a very merry Christmas without Da home), and hopefully, it would stay that way, at least, until the show at Barnaby's was over. Da hadn't been home for almost a month. Patrick and Michael had reported that right before Thanksgiving, Da had been spending a lot of money on drinks for his friends (which could range from him and Plug to him and the whole damn bar). There had also been a rumor that Da was looking to buy a car, which was odd because Da didn't have a driver's license (not that it meant he wouldn't drive, but buying a car would be different); most everyone thought that he had got pinched for something and was in jail somewhere.

Ma Dewey was very excited about the local show. She told all the kids that she would be going to the show and that they would have to fend for themselves that night, including the little kids. It was amazing how the mood of the Dewey household ebbed and flowed with Da's presence.

Jim wasn't so happy about telling Leo. He knew Leo would want to come and listen, even if it meant standing outside the bar again. Jim decided not to tell him because he didn't want him to be forced to listen from the street. He told himself that he would make sure that Leo would get a copy of the record once it was released. But he didn't have the heart to watch Leo standing outside the bar while Frenchy kept him out.

♫♫♫

The night of the show came, and it had the fanfare of another Celtics Championship. There were people lined up outside the bar for hours before the show began. Jim was relieved to hear that his da and Plug were nowhere to be found. Ma was also relieved to hear her husband was absent. He didn't believe that women should be in bars, even Sister Mary Celeste (He felt it made men turn into sissies-- especially with the nun around).

The Deweys were given their own table, as were the Goulds. Franny, Joanie, and Lucy sat with the Deweys while pitchers of beer were passed around. Pudge and the rest of the Webster clan were working the bar and waiting tables. In the back, by the doorway, The Weavils waited anxiously. "Where's Mitch," asked Lenny again. "He'll be here," answered Alley, hoping that it would happen soon before his folks could think too much about what was going on. He was sure that they would leave at any minute. Frenchy had come back and told Michael that they couldn't let anyone else into the establishment; they were pushing the fire code as it was. Jim looked out into the audience and saw his family, and a good many kids that he went to high school with was there (anyone who had a phony I.D. made it in).

Suddenly, "Strings," was whispered from behind Jim. He turned and spotted Leo and Addie standing in the doorway. Jim walked to them, feeling bad that he didn't tell Leo, and now here he was. Jim stepped outside into the parking lot, the Gretsch hanging over his shoulder. "Strings, break a leg," Leo smiled, slapping his hands together. "I'm sorry, I didn't tell you. I didn't want you to have to wait outside," Jim apologized. "It's okay," retorted Leo, holding his daughter's arm in support. "Hey… there boys, rip it up," Leo yelled to the rest of The Weavils. Lenny and Michael came over and shook hands with Leo, telling him how much they missed him up at the beach this year. Leo laughed and rolled his head, enjoying the interaction with the band.

Michael asked Leo if he was going to come in and watch the show. Leo smiled and held his daughter's arm tightly. "Naw, I like it out here. We like the cold air," Leo tried to confirm. "No man," said Michael, taking Leo's other arm, leading him and Addie into the back of the pub, "You can come in. You'll hear better in here." Michael led Leo and Addie through the backdoor and into the large bar area of Barnaby's. The mill men at the bar stopped talking and arguing and drinking mugs of beer to stare at the two Negroes being led in by Pudge's kid.

Pudge came around the bar and walked up to his youngest son, "What're doin', boy?" he asked. "He's my friend, Pa. He wants to see the show," answered Michael, helping Addie sit at a table not far from the exit that they had just come in from. Pudge glared at his son, but he decided not to do anything. There were only two of them... and one of them couldn't see, anyway.

As Pudge made his way behind the bar, Shitty Easton grabbed his arm and started, "Pudge, what the…" But Pudge stopped him quickly, "You say one more thing to me, and I'm throwin' your ass out of here... and not for just tonight!" Shitty thought about it for a minute, but as soon as Pudge turned toward Frenchy standing at the door, carding two young-looking Lawrence High School boys, Shitty decided it wasn't a problem. Michael brought Leo and Addie each a beer, then joined his band outside, waiting anxiously to start the show.

Finally, Mitch, Bork, Vernon, and Sandy arrived. The boys gave them enough time to get to the table that the Websters had been holding for them. Then Lenny and the band rushed on stage and kicked off into *Blue Suede Shoes*, the friendly audience going crazy from the first drum beat. Lenny stood at his microphone and took turns singing to Mary Catherine, who was sitting with Bridie and some of her girlfriends, and Rickie Rooney, who was standing by the door, smiling his effervescent smile. Lenny knew he was probably going to go home with Mary Catherine (to his ma's house), but he would really like to be going home with Rickie.

Jim enjoyed the show; he could show off for his ma and family no matter how much Mary Catherine complained, they had to notice him. Jim was also happy that Leo and Addie got to come in and see the show as guests of Michael's; it was a lot better to see it from a table rather than listening out front. Jim would look over and see Leo smiling, clapping his hands, and stamping his feet along with his music. With his ma and Leo there, it was like he was playing for his teachers, for the two people who led him to this moment. Leo listened proudly as The Weavils rocked Barnaby's.

It was also nice to come back and play for the people of Lawrence. Jim took it all in, realizing that this could be the top of his music career. If they didn't get the recording contract, then they would have to go back to getting live bookings from Rickie Rooney and Mr. Conley. Maybe something would happen, but most likely, they would play together until someone got married or had to get a real job.

Franny enjoyed the show but still couldn't help feeling disappointed by the fact that she wasn't up there with them. She had hoped that they would invite her up for a song or two, but when she saw Mitch sitting with the three guys in suits, she realized that she wasn't getting called up. Franny spotted Rickie at the door, and he winked at her, giving her a big smile. She wasn't really sure if he knew that she was Frankie, the piano player, or just the girl who was in the band before he started booking them.

Rickie saw Franny at the long table with what looked like Jim's family. He noticed that Mary Catherine wasn't sitting with them, but it was pretty obvious that it was Jim Dewey's family. Rickie enjoyed the show and especially the performance that Lenny put on, like a good host at a party and lead singer. Rickie felt proud of the band; he felt that he had a real hand in their success. He also feared what it would do to him and Lenny. Lenny had told Rickie all about his relationship with Mary Catherine, but Rickie knew that the girl wouldn't take Lenny from him...it would eventually be the band. That's the way it always happened.

Sandy Solomon and Vernon Desiletz were very pleased with the performance. It was obvious that this was a very friendly crowd, which just showed the kind of manager Mitch was. But the show was entertaining, and they both had to admit, Lenny really had "it." He had "it" in armfuls. When he wanted to rock, the audience rocked with him; when he slowed it down for something like *Last Kiss,* the crowd came with him-- some of the high school girls were actually crying. Everyone knew that The

Beatles were coming. The Beatles were coming. The Weavils were not The Beatles, but they weren't bad either-- they brought down the house with *Quarter to Three.*

♫♫♫

Jim walked Addie and Leo to the bus; he wanted to make sure that they didn't have any problems on the way back to the Tar Pit. He appreciated that Leo came, it was a trek, and you never know what's gonna happen on Paddy Hill, especially if you're black. Jim went back to Barnaby's and was greeted as a conquering hero; Kevin even bought him a beer (Pudge gave Kevin the stink-eye when he ordered two Schlitz drafts, but he didn't say anything when Kevin gave one mug to Jim).

Jim asked Franny what she thought, and of course, she said they were boss-- the best show she's ever seen. It saddened Jim to hear that from her. They were supposed to play together-- at least, that's how he always felt. The party ran long into the night, and Ma even slept late the next day-- she blamed it on getting old. Even Jack and Hildy Gould stayed till after midnight, drinking beer with the Deweys. Mitch came over to the table just before leaving with Sandy and Vernon; he gave Jim a wink. Jim thought it was a good sign.

The Weavils waited to hear from Mitch. Jim and Franny would rush home from school and listen to Bob Dylan-- Jim had gotten down most of the songs from "Freewheelin." Finally, Mitch called Lenny and asked him and the rest of the band to come to his house in Boston.

♫♫♫

The boys drove to Mitch's Beacon Street townhouse in Lenny's step-father's Continental. All the way into Boston, their excitement had been evident. Though Mitch hadn't said so on the phone, they suspected and expected to hear their single on Woo-Woo Ginsburg's Night Train radio show. When they arrived at Mitch's place, he introduced them to his wife Robin, and his two boys, Arthur and Mitchell, Junior. The boys were ages three and five. After the introductions, Mitch led his band into his office on the second floor and asked them to sit down. Lenny, Alley, and Michael sat on the long Naugahyde couch, while Jim stood in a corner. Lenny was a bit confused about Mitch's mood. He looked like there had been a death in the family. "Boys, I have some bad news," Mitch started. Jim couldn't help thinking that Mitch was going to drop them.

Many of the bands up at the beach and even the ones they played with in Boston had told them stories about signing with managers, and just when it seemed like everything was going good, the manager would drop them. The hair on the back of Jim's neck stood up. Lenny couldn't imagine Mitch dropping them-- it would be so stupid-- they were like Jerry Lee fronting the Crickets or the Fabulous Flames. Michael was regretting coming, he had to ditch work to come to this, and now it seemed like it was going to be bad news. Alley hoped no one in Mitch's family had died.

Mitch turned and took an album off his desk. He held it up for The Weavils to see. It was just the faces of four boys, in black and white, on the cover-- looking like their heads were floating in the air. Unlike most boys of the time, their hair was long and combed down in front of their foreheads, shadows obscuring half of each boy's face. On top of the album, it said "***Meet the Beatles**, The First Album from England's Phenomenal Pop Combo!*" "Cool," exclaimed Jim, reaching for the record, "Can we listen to it?" Mitch pulled the album away. "You don't understand. This isn't good news." Jim pulled his hand back. It didn't look like bad news. "Can we still hear the album… even if it's bad news?" asked Lenny.

Mitch decided they could listen to the album; he would listen to the radio in the other room and let them know when their song was on. Mitch made another announcement before he left, "The Beatles are going to be on Ed Sullivan on February 9th." The guys weren't really listening, they were watching Lenny slide the large black disk from its cover.

Lenny laid the record onto the record-changer of Mitch's hi-fi (high fidelity) phonograph. They watched the disk drop onto the turntable, where the arm of the stylus automatically placed itself on the start of the record. The boys waited as the phonograph hissed and popped...then the music began. The first track was called *I Want to Hold Your Hand,* and that's all it took.

The Weavils sat on the couch and the chair listening intently to the four-piece combo. Jim was very impressed with the way the two or three guys sang together, their voices almost blending into one. Their harmonies were so right on and matched so well it was sometimes hard to determine if it was one person, or two people, or even three people. He was also very impressed with the guitar work; one of the musicians had a real feel for country music. Mitch had said they were from England, and it was pop songs but there were some blues in the songs.

Lenny wasn't all that impressed. Yes, they sounded good, but it was so polished. Lenny felt he could almost hear someone telling them that they needed to be clear and clean. Michael was impressed by the harmonies; they had never really tried any other than "... All Night -- all right" or "... Swingin' with Daddy Gee" but these guys were doing whole songs in harmony. He was also very impressed with the drummer, who seemed very competent and strong. He had a real sense of rhythm. Alley thought the songs were fun. It was about holding a girl's hand and telling a girl that you love her or you want to be her man. Nothing like what was happening under the boardwalk in Salisbury.

Halfway through the second side of the album, Mitch came in and announced that their song was going to play on WMEX next. Lenny and Alley got up and rushed into the other room, where the radio was. Jim and Michael looked at each other and sat down to listen to the end of "Meet the Beatles," they had heard their song in New York.

Jim asked Mitch if he could borrow The Beatles album for a few days. Mitch dejectedly said he could-- like if he got the record out of his house, the dark cloud would be lifted. Jim took the album home, and the next day after school, he brought it over to Franny's house, where it replaced the two Dylan albums on the turntable. Jim and Franny laid on the couch, listening to the record over and over again. Even Joanie took a liking to the album and spent the night with the two kids, listening to the four lads from Liverpool, *The First Album from England's Phenomenal Pop Combo*.

♫♫♫

When the night came, Jim invited Franny to join him at Mitch's house to watch The Beatles on Ed Sullivan. Lenny and Mary Catherine were there, so was Michael and Alley. Robin and the boys were there (Mitch thought they should see this, no matter how miserable he was feeling about it). Bork and an older woman, Ida, were also there, dressed like they were going to the opera. Everyone sat in the living room on the first floor and watched the RCA color console, as Ed talked about the craziness of the last few days. Jim, Franny, and most everyone saw the news film footage of The Beatles landing in New York and the interview after. Jim liked them; they seemed funny and easy-going. It was obvious that Lenny felt threatened.

Lenny didn't want to come, but Mitch had said he was the leader, and it would be important that he be there, and he could bring a date if he wanted. He figured that he would bring Mary Catherine since Mary Catherine was accusing him of caring more for the band than he cared for her. Lenny still cared about her, but he was also splitting time with Rickie... also, Lenny was scared to death about trying to break up with Mary Catherine after hearing about that Christmas dinner with her da. It was also safer to keep seeing Mary Catherine because no one would ever think he was doing what he was doing with Rickie if he was still with her. What Lenny didn't expect was Franny being there.

When Lenny and Mary Catherine entered the living room, Franny almost choked on her orange Fanta. Lenny gave her a surprised look-- then Mary Catherine gave her an equally nasty glare. Franny wasn't able to talk for a few minutes, even though she hoped it wasn't obvious because Lenny and Mary Catherine were there.

Robin was a very fine hostess, making sure everyone had enough snacks, tonic, and beer. Finally, Ed introduced The Beatles, and the audience, which seemed to be packed with girls with high-pitched voices, all screamed at once. The band played *All My Loving, Till There Was You, She Loves You, I Saw Her Standing There,* and *I Want to Hold Your Hand.* Excitement ran through everyone watching; it may have been the girls screaming on television or just the excitement of the moment. Franny didn't know what to do; when they started singing *All My Loving,* she grabbed Jim's hand and squeezed it tight, tears starting to gather in her eyes. No one imagined at the time that this would be one of those "*I experienced that*" moments in their lives.

As The Beatles played, the adults in the room commented mostly on the length of The Beatles' hair and their hairstyle. But it was so different, so refreshing; it was obvious to everyone in the room that this was where music was going. It was also obvious that The Weavils may have missed the boat.

When the show ended, Robin gathered Little Mitch and Arthur, had them say goodnight to everyone, and headed upstairs off to bed. Mitch, Bork, Ida, Franny, Mary Catherine, and the four Weavils sat with the television off. Bork and Ida didn't look impressed. Bork had criticized their *uncouthness,* and Ida had agreed. Mitch and Lenny looked disappointed, Alley looked disappointed also, but he didn't seem to know why he was disappointed. Michael was disappointed; no one told him he could bring a date. Jim and Franny were not disappointed. They secretly enjoyed it (it rated right up there with seeing Elvis on Sullivan and the first time they saw Buddy Holly). "I guess we missed it," commented Mitch to nobody in particular.

Jim wasn't really sure what they had missed-- it didn't seem to have started yet, had it? "We can be the American Beatles," announced Michael, finishing the beer he was drinking. Suddenly, it all changed for Mitch--- that's it. "Yes, we can be the *American Beatles,"* agreed

Mitch. "If you want to be?" asked Bork, not really thinking that would be anything successful, "Maybe you want to wait and see what happens to those young men?" "Yes, wait," agreed Ida, "They might see this show tomorrow and realize how in need of a haircut they are." Mitch wasn't listening; he was planning the American invasion of The Weavils.

♫♫♫

Franny and Jim rode back to Lawrence with Michael in Barnaby's pickup truck. They listened as "Let's Go Dancin" played over WMEX. The song had done well since its release-- Mitch said it was climbing charts. Neither Jim, Franny, nor Michael knew what charts they were talking about, but it sounded like a good thing, so they were all happy that the song was climbing. Jim thought the song sounded good, and Lenny did really sing well on it. He wasn't too crazy about the guitar but felt that if he had more time, he could've gotten it a bit better. But everyone at Lawrence High thought it was cool... just not many believed that Jim wrote it. Most figured that Lenny had written it and gave Jim credit because he wrote the music (Lenny had become an almost mythic former student at the school), and Lenny was kind of like that. Jim could see that Franny hadn't had the best night ever, seeing Lenny stirred up everything from over the summer. Jim was sure that something had happened between her and Lenny. He just wasn't sure what it was (and maybe didn't want to know).

Franny watched the traffic heading north on Route 93, leaving Boston. She had hoped facing Lenny would tie up her feelings for him, but it didn't. She still longed for him, and seeing him with Mary Catherine just re-enforced the idea that this was going to end badly. Lenny still had that great confidence and smile, even when it was obvious that he was disappointed that she was there. Franny felt a pang of jealousy towards Mary Catherine, and she wished that she could find someone who cared about her the same way that Lenny cared for Mary Catherine. If only she could meet someone who would overlook her slights and care for her because of who she was.

She couldn't believe that she had gotten herself into this situation and was sure that, eventually Mary Catherine was going to find out about her and Lenny, and maybe the only good thing that could come of this situation is that Mary Catherine decides to take care of her without the ol' how-do-you-do. Franny fell asleep on Jim's shoulder on the way home. Jim thought it turned out to be a wicked good night.

♫♫♫

The American Beatles-- that's how Mitch pitched them to Sandy and Vernon and then everyone else he told of the fine young men he represented from Massachusetts. That's what he told the bookers at The Ed Sullivan Show, "That they were fine young American boys, not like Jerry Lee Lewis, who had married his underage cousin, but fine wholesome, red-blooded American boys." Mitch had even believed it, but he was just as surprised when "Let's Go Dancin'" went to number forty-nine on the charts, and Vince Calandra, the talent booker for Ed Sullivan, called him back and booked The Weavils on the show.

When Mitch showed up unannounced at band rehearsal that day in Lenny's cellar and told the boys that they were going to be on The Ed Sullivan Show, they were stunned. No one jumped up and down happily-- no one danced around. The four boys just looked at Mitch like he had lost his mind. Finally, after Mitch repeated his good news, did The Weavils realize that they were going to be on television-- they were going on Sullivan.

There was a lot to do before they left for New York and the Sullivan Show. Mitch took the boys to his barber and had all four get the same haircut. Jim enjoyed the barber experience compared to having his ma cut his hair. The barber was slow and meticulous in cutting his hair, trying to get it just right. Ma usually did it over the bathtub, and there was always someone running in and having to poop or pee in front of you and Ma was always yelling at some brother or sister and fighting with someone to get in here so they could be next. Ma would be swinging the scissors around your ears and in front of your face, fighting with some other sibling. Mac, the barber, had a very quiet shop, and every once in a while, some guy would come in and maybe talk about the Bruins or the Celtics, but there was no fighting.

The guys continued to rehearse "Let's Go Dancin'" and "Feel My Heart," which was decided to be the second song they would play on the show. Lenny was very excited, but he really wanted the songs to be special. It was hard for all the guys to compare their songs to the Beatles. They were aware that their songs paled compared to *I Want to Hold Your Hand, I Saw Her Standing There, All My Loving,* and *She Loves You,* even the cover *Till There Was You* was a good ballad. So, the guys tried to put it out of their minds that their songs weren't as strong as The Beatles. They all promised themselves that the next songs they write would be as good as the boys from Liverpool-- it was going to be a tough promise to keep.

♫♫♫

Jim made the trip downtown to Essex Street with his Sears Harmony Supertone to play some songs with Smilin' Leo. He wanted to make sure that Leo knew they were going to be on Ed Sullivan, but he didn't have to tell him, because every time someone dropped a coin Leo's worn guitar case, Leo would stop singing and announce, "Be sure to watch my friend, Strings, on Ed Sullivan with his band, The Weavils, on March 15." Or toss off, "This is my friend, Strings. He's a big shot on Ed Sullivan now. That's it, drop a quarter in there. In a few weeks, it's going to cost ya *dollahs* to hear him play." Jim played with Leo, even though the talk about Ed Sullivan made him more anxious, it was still busking with his friend. "I can't wait to see you on Ed Sullivan-- it's gonna be a miracle," announced Leo.

After it had got dark and too cold to play anymore, Jim walked Leo back to the Tar Pit and Addie's apartment door. As they stood at the doorway, Leo suddenly grabbed Jim's arm and squeezed, "I'm so proud of you, boy-- you're gonna get to give the music to millions. I never got that chance." Jim smiled, surprised, but he didn't know what to say other than, "I will. I'll do it." Addie answered the door; Leo squeezed his arm again and said, "I know you will--

you'll do good." As Jim walked home, he thought about what Leo had said, but he felt even if he could give millions the music, he could never give it to them the way that Leo could.

♫♫♫

The night before The Weavils was to leave for New York City, Jim sat on the kitchen roof, outside of the boy's room window. Tonight, he wasn't playing his guitar. He didn't need to sit out on the roof to play anymore. It was all out in the open that he played the guitar and everyone was okay with it (even Da, since he still wasn't home). Jim remembered the days when he had to hide the fact that he had a guitar-- now it was going to be on television.

He sat on the roof and listened to Franny play the piano downstairs in the front room. Jim could tell that it was Franny; there was no mistaking the way she pounded the bass keys and gently rolled the other end of the keyboard. The music was melancholic and sad sounding. Jim didn't know how to talk to her. What could he say?

When Franny finished, the house was quiet, and Franny appeared in the boy's room window. She slid out the window and scooted down, next to Jim. "Are you ready?" she asked, even if it sounded like she said, "How's Lenny doin'? I bet he's very happy?" "Yeah," replied Jim in a grunt.

They sat quietly on the roof; Franny hugged her legs to warm them because she was wearing only a dress until Jim couldn't take it anymore. "I'm sorry you're not coming with us," he said. "Thanks," she replied, "I know it's because of Lenny and me..." "It's not Lenny," insisted Jim, trying to defend Lenny, no matter what had happened between him and Franny. "It's Mitch." "I thought it was because Lenny didn't want me in the band anymore," confessed Franny. "No," Jim corrected her, "It's because Mitch wants us to be The Beatles... and The Beatles don't have a girl." "Oh," said Franny, realizing that it wasn't Lenny who fired her. Jim thought that this probably wasn't good for Franny, to think that maybe Lenny still liked her and it was all Mitch's fault, but Jim didn't care. He just didn't want Franny to feel bad right now. "The band was better when you were in it," Jim honestly stated. Franny smiled.

It started to get cold on the roof, so they moved inside and went to the girl's room and listened to Woody Guthrie on the portable turntable. Franny and Jim lay on the floor, listening to the beautiful music and wise words play out of the small speaker. Dorrie, Ann, and Teresa came and laid on the floor with them, listening to Woody play his guitar and harp. Ma came by and saw them all lying on the floor, listening to the phonograph. Sometimes, a parent has a moment where maybe it all seemed worth it. To see her children there (she considered Franny one of her children) made her almost get weepy. It's a good thing Da wasn't around to see it.

♫♫♫

The trip to New York City was a long one. Again, Bork drove the large station wagon, with Mitch in the front seat with him, Jim and Lenny in the second seat, Alley and Michael in the backseat. Jim figured he would try to write another song during the trip like this was now part of his writing process, but he couldn't concentrate on writing a song. He consistently questioned whether or not "Let's Go Dancin'" was good enough for Sullivan. But it wasn't really a question-- they didn't have another song, and the "Let's Go Dancin'" single was somewhere around number thirty-two on the charts (he still didn't know what that meant-- he had just heard, Mitch, Bork, and Lenny say it). Even if he came up with a great song like *I Saw Her Standing There*, there was no way they were going to try it out on Sullivan. He had to keep telling himself that "Let's Go Dancin'" and "Feel My Heart" was what they were gonna play.

Lenny was comfortable on the ride to the Sullivan show. To him, this was how it was supposed to go. What Lenny couldn't fathom was what to do about Rickie and Mary Catherine. He didn't think that he was a homosexual. He still liked girls; actually, he liked mostly girls, but there was something about the time he spent with Rickie that was special.

Maybe it was like the forbidden fruit in the Garden of Eden? Maybe it was because he knew that spending time with Rickie would make Mary Catherine crazier than she already was. Messing with Mary Catherine was like shaking a ticking bomb. She could go off at any time. But if she found out that he was fooling around with another man, it's hard to conceive of Mary Catherine's actions. Maybe that's it-- maybe that's why his time with Rickie was so exciting? Because of the danger that comes with it if Mary Catherine found out. Or maybe Father Nelson was right? Was he as much as a degenerate as the priest was? Maybe he should think about becoming a priest again? Lenny decided it was because of the excitement and disregarded the crazy priest thought.

The band arrived at the Essex House on Central Park South. Jim couldn't help noticing how the name of the hotel was the same name as the street that he and Leo busked on. Maybe it was an omen or something? Mitch checked the boys into the hotel, and a bellman took their luggage upstairs (The only paper bag this time was Michael's, Jim's brothers and sisters chipped in and bought him a second-hand suitcase from Goodwill on Merrimack Street).

When they entered their room, the boys were surprised how big the room was compared to the one at The Edison. They would have to sleep two to a bed, but they had their own bathroom and closet. Mitch made them hang their new suits in the closet. Mitch took them out to dinner at Steak and Ale, each boy getting a steak and a beer, except for Jim, who had a steak and Coke.

The guys were very excited when they arrived at the hotel, and there were young girls waiting for them in front. They got out of the car and signed copies of their single, “Let's Go Dancin',” for all the girls present. Lenny loved flirting with the girls; he smiled and hugged them, signing everything they wanted to be signed. Eventually, Mitch and Bork hurried them into the hotel and up to their room for the night.

The next day The Weavils went to the studio where the Ed Sullivan Show was shot. Jim thought it was interesting that the CBS Studio was only five blocks north of where they had recorded their song at the Brill Building and another block away from the guitar stores on forty-eighth Street. New York was a big city, but sometimes it seemed really small and compact.

The director of the show, John Moffit, a tall, dapper, gentleman, smoking a pipe, led them around the studio and showed them where they would be playing and where the "green" room was (which, like Community Auditions was not green, pointed out Alley) and had men help them to move their instruments and equipment in. The band ran through their two songs, and Mr. Moffit told them where the cameras would be the night of the filming. Jim ran the band through "Let's Go Dancin'" a few times, trying to add a bass-run as a bridge to the last chorus. Lenny and Alley weren't very happy changing the song now, but after a few tries, it did make the song sound fuller. Jim also asked Lenny to keep his count on the introduction more consistent. "It's one, two, three," coached Jim, "Not one, two, and three. Or one and two and three." Lenny told him that he knew how to count.

♫♫♫

Mitch took the boys downtown again after the rehearsal, to go to the music stores in Greenwich Village. Michael bought some paperback books that he wanted to read. Lenny and Alley shopped for clothes, finding some boss looking shirts in a boutique. Jim hit a bunch of the record stores, and he bought some albums, Muddy Waters "*Sings Big Bill Bronzy*," Phil Ochs, "*All The News Fit to Sing*," Sarah Vaughn's, "*Sassy Swings the Tivoli*," "*A Little More for Ya,"* Reverend Gary Davis and the new Bob Dylan, "*Times Are a Changin'*." After a spaghetti dinner in Little Italy (it wasn't anywhere near as good as Ma's, in Jim's opinion), they headed back to The Essex House.

When they pulled up in front, the boys thought that maybe the Pope was in town and staying at their hotel. There were about fifty people, mostly young girls, gathered in front. When the car pulled up, the crowd surged towards them, making it difficult for Michael and

Lenny to open their doors to get out. Finally, they pushed the doors opened and started to walk through the crowd of their fans.

At first, they tried signing autographs, but there were too many people, and everyone was pushing and shoving to get to them. Bork grabbed Jim and Lenny, pushing the two boys into the front doors of the hotel. Mitch had Alley by the shirt collar and Michael by the arm, pushing them into the Essex House. They rushed through the lobby and into the elevators that took them to their floor.

Safe inside their room, Mitch called the Sullivan Show and told them that they were trapped in their hotel by fans. "They're going to send some guards over," Mitch informed the boys, who, by now, were over the initial shock of the mobbing and were laughing and pretending they enjoyed the attention. Mitch called down to the front desk and asked them not to allow anyone up onto their floor who wasn't already a guest. The hotel manager said that they were having problems with fans coming into the lobby and bothering other guests. Mitch apologized and suggested that they make any complaints to The Ed Sullivan Show. When Mitch hung up the phone, there was a small smile on his face, under his beard. This was exactly what he was hoping for.

The boys had talked about going to a movie in the evening, but now they realized that they couldn't leave the hotel. The room had a phonograph, so they laid on the beds and listened to Jim's new records. Mitch and Bork went next door to their room to prepare for tomorrow's show. Jim and Lenny stared down at the crowd of people standing on the sidewalk, across the street from the hotel. It looked very cold out there, and some of the crowd stayed all night, sharing that side of the street with the Hansom cabs and their beasts of burden.

"Was that over our song?" asked Jim. "I guess so," answered Lenny, smoking a cigarette and staring down at Central Park South. "Do ya think they all listened to the record?" asked Jim, kind of sure of the answer but trying to conceive of all those people listening to his song. "It looks that way," smiled Lenny, exhaling a long plume of smoke. "As long as they're paying for it." "Not nicking them like Mary Catherine," Jim agreed. "Hope not," replied Lenny.

It was hard to sleep that night, knowing that all those kids were across the street waiting for them to come out. Jim didn't really think about the performance as much as about those people standing outside in the cold. He wanted to call Franny and tell her about the crowd outside, but he knew that Franny didn't want to hear about all the girls who wanted to see Lenny come out of the hotel. He still wanted to call her and tell her about the rehearsal at the Sullivan Show. Besides, if he ran up another phone bill, Mitch would probably beat his bum.

♫♫♫

The next day they woke up, and the crowd had grown to about two hundred people. The New York City Police were out there now, many on horseback, making the people stand on the sidewalk and not in the street or bothering the horses. Mitch let them order room service, and a waiter brought it to the room. They ate French Toast and pancakes sitting on the beds. Alley was disappointed because they had planned to go to Saint Patrick's on 5th Avenue and say a prayer before they went to the show, but with so many people outside of the hotel, Mitch thought it would be safer to go directly to the studio. This was their second trip to New York, and he didn't get a chance to go to any of the famous churches. The other guys were not as disappointed.

After breakfast, they got dressed and prepared to go to the studio to play on Ed Sullivan. Mitch led them to the elevators. They waited in the quiet hall until an elevator arrived, and they all got into the car and pressed the down button to the lobby. The trip to the lobby was quiet and took place with anticipation. Mitch had hoped that the Sullivan show had sent over the guards they promised. When the doors opened, it seemed that the whole lobby turned to them and then funneled to the elevator like water running down a drain. Mitch searched the lobby for the guards; Lenny smiled and waved, while the rest of the band followed him out of the elevator. Bork took up the rear, looking to Mitch for instructions.

The boys pushed their way to the front door. "Get the car," Mitch yelled to Bork, pointing to the front door. Some large men in suits approached the band and surrounded them. Mitch looked to a man in a suit who appeared to be in charge, "Are you the security detail?" "We are," confirmed the big guy in a suit, "Just have your boys stay here. Do you have a car coming?" "I have a man bringing it around, “replied Mitch in the middle of the hubbub. The head of the detail had his men circle the boys as they waited for Bork to bring the car around. "Just like the Beatles," Lenny whispered to Alley, proudly. Alley didn't answer. He just looked scared. The boys were surrounded by a large crowd of about fifty people in the lobby. Many of the people were young teenage girls who were taking pictures of the band and trying to get Lenny's attention. Two men pushed their way through the crowd when one of the men grabbed Jim and hugged him, "Jimmy, boyo..."

"Da, what are ya doin' here?" asked Jim, stunned by the appearance of missing father. "I've come to wish ya and ya friends good luck." "Da???" asked Jim again, still not able to process what his da was doing in the lobby of the Essex House hotel in New York City. Suddenly Plug appeared next to Da. They both looked rumpled and unshaven like they had been on a month-long drunk. Jim could smell the stench of his father, who was still trying to hug him. Besides the surprise of his da's appearance was that his Da was hugging him and seemed glad to see him. This only happened when he had a real snoot on and had won in dice.

A few of the security guys started to move in on Da and Plug, even though it was obvious that Jim knew them. Da looked up from his emotional reunion with his son and spotted Mitch waiting anxiously for Bork by the front door. "Oy, Mr. Sudderfield!" yelled Da to Mitch. Da let go of Jim and ran to Mitch, who quickly spotted him and started to back away. "Mr. Sudderfield, ya son-of-a-bitch! Ya jewed me, ya bastard."

Mitch looked out through the front doors and realized that Bork wasn't there. He turned as Da approached him, Jim hanging onto Da's mussed jacket. "Mr. Sudderfield, I've talked to people. They said you should have given me more money for those songs." Mitch backed away as the security guys followed Da, Jim, and Plug. "We had a deal, Mr. Dewey," said Mitch, nervously, "you signed the papers." "But ya lied to me," yelled Da, looking like he was about to kick Mitch with one of his mule-bucks. Mitch pushed himself up against the door, trying to protect himself as Da broke into a charge.

Jim pushed his father away, trying to restrain him. "Da, not now!" yelled Jim, trying to keep him from Mitch. Da pulled up to a sudden stop and turned angrily on Jim, "Boyo, let go of me, or I'm gonna beat your balls!" Jim didn't stop. He pushed Da further away from Mitch, who was cowering against the door. Suddenly Lenny, Michael, and even Alley charged Jim, his Da, and Plug, who was trying to pull Jim off of his old man. The crowd of teenage girls screamed as they pushed away from the fight.

Lenny, Michael, and Jim pushed Plug and Da, arms pulling and tearing at clothes. "Boy, I'm gonna teach ya a lesson!" Jim ducked his head and drove it into his father's chest, knocking him to the floor. The security men dove into the melee, subduing Da and Plug in a pile on the floor. "Jim, Jim, don't hit him!" Mitch yelled from the front door. "Don't hit him with your hands," he begged over the fight in the lobby, "We're on Sullivan!"

Two of the security guys pulled Jim out of the pile of men, his shirt torn and his wiry hair mussed. "Don't punch him," pleaded Mitch, "Watch your hands." Jim was dragged by the security guys to the front door, next to Mitch, as Michael, Lenny and Alley were led to the door, just in time to see Bork pull up in the station wagon. "Doncha come home, ya ungrateful son-of-a-bitch," screamed Da, from under the pile of security guards restraining him and Plug.

As soon as Bork stopped the car, The Weavils and Mitch rushed out of the Essex House lobby. The crowd that had surrounded the hotel the night before letting out high-pitched screams as Jim, Michael, Lenny, Alley, and Mitch pushed their way through the young girls to the passenger doors of the station wagon. Lenny smiled and waved at the fans. Michael and Alley cautiously slipped into the station wagon. Mitch held Jim's jacket and pushed him into the backseat with Alley. Mitch closed the doors and then took his place in the passenger seat beside Bork.

Mitch closed his door and turned to Bork, "What took you so long?" "It's crazy out here. I couldn't get to the front," moaned Bork, pulling out. "Jesus, Dewey," exclaimed Lenny, "Wasn't that your old man?" The guys sat in the car, watching their fans wave at them and wish them luck. Lenny and Alley smiled and waved. "Are you all right?" Michael asked Jim, who looked as angry as when Mutt grabbed Franny. Jim didn't reply to Michael. He just sat-- pissed.

"Did you give him money?" Jim finally asked Mitch. Mitch turned to Jim and stared at him, trying to decide what to say. "Did you?" Jim asked in a low growl. "Yeah, yeah, he's your father. You're a minor. Someone had to sign for you," confessed Mitch. "You never asked..." started Jim, but decided that he couldn't go on. He just watched the city pass by him as they made their way to 53th Street and Broadway.

♫♫♫

The Weavils arrived at the studio, and that too was chaotic. Mitch and some guards from the studio had to help the boys push their way into the theater. Once safely inside, they prepared for their performance. Jim and Alley tuned their guitars, strumming them unplugged, warming up their hands and fingers. Michael sat on a small couch, tapping on a space pillow with his drumsticks. Lenny paced back and forth in the room. This was always the hard part of any performance-- waiting to go on. Once they started playing, the performance would kind of click in but waiting to go on, whether in a dressing room, a back parking lot, or a storage room, was always the worst part of the night. All four boys were wearing the same black suits, with large, stiff collars and thin ties. Michael had taken his jacket off, but the rest of the band was fully dressed all the way down to their Florsheim shoes.

Alley was feeling really good because unlike Community Auditions, The Ed Sullivan Show had a make-up woman who put pancake make-up on his acne blemishes... he asked her if there was some way to hide his mouth full of braces. She told him coldly to keep his mouth shut. He was determined not to smile during the performance. Alley couldn't stop staring in the mirror at his, now, almost clear complexion.

It had been a very special day for The Weavils. It was the day that they actually got to meet Ed Sullivan. The rehearsals the two previous days had just been with the director of the show, John Moffit and his crew. But earlier in the day, the boys got to meet Mr. Sullivan when he came in with a woman named Lois, who was Mr. Sullivan's assistant. It was very exciting but unfortunately, at the moment that they had Ed Sullivan's attention, no one could think of anything to say except to ask what it was like to meet Elvis, The Beatles, The Everly Brothers, and Buddy Holly. Mr. Sullivan was nice but didn't seem to remember what those guys were like. Lenny asked him what Jayne Mansfield was like (she had been on the show the week before), and Ed spent five minutes telling them what a knock-out she was. He wished them luck and told them to break a leg (Leo had told Jim that this was the way show people said good luck-- which was strange since breaking a leg would definitely be some real *bad* luck).

Mr. Sullivan also told them that they would talk on the show, and he would ask them some questions. Jim had hoped they would ask easy questions to answer. He was still pretty upset about Da trying to get more money out of Mitch... he wasn't surprised he would come back, but he was surprised that he'd come to New York City to do it. Lenny was just hoping that they would go on soon, he didn't care who he had to talk to, besides Ed seemed nice enough and if The Beatles could answer his questions so couldn't The Weavils.

Mitch entered the green room with the woman, Lois, who was about Mitch's age and had her hair up in a bun, like the librarian at the Lawrence Library. "It's time, guys," Mitch announced. Alley, Jim, and Michael stood, like three men going to the firing squad. Michael put his jacket on, and Mitch adjusted Jim's tie. Lois smiled at the boys as they walked to the stage. When Lenny passed her, Lois reached out and adjusted the collar of his jacket. "You look perfect," she said with a smile. "Thank you, ma'am," answered Lenny, with his wry grin.

♫♫♫

Joanie placed a bowl of popcorn on the coffee table in front of the couch where Franny and Mary Catherine Dewey were sitting, drinking their tonics. Both girls were watching a commercial on the television. "It's so nice that you could come over, Mary Catherine," stated Joanie. "Franny and I were almost part of the band, so I felt that we had to see the show together," replied Mary Catherine, smiling warmly at Franny. Franny uneasily smiled back at her.

Franny never thought about inviting Mary Catherine over until Mary Catherine and Bridie cornered her by the gym at school. At first, she was repulsed in ever having Mary Catherine at her house but then realized that it would probably be best to look like she had nothing to hide. "Of course, come to my house; I would never sleep with Lenny," she thought to herself. But now that Mary Catherine was here, Franny realized that this was going to make a painful experience (watching her band on television without her) excruciatingly uncomfortable. "Would you like some more tonic?" Joanie asked Mary Catherine. "Sure, I'll take another Coke," requested Mary Catherine. Franny knew that her mom called it tonic because it wasn't really Coke. It was Stop N Shop Cola. Joanie took up Mary Catherine's glass and went back to the kitchen.

The girls watched the television, waiting for the boys to come on. Mary Catherine leaned closer to Franny and then gently tried to kiss her on the mouth. Franny pulled her head back, surprised. "What are you..." she started to ask. Mary Catherine made sure Joanie was still in the kitchen, "I thought you'd like it," she whispered, trying to take another shot at Franny's lips. Franny dodged away from her, "I don't want to." Mary Catherine looked back into the apartment's kitchen, "I thought since we had somethin' up at the beach, you would wanna..."

Franny looked at Mary Catherine like she had lost her mind. "We didn't have something up at the beach," Franny scolded her, "You stuck your finger in me!" Mary Catherine backed away from her, hurt. "Just sit there and watch the show," grumbled Franny. Joanie arrived from the kitchen with Mary Catherine's tonic and a tonic for herself and sat down beside her daughter.

♫♫♫

The Weavils took their places on the stage. Behind them were black outlined white squares, triangles, and circles, floating above their heads. A large wail of screams rose from the rows of chairs in front of them. The hall was filled with young girls, many of whom probably had been screaming their heads off in here six weeks before when The Beatles stood in the same spot that The Weavils now occupied. The screams were deafening. Jim looked to Lenny in a panic. He strummed the Gretsch once and realized he couldn't hear anything-- he tried turning up the volume, but it didn't make any difference. Alley looked over at Jim when he realized he couldn't hear his bass over the hundreds of young girls screaming.

Jim and Alley looked to Lenny standing at the microphone, waving to the girls in the audience. Bobby, the stage manager, stood between the two large cameras that looked like large one-eyed robots, ready to devour them. Bobby signaled to Ed, standing alone, to the right of the Weavils and started counting down from ten on his fingers. Other stage managers were trying to quiet the girls in the audience so that Ed could introduce The Weavils. Lenny turned to Jim and nodded. Jim tried to point to his guitar and indicate that he couldn't hear it, but Lenny had turned away and prepared to sing his heart out.

Three fingers, two fingers, one finger-- Bobby pointed to Ed. "Quiet down, quiet down, you kids," Ed scolded the audience of girls. "Tonight, we have some fine American boys from Lawrence, Massachusetts, who are going to play a song... THE WEAVILS!"

Bobby quickly pointed to Lenny, who turned to Michael, who counted off, tapping his drum sticks together as Lenny yelled, "One, two, three, and four..." Michael hit the beat with Jim and Alley following him into the song. *Come on, baby. Let's go crazy. Don't be lazy -- let's go dancin' tonight...*

♫♫♫

“Let's Go Dancin'” went okay. Jim, Alley, and Michael didn't hear any of it because of the screaming girls. The second song they played, “Feel My Heart,” was going the same way, the girls screaming at the top of their lungs and The Weavils trying to play over it. Right before the last chorus, Lenny turned to Jim and gave his wry "*Watch this smile*" and turned back to the screaming audience to finish the song. It suddenly hit Jim what Lenny was about to do. Jim stepped to his microphone and waited for the chorus to come around. He and Alley had to do back-up harmonies on the refrain, and when it was Jim's time to come in, he sang as loud as he could.

Television in those days was in its infancy. The medium didn't also have a way of delaying the broadcast, everything on the show was live, and there was no way to avoid an unintentional mistake or even an intentional mispronunciation.

Coda

Jim had become an instant celebrity back at Lawrence High School after arriving from New York City and performing on The Ed Sullivan Show. The boys who had for almost twelve years had been physically and verbally threatening him (though they couldn't actually go through with any real violence because of his older brothers and, or, more importantly, his younger, crazy sister) now shook his hand and said that he and The Weavils were "wicked cool."

Girls would approach him and not be able to talk. Two or three girls would pull up in front of him on his way to class, stand, and move their mouths, but nothing would come out-- then they would do the only thing they could do, scream and run down the hallway. Franny was the most amused by them. Many of these girls had snubbed her and called her "His Boy, Sherman" after Mr. Peabody's boy, now tripped over themselves to ask her what Jim and Lenny were really like. The girls would have liked to have Jim date them, but it was obvious to everyone (except for Franny) that Jim only had eyes for her, so he was left alone, and every girl wished they were Franny.

Ma Dewey never really understood the music that The Weavils played but she realized that every generation had their own music. She got giddy when she heard Bing Crosby and Frank Sinatra, and the big bands, her parents never understood why she didn't appreciate the great Caruso, because he was Caruso.

Ma was so proud of her boys, Jim and Lenny, she had taken to going to Mass every Sunday and sometimes even Saturday night. At one time, walking down the aisle of Saint Tony's was uncomfortable and almost embarrassing, Da wearing his ill-fitting suit and looking like he had to be stuffed in Sunday clothes, children who wanted to be anywhere else. Now she could walk down the aisle, and people would wave, tell her how wonderful it was to see her boy on the tv. They would mention how handsome he was, and what a good musician. Ma would also remind them that she taught Lenny how to play the piano (though he never really did). Most people would go on about how wonderful they were; some would ask if they really heard someone say the word "fart" on the television and if that was legal. Some were against the music they played because it was nigger music, but most were proud that it was Lawrence boys that were on the television.

Jim went down to Essex Street after school and brought his Sears Harmony Supertone with him. He had hoped to play a bit with Leo and hear what Leo thought about the performance. When he arrived at Leo's spot, there was no one there. Figuring that he must have missed him, he headed back for The Tar Pit and Addie's apartment. He hoped that Addie had made some of that fresh cornbread she liked to bake and thought he could smell it when he approached the apartment. When Addie answered the door, Jim knew immediately that something was wrong. Addie invited him in and led him to the kitchen table. She offered him some cornbread, but Jim couldn't eat. Addie told him what had happened.

♫♫♫

Smilin' Leo was very excited that his boy, Strings, was going to play on that Ed Sullivan television show on Sunday night, and on Saturday, he went down to play in front the W.T. Grant on Essex Street. He had been there for a few hours, playing his beautiful F-20 Guild Hoboken

Troubadour as pedestrians dropped coins into his guitar case. In the afternoon, some boys had come along and decided that they would gather a little pocket money by running past the blind man playing the guitar and swoop in, scooping up money as they ran by. The boys made a few sweeps, grabbing some change from the guitar case, while Leo tried to fend them off the best he could while still playing and singing.

As boys do, they got bolder and bolder on each sweep till they just went over and reached into the case to take all the money. Leo could hear them and tried to chase them off, but they kept coming back. It would be nice to think that maybe someone would help Leo stop them, but there seemed to be no witnesses later. As Leo was pushing a boy away from his guitar case, another boy grabbed his guitar, pulled it off his shoulder, tearing the strap, and ran down the street with it. Because the boy ran away with the guitar, the other boys starting running, too. Leo was confused. He tried to separate the footsteps from the one that took his beloved instrument. Leo turned and yelled for them to stop. He then gave chase in the direction that he thought the boy with his stolen guitar went.

The man driving the '59 Thunderbird didn't see the old black man, in the tattered jacket and a worn fedora hat, wearing dark sunglasses, lurch out from between two parked cars because he was turning the T-bird's radio up to listen to that *Dancin'* song those boys from Paddy Hill played on Ed Sullivan. By the time he spotted Leo, he was right on top of him. The screech from the T-bird's tires was heard for blocks. Leo flew over the hood and went headfirst into the street. Smilin' Leo was pronounced dead at Lawrence General Hospital on arrival.

♫♫♫

Addie got up. Jim sat at the Formica table in the kitchen, watching Ruby in the other room playing with a baby doll. The doll was white, and Ruby held it to her chest, singing the *The Crawdad Song* to her baby, softly. Jim couldn't really fathom what Addie had just told him. Did this mean that he would never see Leo again? There would be no music on Essex Street anymore? There would be no busking with Leo ever again? Ruby sang softly to her doll.

Addie exited Leo's bedroom, carrying the closed guitar case that Jim assumed held the Guild F-20, that would always remind him of Leo whenever he would later see one. The very same instrument his friend died for. Addie brought the case to the table and set it down. She opened the lid so that Jim could see the instrument, even though he only saw Leo playing it in his mind and the sound of Leo singing and strumming the beautiful guitar. "I guess he would've liked you to have it," Addie stated, almost as if it was just a picture of Leo playing on Essex Street.

Jim was taken back-- he loved the guitar, but it didn't seem right that he would have it. It was Leo's-- it was the guitar that he dreamed of owning one day, but he saw himself buying it from a store on 48th Street in Manhattan. Not how he was getting it now. He reached down and felt the maple wood of the body of the guitar and then ran his fingers over the bridge, across the strings of the guitar, following them up the neck past the shiny pearl insets to the nut. But he couldn't stop seeing Leo holding the instrument. Jim looked up at Ruby, still singing her song and holding her baby. "You should give it to her," he said, somewhat surprised that he would suggest what he was suggesting, "He would've wanted it that way."

Addie looked at Jim, maybe a little indignant at first that he refused her gift but also a bit relieved that he didn't take it. "Yeah," agreed Jim, with his first impulse, "He would've wanted to pass it on." Addie nodded in agreement. That's what he would want to do. Addie closed the case and turned to Jim, awkwardly, they embraced. "Thank you," she whispered in his ear, "He was so proud of you." Jim took his guitar up and smiled at Ruby, who smiled back at him. Jim left Addie's apartment and walked out of the Tar Pit, back to Paddy Hill.

♫♫♫

The next few days for Jim was a blur. People would stop and talk to him, but he didn't hear what they were saying. School was just moving from one classroom to another, watching teachers talk. He had told Franny about what happened to Leo, and she hugged him, telling him how sorry she was to hear (No newspaper in Lawrence was going to run a story about a stupid blind negro who ran into the street and got hit by a car) and how sorry she was that he didn't get to hear them on television. The Weavils were all saddened to hear of Leo's passing, especially Michael, who went against his own family to allow Leo and Addie's admittance to Barnaby's for the big show.

Da had arrived home a short time after they got back from New York City. He was friendly and gregarious with the family on his arrival, especially with Jim, telling him that he was very proud of his band being on that television show and how the mill men were buying him drinks all over town. Jim figured that he was being nice to him so that he wouldn't tell Ma and the rest of the family he had blown all the money that Mitch had given him... and then traveled to New York to shake down Mitch for more.

Mitch had gotten his record contract, and The Weavils were planning on going back to The Brill Building to start recording their album. Jim and Lenny were meeting to try to work on songs, but Jim had found that it was almost impossible to concentrate on anything other than the loss of his friend. Lenny was disappointed and impatient with Jim. This was important. He was so angry he threatened to write the whole record himself. Jim left and rode the bus over Duck Bridge, back home.

Feeling that he had to do something, Jim took his guitar, and its new guitar case and went down to Essex Street, across from W.T. Grant and took out his Sears Harmony Supertone #319 and slipped the worn strap over his left shoulder. He had opened his guitar case and had even dropped a quarter, dime, and two pennies in. But he wasn't there to make any money; he was there trying to fix something.

He started playing. It was cold, and the strings were digging into the callus pads of his fingertips. But he kept playing-- playing the songs that Leo had taught him, *Key to The Highway, Mannish Boy, Black Snake Moan, Born Under a Bad Sign, and No One Knows You When You're Down and Out.* He played those songs in remembrance of his friend and teacher. The man who called him Strings because he had to help Jim tune his first guitar. He played those songs that Leo believed in, the songs that Leo sang every day, which he did because it was the only thing he could do, "Bringing the music to the people." And as he played, Jim started to understand why Leo played out on the street, in the heat, in the cold, in the rain, in the snow.

It wasn't just to bring the music to the people. It was because the music brought hope. Jim realized then that was what the blues were about-- hope. Hope that your marriage would get better, that your job would get better, and your life would get better. Hope that the world would get better, and that's why people sang. That's why people sang in church, and that's why Leo and Addie sang at the march on Washington. It's why people listened to music, listened to Muddy Waters, Buddy Holly, Elvis, The Beatles, to Dylan, listened to Woody, *for hope*. Suddenly, as he played and sang, Jim realized that he wasn't really in the music business. He was in the hope business. That's what music was all about, and Leo knew it, too.

Leo was the great giver of hope, as he stood on Essex Street in Lawrence, Massachusetts, and sang his beloved blues songs. Leo gave out hope, and the music gave hope back to Leo. Hope that one day his daughter and his grand-daughter would "Be judged on their character, not the color of their skin." That Franny would someday find out who her real father was. That maybe someday he and Franny would play in the same band because she was the best musician he ever played with. He hoped that Franny would someday understand how he really felt about her. Hope that the world would understand what he knew, that we were all in it together and had to get through the best we could and one element that would help was music. Leo knew that the music would save the world. That while there was music in the world, there would always be hope. That the music held what was the best that we could give each other-- hope. Maybe even someday, that a man would land on the moon.

As Jim played on that cold day, he felt hope. He realized that what his Ma was seeing when she closed her eyes when she played the piano in the front room was hope that it would all be better someday. Ma could see (and probably hear) the hope in the music. That was where she went when she closed her eyes when she played the piano. It was that hope that all children are born with, the hope that rises with the daybreak, the hope that comes when the needle is dropped on the record before the music starts, the bass-line that beats throughout the world, in its music, the hope that leaps out with every line of a Woody Guthrie song, the hope that can only come from music.

There was the sound of coins dropping into his guitar case. Jim looked up at a man in a trench coat, staring at him. "Didn't I see you on Ed Sullivan the other night?" the man asked. Jim continued playing his guitar, "Yessir." The man smiled, "What're you doin' here?" Jim smiled broadly and said, "Just bringin' the music to the people." The man continued on his way, as Jim kept playing and singing Bob Dylan's *"The Times are a Changin'."*

The End

My immense thanks to Linda Andrea Rapke for insightful editing help and cover design; also to Debra Bard, Patrick Cannon, Alan Dunlevy, Dave Walsh, Diane Arliqueew, Little Steven's Underground Garage and Professional Musicians, Local 47.

Bill Ryan is a writer, guitar player and union activist. He lives in Los Angeles with his wife and daughter.